T
ASYM[...] [...]
MAN

Alex Rushton

SCRIPTORA

Published in Great Britain 2023 by

SCRIPTORA

42 Brookside Avenue
Polegate
Eastbourne
East Sussex
BN26 6DH

In association with SWWJ (The Society of Women
Writers & Journalists)

scriptora@bigginwords.co.uk

ISBN 978-0-9500591-8-1

Printed and bound by Witley Press Hunstanton PE36 6AD

For Trevor, with gratitude and love

Special thanks and much appreciation go to my editors
Barbara Field-Holmes, Mary Rensten and Pat Alderman of
the SWWJ for their insightful comments on this
manuscript.

Thanks also to Martin Cort, John Havergal, Howard
Schaverien, Guy Blythman, Adam Lewis and especially
Ann Braine for their continuing encouragement and
support during the creation of this manuscript and the
marathon journey to publication.

PROLOGUE

Blake Carter's heart thumped; his nerves were at fever pitch. He clasped his rifle ready to fire. His keen eyes had been scanning the thick foliage for the last ten minutes and he could see the SAS troopers – Jones, Tanks, Taffy and Shorty – crouching hidden behind clumps of bamboo and trees. The enemy camp still looked deserted. Sgt Jones stepped cautiously into the open. There was a thunderous noise. Jones fell to the ground. 'Shit,' said Blake. Bullets were coming at him, fired from unseen directions. Some ricocheted off trees, making a high-pitched zinging noise. Shredded saplings and branches fell from above. Mud splattered up into his face. Something came flying through the vegetation. It made an alien noise, a hiss, smack and a thump as it hit the foliage. It exploded; it was a grenade. Blake's bladder let go, staining the crotch of his trousers. His senses were razor sharp, his breath fast and shallow. A terrified monkey screamed; it lurched away with lightning speed, high up in the canopy, swinging from branch to branch. A sudden silence descended. Even the insect noise ceased. Blake watched as Tanks crawled over to where Jones had fallen and made a throat-slashing gesture – Jones was dead.

A thin cloud of smoke from the gunpowder hung in the still air, its acrid stench filled Blake's nostrils and the bitterness caught at his throat. Out of the corner of his eye he could see an Indonesian soldier emerging from behind a tree, aiming his rifle at Tanks.

'Fucking hell,' gasped Blake under his breath.

With appalling clarity, he knew instantly what he had to do. An icy coldness descended on him. He took aim at the man's chest and pulled the trigger. The Indie spun round, fell to his knees. He looked straight at Blake and raised his rifle once more. Without hesitation Blake fired again, into the man's head; the Indie's body hit the ground with a thud. Blake shuddered at the enormity of what he'd done: he'd killed a man. Before had all been preparation, hours of target practice for something that might happen. Now, with chilling reality, it had. He heard Tanks shout:

'I'm taking command, can't tell what's out there so scoot... back up, towards the river... get ready.'

His edgy voice was absorbed into the vegetation and all was quiet again. Taffy got up from his hiding place behind a bamboo clump and began to run. Shots rang out. Taffy was hit in the head; blood and brains splattered in all directions. He seemed momentarily to hover in space, his arms outstretched, before he too fell to the ground. Blake watched in horror.

'Head to the river,' Tanks shouted.

'When you move, I'll cover you,' Blake yelled.

'Go for it! Then follow up behind me.'

As soon as Tanks moved Blake triggered a barrage of bullets from his automatic rifle into the dense jungle. He heard a distant wail: Tanks had reached the other side of the clearing. Shorty, having made his way round the clearing, crouched beside him.

'Right, your turn,' Tanks shouted, and he and Shorty gave Blake covering fire.

Blake ran for cover as shots reverberated around him. In spite of nausea and exhaustion, adrenalin kept him going as if it had a life of its own. He became aware of a disgusting stench; he had stumbled into a clearing where there were two bodies, already bloating in the heat. Indies. They lay flattened on the jungle earth. One body had a chest wound; a slow river of blood drained over torn clothing. The other was barely recognisable as a body, a grisly mixture of blood and tissue. The ants had already begun to invade. He tried not to look. He had to stay focused and cool. But the stench overpowered him. He retched, then stumbled on, driven towards the goal.

When Blake reached the Emergency Rendezvous by the river, Tanks and Shorty were already there. Tanks' eyes were feverish. Two dark veins in his forehead stood out. His face looked slippery, sheened in sweat.

'I owe you one. You saved my life,' he said.

'You'd have done the same for me,' said Blake.

'Yes, well, I'll make sure they know about it when we get back.'

There were smears of blood on Shorty's trousers.

'I found a couple of bodies on the way here. Was that anything to do with you?' Blake asked.

'Yes, I ran into them, they must have got separated from the others,' said Shorty. 'I managed to deal with them before they knew what was happening. Evens the score a bit.' He sniffed. 'We shouldn't have gone there. Going back to that deserted enemy camp was too risky.'

'Well, that was Jones' decision,' said Tanks. 'And he and Taffy paid for it.'

Tanks spat on the ground and tears welled in his eyes. He blinked them back.

'They'll give you some time out after this, won't they?' asked Blake.

'Shorty and I will recover soon enough,' said Tanks. 'The next mission we go on we'll go at it as hard as we can. The Regiment's in our blood.' He wiped his face on his sleeve. 'Carter, you did well for your first time in combat. Better than I thought you would.'

'Baptism of fire,' said Shorty.

Yes, thought Blake. He felt a wave of grief and revulsion, remembering Taffy's abrupt and gory extinction and Jones' death, but knew that to be effective he would, like Tanks and Shorty, have to put it behind him and press on. They picked up their kit and set off for base.

CHAPTER 1

Cambridge
Eight months earlier. March 1966.

Blake stood for a moment, and looking up at the word HUMILITATIS carved in stone above the archway leading into Caius College. He walked through the gate and across Tree Court towards the south west corner of the quad and an ancient solid oak door. He pushed it open and its hinges creaked. In the gloomy hallway that stretched before him, there was a dark wooden staircase whose intricately carved balustrade gave off a faint smell of furniture polish. As he walked upstairs the steps groaned beneath his feet and he reflected that students like himself had been using the University, and this college, for more than seven hundred years. He wondered how many others had found the conventions stifling, although it had not taken him long to learn to get around them and turn them to his own advantage.

Blake made his way to Professor Dodds' rooms on the second floor. This was only the second time he'd been invited; the first was after they'd been introduced, two years ago. They usually met in *The Rose and Crown*, a quiet back street pub. He knocked on the dark oak door and a few moments later it creaked open.

'Good evening, Professor.'

'Ah, Blake, do come in,' said Dodds, with a hint of awkwardness. 'You're on time, I see. That's good, shows good manners.'

The front of his shirt had slipped out of his trousers and his tie was stained with remnants of food and gravy still wet from dinner. Blake recognised the same smell of roast beef he'd noticed last time. Dodds often appeared

5

to be scatterbrained, rambling from one subject to another, but Blake had learnt that his appearance and distracted manner hid a sharp mind. He followed Dodds into the living room, a dark space with heavy wooden panelling; it was just as he remembered. There was a medium-sized dining table with four upright chairs ranged round it, a two-seater sofa and two leather armchairs. Against the far wall were two sets of tall bookcases stuffed full of books, with layers of books arranged horizontally on top of the upright ones. Two photographs of the Professor in his colourful gowns were displayed in silver frames on top of one bookcase. Document folders and sheets of paper were piled high on almost every surface. Removing his Cantonese/English dictionary from the pocket of his canvas jacket, Blake was ready for another evening of their usual academic conversations, but as he stepped further into the room, he saw a stranger in a grey suit sitting on the sofa, drink in hand.

'This is the young man I was telling you about, Gerry. Blake Carter. Blake, this is Mr Benson,' said Dodds. The stranger rose to his feet, and held out his hand.

'Good evening, sir,' said Blake, shaking hands.

'A pleasure to meet you.' Benson's voice was rich and clear. He was tall and lean, his sharp blue eyes shining like beacons.

'Make yourselves comfortable. Gin and tonic, Blake?' said Dodds, turning away towards a small cupboard used as a drinks cabinet.

'Yes, please.'

Dodds poured Blake's drink and handed it to him.

'Just a minute, let me move some of those out of the way.' He lifted a pile of documents from the seat of an armchair and made space for Blake to sit down. Benson returned to his seat on the sofa while Dodds sat on the other leather armchair, both of which had seen better days. 'I've made some comments on the Chinese article about hydroelectric dams. Now where did I put it?' Abruptly Dodds got up and put his drink on a small table beside his chair. He then did a tour of the room, rifling through different piles of documents and ending up at a pile on a footstool. Picking up a buff-coloured folder, he studied its contents. 'Ah, here it is,' he said, handed it to Blake and sat down again.

'Thanks.'

'Well, Blake, how are you getting on with the Thai translation?' asked Dodds.

'Almost halfway through,' said Blake.

'Good, good.'

'Ah,' said Benson, 'Doddsy here has been telling me he's employed you to do translations for him.'

'Yes.'

'Translations? You're reading Natural Sciences, aren't you? Not much to do with Oriental languages I would have thought.'

Blake wondered where the line of questioning was leading and who Benson was; it seemed unlikely this was just a chance meeting. He shuffled in his seat.

'I was raised in the Far East,' he said.

'Ah, I see. So how did you come across Doddsy?'

Blake felt as if he was being quizzed, but Benson's manner was friendly.

'I asked the Department of Asian Studies to recommend someone who could help me practise, so I wouldn't forget it all. They put me in touch with Professor Dodds.'

'Glad to be of assistance,' said Dodds piously.

'Doddsy tells me you're quite fluent. He enjoys your evenings at *The Rose and Crown* practising... which languages is it now... Thai and Cantonese?'

'At the moment, Cantonese.'

'Wouldn't you prefer the company of your fellow students in the Junior Common Room, a young man like you?' Benson took a swig of his whisky.

'I'm afraid I find the chitchat in the JCR a bit dull at times. They tend to be obsessed with their grades. Anyway, I'm not very good at small talk and the Professor is much more interesting; I think we're both benefiting from the language practice.'

'How many languages do you speak?' asked Benson, with the hint of a friendly smile.

Blake thought for a moment.

'I'm fluent in only three, French, Thai and Vietnamese. But I can get by in Cantonese. My Mandarin is a bit rusty and I have a smattering of some of the local dialects of the Hong Kong region.'

'Hmm...' said Benson; 'Impressive. Have you decided what you want to do after you graduate?'

'Physics is my main subject, so I expect I'll do something in Research and Development. I like the practical lab work. Whatever work I do, I want to make a difference.'

'A noble purpose. And where would you like to work?' asked Benson, 'I mean are you planning to stay in England or work abroad?'

'I don't mind where the work is.'

'You're not averse to working abroad then?'

'No, not at all; I've lived half my life abroad,' said Blake. He studied Benson and wondered if he was a headhunter.

'Hmm... it would be a shame not to make use of your languages.'

'I do supplement my student grant with translations, as Professor Dodds can confirm, but I wouldn't want to work full-time as a translator.'

'Well... there are other options,' said Benson. He swished the whisky around in his glass.

'Oh, can I top you up, old man?' asked Dodds.

'That would be very kind of you, Doddsy.'

Dodds refilled the glass, handed it back to Benson and sat down.

'Tell me, are you planning to take a wife, settle down, that sort of thing?' asked Benson.

Blake was taken aback by the directness of the questioning. He took a gulp of his gin and tonic.

'I don't have any serious girlfriends at present,' he said.

'Not a ladies' man,' said Benson.

Blake threw caution to the wind. 'To be honest, none of them seem to want to stay around at the moment.'

'Why do you think that might be? Man to man,' said Benson.

Blake shrugged. 'I've been told I'm too cerebral, lacking in emotion; a cold fish, in fact.'

'What about Mary? Was she serious?'

Blake's eyes widened. Benson had obviously done his homework.

'That's a bit below the belt, sir.'

'Sorry, I prefer hard facts; I'm not fond of small talk either.'

'She didn't hang around.'

'Did it bother you?'

'Not much, I'm not ready to settle down anyway.'

'Good,' said Benson and a wry smile began to spread across his face.

Startled, Blake glanced at Dodds, who winked at him. Unusually for him, Dodds had nothing to say, but sat back in his armchair with his fingers laced across his small pot belly, relaxed but watchful.

'The Professor speaks very highly of you, Blake. He is impressed with your self-discipline, cool-headedness and mature approach to life,' said Benson, looking over at Dodds.

'Indeed I am.' Dodds' face brightened.

'And Hugh Jenkins, your old sixth form tutor, remembers you as, now, what was it…' he glanced up at the ceiling, gathering his thoughts, 'yes, self-reliant, independent and resilient, usually completing your work ahead of time. You were particularly good at thinking on your feet and problem-solving, running rings around some of your more pedantic masters apparently.' He laughed. 'Just the sort of qualities we're looking for, in fact.'

'We?' said Blake.

'Yes, we,' said Benson.

Blake waited, but Benson did not elaborate. However, Blake's suspicions had been confirmed: this was an interview, and his references had already been taken up.

'How's your father?' asked Benson suddenly.

'He was OK last time I saw him, a few months ago,' said Blake, cautious now.

'And your mother's dead, I believe.'

'Yes.'

'And you have two brothers?'

'Yes,' said Blake.

'Your father worked in the Far East, in various Embassies, didn't he?' said Benson.

'Yes, he was an accountant,' said Blake.

'Amongst other things,' said Benson, so quietly that Blake almost missed it. Blake stiffened.

'Would you consider working in one of our Embassies in the Far East?' asked Benson.

'As what?'

'Shall we say… translator?'

'But my interest is in R&D. I don't want to work as a translator,' said Blake levelly. He felt hot. He ran a finger under the collar of his shirt.

'So you said.' Benson's smile broadened.

'Are you saying that I'd be in the Diplomatic Corps?' asked Blake.

'Not exactly,' said Benson, 'sort of attached to them.'

'And working for whom exactly?'

Benson smiled even more broadly and tapped the side of his nose with his forefinger.

'Let's just say Her Majesty's Government, shall we,' he said.

Suddenly it all made sense. Blake nodded slowly. He took a long swig of his gin and tonic.

'You will be on the normal Civil Service salary scales, which, as you may know, are not over-generous. But there will be opportunities for advancement. And I can promise you the work will not be boring; in fact sometimes you may feel the need for some routine. You'll need to undergo training, of course.'

Blake took a deep breath.

'Presumably this training doesn't take place here at Cambridge, in one of the colleges?'

'Good Lord, no. We have our own training facility, tucked away in a discreet location.'

'Am I the only one who's been approached like this?' asked Blake.

'No, actually, you're the fourth. But two of them weren't up to scratch.'

'What do you mean?'

'Failed their training, as many do.'

'I see.'

'Any more questions, Blake?'

'No, not at the moment. I need to think it over.'

Benson put down his glass.

'Of course. Let Doddsy know what you've decided. But don't take too long about it. We'd want you to finish your degree first, so you'd join us after that... I can assure you the work you do for us will make an important difference, with potentially far-reaching consequences. Oh, and we haven't met and we haven't had this conversation, if you follow me.'

'I understand,' said Blake.

All three got up and Benson extended his hand.

'It's been a pleasure meeting you,' he said and shook Blake's hand firmly.

'I'll see you out,' said Dodds, opening the door and ushering Benson out.

A few moments later, Dodds returned and stood awkwardly in front of the fireplace.

'Would you like another drink, Blake?'

'Not now... So you told MI6 all about me then?'

Dodds flicked his tie and looked at it briefly. 'Good Lord, I must stop being such a messy eater. I'm very partial to gravy you know, beef gravy in particular; sloppy stuff.' He scraped the stain with his thumbnail.

'Professor?'

'Er, yes, where was I?'

'Are you in MI6 as well?'

Dodds frowned, scratched his ear, picked up his gin and tonic and downed it in one gulp.

'Well, not exactly. Some years ago they asked me to keep an eye out for potential recruits; if I came across someone outstanding I thought was suitable I'd let them know, which is what I did in your case.' Dodds flattened the tie on his shirt with his hand and patted it. 'You know, Blake, I wouldn't have put your name forward if I didn't think you were exceptional. I've been very impressed with your abilities, and not just with languages. There have been few, very few indeed, who have measured up.'

Blake shrugged. 'Were you involved in recruiting the other three?'

'No, I don't know anything about them. I'm not surprised that two have failed to make the grade, though; the training is very tough I understand.'

'I like a challenge.'

'I know you do, Blake. You've got your quick mind around the most obscure Cantonese.'

'Do you know what's involved?'

'They haven't gone into detail. I expect it's the usual Secret Service stuff. I do know that the ones who show the most aptitude get some sort of military training as well.'

'Hmm… now that's interesting.'

'So that aspect appeals to you, does it?'

'I was an army cadet before I came to Cambridge. Also, several of my ancestors were military men.'

'Oh, were they…?'

'My great-grandfather Captain Montgomery Carter fought in the 2nd Boer War, and my grandfather Major Douglas Carter in World War I.'

'I didn't know that.'

'Yes, my grandfather was at Passchendaele. Most of his regiment was killed, and he was wounded but survived. He didn't like to talk about it, understandably, but he was proud of what he did. He got a DSO for it.'

'My goodness, he must have been a brave man.'

'Yes, he was. So military service is a bit of a family tradition. However, it's a big step, and it's completely different to what I saw myself doing.'

'But you'll consider it?'

'Yes, I'll give it serious consideration. But I'm not going to make a snap decision; I need to mull it over for a while.'

'Fair enough. Sure you won't have that drink?'

'Perhaps next time.'

Blake drained his glass and put it on a stack of files.

Dodds looked relieved. 'Yes, certainly. Next time,' he said eagerly.

Blake walked to the door. 'I'll see myself out.'

'See you soon then.'

'Yes.'

Climbing down the wooden staircase, strangely Blake couldn't remember Benson's face at all, only the bright eyes.

Dodds went to the window and watched as Blake crossed Tree Court. I knew I was right, he thought.

CHAPTER 2

London
February 1967

'Excuse me, sir, we're beginning our descent into Heathrow.' The male voice was clear and close. 'Would you fasten your seat belt, please?'

With a start Blake opened his eyes. 'What? Oh, right,' he said. He heaved himself upright and clicked the belt into place.

At passport control he noticed the official looking intently at him as she compared his face and the photograph. She turned slightly and nodded at a man waiting in a nearby doorway. The man returned the nod, went into the office and closed the door. The woman gave Blake his passport.

'Welcome back to England, Mr Carter,' she said and looked at him with interest.

'Thank you,' said Blake.

In the taxi he took out the envelope the official had put in his passport. Inside was a piece of paper with an address and an appointment time for the following day, with instructions on where to enter the building. He memorised the details, tore the note into fragments and stuffed them into the cab's ashtray.

* * *

Next day, Blake got out of a taxi outside Century House at 100 Westminster Bridge Road, Lambeth. He noticed with some concern that the taxi driver gave him an exaggerated wink before driving off, which made him suspect that although MI6 officially didn't exist, the site of its headquarters seemed to be known to London taxi drivers. Proceeding according to his instructions, he made his way through a tradesman's entrance and identified himself to a member of staff. An officious receptionist led him up a narrow beige staircase, through long blank corridors, onto the second floor and into a featureless committee room. There was a smell of cigarettes. Two men were sitting at an oval table. When Blake entered they got to their feet, introduced themselves and shook his hand.

Mr Marshall, the older man with an air of authority about him, had obviously been educated at a public school, which was true of most of the people Blake had met at Cambridge. Mr 'Smith' was shabbier. He had shrewd, intelligent eyes that missed nothing. He held a cigarette between fore- and middle fingers and flicked ash into the nearby ashtray. A field operative, Blake guessed.

Marshall paced up and down the room. He held a set of documents in his hand.

'Do sit down. Blake Carter, isn't it? Don't mind if I stand up, do you, a habit of mine, keeps my mind on track, you know.' Smith sat down and Blake took one of the other chairs. Marshall continued, 'You've got an impressive background, Carter, Combined Science and Languages. It's your Oriental languages we're interested in. You're fluent in Thai, Vietnamese and French, I understand.'

'Yes, sir, and I speak some Cantonese as well.'

'I hear you're an excellent shot.'

'They thought so.'

Marshall brandished his clutch of papers. 'According to the reports in here, you scored remarkably well with all the weapons you've used.' Blake shrugged. 'Your father was a marksman as well, I believe.'

Blake flinched. 'I wasn't aware of that,' he said.

'Well, that was some time ago. Let's get back to you. I want to talk about your training, which you have now completed. Very successfully, I might add.'

'Yes, sir.'

'All your instructors for basic fitness training and tradecraft were very impressed with your abilities. You passed all the exercises with excellent marks. Not just scraping through, as some of the others did. Did you find that part of it a struggle?'

'No, not really. It was challenging, of course, but I felt it was something I could master.'

'Did you form any friendships with your fellow trainees?' asked Smith. 'Sometimes these sorts of shared experiences bring people closer together.'

'No, I'm afraid not. Was I supposed to?'

'Well, it's not required but it does happen, naturally,' said Marshall.

Again, Blake shrugged. 'Not with me,' he said.

'There was one aspect of our observations that interested us. Your rejection of Claire Brendon,' said Smith.

Blake sat up straighter. 'Pardon?'

'Did you form a special attachment to her?'

'No.'

'She asked you for help with some of the exercises, didn't she?'

'How did you know that?' asked Blake, before realising that of course they would know – they would let nothing escape them. 'Yes, she did.'

'But you didn't help her, did you?' continued Smith.

'No, I didn't.'

'Was there a particular reason?'

'Yes.'

17

There was a pause.

'Go on,' said Marshall.

Blake sighed. 'I liked her, but she was struggling. If I'd helped her, she might have made it through the training. But when it came time for her to be deployed... I thought she would have been a liability. So I thought it best not to prolong the agony.'

Marshall looked across at Smith, who just raised one eyebrow but said nothing. Blake couldn't read Marshall's expression.

'Sink or swim?' said Marshall. 'It was a very Oriental reaction, and one of which we approve.'

'She didn't get through, did she? I didn't see her again after we finished tradecraft.'

'We don't discuss an applicant's results, Blake, at least not within the applicant's team,' said Smith.

Blake nodded.

Marshall leafed through some of his papers. 'Your performance in the desert was impressive as well, it seems. Were you pleased with how it went?'

'I found the sand tiresome. It got into everything, every nook and cranny. Too gritty for my liking.'

'And Scotland, bit nippy up there I expect.'

'Yes, we didn't get properly warm the whole time.'

'Even so, you impressed again.'

Blake gave a slight smile.

'Now, we come to the real meat of your training, with the SAS in Borneo, and your baptism of fire. There is an incident we'd like to know more about, your lost map. In the jungle, where you're not supposed to leave any traces to show that the SAS are patrolling out there.'

'Yes, Blake,' said Smith. 'The loss of a map is not just inconvenient to the operator, but if such an item ends up in the hands of the opposition it could mean the collapse of the whole scheme you're engaged in.'

Blake squirmed slightly on his chair. 'I understand that, sir.'

'How did you come to lose it?' asked Smith.

'While we were taking a rest, it slipped out of my pocket,' said Blake, uncomfortably.

'Bit damned careless of you, wasn't it?'

Blake stared hard at Smith. 'Yes, it was.'

'We can't have you chucking sensitive material about, leaving it for anyone to find.'

'I've learned my lesson,' said Blake. 'I'm more careful now, it won't happen again.'

'You lost the map, but were then able to navigate through the jungle by dead reckoning and retrieve it, I believe?' said Marshall.

'Yes, I did.'

'Good recovery,' said Marshall, looking at Smith, who nodded.

'You must realise how important things that seem like trivial events are. They can have serious results all round. It can be a matter of life and death,' said Smith.

'Yes, sir, it won't happen again.'

'Then we come to the ambush by the Indonesians. Two SAS troopers killed. Three of you made it back to base. You saved the life of one of them, for which you must be commended.'

'Thank you, sir.'

Blake noticed Smith scrutinising him while rubbing his finger across his mouth.

Marshall looked at Blake; his black eyes glinted. He brandished his documents. 'The officers who debriefed you described the speed of your reactions under pressure as, I quote, "very fast, highly effective...".

They were impressed with your tenacity and bravery. You've made mistakes, but you're a fast learner. Usually a man has weaknesses, but I must say, in your case we're having difficulty finding any. In fact, it's been reported to me that you weren't thrown off balance at all, as some inexperienced men are. Tell me, are there any after-effects from the incident?'

'No, none,' said Blake, puzzled.

'You killed a man in that ambush, albeit to save the life of your colleague. How do you feel about that?' said Marshall.

Blake shrugged. 'It was an instant reaction, automatic, I didn't have time to think about it; at that moment you don't think of him as a human being, just a threat. It was a matter of kill or be killed. There wasn't a choice.'

Marshall put the documents on the table, stopped abruptly with his back to the window and looked straight at Blake. Blake could see the light from the window pink through his ears.

'That's what I expected you to say and why, given the timing, we're considering you for a special assignment in Vietnam,' he said crisply.

'Vietnam?' said Blake, surprised. 'We're not operating out there, are we?'

Marshall paced around again. A floorboard creaked.

'Yes, we are, in a small but crucial way,' he said in a matter-of-fact manner. 'We're not officially in Vietnam. Our Government has been trying through diplomatic channels to help the Americans by offering military expertise, hoping this will help to strengthen our bargaining position with them in the Far East. However, while these negotiations have been going on we've been having other talks with our American military counterparts. There's a very well-organised and effective secret Viet Cong infrastructure which has infiltrated South Vietnam. It has been responsible for a damaging campaign of terror against South Vietnamese officials and American military personnel. We've agreed that we would take an active part in removing their most senior Viet Cong commanders, decapitating the organisation... temporarily, at least.' Marshall's affected voice sounded shrill and jarring and as he walked about it echoed around the room. He stopped and looked out of the window.

'Removing? As in?' said Blake.

Marshall spun round. 'Yes, assassinating.'

Blake took a deep breath. 'So that's where I come in?'

'Precisely,' said Marshall.

'I don't understand, why is MI6 doing this? Isn't this the sort of thing the SAS are used for?'

'We can't be seen to have any military personnel at all in Vietnam. If it became known the SAS were out there it would cause a frightful row.'

'I see.'

'Do you think you can do it?' asked Smith. 'It won't be the same as in Borneo. This will be cold, calculating, targeted but necessary killing.'

Blake took another deep breath. 'This isn't the sort of assignment I expected to be given.'

'What did you expect?' asked Smith. 'A nice cushy number shuffling papers in an office?'

'No, I expected to do field work, but this, this is murder. That's a completely different situation.'

'Did you enjoy it?' asked Smith.

'What do you mean?' said Blake.

'Shooting that Indie? Did it give you a thrill?'

Blake reddened. 'As I explained, sir, it was an automatic reaction. And no, I bloody didn't enjoy it. I took no pleasure in killing him, if that's what you want to know. Why, does that disqualify me for the assignment?'

'No, on the contrary,' said Marshall. 'We don't want pathological killers, they're likely to go off-script and kill people for the hell of it, causing all sorts of mayhem. Wouldn't do at all.'

'I see.'

'No, we need someone disciplined, who'll follow orders. These VC commanders are ruthless murderers themselves.' Marshall looked at Blake intently. 'Throughout history there have been attempts by good men to overthrow bad and the downright evil. On 20 July 1944, Claus von Stauffenberg and his fellow conspirators attempted to assassinate Adolf Hitler. It was because of a slight miscalculation that their bravery and daring failed. Their actions might have shortened the war and saved thousands of lives but for a table leg. This kind of mistake you cannot afford to make.' Marshall threw back his shoulders and stood with his hands behind his back. 'They tell me you want to make a difference. Here, you will be. Will you be prepared to join us in making a difference with our American friends in Vietnam? As you've already found out, this is no parlour game. Well, what do you say? We need a definite answer.'

Blake sat back on his chair, considering. He thought back to the firefight in Borneo. This would be different, he knew. Not a kill-or-be-killed situation but a calculated, cold-blooded execution. Was he ready for this?

There was a knock on the door and Marshall opened it. A middle-aged woman dressed in an apron wheeled in a trolley laden with coffee and biscuits and parked it between them.

'Thank you, Janet,' said Marshall, impatiently hurrying her out and closing the door behind her. 'Coffee, gentlemen?'

'Black for me,' said Smith. He dropped two sugar lumps into his coffee. As he stirred them in, the spoon clinked against the side of the cup.

Marshall made eye contact with Blake. 'The same, thanks,' Blake said.

Marshall poured and handed a cup to Blake. The steam rose and there was a strong smell of coffee. They were quiet for a few moments.

'OK, I'll do it,' Blake said.

Marshall looked inquiringly at Smith, who nodded firmly.

'Mr Smith agrees with me you're the right chap for the job,' said Marshall and began pacing around the room again. 'Our involvement appeals to the Americans because it makes it easier for them to deny all knowledge if discovered. The American public are squeamish, they wouldn't stand for their boys carrying out targeted assassinations, even of the VC, if you see what I mean. Especially as there is already a lot of anti-war feeling, particularly among youngsters. Growing all the time: protests in the US and of course here, mostly in Grosvenor Square, outside the US Embassy.'

'Yes, I've noticed.'

'We have been successfully running the operation, code name Hunter, for a while now. All off the record, of course. It's just one of a battery of measures being used by the Americans to counter the Viet Cong. The situation is this,' said Marshall and coughed, clearing his throat. 'We did have an operative in place, named Coulter, performing this role. Six weeks ago Coulter was found dead, killed. We know he was planning an assassination at the time. We want you to take on his work.'

Smith took a vicious drag on his cigarette and blew the smoke high into the air. It formed a thin cloud as it hovered in the airless room. Both men stared at Blake, their expressions intense. Blake had an uncomfortable feeling of foreboding; he didn't relish the thought of walking in a dead man's shoes.

'Can I change my mind, now you've told me my predecessor was murdered?' asked Blake.

'Do you want to?' asked Smith.

There was a pause. 'No,' said Blake. 'I'm in.'

'Good. Your first task will be to re-establish relations with Coulter's contact,' Marshall continued, pacing around again. 'Coulter was the cut-out between the service and the contact and nobody else knows the identity of his informant who gave him the names and movements of his targets. Coulter liked his drink, spent time with prostitutes and other shady characters in the more disreputable part of Saigon... so you might like to start looking there. He was also a bit of a maverick, lax about keeping London up to date with his activities... hence there are vital gaps in the files here. Not much to go on, I'm afraid,' he said in a dry, business-like tone.

'So, what's my cover?' said Blake.

'Your role in the Embassy will be translator. Plenty of work there, I'm told. You'll be living in a flat above a firm of accountants. The flat is owned by Duong Khien, a useful and reliable supporter of the South Vietnamese government. Khien knows you're working for us, but he doesn't know any details of what you're up to. He is trained in arms and may be able to help you out if you need it.'

Marshall picked up his coffee cup. So did Blake and Smith and they swigged in unison. Blake noticed the coffee tasted bitter.

'Khien has had some personal tragedy himself at the hands of the Diem regime and believes that the Americans present the only hope for establishing true democracy and freedom. He's been helping us out,' said Marshall. 'Any questions?'

'Yes,' said Blake, 'how did Coulter die?'

'Gunshot wounds, I believe. We've little information about that.'

'Any idea who killed him?'

'Nothing to go on, I'm afraid. Anything else?' he asked briskly.

'Yes, I'd like to see the dossier on the Viet Cong infrastructure if there is one,' said Blake.

'Yes, there is. I'll make the official one available to you. After reading it I don't think you'll have any doubts about the importance of the mission. Any other questions?'

'No.'

Marshall inhaled deeply and stared long and hard at Blake.

'A challenging first assignment, I'm afraid, but you've got strong credentials, and you'll be working alone, which, from what I've heard, will suit you. Mr Smith will give you your legend… Oh, and we've given you a new name and passport – you'll be known as John Miller. We'll be in touch again soon. So, if there are no more questions, I'll detain you no longer.'

They shook hands. Blake left the building aware of the challenge of the assignment. I can do this, he thought.

CHAPTER 3

Saigon, Vietnam
March 1967

As Blake stepped off the plane at Tan Son Nhat Airport the heat and humidity hit him like a slap. Inside, the airport bustled with activity; people were speaking in both French and Vietnamese. Most of the men looked lean and physically fit. The women were petite and slender, many of them wearing *ao dai*, a high-necked, close-fitting tunic cut to the ankle with a slit on each side to mid-thigh, over loose-fitting flowing trousers.

Blake hired a rickshaw and was driven through the heat, smells and a cacophony of noise to the heart of the city. The driver stopped at Rue des Fleurs, a busy side road with a scattering of market stalls set out on the pavements. Blake followed the instructions and found the entrance to his flat up a communal stairway tucked between a barber's and a shoe shop; as he went up the stairs he saw a Vietnamese man on the landing.

'Mr Miller? I have been expecting you. My name is Duong Khien,' he said in English, and shook Blake firmly by the hand. His eyes were bright and his cheeks ruddy.

'John Miller, nice to meet you,' said Blake.

'Which language would you prefer, English, French or Vietnamese?'

'Vietnamese is fine with me.'

'Do come in,' said Khien in Vietnamese, leading him inside and shutting the door. 'I hope you will be comfortable here. My accountancy office is downstairs, a small door on the left. Please find me if you need anything. Now, let me show you round the flat.'

Khien was taller and larger built than the average Vietnamese. The buttons on his tight shirt strained over his paunch and the dark hair on his stomach showed through the gaps. Inside the flat was cooler than outside. Blake looked round. In the main room, a bamboo dresser was set in one corner with china displayed on shelves. Four wicker chairs with faded green cushions surrounded a wooden table. Thick net curtains at the windows made the rooms seem dark and dingy. There was a faint smell of cigarette ash in the air. The flat had a well-used, slightly dilapidated feel about it.

'The flat is simply furnished, as you can see.'

'It seems to have everything I need.'

'Good, but it also has a few surprises,' said Khien. 'Saigon is an uncertain place these days. We need to be vigilant.'

Khien led him into the bedroom. An insect net, suspended from the ceiling, surrounded a double bed.

'Here, let me show you this.'

Khien squatted down and lifted the carpet. He pushed his stubby finger between two floorboards and lifted one of them clear of the floor. A cluster of firearms of different shapes and sizes lay in the cavity.

'I collected these over the years,' said Khien proudly. 'Automatics, handguns, silencers, you might like to try them out, some are in better condition than others.'

Blake took a quick glance at the motley group. 'Interesting,' he said.

Khien replaced the floorboard. He stood up, pushed his shirt in and pulled up his trousers.

'I'll give you some time to settle in, then maybe you'd like to accept my hospitality and have dinner with myself and my family; we live in the next street. I've written down my address and left it on the table for you; say seven o'clock.'

'Thanks, I'll be there.'

Khien let himself out.

Blake walked from room to room. There was another bedroom, a compact kitchen and a large bathroom. The flat was spacious and the location discreet. On first impression he thought he would be able to get along with Khien, who seemed welcoming and helpful, and on the surface, reliable. However, in his risky business appearances could be deceptive; he would need to be cautious. He walked over to the window and pushed back the net curtain. It had a yellowish tinge through years of accumulated cigarette smoke. He pulled on the rope to open the sash window; with force it yanked free. Outside the air was hotter. A smell of spices and leather wafted up from the market. There was a barrage of shouting, banging and traffic from the street. A café called *Les Croissants* was directly across the street; people sat at tables outside, drinking coffee. Blake lifted the loose floorboard again and examined the firearms. A battered-looking AK-47 rifle issued to both the VC and the NVA, an M-16, standard American issue, a No.4 Mk1(T) with telescopic sight and a Colt AR15 5.56mm. A few handguns lay amongst the heap. He noticed the Browning 9mm high power semi-automatic. He liked the Browning; he'd used it extensively during his training. This one looked in good condition.

* * *

Khien ushered Blake into the room.

'Come in,' he said. 'Sit here, please.'

Khien sat at the head of the table and gestured Blake to sit beside him. As Blake pulled in the chair, the wood screeched on the floorboards. Bowls of steaming fresh food were set out on the table; there was a smell of spices. The sound of crockery clinking and female voices echoed from the kitchen. A short, plump woman came in; she had dark hair streaked with grey and wore a colourful apron. She carried a bowl filled with what looked like papaya and set it in the centre of the table.

'This is my wife, Ming,' said Khien. The woman bowed slightly, and as she smiled Blake saw a flash of gold teeth.

'Welcome,' she said, and took her place at the other side of Khien, opposite Blake. A striking, much taller woman followed Ming. She was pale and wore no make-up. Her black hair was piled up high and held in place with an ivory pin. She held the biggest bowl of white rice Blake had ever seen.

'And this,' said Khien, 'is my daughter, Hoa.'

Hoa met Blake's gaze steadily.

'Pleased to meet you,' she said.

Hoa put the rice in front of Blake and sat down next to her mother. Two small girls and an even smaller boy came in and sat at the other end of the table. Khien smiled at them indulgently.

'Hoa, would you please serve Mr Miller some food,' he said.

She looked at Blake demurely and her lip curled.

'I'm sure Mr Miller can manage to serve himself,' she said with a coy smile. The children giggled.

Khien frowned. He was about to speak.

'It does look delicious,' said Blake and reached for the serving spoon balanced on the papaya. 'Are these fried in shrimp sauce?'

'Yes,' said Ming, 'an old family recipe.'

'And please, call me John.'

Blake added a generous helping of rice to the mixture on his plate together with some of the shredded duck and also a couple of meatballs.

'As you know, Vietnamese society embodies the principles of Confucianism. Deference is central to this. People obey without question at all levels of society. Citizens obey the rules, students their teachers, wives their husbands and children their parents. As you can see, Hoa has some problems with the last one. Perhaps her husband will find her different.' Khien said this sternly, but Blake sensed that he was in fact more indulgent than his tone suggested.

'Is there a particular religious tradition that you follow yourselves?' asked Blake.

'Yes, Buddhism,' said Khien. 'Ajahn Kai-Luat is the Abbot of the monastery An Lac that we visit. It's in the Central Highlands.'

'He's a distant cousin of my father,' said Hoa.

'I see,' said Blake. 'Which branch of Buddhism?'

'It is based on the Theravada tradition, but Ajahn Kai-Luat doesn't always follow the rules. Some people call him a rebel, but I call him a visionary,' said Khien. 'We visit as regularly as we can, although it is a long and difficult journey, especially now. But it is worth it, if only for the weekend. It is very quiet and peaceful.'

'I see.'

'You are welcome to join us on our next visit. After you've been here for a while you may want a break. There are so many Americans in Saigon. It's like a market-place, twenty-four hours. So different now the war is on.' Khien frowned.

'Thank you,' said Blake. 'I will.'

'Tell me, Mr Miller...' began Ming, her voice soft and low.

'John, please.'

'Yes, forgive me, John. Is your wife still in England?'

Blake cleared his throat. 'I'm not married.'

'Oh, really?'

'Yes. I haven't found the right girl yet.'

Ming looked at him. She placed the tips of her fingers together, as if praying. 'Well, perhaps you will meet her in Vietnam.'

'Perhaps, but I'm a bit of a loner,' said Blake.

The children giggled again. Ming put her finger in front of her mouth and gestured for them to be quiet.

'Hoa teaches at the local primary school,' said Khien proudly.

Hoa tossed back her head.

'Do you enjoy it?' asked Blake.

'Yes, it's very rewarding,' said Hoa. 'My children are always very respectful and obedient.'

'That's fortunate,' said Blake.

'Unlike my daughter,' said Khien.

Hoa, Blake and Khien spent the rest of the meal discussing Vietnamese schools and the villa Khien sometimes visited on Lang Doc island. Ming and the children listened and watched. When they had finished eating, Ming cleared away the dishes. Khien led Blake and Hoa into the living room, where Hoa pointed to an altar in the corner of the room.

'Here, let me show you this,' she said.

A table was draped in an orange cloth with a gold rim. On it lay an incense holder, photographs of two women and a man, all sepia-coloured, and a small pile of sweets in an ornate dish.

'I presume this is a shrine for your ancestors,' said Blake.

'Yes,' said Hoa, pointing to the photographs in turn. 'This is my grandmother, Ly, my grandfather, Chinh, and my aunt, Thuy.'

'I see, thank you for showing me,' said Blake.

'And here are my cards,' said Hoa, picking up a colourful deck from a nearby table.

'Cards?'

'Yes, tarot cards.'

Khien laughed heartily.

'Hoa uses the tarot, she thinks it can help her to get in touch with the ancestors,' he said. 'But it's all nonsense.'

'It's not,' said Hoa forcefully. 'It's more direct than just burning incense at the altar. And it's not the only use of the cards.'

Khien wore an expression of weary resignation.

'It's just superstition,' he said dismissively, 'like the ace of death cards.'

'What are they?' said Blake.

'The Americans think that the ace of spades creates fear in the North Vietnamese forces and the Viet Cong,' said Hoa. 'So, some wear it as a symbol on their vehicles and their helmets. They also leave them on dead bodies for the Viet Cong to find. They're wrong, of course. The ace of spades has no significance for Vietnamese people. The tarot is different, though. That's not superstition.'

'Why is that?' asked Blake.

'The tarot is sensitive to the energy around people. When you throw the cards, you can predict the future because of the pattern of the cards. It has been right so many times. I am convinced it works.'

Khien propped himself up against a wall and shook his head.

'My father, he doesn't believe in it, but he is so fixed in his ideas. I hope you're not so sceptical, Mr Miller.'

'I agree with your father, it does sound irrational.'

'Hoa, you're naive. I don't know who told you all this nonsense. Your ideas are misguided and have no place in Vietnamese culture.'

'Father, like Ajahn Kai-Luat, I am an independent thinker. I read, I observe and I am not mistaken. One day I will show you I am right,' she said defiantly.

'Ajahn Kai-Luat uses reason, he doesn't believe in superstition,' said Khien in an exasperated tone.

'Father, this is not superstition.'

Khien gave her a long, hard look, sighed, then his expression melted into one of affection.

'Fortunately, the tarot isn't the only cards Hoa likes to play with, she plays excellent pontoon.'

'Maybe we can have a game sometime,' said Blake, looking at her.

'Maybe, Mr Miller, but I will beat you,' said Hoa demurely.

Swiftly she left the room; moments later they heard her talking in the kitchen with Ming.

'She started with the I-Ching, and then became interested in the tarot. She needs a strong guiding hand to keep her grounded.'

'Does she get guidance from Ajahn Kai-Luat?'

'No, she respects him, but will not listen to him. She needs a husband. There have been a couple of suitors; they both proposed, but she rejected them... they had weaknesses, she said. Ming despairs that she is hot-headed, will get a bad reputation and never settle. Modesty and dignity are not Hoa's qualities. As a father, this is difficult. She needs a strong man to take her on. Hopefully we will find one... Anyway, I have said too much.'

CHAPTER 4

In the morning Blake made his way to the British
Embassy. It was a few streets away, in a nineteenth-
century terraced building set back on a wide boulevard.

'This is your office,' said Gerald Flint, the
Ambassador, in a crisp, commanding voice. He was
slim and grey-haired, dressed in a pressed white shirt
and a silk tie. He opened the door and turned on the
ceiling fan, which whirred gently. 'You'll find it quieter
at the back here.' He took a few paces across the room
and opened the window. 'There's not much we can do
about the heat, I'm afraid.' He loosened his tie. 'I expect
you may want to use the safe.' He pulled open the doors
of a wall-mounted wooden cabinet situated above the
desk and removed a dozen books stacked up on shelves.
Set into the wall was a rectangular metal plate. He
turned the wheel of the combination lock and the door
opened with a click. It was empty. 'You can set up your
own code.'

'Has this office been vacant for long?'

'A few months. A chap named Coulter. He's no
longer with us, sadly.' He cleared his throat and
frowned. 'I'll set up secure communication with London
for you. If you need anything else, just ask.'

'Thank you, sir.'

'In the meantime, come with me and I'll introduce
you to some of the Embassy staff.'

Blake followed Flint back to the main office. It was a
hive of bustling activity: there were a dozen or so desks
arranged in two rows. The ones at the front were
occupied by Vietnamese women, busily typing.

As they entered, an older, smartly-dressed
Vietnamese woman came up to them. 'Mr Flint, I need

you to sign these letters, please,' she said, holding out a bundle of papers.

'Put them on my desk, please,' said the Ambassador. 'I'll sign them later.'

'Yes, sir,' she said, and turned to go.

'Wait a moment,' Flint said. 'I want you to meet Mr John Miller, he's joining us as a translator. Miller, this is Pham Hieu, without whom I would be lost. She keeps all the Vietnamese staff in order for me.'

'Pleased to meet you,' said Blake in Vietnamese.

'You speak Vietnamese very well,' said Mrs Hieu. 'Have you been in Vietnam long?'

'No, I've just arrived. I learnt Vietnamese when I was child, from my nursemaid in Thailand: she came from Saigon.'

'You lived in Thailand when you were young?'

'Yes, for many years.'

'Well, I hope you like it here,' she said.

'Thank you,' said Blake. 'I'm sure I will.'

'If you need anything typed, Miller, give it to Mrs Hieu and she'll get one of the girls to do it,' said Flint.

'Thank you,' said Blake. 'I appreciate it.'

'See you later, Mr Miller,' said Mrs Hieu as she turned and walked away.

Flint guided Blake towards the desks at the back of the office. One was occupied by a young European man. 'This is Parker, he's my assistant, gets all sorts of boring and tedious jobs. Don't you, Parker?'

'Don't believe him,' said Parker. 'There's always something interesting going on.'

'John Miller's joining us as a translator,' said Flint. 'Why don't you introduce him to the other chaps? I've got to go and make some telephone calls.'

'Righto,' said Parker.

'See you later, Miller,' said Flint.

'Yes, sir,' said Blake. The Ambassador went into his office and closed the door.

'Well, what do you think of Old Thunder?' asked Parker.

'Too early to say,' said Blake. 'I'll let you know when I've been here a bit longer.'

'Anyway, come and meet the other chaps, they'll be pleased to see a new face, I expect. They're normally at these desks next to mine, but I think they're all outside at the moment. Come on, let's go and see.' Parker ushered Blake through a set of French windows at the rear of the office. There was a small garden outside, with a few small trees giving some shade. Under the trees were three men sitting on rattan chairs round a wooden table.

'Chaps, this is John Miller, he's joining us as a translator,' said Parker. 'Take a seat, why don't you?' Blake and Parker sat down on two vacant chairs.

'Welcome, Mr Miller,' said one of the men, reaching out his hand. Blake shook it. 'I'm George Mason.'

'Please, call me John,' said Blake. 'I don't like formality.'

'These other chaps are Roger Sinclair on my left and David Anderson over there,' said Parker.

'I may have trouble remembering all your names,' said Blake, who had already committed them to memory and made a careful note of their respective appearances, particularly Anderson, whose bright red hair stood out like a beacon.

'Oh, I'm sure you'll not have much trouble,' said Mason. 'After all, there's only a few of us.'

'How long have you been here?' asked Blake.

'Roger and I are new, we were posted here about a month ago,' replied Mason. 'I'm out from London, Roger was in Vienna. The FO are beefing up the contingent here because of the hoo-ha that the Americans seem to have got themselves into. Makes more work for all of us. David's been here the longest, I believe. In Moscow for a while, weren't you, David?'

'That's right, I was there about four years,' said Anderson. 'It could be bloody parky there, but give me the cold any time rather than this wretched heat and humidity. Came here about two years ago. Not my idea of an ideal posting.'

'Where was your previous posting?' Blake asked Richard Parker.

'I was in Washington DC until a year or so ago,' said Parker. 'The climate's not wonderful there, but at least you don't feel as if you're permanently soaking wet.'

* * *

Blake shut his office door and looked round the room that had been Coulter's office. He had the same unsettling feeling of walking in a dead man's shoes. He spent the rest of the morning gathering information. At mid-afternoon he left the Embassy, purchased a street map and went in search of Coulter's flat. The streets around the Embassy bustled with activity. Street vendors, pedestrians, cyclists and motorbikes jostled for position, people pushed and shoved each other as they made their way through the crowds. Blake counted three noodle cafés, two boutiques, three bars, a grocery shop, a launderette and two street kiosks selling books, newspapers, magazines and sweets. A thriving and obvious black market sold everything from Zippo lighters to Levis to Budweiser beer. He stopped at a noodle café overflowing with people and found a vacant seat on an outside table. They were jammed together and there was barely room to get in and out. He ordered coffee. A small boy came up and waved an empty, broken plastic cup at him. The boy's fingernails were ingrained with dirt and his tunic was stained and tattered; he had a farmyard smell. He looked up at Blake, his eyes demanding and intense. Blake emptied his pocket of his small change and the boy ran away, satisfied. Some moments later a swarm of mangy pigeons picked greedily at the spoils under the table until they had completely cleared them, then just as quickly disappeared. He studied the map, gulped down a black coffee and moved on. Coulter's flat was set in a busy market area. Rows and rows of rickety old stalls were bunched up against each other, many with live animals in cages, including songbirds, wildfowl and native rodents. As Blake walked by, one overpowering smell blended into another. An enormous pungent stench hung in the airless street. Rickshaw drivers shouted and rang their bells as they dodged and weaved through the crowds looking for customers. A hawker dressed in a grimy overall approached him, trying to flog his savoury rice takeaway.

'Here, you can enjoy your evening meal!'

Blake studied it; unattractive pieces of grey meat were mixed in.

'What's in it?' he asked.

'Pig, slaughtered this morning,' the hawker grinned.

Blake looked at the glistening meat; it was impossible to tell what animal it had come from.

'No.'

He walked on. The flat was on the first floor up a dimly lit staircase between a restaurant and a grocer. There were six weeks left on the lease. He let himself in. It was like entering a boiler room, airless and baking; the late afternoon sun poured in through closed windows. Dust particles shimmered in shafts of sunlight. Blake closed the door behind him and removed his shirt; he'd just have to bake. The place had been shut up like a mausoleum. He took a brief walk round the flat and realised he wasn't the first person to do a search. Empty drawers had been left open and rugs folded back. It seemed like the person doing the search had left in a hurry. If Coulter had left documents here rather than in his office, he just hoped they hadn't been found so far. The kitchen smelled of mould and dustbins. Tiny flies, which had bred in the humid atmosphere, hovered around like helicopters. As he moved about, disturbing the still air, the flies were pushed aside like objects floating in water. The furniture was cheap and sparse. He examined every drawer and cupboard, the wardrobe, shelves, and desk in minute detail, searching for secret compartments, just the smallest of clues. Spilt red nail varnish lay shining in the bottom of a drawer. He rubbed his finger over it; it was set in position like volcanic rock. He removed the one picture from the wall, a fading black and white scene of old Saigon, and turned it over. The brown sticky back paper holding the cardboard backing in place had peeled at the edges but was still securely attached. The rectangle where the picture had hung was distinctly lighter than the wall around it. It had probably hung there untouched and unnoticed for years. Blake replaced it. He completed the first search. Nothing was remotely significant. Sweat dripped into his eyes and the waist of his trousers was saturated. He wanted the job over quickly, but this was long, laborious work and the answer he desperately needed wouldn't yield easily, if indeed it was here at all. He wasn't prepared to leave without having examined every inch of the place.

Blake started a deeper search. He unscrewed the cheap kitchen units. They fell apart readily enough, but yielded no clues. He put them back together with more difficulty and spent more time than he wanted replacing them exactly as they had been. He removed the carpet from the main room and shone his torch down the gap between each floorboard in turn, examining them at the same time for evidence of unnatural shift. One of them moved; he levered it up. Nothing. He examined the toilet cistern, took the panel off the bath, removed the mirror in the bathroom, unscrewed all the light fittings, then put them all back together. He rapped on the walls with his knuckles, listening for hollow sounds made by holes hidden behind the plaster – it drew a complete blank. Somebody else had ripped apart the upholstery and soft furnishings. This didn't put him off, he did his own minute search, but it revealed nothing. The deeper search was physically more demanding. Gasping for breath, Blake found an old chipped and cracked cup and gulped down some tepid water at the kitchen sink. He got back to work, crouching at floor level in the other rooms. He heard a Vietnamese family on the stairs. Children laughed and a woman shouted at them to behave. He heard a key in a lock and a door slam. Hours passed. Evening light dipped in through the windows.

He found a half-full bottle of cheap American brandy in one of the kitchen cupboards and poured himself a drink into the same cracked cup. The chair creaked as he sat down. He allowed his body to relax but his mind was razor sharp, racing. He tried to get into Coulter's mindset. Born in Aberystwyth, London University, Mathematics. Blake had studied his file in minute detail only a few hours ago and found nothing significant. Coulter was experienced, a professional, he would have been inventive, creative. Blake shouldn't look in the obvious places. These ideas passed quickly through his mind as he gazed up through the upper part of the window at the setting sun. Almost by chance, he noticed something. It dawned on him that there was something peculiar about the bamboo curtain rail. He took his time, studied it, his eyes scanning it from one side to the other. It looked ordinary enough, he couldn't put his finger on it; it was just out of place, askew a fraction. He took it down from its fixing and noticed that the end was plugged with a cheap plastic screw. His optimism returned. If only. He tipped it up. There was the faint sound of something knocking up against the screw. He tried to yank it off but his sweaty hands failed to grip the slippery plastic. He used a piece of discarded upholstery as friction and the screw came off with a pop. He looked inside and tilted the pole; the contents fell out. A bundle of rolled-up papers was tied together with red string. He examined them quickly. This was the cache. He tidied up and made sure the flat looked no different from when he entered, then made a quick and discreet exit and returned to his office in the Embassy.

The files were written in code more complex than he would have expected, but amongst them he found an un-encoded note, which contained a hint as to the keywords needed to decode the files, which were peculiar to Coulter's past. He had to revisit Coulter's personnel file more than once, looking for more than one significant word. Blake had a new energy, but it was well into the night before he discovered the code. Only Coulter, or somebody with access to Coulter's file, could have known it. Blake worked for hours in the silence of the night. His concentration was broken only by the sound of distant footsteps and the click of a light being extinguished. He listened intently as the footsteps got louder and stopped at his door. There was a momentary silence. Then there was a knock.

'Come in,' said Blake heartily.

The night porter opened the door and stood in the entrance, frowning.

'Can I help?' Blake smiled.

'We don't expect people to work this late,' the porter said.

'What is the time?' said Blake. 'I've been so involved with my translation I've lost all track of it.'

'Three forty-five,' the porter responded, glancing at his watch. 'Are you expecting to be here much longer?'

'Could be all night, I've got some urgent papers due for tomorrow.'

'It's not in the regulations for people to stay all night,' he said.

'I'm new here, I didn't know that. Tell you what, do you like Budweiser?'

'Yes.'

'I've got a crate of it in my flat. I'll bring you some tomorrow. Shall we say a dozen?'

The porter sniffed and stood there for a moment, considering.

'I'll look forward to it,' he said eventually with a satisfied nod.

He closed the door and Blake heard his footsteps disappear into the distance. He refocused on his work. He painstakingly decoded every letter, every sentence, and double-checked it. The files contained lists of Coulter's contacts and detailed instructions on the positions of the dead letter drops and the signals involved. They included personal comments on the reliability or otherwise of his contacts, people he had suspicions about, people who could be approached in an emergency. Most important, there was a description of the main contact, an Englishman by the name of Tranter, a mercenary character with a shady past but still something of a patriot who frequented the *El Paraiso* bar in downtown Saigon, and the recognition signals. Blake worked until he found himself nodding off at his desk; his eyes began to shut of their own accord, pre-sleep, dream-like images flooded his mind. He jolted himself to and locked the papers in the safe until he could complete them, then rested his head on his desk and woke at daybreak when the sun streamed through the window. He fixed himself a thick black coffee, went back to the flat and got another couple of hours' sleep. He had got used to the quirky bed and was able to sleep despite its groans, pits and bulges. By late morning he was back at his desk, and a couple of hours later he'd finished.

CHAPTER 5

Blake made his way down the broad tree-lined boulevards and past solid grandiose and graceful buildings to the imposing nineteenth-century *Hotel Continental*. The centre of Saigon was architecturally impressive and he understood why it had been named 'the Paris of the Orient'. But it now had a war-ravaged feel about it, some of the buildings decaying. He made his way to the Terrace Bar, he ordered himself a *citron presse*, a tart French drink, sat down in a dark green wicker chair and took in the atmosphere of faded elegance. The bar was decorated with distinctive black and white tiles; cooling ceiling fans whirred and hissed. There were a few local men in suits, a well-dressed American couple and some scantily-dressed women perched on high bar stools. There was a pervading smell of Gauloises. He worked his way further down Tu Do Street, and stopped at a plaque stating that this street was formerly known as Rue Cadinet under the French. He ordered a drink at another bar and listened to a conversation between two inebriated US war correspondents. Teasing out the useful bits from the long rambling sentences and laboured slurs, he got the gist. They weren't there by chance. This street had a second name in certain quarters: 'Radio Cadinet', because of the military intelligence they could pick up there. Blake visited a few more bars, got a sense of the place and then continued downtown, where the streets became narrower. As the day turned into evening the American G.I.s appeared in greater numbers. He walked through a maze of litter-strewn alleyways with ramshackle houses on either side. The place was bustling with people, bars and cafés. American G.I.s were standing in groups on street corners. Some were lolling about on their chairs in front of pavement cafés loaded up with beers and thick black Vietnamese coffee. Their drunken laughter mingled in with the tinging of bicycle bells, roaring motorbikes and Jimi Hendrix taped music. Street corner drug-dealing was rife, not even disguised. The prostitutes were also out in force looking for business. One G.I. stepped out of a doorway doing up his flies. The occasional US Army Jeep crept up the busy alleys, displacing the crowds on to the pavements. A smell of beer and cigarette smoke hung in the air. Blake found *El Paraiso*. From the outside it looked like one of the seediest bars. He came through the doorway and spent a few seconds evaluating, working out possible escape routes. He took a closer look at the finer details, the décor, potential hazards, the customers and the atmosphere. There were mainly locals, a few G.I.s, a few prostitutes. The dark, oppressive atmosphere was thick with smoke and heavy with the smell of booze. It signalled a general sense of debauchery and low life, Coulter's world. He ordered himself a whisky; it was large, cheap and strong, the kind of stuff which would go to your head quickly, making you dull and reckless. Its sharpness left a burning sensation in the back of his throat. He decided one was enough, but judging by the number of empty glasses on the table, not enough for the locals or the G.I.s. He noticed one get up and follow a woman into a stairway.

A young woman wandered over, walking awkwardly in over-sized stilettos. Her tight mini skirt was split at the seams. She propped herself up at Blake's table and flaunted herself at him. Her perfume was thick and heady. He looked away and waved his hand; she walked off. An older Vietnamese man in dark glasses entered, bought a drink and sat at a table by himself. Blake regarded him for a while out of the corner of his eye before making a strategic exit to watch the bar entrance from a concealed position inside a doorway on the other side of the street. The man emerged, scanned the street, turning his head from left to right, then walked off towards the town square. Blake decided to spend the next few weeks getting familiar with Tu Do Street and downtown Saigon.

* * *

'Mr Miller?' Blake looked up. Mrs Da Quang, the cleaner, was standing in the doorway. 'I disturb you?' she said.

'That's OK. I was just about to have a break anyway. Come in. Sit down.'

Over the last two weeks Blake had got used to Mrs Da Quang fussing around his office with her feather duster and furniture polish. He'd made a point of being pleasant. She had an engaging smile and was a good source of office gossip. Mrs Da Quang came in hesitantly and stood in front of the desk. Blake drew up a chair for her and she sat down.

'What can I do for you?'

'You very good language man,' she said. 'Everyone says so.'

'Well…'

'I want to speak more good English. You give me lessons. Yes? I pay you.'

Blake thought for a moment. 'Well, I suppose I could do the occasional lesson,' he said. 'If you really want to do this.'

'Oh yes, Mr Miller. Speak good English, get more good job. More money.'

Blake studied her for a moment. 'OK then. I'll do it,' he said. He thought it might be an interesting diversion. 'It'll have to be in the evening, though. There's no time during the day.'

'Evening good. Thank you, Mr Miller.'

'Is once every two weeks OK for you?'

'Very OK,' said Mrs Da Quang. She beamed.

Later that afternoon Blake found that he had acquired two more pupils also anxious to improve their English. One of the ex-pat secretaries offered to host the lessons, to relieve the tedium of the long evenings while her husband explored the nightlife. To his surprise he found he enjoyed the sessions, and being only once a fortnight, they didn't interfere too much with his own clandestine explorations of downtown Saigon.

* * *

Blake decided it was time to make contact with Tranter, using the recognition protocol described in the file he had found in Coulter's flat. He was aware of the risk; the file might have been found, decoded and replaced for Blake to find, in which case tonight's meeting would be a trap. However, he had no choice. To approach Tranter in any other way than the one agreed would only raise his suspicions. Blake entered *El Paraiso* bar on the first Wednesday in June. As before, it was thick with cigarette smoke and smelling of alcohol. Blake stood at the bar. He had a drink and surveyed the area, again evaluating possible escape routes. He immediately recognised Tranter from Coulter's description, a portly, balding man in a crumpled soiled white suit, with a cigarette between his fingers. The only other people were a few locals, absorbed in conversation. It seemed like as good a time as any. Blake took a deep breath and seized the moment.

'Mind if I share your table?' said Blake.

'Of course, old chap,' said Tranter in a slow English drawl, retaining the remnants of a public school accent, 'glad to see a new face.' He leant across the table extending his hand. 'Name's Tranter, by the way.'

'I'm John, John Miller,' said Blake, and shook the wet limp hand. He brought the recognition protocol sharply to mind.

An inebriated waiter in a stained apron walked up and hovered nearby.

'Can I buy you a drink?' Blake asked. 'I'm new in town, what's the local brew like?'

'Poison,' said Tranter, 'I'd stick to Coors if I were you.'

'OK, two Coors, please.'

The waiter nodded his head vacantly and wandered back to the bar. Tranter took a drag on his cigarette and puffed the smoke up into the air. Blake noticed that his white suit had a faint ash-grey tinge to it.

'What do you get up to in Saigon?' said Blake. At first impression, Tranter looked ineffectual, unkempt and the worse for too much dependence on alcohol or chemicals or both, but as Tranter's eyes bored into him they were as sharp as razors.

'I'm in import-export mainly, but my cash flow situation has been a bit poorly recently.'

'Well, I hope that will pick up again now.'

'What about you?' Tranter's voice started to rasp. He coughed.

'I'm a translator at the Embassy.'

'What languages do you speak?'

'Mainly Vietnamese, Thai, French, with a bit of Cantonese.'

'I've picked up a bit of Vietnamese over the years. I've been here over twenty years now, after things got a bit warm in Germany.'

Tranter flicked the ash off the end of his cigarette and it landed in the ashtray a few inches away.

'You married?' said Tranter.

'No. What about yourself, are you a family man?'

'No one regular. I'm on my own.'

The waiter approached, struggling to balance the bottles and glasses on the tray he held precariously in his right hand. He placed them slowly, one by one, on the table. Standing upright was a greater challenge; he leaned backwards, almost keeled over and swayed from side to side until he found his balance. Blake eyed him curiously. Tranter didn't react. The waiter staggered back to the bar and propped himself up against the counter. Blake poured the beer into his glass. Tranter drank it straight from the bottle, then took a final vicious drag on his cigarette, extinguished it between his fingers and threw it into the ashtray, where it lay smouldering with several others. Blake felt the smoke tickle his throat and took a few swigs of his beer.

'Any good places to eat?' said Blake. 'I haven't had a decent meal since I arrived.'

'If you want French food, the place to go is *Chez Jacques*. If you want local cuisine, you need to go to *Pok-choy*; it doesn't look good from the outside, but inside it's always full of locals. The food's good, not expensive, authentic Vietnamese cuisine.'

'Thanks, I'll try one of those. Is there anything particular to see in Saigon?'

'I like the Botanical Gardens, an interesting array of plants. I often spend my afternoons there in the café, reading *The Economist*,' said Tranter.

'Maybe I'll see you there,' said Blake.

Blake got up and shook Tranter's hand. He felt something transfer into his grasp, a flimsy piece of paper; he put it straight into his pocket. Once inside his flat he read the scrawny handwriting. It was a list of signals for clandestine communications between himself and Tranter. Blake memorised the details then burnt the paper, turning it into ash under his fingers. He had a shower, wrapped himself in a towel, poured a stiff whisky and sat in one of the wicker chairs. His head was heavy with the drunken, debauched atmosphere, his mind alert to the dangers, risks and realities of his undertaking.

* * *

The Zoo and Botanical Gardens may have been impressive in their heyday, but, like everything else in Saigon, now had a sad and neglected look. Just inside the entrance was an amusement ride where people sat upon real animals. Stuffed bears, large cats and deer followed each other around the revolving platform. The children seemed to enjoy the ride despite the threadbare, tatty appearance of the animals. There was something macabre about it. He made his way under the giant tropical trees and past the lawns and flowerbeds to the café set with a view of a kidney-shaped pond. There were only a few customers. Tranter sat at a table, alone, smoking. *The Economist*, front cover up, was set out in front of him. Blake walked on, sat on a bench beside the pond and watched the white-winged ducks for a while.

As far as he could tell, there was nobody taking any interest in Tranter. He pulled out a Gauloise cigarette from the packet he had bought that morning and wandered over to the table.

'Excuse me, do you have a light?' Blake said. He put his own *Economist* down on the table.

'Pleased to oblige, old chap,' said Tranter. His cigarette waggled up and down as he answered without taking it out of his mouth. He pulled his Zippo lighter from his pocket and lit Blake's cigarette.

'Thanks,' said Blake. He picked up Tranter's *Economist* and left his behind, with $10,000 hidden inside. He made his way back to the park entrance, stubbed out the cigarette and threw the packet of Gauloises into the litter bin. He hated cigarettes.

Later that afternoon Blake made his way to the Tan Dinh Church on the northern outskirts of central Saigon. It was silent, still, dark and cool inside. He walked up to the altar of Our Lady on the left-hand side. There were ten lit candles in the sign of a cross. Blake lit a few more in a diagonal, made an offering and walked to a pew at the back. He kneeled and waited. He remembered as a small boy sitting next to his mother in the church in Pukhet. She had whispered to him to be silent. Her face was pale and she brushed her finger across her cheek to wipe away a tear. He remembered how he felt confused and unhappy. The contrast to now was stark. He experienced a sudden pang of doubt and guilt. The duality of his role hit him. On the one hand there was deception, betrayal and duplicity, and on the other patriotism, duty and self-sacrifice. There was only one moral law – justification by results, even if the means were dubious. This is the work he had been trained to do, this is what he'd learnt and this was his

53

choice. He heard footsteps. A man in a crumpled white suit walked in, sat for a while in a second-row pew, wandered up to the altar of Our Lady, crossed himself and stood in silence. Blake knelt down, head bowed, his hands flat against each other. He heard the echo of more footsteps. After ten minutes he looked up; the candles making the sign of the cross were extinguished. Blake walked carefully to the pew in the second row, knelt down and retrieved the envelope that was stuck with Sellotape to the underside. After some more 'prayer', he returned to the front of the church and snuffed out the candles making the diagonal. He went back to the Embassy and decoded the message. Now that Tranter was back on the payroll, he had wasted no time in identifying Blake's first target, Major Phan Nam. Blake had already heard of him. A black-and-white photograph of the Major was included. *A small group of Viet Cong commanders, south-west division, are to meet in the Old Town Square Hotel conference room. Sunday next, 5.00pm.* Blake opened his filing cabinet, took out his list of names and checked that Major Phan was listed as a VC commander. The photograph Tranter had provided matched the one in his own file. Thanks to Tranter, Blake could now get him. Tranter was obviously more efficient than he appeared.

* * *

Blake made his way to the *Old Town Square Hotel*, bought himself a drink and sat at the bar. Rows of lamps were set out on tables. The seats were covered in red velvet upholstery. A selection of Vera Lynn classics played endlessly on an automated jukebox as if stuck in a time warp. Blake followed a group of businessmen upstairs and did a tour of the hotel. He found the conference room on the first floor, overlooking the Old Town Square. He looked out of the large window. The smaller *Hotel Oriental* stood directly opposite. Blake walked across the square and into the reception. He flicked through some brochures. The room keys were arranged in rows on hooks behind the desk. The pretty Vietnamese receptionist flirted with an American G.I., oblivious to the smartly dressed man who was waiting impatiently. After arranging a date, the American left. When the guest finally got her attention, he vented his frustration with a barrage of angry words. Blake walked upstairs unnoticed. There was the abrasive noise of a vacuum cleaner and a cleaning trolley in the corridor; the room doors were open. He identified several rooms which would give him a satisfactory view of the hotel opposite.

Two days later Blake waited in the lobby of the *Hotel Oriental* until reception was deserted, then stole the key to a vacant room overlooking the square. He locked himself in and wedged a wooden chair against the handle of the door. There was a good view of the conference room from his vantage point. He removed the Mk1(T) rifle from his rucksack, screwed the silencer into place, drew up a wooden chair, opened the sash window a few inches and waited. They were fifteen minutes late. He could hear the floorboards creak as people walked in the corridor outside his room. There was a brief interlude of silence then more footsteps, some chatter and laughter, the jingling of keys. A door banged. Across the square five or six men entered and milled about the room. Blake used his telescopic lens and identified the Major from his photograph. He was distinctive, tall and thin, with a close-cropped beard.

The subservient behaviour of the other men in the room was obvious. The Major sat down at the head of the table and the others took their places around him. A waitress entered and served coffee. Blake felt adrenalin coursing through him. His heart pounded; he didn't have much time. The icy coldness he'd experienced in the jungle descended upon him. He controlled his breathing and his heart rate dropped. He blocked out everything around him. Nothing else existed apart from what he could see through the optic. He was focused, absolutely still. His right hand extended over the rifle stock; there was a perfect alignment between his eye, hand and gun. In that instant, both he and the gun were made of steel. He took aim, inhaled and pulled the trigger. The window smashed. He heard a muffled yell and watched down his lens as the men inside the room started to move. Blake worked the bolt, sighted, took aim and squeezed the trigger again. The Major went down, his blood splattered on the broken window. Blake rapidly dismantled the gun, stuffed it in the rucksack, made a discreet exit and hastened back to his flat. He poured himself a large whisky; as he flopped into the wicker chair it creaked. For a moment he thought of nothing. He drank the whisky. The strong, bitter taste felt good. He did a mental assessment of the whole operation. The meeting was late, but apart from that everything had gone according to plan. Relaxing in the chair, the sickly-sweet burden of success suffused him.

The next day he used the secure communications at the Embassy. Then everything was back to normal, his early morning run, the translations, the weekends with Khien and his family, the evenings downtown, the English class. A nice, comfortable routine, which included both the respectable and the seedy, although he felt no sense of belonging in either. He was a fraud in both.

* * *

The streets, the bars and the G.I.s became familiar, almost routine. He made a point of striking up trivial conversations with fellow customers. He even grew to like the cheap whisky, bought drinks for others, accepted drinks, and still felt sober after a few. After the eighth approach from a prostitute one evening he felt his resistance weakening and accepted. He followed her through a dark narrow corridor and into a small, seedy back room. The only furniture was a bed. Mouldy dark patches showed through the plastered walls. A single lamp resting on a bamboo mat dimly lighted the room. There was a strong smell of incense and a hint of cannabis. He negotiated the price for the service. The girl removed all her clothes without the least embarrassment and lay down on the bed. Blake removed only the minimum clothing necessary. It was over quickly. He paid her extra as a kind of compensation, aware that he had barely even acknowledged her humanity. It was a satisfactory, uncomplicated transaction, one that became increasingly habitual. At its basest the sex was as satisfying as an urgent piss. And he never went to the same girl twice. It felt sordid; mostly, the women were sad and wretched, their faces like masks beneath layers of thick make-up. Their eyes were dead and distant. But then his work was sordid. Once a young woman smiled sweetly at him as she walked him to the door. He flattered himself that she'd enjoyed the experience until she asked for more money. He recognised he was slipping into the same low life as his predecessor and wasn't proud of it, but he had nobody to account to, only the nagging, troubling reminder that Coulter was dead.

CHAPTER 6

London
Twelve years later. April 1979

Cathy's insides had been churning for the last ten minutes and now she felt as if she was burning up. She was perched, bird-like, on the edge of a hard-backed grey chair, halfway along the office corridor. It wasn't a good place; a radiator directly behind her was throwing out heat like a furnace. She dared not take off her jacket; her shirt underneath had a coffee stain and she hadn't had time to wash it. Men in smart suits and women in drainpipe skirts and polished shoes walked past her. Their shoes made a sharp, officious sound on the linoleum floor. Her skirt had swivelled round a bit, with the seam out of place. She tugged the material around, moving her weight from one buttock to the other.

She'd worn the grey pinstripe suit three times and cut her thick dark hair short to look business-like, but she still hadn't been offered a job. She tried not to take it personally. The tutors had told them it would be difficult. The economy was in chaos. Some said it was the result of Jim Callaghan's useless policies, but the malaise had preceded him. Cathy really didn't care why it was; she only wanted a job. In their last term at university she and her flatmates had papered the kitchen walls with letters of rejection. They gave each a different-coloured star depending on how polite it was. Gold - very polite, green - indifferent, red - curt and short, enough to kill your confidence stone dead. A novel kind of wallpaper had been born.

She was optimistic about this job as a 'Research and Administration Support Assistant'. 'Typing skills essential,' the advertisement stated. She had a real chance with this one. Relax, for God's sake relax, she thought. Have confidence; be confident. It's only an interview after all. I'm not scaling a rock face with a 200-foot drop. She absent-mindedly picked a piece of fluff off her skirt and flicked it onto the floor. Fumbling in her handbag, she withdrew the job description. She read it again and checked the details.

Out of the corner of her eye she noticed a striking-looking man striding purposefully towards her. As he approached, he adjusted his tie. He had small, wide-set eyes, a neat short beard and wavy, dull brown hair. She caught a strong whiff of aftershave.

'Hello, I'm Norman Wells, Research Officer. You're Cathy Simpson, I presume?' he said.

'Yes.'

Cathy stood up and shook his extended hand, which was a touch clammy. She noticed him scanning her up and down, which was slightly unnerving. She pulled the jacket closer.

'Follow me,' he said.

She tried to readjust her skirt as she walked along, discreetly pulling it round. He led her through a busy, open-plan office noisy with the click-clicking of electric typewriters and into a small, bright office. As they entered a tall man stood up from behind a desk. He smiled and shook her hand; his own was warm and his grip was firm.

'Hello. Cathy Simpson?'

'Yes.'

'I'm Blake Carter, I'm the Applied Research Manager.'

'Nice to meet you,' said Cathy.

'Do take a seat,' he continued.

She and Norman sat down on the chairs opposite his desk.

'I see from your CV that you live in Dulwich, Forest Hill.'

'Yes.'

'How was your journey?'

'Easy, I got a direct train to London Bridge station and walked.'

'And you found us without any trouble?'

'Yes, thank you, it was quite straightforward, Personnel sent me a map.'

'Good.'

She was struck by Blake Carter's deep, mellow voice. There was something in the way he looked and moved that grabbed her attention. He consulted a checklist in front of him, pen in hand. She guessed she would have to jump through some of the hoops on his list to get a chance at this job.

'I see you're rather over-qualified for this position,' said Blake Carter, studying her. 'Your science background will be useful. After some training you'll be able to understand the research we're doing here, but the job you've applied for is a support position and some of the work will be secretarial. Will this suit you?'

'Oh yes,' replied Cathy, 'I did the secretarial course to increase my range of skills. I'm perfectly OK with this. And I don't mind typing. In this job I would be learning so much and gaining invaluable experience.'

'Good,' he said, and smiled. 'And your plans for the future?'

'I'd like to do pure research.'

'So you see this job as a stepping stone?'

'Yes.'

'I see.'

Cathy had no intention of being stuck behind a typewriter. Once established in her career, hopefully in scientific research of some kind, she hoped to settle down, get married and start a family. But she'd carry on with her work and her hobbies. Being a full-time housewife and mother wasn't for her. Most of her friends wanted the same. There was no reason in her mind why it shouldn't all happen as she envisaged.

'We undertake a number of research projects with different sponsors. Some of our projects are partly funded by the European Research Council, the Science Research Council and the Science and Engineering Research Council. Have you heard of them?'

'Yes, I have.'

Blake Carter consulted his checklist again and then relaxed back in his chair.

'The project that we'd like you to work on initially involves developing compact discs, or CDs for short. It's a new project in collaboration with the Science Research Council. They're a new data storage medium for computers and will probably replace floppy discs eventually. BCS wants be at the forefront pioneering this research. We've a budget of around 80k in the first stages and this should keep us going for about two years,' he said.

'I see,' said Cathy, 'that sounds interesting. Technology moves so fast.'

He looked at her attentively for a few moments, then sat forward and studied his checklist. He was in his mid-thirties, she estimated. His brown hair was cut short and his eyes were grey. He was not good-looking in a conventional way; his nose was too long and his eyes too close-set. His face was pitted and blemished, giving him a rugged look as if he'd been living in a harsh place, in the open air among the elements. He wore a white shirt with a blue tie; his grey jacket clung comfortably to him. The creases around the elbows were set in. He didn't look like a typical businessman, or a scientist for that matter, but there was something very attractive about him.

He asked her questions and made a column of neat ticks down the page. She had the impression he was perceptive and astute, and that it wouldn't be easy to pull the wool over his eyes. Not that she wanted to. Blake Carter turned to Norman Wells.

'You'll be working with Norman for some of the time on various other projects, so, Norman,' he said, 'it will be helpful if you give Miss Simpson an account of your current research projects.'

Norman Wells cleared his throat and scratched his ear.

'Certainly,' he said, and then launched into a seemingly interminable monologue, his eyes fixed on a spot on the wall above the door. Cathy looked over at him and tried to appear interested but his account was rambling and full of confusing terminology. She only half-heard and soon her attention refocused on Blake Carter, who also appeared uninterested, his own attention focused on his checklist. He began writing. She noticed that his handwriting was small and neat with the occasional wide flourish. Norman Wells sighed loudly. He was finished at last. Blake Carter looked up.

'And that's why my research is vital to the profitability of BCS,' Norman Wells announced. He threw back his shoulders and stretched. 'Scientific collaboration is commendable, but we are, first and foremost, a commercial enterprise.'

A corner of Blake's mouth contracted.

'Thank you, Norman,' he said, and turned over some papers. 'Your CV says that you can speak French,' he said.

'Yes, but not fluently.'

'And you have an unusual hobby, rock-climbing.'

'Yes, I learnt it at university.'

'Tell me about it.'

'I've been climbing for about two years, mainly in Yorkshire. I learnt with ropes, but I prefer not to use ropes on cliff faces I'm familiar with.'

'That takes courage,' said Blake Carter. 'So why do it?'

'I like the challenge, the feeling of achievement when I've reached the top. It's energising.'

'And how far is the top, usually?'

'About 100 feet. I'd like to go higher, but much above that and it becomes a lot riskier.'

'I see,' said Blake Carter.

People had told her she looked too fey and slight to be indulging in such a dangerous sport. Perhaps that was why he was studying her.

'Is that the only time you take risks, on a rock face?' said Blake Carter.

'I like a challenge.'

'Then I hope you won't be too bored here at BCS,' he said with a slight smile.

'Research is never boring,' said Cathy.

He sat back in his chair. 'Do you have any questions for us?'

She found herself gazing into his eyes and was momentarily speechless. Perplexingly, her face burned and her heart pounded. Norman Wells coughed. Cathy blinked and looked away. She came to her senses. God, what was all that about, she asked herself.

Any questions… 'Yes,' she thought quickly, 'what are the hours of work?'

'Just nine to five, with some flexibility if you're able,' he said. 'We may ask you to work late if we have deadlines to meet. You'll be given time off in lieu.'

'Oh yes, that's OK.'

'Any other questions?'

'No, not really, I think you've covered everything I was going to ask about,' she said.

Blake Carter stood up. He reached for her hand and shook it again. She was aware of the warmth of his grasp. 'Thank you for coming, Miss Simpson,' he smiled. 'We'll let you know as soon as possible.'

'Thank you,' said Cathy and smiled back.

She left the building, walked out into the bright sunlight and took off her jacket. The cool air felt refreshing and her skin tingled. She exposed her stained shirt to the world. It didn't matter now. Damn, Cathy thought, I really messed that up at the end. God, I hope he didn't notice my burning up. Why did I do that? What a fool! She turned it over and over as she walked towards London Bridge station, her agitated thoughts skittering everywhere. Deep in thought, she nearly banged into an old woman on a bicycle. The brakes squeaked abrasively and the overloaded basket at the front wobbled from side to side. She watched helplessly as some apples toppled out onto the pavement, then stooped down and picked them up.

'Watch where you're going,' the woman snapped and glared at her from behind horn-rimmed spectacles.

'Very sorry,' said Cathy, 'I'll pay for them. How much?'

'No need, but be more careful next time,' she said curtly.

Cathy placed them back in the basket. The woman didn't object.

'Yes, I will,' said Cathy, and walked on.

Cathy took stock, surprised to be so preoccupied considering she'd probably never see Blake Carter again. She wandered back to her flat, quickly changed out of her starchy clothes and made a coffee, still deep in thought. Two hours later she got the phone call: it was the BCS Personnel Department, offering her the job. She accepted, of course; she had little choice.

CHAPTER 7

'Hello there,' said a coarse female voice.

Cathy looked up from the dreary Health and Safety document. A young woman in a bright pink blouse stared down at her. Cathy smelt a strong, sickly-sweet perfume.

'I'm Rose. I work over there,' she said, and pointed to a cluster of desks at the other side of the office, where another woman was standing. 'You must be the new girl, Cathy.'

'Yes, I am. Nice to meet you, Rose,' said Cathy.

The early morning sun streamed in through the large picture window behind Cathy. The last two days she'd arrived early. She liked it when the office was quiet. Rose's brass bracelet caught the light, shimmering and sparkling. Rose turned round.

'Over here, Margot,' she called.

Another woman wandered over. Her cleavage was low cut; she tottered on stilettos and her breasts bounced along, heaving and generous.

'Margot, this is Cathy,' said Rose.

'Hello, Cathy,' said Margot in a high-pitched, sing-song voice. 'We've been wanting to have a chat with you.'

'Oh. What work do you do?' asked Cathy; she looked from one to the other, smiling.

Rose sat with one buttock on the side of Cathy's desk. Margot leant against a tall filing cabinet. They made themselves comfortable.

'We work for Paul,' said Rose. 'We're the data entry clerks for the Nuclear Physics team. It sounds posh, but our work's the same all the time. It can get boring sometimes.'

Cathy took a deep breath.

'I see. I'm in the Research team,' she said.

'We know,' said Rose, and her eyes twinkled mischievously, 'you're working for Mr Mysterious.'

'I'm sorry?' said Cathy. Her eyes widened.

'Blake Carter, the guy with the voice and body to die for. He's been working here for years, but we know hardly anything about him except he lives alone.'

'Oh,' said Cathy, and sat upright.

'No one's ever heard him take a personal call. Strange, isn't it?' said Margot. 'He used to spend every evening here working into the night. He leaves earlier now. But whenever anyone asks him, he always says he's going straight home. He won't say anything about himself, nothing.'

They stared at her.

'What do you think of that, Cathy?' said Rose.

'Well, I don't know what I think, if it's true.' Cathy shrugged and thought for a moment. 'Perhaps he likes his own company,' she said.

'Well, it's a bit unusual like, isn't it?' said Margot. She gently touched her blow-dried peroxide bouffant and repositioned it.

'We think he must have loads of money. He only takes one long holiday a year in the Far East,' said Rose. 'He hardly ever wears any new clothes, and he only drives a conked-out Cortina.'

Cathy took a deep breath and frowned.

'You jump to conclusions too quickly. God knows, he could have any number of financial commitments. He could be in debt, or maybe he's just frugal.'

Rose and Margot looked at each other, and then back at Cathy.

'Is it anybody's business? Why is anyone interested? He's entitled to some privacy, surely,' she said. She was beginning to feel hot. She rolled up her sleeves.

Rose looked intently at Cathy and twisted her long dark hair between her fingers; her nails were carefully manicured and painted with bright red varnish.

'Well, look,' said Rose. 'He's the sexiest man at BCS. And he's single. Of course we're interested.'

Cathy bit her lip.

'Maybe he's…you know what I mean, and that would be the end of it,' said Cathy, hoping to close the conversation.

Margot shook her head. 'No, he isn't,' she said. 'There's a rumour going around that he had a wife who died some years ago. And someone here said he had a girlfriend once, but she was really ugly.'

Margot removed a small mirror from her pocket, looked at herself in it and carefully patted her hair.

'It seems you know quite a bit about him then,' said Cathy.

'Only bits,' said Margot.

Rose's expression hardened and her eyes narrowed.

'Don't get any ideas about him, though,' she said. 'You won't get anywhere with him. We've all tried.'

'Goodness. It hadn't even crossed my mind. Why should it?' said Cathy, frowning. 'Perhaps he's mourning his dead wife.'

'Well, I hadn't thought of that,' said Rose, spinning her bracelet between her fingers.

Cathy had been pleased to be given the bright corner desk. Now she wasn't so sure. She felt trapped and neither woman seemed ready to move. Cathy looked down at the document in front of her and turned over the page. She picked up her pencil.

'Look, I've got a lot of reading to do,' she said.

'Anyway, Blake might be pushed out soon,' said Margot.

Cathy looked up. Margot put the mirror back in her pocket.

'Norman thinks he should be the manager,' continued Margot. 'He's friendly, not sexy and mysterious like Blake. He's married, his wife works in a department store, long hours. I think he gets lonely; he likes to go to the pub with us after work and buys us drinks... not just us, sometimes other people come as well.'

Cathy sat stiffly, twisting the pencil between her fingers, not knowing what to do.

'Norman went to Bristol University and came top at everything,' said Rose. 'Like Blake, he's got a first-class degree, and he's made friends with one of the directors. Norman says we should all "wait and see". He's "got plans". There's going to be a showdown... but who could you choose?'

'I know who I'd choose,' said Margot, 'the one with the voice, even if I don't really know him.'

'Your work might be boring but BCS isn't then,' said Cathy.

Both Rose and Margot giggled.

'There's more,' said Rose. Her restless eyes scanned the office. She curved her hand around her mouth. 'We've got a friend in Personnel, called Barbara,' she said excitedly, and leaned towards Cathy. The scent of the sickly-sweet perfume was unpleasantly overpowering now. Cathy could feel it in her nose and throat.

'Look, really, I don't –,' said Cathy and leaned away.

'Wait – you must hear this. She's told us Blake has got five years missing from records where he was, it says, "travelling in the Far East". I mean, how can anybody "travel" for five years?' Her eyes flashed. 'Margot thinks he's been in prison, don't you, Margot?'

'Well, what else could it be?' said Margot.

Someone walked into the office. The two women suddenly stood up and walked purposefully towards their desks. Cathy scanned the Health and Safety document again, trying to take it in, but it was hopeless. The text might as well have been in Japanese. Her mind was a whirl: she couldn't concentrate.

* * *

Cathy put down the phone and looked at the clock. It was four forty-five. She made her way up from the second floor to the fourth and followed the directions to the Personnel Department. The double doors were held wide open with grey rubber wedges. It looked and sounded deserted, but as she walked in she heard someone cough. A rotund woman with a red face sat at a desk in a large recess behind the door.

'Hello, I'm Barbara, the Personnel Office Manager, and you must be Cathy Simpson.'

Barbara studied Cathy for a few moments.

'Yes.'

'You're just as they described you.'

'Who described me?' asked Cathy.

'The girls, of course, the girls, we're all friends here' said Barbara and giggled. 'Don't worry, it was all complimentary.'

The open-plan office was the same size as the one downstairs but arranged differently. One long wall was filled with filing cabinets, floor to ceiling, complete with alphabetically labelled hanging files.

'I see you're looking at our Personnel files,' said Barbara. 'Everyone has one, and we're about to create yours.'

Barbara opened a drawer of her desk, removed some forms and put them in a grey plastic tray. She leant on the desk and heaved herself out of the chair.

'Sorry to phone you so late in the day, I almost forgot, but these forms are now urgent,' said Barbara. 'We need you to complete them. One's for medical records, one's for security purposes, one's for payroll and one's for the lab.'

'Yes, of course,' said Cathy.

Barbara held her handbag in one hand and the tray in the other. She walked over to Cathy and placed the papers on a nearby desk.

'You can sit here,' she said. As she came closer Cathy could smell stale cigarettes. 'They may take some time to complete, but it would be good if you could do them before tomorrow.'

'OK, that's no problem,' said Cathy, sitting down.

Barbara put one hand on the desk, looked at Cathy and smiled weakly.

'I need to rush off to see the GP, could you do something for me? It'll only take a minute.'

'Well, in that case I don't see why not.'

'When you've finished, could you put them in this tray,' she said, tapping her stubby, nicotine-stained finger on the edge of the grey plastic tray. 'And then lock it away on the empty shelf under Z in the main Personnel records filing cabinet,' she pointed, 'and then lock all the filing cabinets with these keys.' She withdrew an enormous bunch of keys from the pocket of her voluminous dress and placed them on the desk. 'And then take the keys to Reception. Each of the cabinets and keys are colour-coded so you won't have a problem working out which key goes where.'

Cathy frowned.

'Oh, don't I need security clearance for this?'

Barbara hesitated and took a deep breath.

'Well, nobody will know, just this once' she said, and winked at Cathy. 'It's between you and me, huh?'

Cathy's eyes widened.

'I don't feel comfortable about this...'

'It's fine,' said Barbara dismissively, 'I'm sure I can trust you.' She walked towards the door. 'Thanks, great, that really helps me out; if you've got any questions about the forms we can talk about them tomorrow.' She slung her handbag over her shoulder and walked out of the office. 'Well, goodbye.'

Cathy sat for a while in the silence. She settled herself at the desk and laboriously completed the forms. Ten or fifteen minutes passed. The lifts whirred and thumped as they took people to the ground floor, but she couldn't see or hear anybody. The place seemed strangely cold and eerie and abandoned, like being inside an enormous aircraft carrier in dock.

She continued form-filling. Another ten minutes passed. She was alone. She completed the last form and placed it in the plastic tray. She sat for a few moments, thinking about the opportunity that presented itself. She knew she shouldn't, but it was tempting. She agonised for a few moments, lost in indecision, turning it over in her mind. It seemed harmless enough; she was only curious, after all. She put the bunch of keys in her trouser pocket, stood up and walked around to the filing cabinets. They were open and inviting. She slowly made her way to the cabinet labelled A – D and stood in front of it for a few moments in silent deliberation. She listened; she could hear only her own breath. Go on, she said to herself. She walked right up to it: it was now or never. She fingered the files with the surname 'C' and quickly located Blake Carter's file. Her heart started to beat fast, her fingers trembled a little. Carefully and silently she pulled it out. She flicked through the pages, her heart heavy with guilt and trepidation at the fear of discovery. She found a copy of his degree certificate. Cambridge, first-class honours Natural Sciences 1966. She kept thumbing. She found his CV and quickly skimmed the pages, noting his address was Brandon Wood, North London. There it was in black and white: 1966-1971 'travelling in the Far East', 1971-72 maintenance driver, followed by Senior Technician, Institute of Developing Technologies, then 1972-74 Research Assistant, Cambridge University, Physics. In 1975 he had joined BCS. There were several pages with details of his various promotions. She had a quick look at two of his references: 'a capable and independent thinker' and 'outstanding ground-breaking work' stood out. She glanced around quickly and listened. She heard the ominous sound of distant footsteps and the jangling of keys. Somewhere nearby the caretaker was moving about; he began whistling *Summertime*. The sound reverberated with a distant echo off the whitewashed corridor walls. She was rooted to the spot, her heart thumping. The file felt like a hot potato, burning her hands, yet she couldn't move. She waited. The sound got softer. All was still once again. She silently placed the file back in its holder. Boldly now, with renewed confidence, she walked over to the filing cabinet labelled W – Z. She looked for 'W' for Wells and quickly found it. She thumbed through and found the copy of his degree certificate. Salford University, third-class degree Chemistry and Physics 1971. Her heart skipped a beat. She found a reference: 'Outgoing and a good communicator... resourceful and ambitious'. She carefully placed it back in its holder.

As she had been instructed, she put the grey tray on the empty shelf under Z and with trembling hands she locked all the filing cabinets. She dashed out of the office like a thief in the night.

* * *

'It was unfortunate I was away in Brussels your first week. I hope you've been able to settle in,' said Blake.

'Yes, everyone's been really friendly and helpful,' said Cathy.

'I'm pleased to hear it. Has Barbara contacted you about the induction forms?'

'Yes, I've completed them all,' said Cathy.

'Good,' said Blake.

She remembered her covert look at his Personnel file and felt a surge of guilt.

'Cathy, I'd like you to meet Robert,' Blake said. 'He's one of our laboratory technicians. Robert, this is Cathy, our new Research and Admin. Support Assistant.'

'Pleased to meet you,' said Cathy. Robert was a tall, gangly youth, with a pale face and close-cropped curly hair. He looked away as Cathy shook his hand and seemed too embarrassed to speak.

'Robert, I'm going to introduce Cathy to the work we're doing with the lasers in the laboratory. I'd like you to come with us and take a look at the wiring on the secondary transformers. The current has been a bit erratic lately.'

'Will do, Mr Carter,' said Robert. 'I just need to fetch my toolkit.'

'OK. Cathy and I will go on ahead now, and we'll see you there,' said Blake, leading the way. 'The laboratories are in the annex,' he said to Cathy.

At the end of the corridor, a set of double doors confronted them. Blake tapped a code into a keypad, there was a click and he swung the door open; he motioned for her to go first.

'I'll make sure you get the codes for all the secure areas,' he said.

'Thanks,' said Cathy. The corridor stretched away into the distance. As they walked along, their footsteps sounded dully on the concrete floor. Water gurgled in hidden pipes. 'This is a big, meandering place.'

'This old building was used for storage for decades, now it's mainly laboratories,' he said. 'The corridors all lead off from each other. It's a bit like the Minatour's labyrinth. You can get lost, but I'm sure you'll get used to it.'

'I expect so,' said Cathy.

Two men and a woman, clad in white coats, came towards them. As they passed, they nodded to Blake. They turned some corners and walked on. He stopped, removed a key from his pocket and opened a door with a chrome plate on it labelled 12; she followed him inside with the door still ajar. It was a bright space, with several large windows. He removed his jacket and hung it carefully on a hook. Not consciously wanting to, but seemingly unable to help herself, she took in the shape and size of him; the white shirt hugged him, she could see his muscles move under the fabric. Cathy looked around the spacious room. The shelves were full of labelled cardboard boxes; large instruments and equipment were scattered around on benches. Robert came in, carrying a blue metal toolbox. He shut the door behind him.

'Hello, Robert,' said Blake.

'Shall I start with this one, Mr Carter?'

'Yes, fine.'

Robert removed a metal plate at the side of one of the instruments.

'This is one of the laboratories we're using to test the compact discs,' Blake said. 'Tell me if you don't understand anything.'

'Yes, of course,' she said.

She wished she wasn't wearing the dowdy brown culottes, stripy shirt and flat sandals. She felt like a frump, but her rational voice said: come on, get over it, what does it matter? Blake walked across to the other side of the laboratory.

'We've got three lasers in here and they're all set up differently,' he said. 'Come here and I'll show you the first one.'

He turned on some switches and she walked over and stood beside him.

'It looks like a mini rocket launcher,' she said.

'Yes, it is a bit space age.'

'I always did like science fiction.'

He smiled at her. She liked his smile, it was spontaneous and natural.

'In the future people will be using compact discs every day,' he said.

'What will they use them for?'

'Well, most people in the field are working on using them for recording and playing music. But I think that in the future we'll be able to use them for storing images and data as well.'

'And here we are – pioneers. That's an amazing thought,' said Cathy.

She could hear muffled voices and footsteps from the corridor outside.

'The different lasers have different characteristics, different energy pulses and wavelengths,' he said. 'This is the laser we're spending most time with at the moment.'

'Mr Carter, I think I've found the problem with the wiring,' said Robert.

'Good,' Blake replied. 'When you've finished, can you check the other lasers, make sure it's an isolated problem.'

Robert nodded. Blake bent down and pushed a plug into a socket in the wall. The steel gun-like instrument was positioned on a pivot. A large circular silver disc like a vinyl LP lay flat underneath it.

'This is a very crude demonstration,' said Blake, 'just so that you get the idea. I'm going to position the gun and aim it at the disc. When I turn on the switch the laser will come on and the disc will start spinning at the same time.'

'OK,' said Cathy. She stood nearby, watching.

Blake placed one hand on top and one hand underneath the gun and swung it just a few inches into position. His movements were precise, fluid, supple and lithe. He was slow and careful. God, I can see why Rose and Margot are impressed with Blake, she thought, and so am I. God help me, I must resist this. He reached behind him and turned on a switch. The laser gun produced a dazzling beam of red light that shone directly at the spinning disc.

'It's very bright,' said Cathy.

'We can control the intensity of the beam, making it brighter or dimmer,' he said. 'We're trying to work out the optimum level needed to burn the holes efficiently.'

She watched as the beam of light changed from bright to dull.

'How are you doing that?' she asked.

'I'm turning this dial,' he said, pointing to a dial fixed to the bottom of the laser. 'Would you like to try it?'

'Yes.'

'Put your hands here, Cathy,' he said.

Blake stepped back, giving her space. She followed his instructions, the gun slid into position, then she spent some time moving the gun around on the pivot, trying out the laser.

'You can position it precisely,' said Blake.

'It's very smooth,' she said, and continued, engrossed. She caught his eye.

'Carry on experimenting and you'll become familiar with it.'

'OK.'

Blake walked across to Robert. 'Robert, how is it going?'

He and Robert spent some time discussing the electrics; several minutes later Blake returned.

'What's happening here?' asked Cathy, pointing to a second laser and compact disc set-up.

'With this one, what we're trying to do is find the optimum wavelength for the particular compact disc we're using. The laser burns holes into the surface of the disc as it spins, in a binary nought or one pattern; the shorter the wavelength, the closer together the holes.

The closer the holes, the more data you can get on the disc.'

'How do you know how close the holes are?'

'Good question. We use a microscope, record the results and the computer does the calculations.'

'Will I be able to do that?' said Cathy.

'Well, that's another lesson for another day. What I'd like to do for the rest of the afternoon is show you the other lasers and the prototype compact discs. When you're ready.'

'I'm ready,' said Cathy and turned off the switch.

The instruction continued. She watched as he took the equipment apart and put it back together. He explained how things worked, was attentive and made sure she understood. His conversation was fluid, easy and natural, his explanation clear and concise. The afternoon passed rapidly.

'You picked all that up quickly, Cathy,' he said as they were packing up.

'Now I'll be able to understand the technical reports I'm typing.'

'That's the idea. And it will also make the secretarial work more interesting, hopefully. We don't want you scaling the walls with boredom, do we?' he said and grinned.

'I don't get bored, I always find things to interest me.'

'Good,' he said. 'Once you've mastered the basics, I want you to take on some of these investigations yourself. We'll need to arrange some more sessions.'

'OK.'

'I'll blank out some time in my diary.'

'Thank you,' she said.

'How are you getting on, Robert?' asked Blake.

'I'll stay for a while if you don't mind, Mr Carter. But I think I've fixed it.'

'OK, good,' said Blake, turning to Cathy. 'Can you find your way back to the office? There's something else I need to do now.'

'Yes, sure.'

As Cathy walked down the corridor, she had a feeling of warmth and contentment but at the same time a kind of tightness in her belly. That was OK. He really made that so OK, she thought at the end of the day. I like this man. Oh God, whatever secrets he has, I really like this man.

CHAPTER 8

Saigon, Vietnam
August 1967

Nobody else would have noticed the white chalk mark
on the wall outside the *Banque de France*, but Blake
saw it from a distance and felt the adrenalin pump
through his body. He slowed down from a run into a
trot, searched in his pocket for the red chalk and made
his own mark as he passed by. He jogged slowly round
several blocks, giving Tranter time, then passed by the
traffic light where Duong Nguyen Du and Duong Huyen
Tran Cong Chua intersected at the south side of the
Presidential Palace. Chewing gum was attached to the
post. He jogged on until he found the street and the right
bench and sat down, as if catching his breath. As the
early morning sun rose, the graceful, tall buildings cast
long, deep shadows. He looked around and listened for
signs of life. A few odd pieces of litter wafted through
the street, caught by the wind. The place was deserted;
he was alone. He collected the package taped to the
underside of the bench and put it deep in his pocket. In
the next street he left his red chalk mark on the wall
outside the *Café Splendide.*

Blake returned to the flat and decoded the message.
*Colonel Pham Quang Giap will be driven by car from
Saigon to the town of Ben Luc next Wednesday morning,
arriving after 10.00am.* There was a photograph of his
quarry and a description of the car, plus the address
which the Colonel was going to visit. He poured himself
a stiff whisky, threw his head back and gulped it down.
Checking his records, he found Colonel Pham Quang
Giap was on the list he'd devised from his networks and

contacts. How to do this? It needed careful planning; he had five days. Blake hired a car and reconnoitred the route through the suburbs and outskirts of the city. The road was flat for miles past paddy fields and small villages until it approached the town of Ben Luc where it became mountainous. The steep road wound and twisted through jungle forest until its descent into the town. He passed only one vehicle after ten minutes and another fifteen minutes later. On the way down into the town ramshackle structures were set back from the road. Vapoury shimmers of heat rose from their corrugated tin roofs. The town was a sleepy place with a main street, some pedestrians, a few shops, and a noodle café. There were several parked cars. He sat at a table on the pavement outside the café, considering. A little old man shuffled along on the other side of the road; his back was bent, laden with sticks for firewood. Two children skipped across the road, mother in tow. In the shade of a palm tree, a group of men sat around a table, absorbed in a game of Mah Jong. A dog lay in the shade under a nearby table. It yapped softly in its sleep, wagged its tail and twitched. He heard a high-pitched shrill laugh and a shuffling of feet. A plump waitress emerged from inside the café and approached his table, her hair scooped up in a high ponytail. She dried her hands on her white apron, smearing it with streaks of yellow moisture. There was a smell of fresh fish.

'*Oui, que voulez-vous ?*' she said.

Blake ordered *Goi Cuon*. A short while later the woman plonked down a plate of steaming noodles with *nuoc mam* sauce. She waited while he tried some.

'*Très bien,*' he said.

She nodded, pleased, gave him a curious but distracted glance then went inside. Soon the laughter started once again. Blake realised he would not go unnoticed in this town. He would have to ambush the Colonel en route. He drove up and down the road alongside the ravine looking for the best ambush point. He needed to have a good view of the car for some yards as it approached. He assessed different vantage points and watched the passing cars through his binoculars. It was evening by the time he'd decided on his plan of action. He felt the familiar steely cold hardness descend on him. It helped him remain focused, calculating and determined.

Three days later, Blake purchased a battered pick-up truck from a local dealer, paid cash and parked it on the other side of town. In the early hours of the following morning he collected it and drove to the ambush point. He parked in a clearing on the opposite side of the road just out of sight of any oncoming vehicle and waited. The night-time howl slowly gave way to the noises of insects and birds. There was a mist in the air; it wafted like clouds through the tall trees. As the sun rose behind him the long shadows contracted and the road was bathed in sunlight. In the distance he heard a car approaching and examined it through his binoculars. It didn't fit the description of the target car; the driver was a peasant with a weather-beaten face and there were no passengers. He was pleased with the clear view of the driver. For hours he waited and watched, like a panther ready to pounce on its hapless prey. Several other cars passed before he heard the engine of a different car, a smoother sound. The black car fitted the description. He adjusted his binoculars and scrutinised the driver and passenger. In the centre of the field of view was the man in the photograph, his quarry. Blake fired the ignition of his pick-up truck. He took a deep breath, felt his muscles tighten and his heart thump. As the car drew level he estimated the position of impact, his foot poised on the accelerator. At the right moment he shot the truck forward; it smashed into the side of the oncoming car. There was a screech and a bang. The driver's face was gripped with terror. Blake was pushed hard back then thrown forwards in his seat. Just as he'd planned, both vehicles toppled down the side of the road and into the ravine. At the last moment Blake threw himself from the truck and rolled over and over in the forest undergrowth. A thorny vine clung to his shirt, ripping the fabric and his flesh. He tore off the vine and drew blood on his fingers, but was oblivious to the pain. He heard the vehicles continue to roll, then an enormous splash. He peered over the edge of the ravine; his truck was lying on its side in a ditch, wheels spinning. A slow stream of water cascaded around it. Jungle animals shrieked as they scurried from the scene. Dark grey smoke began to billow from the truck's exhaust and wafted into the forest; there was a strong smell of petrol and burnt rubber in the air.

Blake scrambled down the bank. The battered body of the driver was spread-eagled on a rock, his head lolled at an unnatural angle, his neck broken. But the Colonel was nowhere to be seen. Blake spotted a movement inside the wreckage of the car. He watched as the Colonel slowly dragged himself out of the gap where the door used to be. The man gasped and cried out in pain as he crawled a few feet away from the car. It seemed as if the life of the forest had been switched off; a silence descended. The Colonel turned his head and looked up at Blake, mouthing something unintelligible. Blake avoided his gaze; he hesitated only for a moment, then took aim and fired six shots in quick succession straight into the Colonel's head, as if he was on the firing range. The sound of the shots echoed through the valley, shrill and painful to his ear. He looked at the place where the man's head had been, now a mass of blood and gore. Blake stood still. He seemed strangely disconnected from the scene before him. He watched, as if in suspended animation, as the wheels of the truck slowed to a halt. The hot metal ticked and creaked. Boiling water spluttered from the shattered radiator to rise as steam. Looking up, he could see grey smoke hanging motionless in the higher levels of the canopy. He quickly came to and climbed back up the bank. There were tyre marks in the tarmac. Somebody would find them, sooner or later. He began the long trek back to Saigon, keeping away from the road and arrived back in the outskirts in the early evening, exhausted. His clothes were saturated with sweat, his back and his fingers hurt. A woman in a coolie hat and baggy trousers carried two huge baskets hanging from the end of a pole across her shoulders; she leant down and set the baskets on the pavement. A young man purchased a chicken noodle takeaway. Blake ordered the same and washed it down with a beer from a nearby kiosk. Back at the flat he took a cathartic cold shower. He placed a flat dressing over his shoulder, secured it with medical tape, wrapped a handkerchief round his fingers and poured himself a stiff whisky. He'd grown quite partial to the strong, sour taste over the months: it mirrored his state of mind. He gulped it down and let it burn his throat. He lay on the bed, relaxed, and carried out a mental post-mortem of the operation, down to the most minuscule detail. What had gone badly, what well, what could have gone better, what he'd learnt, what he'd do differently next time. Tomorrow, communication with

London, then back to normal: running, office, downtown. He remembered he needed to shop for some groceries, he'd fit that in midday. He made a mental shopping list – tea, coffee, condensed milk, palm sugar and bread.

* * *

The next day Khien invited him round for dinner. Afterwards, while the women were tidying up in the kitchen, Blake shuffled some cards at the table in preparation for a game of pontoon with Hoa. Khien looked up from his newspaper and waved it in the air, laughing exuberantly.

'Here,' he said, 'read this,' and pointed at an article on the front page: 'Senior Viet Cong commander found dead in ditch, killed by unknown assailant'.

Blake didn't raise his head, but looked up at Khien, who held his gaze and grinned.

'I propose a toast,' Khien shouted. 'Everyone in here. Wine for everybody.'

'Not for the children,' said Ming.

'Yes, wine for everybody, this is a celebration,' said Khien.

Ming said nothing; she quietly poured the wine into seven glasses. The children gathered round obediently. Blake stood up and joined the circle.

'For the future democratic Vietnamese Government and our American and British friends,' Khien announced exuberantly.

'For the future democratic Vietnamese Government and our American and British friends,' his family echoed with equal exuberance, in unison.

The glasses clinked, the children giggled and the wine was swigged back. Khien held Blake's arm and patted him fiercely on the back.

'My friend,' he confirmed vehemently and with pleasure. The children jumped and threw their arms in the air with excitement.

CHAPTER 9

As the car bumped through the potholes they were shoved from side to side. Blake's back ached and his teeth were set on edge. Over the last two miles the road had become narrower and rougher. Khien did his best, but this road would have tested the most skilled driver. Blake turned to Hoa in the back.

'How often do you visit An Lac?'

'We try to go every few months, usually it's just father and I. Have you visited a Buddhist monastery before?'

'Once or twice when I was a boy, growing up in the Far East, but I don't remember much about it.'

'I want you to meet Ajahn Kai-Luat. I think you'll be impressed by him,' said Hoa.

Monks intrigued Blake and he was interested in how they lived, but doubted that he would be impressed. Nobody had ever impressed him.

'It is good to have your company on the journey,' said Khien.

'Yes, it is,' said Hoa quietly.

'You know, John, you have this strange effect on Hoa. Hoa, you are always polite with John, but you always answer back with me.'

'I respect John.'

'So you respect John, but not me, your own father?'

'Yes, I do respect you, father, but in a different way.'

The car spluttered and laboured for the last mile. Its headlights lit up the delicate tree ferns. They looked like grasping, spindly fingers reaching towards the car in the blackness. They reached a clearing in the jungle where a bright fire lit up a central courtyard. Khien killed the engine and got out. A few minutes later he returned.

'I've arranged three huts, one for each of us,' he said.

They unpacked a few things and put them in the huts, then went to the fire. There were three other people there: one man and two women, sitting on stout logs, tending steaming pots of rice and fish. The man stood up.

'Welcome,' he said, smiling at them. 'I am Sinh and this is Thu and Chi.' He indicated his companions. 'Please, join us for supper.' He gestured for them to sit down. Khien introduced himself and Blake and Hoa.

Chi smiled and handed out wooden bowls and chopsticks. They gathered round in a circle. It was a noisy affair; the chopsticks clinked, they all slurped their food and the fire crackled. When they had cleared away, the other travellers went to their huts. They were also on their way to An Lac monastery and were anxious to make an early start in the morning. Khien and Blake sat on a damp, decaying log round the dying campfire well into the night. The high moon was full and bright and bathed everything in a very faint white glow.

'A few years ago Kiko, my niece, was injured during Buddhist demonstrations against the Diem regime,' said Khien. 'It was a terrible time for us. The Buddhists were being repressed in favour of the Catholics in the land reform program. There was a lot of violence. The nepotism became even more blatant.'

'Diem was very unpopular; being a Catholic made people even more hostile. I was in London at the time. I read in a newspaper that he was betrayed by his own Generals and murdered.'

'Yes, that was about six months after Kiko's injury. I remember that happy day, November 2nd 1963.'

'I read that the whole of Saigon celebrated,' said Blake.

'Oh, how we celebrated! Anyway, that was later. Kiko… she spent three months in hospital. She survived, but now she's disabled, cannot walk, needs help with dressing, washing,' he said and swallowed hard, his expression anguished. 'In the months that followed I felt so angry I was murderous. If I had been a younger man, I would have joined the new Buddhist army under Tri Quang and mercilessly torn those Diem supporters apart. War can turn an ordinary man bad.'

Khien stopped talking and looked into the fire, absorbed in his own thoughts. Blake could hear Hoa shuffling her cards. She knelt on the ground a few yards away with a candle beside her.

'Perhaps there are no wholly good or bad men,' said Blake.

'Maybe, maybe,' said Khien, thoughtfully. 'We could talk all night about this. As a Buddhist I try to do right action, but it's hard to feel compassion when those you care about are hurt. It's one thing having an ideology, it's another being tested personally.' He took a deep breath and looked directly at Blake. 'And you? Do you ever get angry?'

'Emotions get in the way of doing your job,' said Blake.

'Then for you it's simple. You don't strike me as an emotional man. You are clever, detached and clear-headed. I admire that.'

The dying embers of the fire crackled and hissed. A thin, steady stream of smoke wafted up into the darkness.

'Vietnam is your country. It's difficult for you to be detached from what's going on.'

'It is. I do what I can, but much of the time I feel powerless, both for myself and as a Vietnamese citizen.' Khien sighed and shook his head. 'The South would be overrun without the help of the Americans. Since Diem we have only had ineffectual Governments, no match for the Viet Cong under Ho Chi Minh. He's strong and his people admire him. I am thankful the Americans are here. With their help I believe democracy is possible. I want to see re-unification of Vietnam, where all Vietnamese citizens can live peacefully together. We are all worried what will happen to the Buddhist way of life if the communists take over.'

'What about Ajahn Kai-Luat, is his monastery vulnerable? The Viet Cong are moving their way southward and taking territory at night. They can't be far from An Lac.'

'Ajahn Kai-Luat has many friends in high places. He is the spiritual guide to Ho Chi Minh's brother-in-law, who has been following him for decades. Although Ho Chi Minh is implacably opposed to religion and Buddhism in particular, his brother-in-law is still family. So the Viet Cong need to be very careful in their dealings with him.'

'Ajahn Kai-Luat is in an interesting position,' said Blake.

'A more shrewd and wise man I've never met. And he can also see the bigger picture, in so many ways. Most of the ethnic people around here are Theravada Buddhists. He likes his monks to follow the 227 precepts, but he is unconventional. Monks at the more traditional Theravada monasteries believe he should become independent, but still the young monks flock to him.'

A night creature howled. Branches cracked and leaves rustled as it lurched between trees in the darkness.

'Unconventional. In what way?'

'He travelled in India and Tibet and spent time with philosophers and so-called mystics. He uses some of their wisdom in his teachings rather than just sticking to the conventional texts. When he set up the monastery, two Europeans he met in India came with him. There's an Indian as well who arrived a couple of years later. They've all been with him for at least a decade.'

'What do the locals make of all this?' said Blake.

'They are reverent towards Ajahn Kai-Luat. Many of them are simple, illiterate farmers. They wonder, but they don't ask questions. Ajahn Kai-Luat's reputation is enough.'

'The cards are prepared, would you like to have a reading?' called Hoa. She had unclipped her hair and it fell about her shoulders in a thick black cascade.

'No, that isn't my kind of thing,' said Blake.

'Oh please, the night is beautiful and the conditions are right for the reading.'

'You will offend my daughter if you do not accept her offer,' said Khien and laughed heartily. Slowly and reluctantly Blake got up, walked over and sat cross-legged on the ground opposite her. She smiled demurely and passed the pack of cards to him.

'Shuffle the cards, holding in your mind an important question, and then pass the cards to me,' she said.

Blake followed the instructions unenthusiastically. He watched as she laid the cards out, very slowly and carefully, one by one. Her loose hair softened her features and in the dim light she looked tantalising.

'I see you going on a long journey,' she said.

'Yes, that's this one to the monastery,' said Blake, 'I'm already on it.'

Hoa gave him a quick glance and ignored his comment. She turned over some more cards and was silent for a while, deep in thought, as she studied them.

'And an older man will be important in your life,' she said.

'Yes, that's your father and I'm living in his flat,' said Blake.

They made eye contact and laughed together.

'You are making fun of me,' she said coyly, and smiled at him.

'No, not at you, at the cards.'

She looked down at the cards again and continued turning them over. The last one she uncovered was *The Lovers*. She drew her breath in sharply and, looked into his eyes, regarding him seductively. 'You can see for yourself what this one is,' she said.

'Um... not sure how to respond to that,' said Blake.

'What is it... what is the card?' called Khien.

'*The Lovers*,' replied Hoa.

Khien laughed heartily.

'The reading is now over,' said Hoa. 'Have I answered your question?'

Blake stood up. 'Thank you,' he said. 'You've left me with more questions than answers.'

As Hoa gathered together the cards he walked back to the fire and sat down next to Khien.

'You are good for her,' Khien said, still laughing. 'She needs a practical man in her life.' He slapped at a mosquito that had landed on his neck, inspected the carcass briefly, then leant over and wiped his hand on the log. They sat together in silence. 'What does a man like you do without a wife?' said Khien tentatively.

'You are a young man; surely you cannot happily live a celibate life?'

'There are plenty of available women if you have the cash,' said Blake.

Khien gave Blake a long and thoughtful stare.

'But that is not a satisfactory way to live.' He thought for a moment. 'I have watched you and Hoa playing cards together; you are happy, content in each other's company. Over the past few months I have realised that you and Hoa have many interests in common. I think you complement each other.'

Hoa had overheard the conversation.

'I like you, John Miller.' After a long moment she said, 'My father wants me to marry you… if you ask me I might say yes… if you are very lucky.'

She wrapped the cards in red silk, put them in a silver box and into her pocket. Watching Blake out of the corner of her eye, she picked up the candle and slowly walked to her hut. She lit several candles inside, opened the shutters and closed the curtains. Her windows radiated a warm yellow glow. Khien and Blake remained silent as the embers from the dark red flames died away and sparked in the night.

'She needs a strong man like you, John, and you will make her a good husband,' said Khien. 'You could go to her; for Hoa the cards have foreseen the future and she is expecting you.'

Blake considered his options. He couldn't use Hoa without making a respectable woman of her. Going downtown was beginning to pall and he didn't like covering up. However, taking a wife brought its own complications and could interfere with his independence. She was not unattractive and she had an engaging smile. Apart from the odd challenging comment he had found her company surprisingly pleasant and he enjoyed playing cards and chess with her. Once she was married she would, most likely, behave like her own mother and fall into a subservient role, in which case she would probably be an asset rather than a hindrance. On balance, it seemed to have more benefits than disadvantages. Anyway, despite all reasoning, at that moment his flesh was weak. He watched the fire for a while longer. He stood up and wandered over to Hoa's hut. And it was a welcome relief from paying for the service with a stranger. He'd have to marry her now, of course.

* * *

'This is John Miller,' said Khien.

'Welcome to An Lac,' said Ajahn Kai-Luat and bowed, holding his palms together in front of him as if in prayer. Two other, taller monks, also dressed in saffron robes, stood a few feet behind him.

'Thank you for your hospitality,' said Blake, returning the bow.

'I hope you will find some peace and quiet while you are here.' Ajahn Kai-Luat's features were similar to Khien's, but he was smaller and thinner. As he studied Blake with his intelligent eyes his expression was inscrutable. There was something indefinable in Ajahn Kai-Luat's bearing and the way he spoke that held Blake's attention.

'I'm sure I will,' said Blake.

'We have a library with texts written in various languages. Please feel free to use it. Khien has been telling me about your translation work.'

'Thank you. I would like that.'

Ajahn Kai-Luat smiled almost imperceptibly, bowed again, and took a pace back. Blake bowed in response. As Ajahn Kai-Luat withdrew, the two other monks followed him. Blake watched them walk away.

CHAPTER 10

October 1967

Blake ran a finger round the collar of his *ao dai* in a vain attempt to loosen it.

'Collar's a bit tight, Khien,' he said.

Khien nodded. 'Sorry. But it's the best I can do at such short notice. The tailor is a good friend of mine. He did the job very quickly; there was no time for a proper fitting.' He looked appraisingly at Blake. 'You look good in that outfit. Blue is a good colour for you.'

Khien's *ao dai* was a dark green. The fabric was stretched tightly over his paunch.

'You're looking good in yours,' lied Blake. Khien beamed with pleasure. 'Thanks for your efforts, Khien. I appreciate it.'

'No trouble, particularly for Hoa's husband.'

'Well, I'm not her husband yet, Khien. Soon, but not quite yet.'

'No, you are her husband. Here, I have your certificate.' Khien handed Blake a document, which he unfolded and scrutinised. He looked up, peering quizzically at his companion.

'Don't we have to go to the authorities, make statements, sign papers and all that, in order to be married?'

'Yes, but you and Hoa have already done all that.' Khien winked at him. 'At least, as far as the officials are concerned, it's all been done, all in order.'

'How is that possible?'

Khien smiled broadly. 'You just have to know the right people to give the money to. One of them is my wife's cousin. I had to give him a bit more than usual because of the short notice, but it's all taken care of – you and Hoa are now husband and wife. Now we have the reception and drink toasts to your future happiness.' He clapped Blake on the back. 'Congratulations!'

'So presumably we're having the reception here?'

'Yes.'

Blake looked round the room. Sunlight was streaming in through the large windows. At one end of the room was a long low wooden table, laden with food and drink. Bowls of rice piled high were laid out in an elaborate display with bowls of salad. Jugs of iced water and red and white wine were at one end of the table behind a row of sparkling glasses. At the other end was a large vase of flowers. Blake recognised yellow apricot flowers and peach flowers, together with others he didn't remember seeing before. The rest of the room was bare, save for several cushions ranged on the floor around the table. Near to the table was a closed door.

'What's through there, Khien?' asked Blake.

'Madness.' Blake looked quizzically at Khien. 'My wife's through there, panicking about everything. My aunt is there as well, helping. Hoa and my other children should be there, getting dressed. Best to stay out of it, it's complete madness.' As he spoke, the door opened and a small grey-haired woman came into the room carrying a large bowl of fruit, which she placed on the table. Khien called to her and she approached, grinning.

'John, this is my aunt, Mrs Cuc.'

Blake and Mrs Cuc bowed to one another. 'Very pleased to meet you,' said Blake in Vietnamese. Mrs Cuc smiled at Blake.

'I'm very pleased to meet you, Mr Miller. Congratulations on your marriage.'

'Thank you,' said Blake.

The door opened again and Khien's youngest children spilled into the room, chattering excitedly. Each was dressed in an *ao dai*, one gold-coloured, one yellow and one white.

'Behave yourselves,' Khien called. 'This is an important occasion.' Once more the door opened and Ming and Hoa entered. Ming was wearing a red *ao dai* and Hoa was wearing a pale blue one, matching Blake's.

'Now we're all here,' said Khien, 'we can begin. As everyone knows, for many reasons this could not be a completely traditional wedding: John is a stranger in this land, with no relatives in this country. Also, he has no family home here. So the traditional *le dam ngo,* proposal ceremony, and *dam hoi*, engagement ceremony, cannot take place. Anyway, they are now married...' Hoa looked up, startled. Blake nodded at her. 'And we can start the reception!' Ming and Mrs Cuc swiftly exited the room and shortly came back in carrying trays laden with dishes of steaming food, which they distributed on the low table. While they were doing that, Hoa drew Blake to one side.

'What's this about already being married? I thought we were going to have a proper ceremony.'

Blake shrugged. 'So did I, but it seems your father had other plans, which I knew nothing about. It's just as much a surprise to me as it is to you. Are you very disappointed?'

'You know I don't care for tradition, I'm not at all bothered, it's all the same to me. Obviously he's desperate to get me off his hands, which is why this is all so rushed. He wants to pass me off on to you. Husband.' She grinned wickedly at him.

'Come on, everybody, it's time to eat!' Khien bustled about, directing where each person should sit, with Hoa and Blake at the head of the table. When all were seated on their respective cushions, and supplied with drink, he rose again to his feet. 'I propose a toast,' he said. 'Raise your glasses.' All lifted their glass of water or wine. 'To the bride and groom!'

'To the bride and groom!' everyone responded before taking a drink.

'Now, eat and enjoy,' Khien commanded.

Squatting on his cushion next to Hoa, Blake was aware of her delicious patchouli scent. As he gazed at her tightly-fitting *ao dai*, he could see the truth of what people say about the *ao dai* – that it 'covers everything but conceals nothing'. Hoa leaned forward and kissed him gently on the lips. He kissed her back. Khien looked over at them and beamed.

CHAPTER 11

London
September 1979

A shadow passed across Cathy's electric typewriter and she looked up. Rose perched herself on the desk, removed an emery board from her pocket and smoothed her nails. Cathy could detect the same sickly-sweet perfume.

'I thought we'd have a chat,' she said, 'I'm on my coffee break.'

'But I'm not,' said Cathy, glancing up at her and frowning.

'Come on, take a break. You work too hard. You're always typing or in the laboratories – with Blake,' she said.

Cathy finished typing the page and removed it from the typewriter. She prepared a new piece of paper, put the carbon copy paper behind it, aligned them, slotted them into the typewriter and turned the dial. It clicked as the papers slipped into position.

'He's been spending a lot of time with you, hasn't he?' said Rose.

'No, hardly any time. If you pay attention, you may notice that most of the time he's out of the office.'

'But when he is here, you're in the labs.'

Cathy said with irritation, 'Of course we're in the labs, it's my job, and we're working.'

'What have you found out about him Cathy?'

Cathy heard the question. It seemed to reverberate inside her head. She didn't look at Rose. She looked up and her eyes wandered over to the window. She stared, as if transfixed, at the oak tree swaying in the wind.

Over the last four months they'd spent exactly twelve afternoons together in the laboratories. It hardly seemed any time at all. The abrasive scraping of the emery board hauled Cathy out of her trance.

'As I said, we've been working.'

'Working?' Rose's eyes narrowed and she stared at Cathy suspiciously.

'Well, if you must know, I've learnt how to operate the lasers, how to categorise the compact discs, how to use the microscope, how to set up the computer to record the calculations and how to produce reports.'

'Does he talk?'

'Of course he talks.'

'What about?'

'About BCS and its European offices and its partners, the future of satellite technology, the paper he's preparing to present at the 'Emerging Technologies' conference in Madrid, what I should do when he's away. For goodness sake, where is all this leading, Rose? I really don't need to explain myself.'

'Yes, but what have you found out about him?' said Rose.

Cathy looked up. Rose was smiling, but there was frustration, impatience and hostility in her eyes and her voice.

'Nothing,' said Cathy.

'Nothing,' said Rose, and laughed. 'You spend hours alone with him in the labs and you know nothing about him?'

Cathy paused.

'Nothing... personal,' she said. She heard her own voice; it sounded disconcertingly pensive and wistful. 'And if you think we're alone you're mistaken, there are technicians everywhere, and if you think I want to be alone with him you have an overactive imagination,' she added forcefully. 'Come on, Rose, get real.'

Cathy looked into the distance again. In that moment she felt disconnected from the office. Spending time with Blake had become the highlight of her work. There was a naturalness and spontaneity about him that made her feel easy and relaxed. Sometimes they'd laughed and joked. She'd sensed the chemistry between them. But when they parted she felt the usual confusion of emotions. The effect was like a drink of cold water in a blistering desert and being eaten alive by ants, both at the same time. He'd never strayed across that professional boundary. Never. She was relieved that he hadn't and at the same time she wished he would.

'You all right?' said Rose.

Cathy came to. She felt annoyed with herself for letting down her guard, even momentarily.

'You'll be ready for your coffee now, won't you?' said Cathy.

'God, I get the message,' said Rose and walked off disgruntled, with her head in the air.

* * *

Cathy's fingers were stiff from so much typing. She had two more pages to go; she rubbed her eyes. She'd grown familiar with the clean, neat lines of Blake's handwriting and she drew her fingers over his script. It made her feel oddly sensuous and affectionate; he was a prolific writer. People clattered around her as they gathered up their belongings and drifted out, one by one, on their way home. Blake had had one meeting after another in his office; Mr Zachary was the last person who had gone in. As the office quietened, their

104

conversation became more audible. She couldn't help but listen and stopped typing.

'Well, Blake, how are you getting on with your research proposal?'

'I've been in contact with the SERC and they've already agreed to put in 20% of the funding.'

'Good,' said Mr Zachary.

'There's quite a bit more to do. I'm working on the overall scheme at the moment. Then I'll detail the time scale over which we will see the benefits and when we can expect to see a profit.'

'You'll be able to meet the deadline of the 17th?'

'Oh yes. In fact I'll be able to let you have it by the 11th or 12th of October. That'll give you time to go over it and make any changes you think it might need before presentation to the Board of Directors.'

Ann, the Department Secretary, was the last person to leave the office. She placed the blue plastic cover over her typewriter and pushed the drawers of her desk shut. They rolled and banged noisily into position. She picked up her handbag and left.

'There's likely to be quite a while before your research generates any profit for us. Isn't that so?'

'Well, yes. This is leading-edge work. Information technology and satellite communications will transform people's lives, the impact will be enormous. BCS is in at the critical stage here. We will be a market leader. It will be profitable, eventually.'

'Perhaps not soon enough for Dr Shaw,' said Mr Zachary.

'What do you mean?' said Blake.

She heard Mr Zachary clear his throat.

'I mean he's asked Norman to submit a proposal as well. On something new.'

'Norman?' Blake's voice rose. 'But he's not working on anything new. Nothing I'm aware of anyway. What is this something new?'

'It's just a joint thing with Porton Down.'

'Porton Down?' Blake's voice rose even higher. 'But they make nerve gases for the military. What's that got to do with us?'

Cathy took a deep breath. She could see Mr Zachary's bulky shadow pacing up and down through the frosted window of the office.

'Apparently Porton Down has come up with a new nasty that the MoD wants in bulk. Our part would be to work with them to devise a manufacturing process that could be scaled up to produce industrial quantities of it. All completely hush-hush, of course, by the way.'

'I doubt that Norman's up to writing the proposal, never mind doing the research,' said Blake.

'Well, Dr Shaw obviously does. And as he's the Research Director, his word goes.'

'Well, he's not as familiar with Norman's work as we are.'

'That's true, but there it is,' said Mr Zachary.

There was a moment of silence.

'I've noticed Norman and Dr Shaw talking together, and Norman has been behaving a bit strangely,' said Blake, his voice tense with irritation. 'It makes sense now. He's gone straight over my head.'

'Didn't you see something like this coming?'

'I'm not surprised about Norman, but I didn't think he was capable of it,' said Blake. 'Why are we considering getting mixed up with the MoD anyway?'

'Money, Blake, money. The MoD will pay handsomely for bulk supplies of their new toy, and we wouldn't have to wait years for a profit.'

'So I'm wasting my time preparing my proposal then.'

'Well, I wouldn't say it's a complete waste of time,' said Mr Zachary. 'But as Mr Shaw has asked especially for Norman's proposal to be included in the ones to be put forward for funding I think you can safely say that yours is not top of the list.'

Cathy swallowed.

'Great,' said Blake, 'and is Norman going to take over from me as Research Manager as well?'

'Well, I won't say it's not a possibility,' said Mr Zachary after a pause. 'Dr Shaw likes Norman, he fits in well.'

'And I don't?'

'No, frankly, you don't.'

'What, just because I don't go toadying to the directors?'

'It's not a question of toadying, it's a question of... well, apart from anything else, Norman's wife and Shaw's wife are best friends, go everywhere together.'

'As you know, I'm not married, so I don't have a wife to go sucking up for me.'

'It's not a question of sucking up,' said Mr Zachary. 'It's a question of getting on well with the people who count.'

Blake said nothing.

'Blake, your proposal would probably be good for us, and our profits, in the longer term, but there is another more pressing matter for the company that takes priority.'

'And what's that?'

'Shares, Blake, shares. We've had a few lean years, as you know. The directors are keen to give out a substantial dividend this year.'

'So, it's more important to turn a quick profit than to develop something of lasting benefit to BCS, and to the wider community? Not to mention dealing in dubious weapons for the military.'

'Look, Blake, you're more than capable. You could have a great future with this company; become a director, have a company car, a company account, share options, but you've got to fit in. And if you don't change your ideas, well, I don't need to spell it out.'

She watched Mr Zachary's shadow turn and walk towards the door.

'Change my principles, you mean,' said Blake as Mr Zachary left the office. He didn't look back and he didn't notice Cathy hidden in her corner.

Cathy grabbed the blue plastic cover and shoved it on the typewriter as quickly and quietly as possible. She placed Blake's handwritten papers in a document wallet and pushed it in a drawer. It made a rolling sound. She flinched. She wanted to slip out unnoticed but she was too noisy and too slow. Blake emerged from his office, saw her, walked straight over and stood at the other side of the desk. She noticed he'd loosened his tie and undone the collar button. Cathy felt her cheeks burn.

'Hello, Cathy, have you managed to finish the report?' he said hurriedly.

'Yes, I've just done it… I mean I've nearly done it.'

He stood for a moment in silence while she tidied her desk.

'You got sidetracked?' he asked.

Cathy looked up at him.

'I'm sorry, I didn't mean to eavesdrop… I just saw Mr Zachary leaving.'

'And no doubt overheard the whole conversation.'

'I'm sorry, yes.'

'The soundproofing in my office has always needed attention,' he said. He sighed and put his hands in his pockets.

Cathy rummaged around in her desk, put the papers and pens away and searched for the key to lock it.

'I'm sorry, Blake. I'll keep it to myself,' she said, looking up at him.

Their eyes met for a moment. She looked in every drawer, searching for the key, but she couldn't find it. She was aware of Blake still standing there.

'Is this what you're looking for, Cathy?' he said.

She looked up. He bounced the key in his palm.

'Oh yes,' she said. 'Where did you find it?'

'It was right here on the desk.'

'Oh, I am stupid,' she said, feeling self-conscious and idiotic.

She locked the drawers.

'Which way do you go home?' he asked after a few moments.

'Usually I get the train.' She put the key in her handbag. 'But on a nice day, like today, I like to walk by the river, then I get the bus.'

'I could do with a breath of fresh air.'

'So could I,' she said.

'Do you mind if I walk with you?'

'No, not at all,' she said.

They walked down to the Embankment. The evening was warm. A cool breeze swept off the water and blew her hair into her face; she swept it back. The trees billowed in the wind; a tin can clattered down an alleyway. They passed a busy, noisy pub forecourt where people spilled on to the walkway. A man laughed so loudly the beer slopped out of his glass and splattered onto the pavement. A group of girls in mini-skirts eating crisps eyed up a group of men in suits.

'I believe this is one of Norman's favourite pubs, have you been here for a drink after work?' asked Blake.

'Not this one, I'm not very keen on pubs myself,' replied Cathy. 'I went out with them once, though, because they asked me so many times. We went to the *Hand and Arrow* in Bule Street, but I didn't enjoy it much.'

'Why was that?' asked Blake.

She hesitated for a moment. 'It was difficult, really.'

'Oh... go on.' He looked at her searchingly.

'They were drinking a lot and getting a bit inebriated and uninhibited. They asked me probing questions about myself, it made me feel uncomfortable. Norman told some crude jokes. I don't think Paul liked it much, but he kept smiling; he left early,' said Cathy.

'Paul's a decent guy, but the rest of them... can be intrusive,' said Blake.

'I'll do what you do, Blake, I'll stay out of it.'

'Do what's right for you, Cathy. I've never really fitted in. I'm not a company man. Today has confirmed it for me. I'm not keen on the profit motive when the product has no real use, or, as in this case, is potentially lethal.'

'I'm sorry. Would you prefer to do something else... some other sort of work?'

'Not if the development work has value and is something I want to do, like the SERC project. They expect me to toe the company line, that's the difficulty,' he said.

'I think your development work is important, Blake,' said Cathy. 'Damn their short-term view.'

'Thanks,' he said and smiled warmly at her.

They stopped walking and leant over a balustrade. The metal felt cold on her skin through the thin shirt. They looked out over the river and watched as the boats chugged up and down. A speedboat zipped past, tossing over the waves. It had the word 'POLICE' written in bright yellow paint on the side. Three men in luminous orange jackets stood inside.

'Do you get much chance to do rock-climbing?' he asked, turning to her.

'Not the physical kind, but I need nerves of steel to cope at BCS.'

He laughed, then turned and looked towards the river, deep in thought.

'Where do you live, in a house, a flat share? If the question's not too intrusive...' he asked after a long silence, his voice soft and tentative.

'I'm renting a small flat. I'm quite lucky, I've got it all to myself. It belongs to a friend of my father.'

'I see,' he said.

'What about you? Where do you live?'

'I have a flat in Brandon Wood, north London. I bought it some years ago.'

'It must be quite a journey to Southwark every day.'

'No, it's easy, forty minutes on the Northern line. If I'm going to a conference or need to get to Heathrow later in the day I drive through London and park at the office.'

'That can't be easy, driving through London.'

'I'm used to it now.'

'You seem to go to a lot of conferences, give a lot of presentations.'

'I need to; BCS encourage it, and it's particularly important if the research is being part funded by Government-sponsored bodies.'

'Do you enjoy it?

'Yes, and it's good to meet others doing similar work.'

'Do you know that Norman uses your office when you're not there?'

'Yes... I was aware of that.'

They watched the activities on the river for a few moments.

'So, your flat, do you... share it with anyone else?' asked Cathy.

'No... I'm on my own.'

'So... what do you like doing?' said Cathy after a few moments.

'What, apart from writing reports?' he said and laughed.

'I can't imagine that's all you do.'

His expression became thoughtful.

'In my spare time I do translations,' he said.

'Translations?'

'Yes, I speak a few Oriental languages. I lived in the Far East while I was growing up. I supplemented my student grant by doing translations when I was at university, but it's a hobby now.'

She felt a tickling sensation on her hand. She looked down; a ladybird was crawling over her skin. She blew it off.

'What languages do you translate?' she asked.

'English to Vietnamese, Vietnamese to Thai, Cantonese to French. It varies. I have a friend at the School of Oriental Studies at London University. We keep in contact, share our ideas.'

'OK... Is it difficult, doing the translations, I mean?' she asked.

'It can be challenging. A single recurring word can make a big difference to a translation. English is a rich language and you can usually find exactly the right word or phrase to convey the meaning. It's more difficult with other languages. I've sometimes spent days just looking for one right word.'

'Wow,' said Cathy.

Blake grinned at her. His eyes sparkled.

'We'll have to have a conversation in French one day,' he said.

'Oh no. No you don't. Pidgin French, that's all I speak, and I'm not going to look a fool in front of a linguist,' she said and backed away, waving her hands in the air. They laughed.

'Come on, let me show you the market,' he said.

They walked on and reached a bustling and colourful street market. Stalls were laid out in neat lines and a busy throng of people milled about.

'Once we get past the food and groceries there are artisans and vendors with antiques and other works of art,' said Blake.

The aroma of sweet toffee hit her nostrils. She loitered at a stall where a machine was making doughnuts. As they fell off the conveyor a man covered them in white sugar. They walked past stalls selling olives, French cheese, Indian spices and freshly made apple juice. They eased their way through the throngs of people; everyone was jostling, barging, shouting. It was a symphony of sights, smells and sounds. Eventually the crowds petered out and they reached the antiques end of the market. They browsed from stall to stall and stopped at a colourful one packed with gadgets, watches and ornaments. Lengths of colourful silk and cotton scarves suspended from the roof of the stall waved in the wind. She picked up a green stone vase, the length of her finger with delicate intricate curves.

'I wonder what this is made of?' she asked.

'That's jade, luvvy,' said the stallholder.

'Oh, it's exquisite,' said Cathy and put it back.

'Five pounds for you,' said the stallholder.

'Here,' said Blake, handing a note to the stallholder, who promptly wrapped the vase in tissue paper and placed it in her hand.

'Oh thank you, you didn't need to,' said Cathy.

'Why not have it… if you like it,' he said.

They continued walking down the Embankment. There were fewer people. They passed a couple hand in hand, a jogger and small groups of businessmen in the street outside a bar swigging beer.

'Do you think it's really jade?' she asked him.

'I'm not sure, let's have a look at it in the light.'

They reached the end of the promenade and sat down on a bench. She pulled off the tissue paper and turned the vase over. It felt hard and cold and smooth.

'I can't see any markings,' she said.

'Can I see?'

'Of course.'

He leant over to have a look. The cool breeze had now turned into a cold wind; goose-bumps appeared on her arms and she rubbed herself to keep warm.

'You're shivering,' he said, removed his jacket and put it around her shoulders. 'Here, is this better?'

'Thank you.'

She turned the vase over and over in her hands while they both peered down at it.

'Difficult to tell,' said Blake, 'you can't be sure with jade. Hmm... jade...' he mused, rubbing his chin. 'There was a story from China I read once about a jade master...'

'Tell it to me,' she said.

'I'm not sure I can remember it.'

'If you can I'd like to hear it.'

He looked into the distance for a few moments. 'Yes, I think I can. It's quite long and involved. Are you sure?'

'Yes, I like stories.'

'Alright then... There was once a young man from a poor background who was determined to better himself. He was clever and shrewd and by the time he'd reached early middle age he had amassed a great wealth and was a millionaire with houses and servants. Yet because of his lowly birth he was not accepted into the society of other wealthy people who also knew about culture, the arts, theatre and history. So he decided to educate himself. He heard there was a jade master living nearby and decided it would be good to learn all about jade and impress the other wealthy people. He asked the master to teach him. The master was unimpressed by the unprepared and impatient young man, but the millionaire offered to pay him very well and he agreed. Eight lessons, one hour each, at the master's house at the same time each week.' Blake paused.

'Go on,' she said.

'So, on the first lesson the millionaire arrived at the appointed time at the master's house and was led by a servant into a room filled with jade pots, saucers, vases, figures of every size and description. The millionaire was encouraged and thought he would be learning all about the mineral, where and how it was mined, the colours, the composition, etc. However, after a short time the servant reappeared and led him into a further room. It was completely empty except for a chair in the middle. The millionaire, somewhat bewildered, sat down on it.'

Cathy looked up at him; he caught her eye and smiled back warmly.

'Anyway, after a further delay the master appeared, smiling and bowing, and placed a small jade bowl in his hands. Then he bowed and backed out of the room. The millionaire was puzzled. When he looked at the clock one hour had passed and the lesson was over. The servant led him to the door. The next lesson the same thing happened: the master entered the empty room as before, but this time placed a jade vase in his hands, bowing and smiling, then left the room. This wasn't the kind of lesson the millionaire was expecting, but he persisted, expecting that the real lessons would start soon. The same things happened for the next six lessons. The master always placed a different object in his hands, then left the room. At the end of the last lesson the master came in and presented his bill. The millionaire exploded with anger and disgust: "What do you think you have been teaching me, what a waste of money and time. Why the object today wasn't even real jade. It was a fake!" And suddenly he realised he knew the difference between what was "real" and what was "unreal".'

Blake caught her eye, smiled at her again and his eyes twinkled. They both burst out laughing.

'Well, what should I think of that then?' she said.

'Food for thought.'

'It's like a sort of Aesop's fable.'

'Or a Zen koan.'

The sun was beginning to set. The sky was so clear that they could almost see flames licking the skyscrapers on the horizon. The jade vase she had been twisting in her hands was warm now; it caught the sun and cast a long shadow over her shirtsleeve.

'I think this is real,' she said, looking at the vase.

'Do you?'

She looked into his eyes. They were silent for a moment. Cathy didn't want the moment to end, but she suddenly felt tongue-tied and silly. She removed his jacket and handed it to him.

'Well, I better get my bus. See you tomorrow?'

'Not tomorrow, I'm going to the Madrid office for a few days, I'll be in next week.'

'OK, goodbye.'

'Goodbye, Cathy.'

He looked deeply into her eyes, holding her gaze undemandingly for a moment. She walked away quickly. Oh God, what do I make of this? she thought. He didn't make this happen, it just happened because of Mr Zachary's conversation. Or did it? I just happened to be there and he trusts me, which is nice. He didn't have to buy me this vase, it was spontaneous, what does it mean? He's a linguist, so that ties in with his CV, 'travelling in the Far East'. I wonder if he's told anyone else that. He confided in me… but maybe this was just a one-off, because of Mr Zachary's conversation. I mustn't read too much into it. I have to keep cool, for goodness' sake. He mustn't see that I like him so much… he really mustn't. She arrived at the bus stop and got on the bus.

'Dulwich, please,' she said to the conductor.

'You're on the wrong bus, Miss, you need bus 65, we're going to Peckham. Get off at the next stop.'

She got off and looked round for the stop for bus 65.

Damn, I can scale a rock face but this is frazzling my brain! Keep cool, Cathy, for goodness' sake, keep cool!

* * *

Cathy knocked on the door of Blake's office, and hearing 'Come in' she entered, leaving the door open.

'What is it, Cathy?'

She held out a buff-coloured folder to him. 'I've finished typing that latest report.' Blake took the folder, opened it and skimmed through the contents.

'It looks at first glance to be up to your usual standard,' he said, smiling.

'Thank you. How was the conference, if I may ask?'

'You certainly may. A lot of the sessions were quite tedious, given by people with high technical ability but zero presentation skills, but there were one or two interesting ones. And I met some helpful people in the bar afterwards.'

'Oh? Helpful, in what way?'

'Some of their research is in the same area as ours. We were able to compare notes: I've got a few new ideas I'd like to try out sometime.'

'Isn't it commercially sensitive?'

'Well, some of my colleagues here may not agree with me but I think we've got more to gain collaboration and openness than being secretive and trying to do everything on our own. Besides, some of it is basic research and no-one's anywhere near producing anything of commercial value from it.' He closed the folder and pushed it to one side on the desk. 'Later today, I'd like you to come to the lab with me. We've just acquired a new laser, direct from the United States.

118

It's more powerful than the ones we've been using and I want to try it out.'

'Of course.'

It was three weeks since they'd walked together along the Embankment and she'd noticed a change in him. Sometimes during the course of the working day she thought she felt his eyes on her, but when she glanced at him he was always looking away. Other times he was sensitively attentive, and would say her name more often. But whenever anyone else was around he always addressed her with formality. There had been no repeat of their walk by the river and he had made no attempt to ask her out. No one would have guessed the agony of longing that sometimes gripped her. She'd successfully concealed her feelings; there was nothing else she could do. Outwardly everything was normal, professional.

In the laboratory, Blake handed Cathy a pair of safety goggles. 'Put these on,' he said as he slipped on a pair himself. He pointed to a rectangular grey metal box about three feet long with a stubby plastic cylinder protruding from one end. 'This is the beast,' he said, switching on the mains power. A thin red beam of light emerged from the cylinder, shining a small red dot on the far wall. 'Not much to look at, but it is pretty powerful. They altered some of the electronics inside to cater for the fact that their mains voltage is 110 and ours is 240.'

'What would it do if they hadn't?'

'Well, burn out the circuits probably. Make a nasty mess of the insides. The first thing I want to do is measure the width of the beam. Pass me that lens, please.' Blake pointed to a circular black-rimmed object on the bench nearby. Cathy picked up the lens and handed it to him.

'It's quite heavy,' she said.

'Yes, there's a lot of solid glass in there.'

'What's that smell?' asked Cathy. 'Smells like something's...'

Suddenly there was a loud bang and Cathy felt something graze the skin of her forehead as it flew past her and thudded into the wall. She looked down. A jagged hole had appeared in the side of the box. Flames and a small plume of acrid smoke issued from the hole. Cathy ran across the room, scooped up a fire extinguisher from its mount on the wall and sprayed the box with the carbon dioxide from it. Moments later the flames were gone and the smoke had dispersed.

'Well done, Cathy,' said Blake as he switched off the power to the laser. 'That was very quick-thinking. Are you alright? You had a lucky escape there.' He looked at her with admiration. Cathy returned his look, but under his steady gaze she felt herself blushing. She shrugged, at a loss for words.

'I'm OK,' she said eventually.

'I heard a bang,' said Norman, walking in. 'I was just passing. Is everything OK? What's that smell?'

'There was a problem with the voltage to the new laser. It's all under control now,' said Blake, opening a window.

'I'll tell Health and Safety,' said Norman.

'No need. I'll be completing an incident report. I need to follow protocol and go through the correct channels. This has to be fully investigated.'

'Oh, OK,' said Norman, looking carefully at them.

'Thank you, Norman,' said Blake.

* * *

Two days later.

'It's a nice evening, would you like to walk along the Embankment?' asked Blake.

'Yes, good idea,' said Cathy, clearing her desk.

They walked amongst couples holding hands, cyclists, joggers, business people and tourists. The place was alight with activity, in some places crowded. She almost lost him in the crowd, then felt his hand take hers. It was warm, firm and reassuring, and he led her through the thickest part of the crowd. They arrived at the bridge. At the foot of the steps there was an old tramp. His legs were outstretched; a dirty grey upturned cap rested on them. A few coins glittered in the sunlight. Blake walked up to him.

'Hello, how are you today?' said Blake.

'Me arthritis in me knee 'urts, but not too bad, sir,' he said with a thick East End accent. He had an ingrained woebegone look.

Blake put his hand deep into his pocket, took out a £10 note and put it in the cap.

'Here.'

'Thank you, sir.'

'He knows you?' Cathy asked, surprised, as they walked away.

'Yes, I always give him something when I pass. When he has enough money, about once a fortnight or so, he spends a night at a YMCA hostel on the other side of the bridge. He gets himself cleaned up and a nurse looks at him. He likes it by the bridge, watching the people go by.'

'What a shame, poor man. Such a strange way to live, begging, with no fixed home or comforts.'

121

Blake regarded her, a strange, enigmatic, distant expression in his eyes. They wandered over to the steps of the bridge and looked out over the river.

'He won't change, will he?' said Cathy.

'I doubt it. He's lived this way for decades, he's an old codger,' said Blake and looked at her mischievously.

'Ten pounds is a lot of money.'

'It is to him.'

'You must be one of only a few people who bother with him.'

'Do you think so?' he said.

'Yes. Look. Most people don't even notice him. They're just walking straight by.'

There was a high-pitched whine followed by a roar as a speedboat zipped off from under the bridge. It left a white frothy wake behind it.

'Look over there. It's going at full throttle,' said Blake. They stopped walking and watched the boat as it disappeared into the distance.

'I've been thinking about the story about the jade master. Have you got any more stories?'

'Yes, there's a few more where that one came from.'

'Where did it come from?'

'I read it a long time ago. It feels like another lifetime.'

'I liked that story,' she said. 'You could come back for a coffee sometime at my flat in Forest Hill if you're passing. Tell me some more.'

She said it flippantly, as if it was an afterthought. But it wasn't. The idea had been brewing just below the surface of her consciousness and now inadvertently spilt out. And as soon as she voiced it she regretted it. You idiot! I shouldn't have said that, what he must think! she said to herself. Her heart pounded and she felt her face burn. He hesitated.

'I might do that sometime,' he said, without looking at her.

She felt like a shy, ridiculous schoolgirl. Then he caught her eye, and this time his expression was serious. They gazed at each other and, if just for a moment, she felt him looking at her with love.

'I need to catch my bus now,' she said, looking at her watch.

'Goodbye, Cathy.'

She rushed down the steps and through an alleyway. She crossed a main road, hardly looking at the traffic, and dashed through a Marks and Spencer's shop and out through the other side. Her throat started to constrict, her heart thumped and there was a tight knot in her stomach. She began to feel nauseous. She was almost beside herself. Oh God, I'm in love, she realised, as if she hadn't known it before. I'm out of my depth... at least I think I am. I need to climb a rock face, find my grit, my courage, my strength; because I know I'll need it. I don't know why. But I just know.

CHAPTER 12

Saigon, Vietnam
April 1968

At 7.00am Blake entered his office and closed the door behind him. He looked around. He didn't feel right and the office didn't feel right; something was different. Quite what, he wasn't sure. It was just a feeling that somebody had been there. Everything seemed to be just as he'd left it, but intuitively he felt there was something amiss. Whoever had been there was very good because nothing seemed to be definitely out of place. This was the second time that he'd had this feeling. He decided he needed to know for certain if somebody was going through his things. From now on the last thing he did before he left his office each day would be to wipe down everything he had touched in the room and on arrival the next morning quickly check strategic areas such as the drawers and filing cabinets for fingerprints. Three days later he looked in satisfaction as a set of very clear prints became visible on his desk drawers. Somebody had obviously been taking a close interest in his affairs. He guessed it must be somebody in the Embassy, possibly the same person who had dealt with Coulter. Sitting in his desk chair, Blake mentally ran through the members of staff. He knew that all the Vietnamese staff would have been vetted as thoroughly as possible, but like most Vietnamese they would be part of large extended families with relatives on both sides of the conflict. You could never be certain where their real loyalties lay. Any of them could be an informant for the Viet Cong.

Blake turned his attention to the Western members of staff. He quickly dismissed George Mason and Roger Sinclair from consideration: they had not joined the Embassy staff until after Coulter's demise. For a moment Blake considered the Ambassador, whom he couldn't rule out at this stage, but felt it very unlikely that he was involved. That left David Anderson and Richard Parker, so he set about getting hold of their personnel files without raising suspicions. Later, back in his office, he opened Parker's file. The photograph showed a confident young man, his dark hair flopping over his forehead. Blake took out the fingerprint card, and placed it on his desk next to the card he had made from the prints found in his office. He could see immediately that there was no match at all between the two sets. Anderson's photograph, being in black and white, did not do full justice to his shock of unruly ginger hair. Blake placed Anderson's fingerprint card next to the one of the unknown intruder. There was a perfect match. He sat back in his chair. 'Got you,' he muttered.

* * *

'Hello, old boy. Not interrupting you, am I?' Blake recognised Tranter's distinctive voice.

He took a deep breath and paused for a moment.

'No,' said Blake, surprised at the sudden phone call. 'Actually I could do with a break. I'm up to my eyes in boring official translations. I've been working on the same tedious document about Embassy procedures for two days.'

'Thought you might like a spot of decent Vietnamese food,' said Tranter, his voice more hoarse than usual, 'makes a change from that slop they serve in the cafés and bars. My treat.'

'Yes,' said Blake, 'sounds good. When?'

'How about tonight, old chap, short notice I know, sorry about that, but I'm off out of town for a week, maybe longer. Not busy tonight, are you?'

'No, I've nothing special arranged. I'd be glad to have dinner. Where is it?'

'It's at *Mrs Ca Doi*. You can get the best crêpes there. All the rickshaw drivers know it. Shall we say seven o'clock?'

'See you there.' Blake put down the phone and stared blankly into space for a few moments, considering.

* * *

Blake got out of the rickshaw outside *Mrs Ca Doi's* restaurant. Although it was early in the evening it was already busy. As waiters dashed about with steaming plates of food, his nostrils were assailed with the aroma of pungent spices. He saw Tranter, in his signature crumpled white suit, sitting at a table near the back of the restaurant. He noticed a half-empty bottle of Jack Daniels on the table. Tranter had obviously started early.

'Hello old boy, glad you could make it,' said Tranter.

Blake pulled out a chair and sat down.

'Apologies again for the short notice, but something special has come up and I have to leave town for a week or two. I wanted to see you before I went.'

A waiter approached and took the order for drinks. Tranter passed a menu to Blake and they spent several minutes in silence, looking it over. Blake closed the menu and put it down.

'What would you recommend?' he asked.

'Well, you could try the *Nem Ran.*'

'What is it?'

Tranter looked up at the waiter. 'Can you tell him what's in it?'

'It's a fried roll. It's got chopped vegetables mixed with soybean curds and sliced mushrooms wrapped in rice, then fried in oil. It's very popular,' said the waiter confidently.

'Sounds good, I'll try that,' said Blake.

'And I'll have the house speciality, *bahn xeo*,' said Tranter.

The waiter brought the drinks, a daiquiri for Blake and a fresh small jug of water for Tranter to mix with his whisky.

'How's business?' said Blake.

'Couldn't be better, old boy, hence the trip. I'm off to arrange a special consignment which will be very profitable indeed,' Tranter said and grinned with satisfaction. His perfectly even teeth were stained yellow and brown with nicotine.

'Do you think it's safe to travel?' asked Blake. 'Hué has only just been retaken, and as you know there was fighting for three days in Saigon itself. Perhaps the Tet offensive isn't over. Who knows if or where they'll attack again.'

'No need to worry, old boy, I shall take all the necessary precautions: I know what I'm doing.'

Blake decided not to probe further.

'Have you noticed much difference since Nguyen Van Thieu has been in power?' he said. 'What do you think of him?'

Tranter snorted into his drink.

'Corrupt lot all of them,' said Tranter, 'you couldn't push a razor blade between them. All of them as corrupt as each other. Don't care a fig for the population just so long as they're alright, raiding the Treasury and salting it all away.'

Blake was surprised by the vehemence of Tranter's reaction.

'Thieu has made no difference on the ground then,' he said.

'No,' said Tranter, 'just the same old story.'

'Do you think he'll last long?' asked Blake.

'Depends,' mused Tranter, sloshing the whisky around in his glass and looking down at it. 'If the Americans withdraw their support he wouldn't last five minutes.' He put his glass down and looked up at Blake. 'Anyway, the bottom line is the Americans will do anything to stop the spread of communism.'

'Yes, they call it the domino theory,' said Blake, 'they think that if Vietnam falls for communism, then one by one the other Asian countries will become communist.'

'That's right, it's their biggest fear, and they're determined to stop it, even at the risk of destroying the country in the process. The Vietnamese people are the victims. The peasants don't know what it's all about. They're scared of the Americans and of the Viet Cong.'

'The peasants are piggy in the middle, aren't they? Distrusted by the Americans and intimidated by the Viet Cong.'

'Yes, but the merchants and the entrepreneurs are riding high on the backs of the Americans, earning lots of money. They've never had it so good. They've got no interest in peace. Then, of course, there are the idealists who want democracy and re-unification, no chance of that... Actually old boy, they've got two chances... fat and slim,' chuckled Tranter, swigging back his whisky. He lit himself a cigarette with his Zippo lighter then droned on in the same monotonous tone: 'The Americans are trying to catch a fly with a machete. They don't know their enemy and they can't even see him.'

'I've heard rumours about the Viet Cong using concealed tunnels,' said Blake.

'Not just rumours, fact. No wonder those poor misguided boys are demoralised. They thought they were fighting for freedom. Now one-third of them are drug addicts. They're just trying to stay alive,' said Tranter ponderously.

'It must be difficult for them,' said Blake. 'Most of them have never been out of the country before and now they're experiencing an alien culture, different in every way to what they're used to. And suffocating heat.'

'They are indeed,' said Tranter. 'These Viet Cong are an elusive unpredictable lot and the Americans can't get themselves together.' His voice began to rasp. He coughed, took another drag on his cigarette, then continued. 'They could have won by now with half the force if the commanders had had more sense and they'd been a proper fighting force. Anyway, old chap, it's no skin off my nose if the Americans are in trouble, I've got my own business to run...' He seemed to have run out of steam: his voice, which had become increasingly croaky, trailed off.

The food arrived. Tranter extinguished his cigarette in the ashtray and smothered the glowing fragments one by one. Blake could see that Tranter's *bahn xeo* was a large omelette stuffed with prawns and bean sprouts. His *Nem Ran* covered most of the platter. He and

Tranter fell silent as they ate the spicy food. Tranter began to perspire, beads of sweat appearing on his forehead; eventually he sat back and sighed, replete.

'How was it?' he asked.

'Very good,' said Blake and took a final bite out of his crisp roll.

'Glad you liked it,' said Tranter.

Then the conversation turned to other matters. After a while Blake experienced a distinct stomach disturbance, but a Coors helped settle it. As he turned to leave, Tranter handed him the menu.

'Just a little reminder of our meal here for you to keep,' Tranter said and his eyes flashed.

'Thanks,' said Blake, 'hope the trip's a success.'

He pocketed the menu and took a rickshaw back to his flat.

Once safely inside, he opened up the menu. Taped inside it was a thin piece of paper covered in typing and beneath it a photograph. He spent the evening decoding the message. It spelled out the details of his next target, but time was short. He only had a twenty-four-hour window, which explained the sudden dinner invitation. As Blake read the message it became obvious that this one was big, very big. After he finished the last sentence he sat back in his chair, his mind racing. The target was a high-ranking officer in the Viet Cong. Colonel Lee Ho Quock, commander of the Fourth Regiment and one of the leading organisers of the Tet offensive, was due to make a lightning visit to a secret Viet Cong encampment located thirty miles north-east of Saigon. Tranter had detailed the exact location. Lee Ho Quock was one of their best, an outstanding strategist and a brilliant tactical commander. He had been responsible for several defeats suffered by the South Vietnamese

Army over the last couple of years. The Americans had been trying to get to him for months. They had even considered, according to Blake's CIA source, mounting a combat mission to eliminate him, into North Vietnam if necessary. That had not been possible though, because he was continually on the move, changing the location of his headquarters every other week. By the time the Americans had found out where he was, he had moved on. Now here was the chance to get him. If the information that Blake had was accurate, Lee Ho Quock would be at the camp for about thirty hours, taking one of the local commanders to task for not pressing the South Vietnamese Army hard enough. Blake would have to move fast if the opportunity was not to slip away. Sudden changes in routine can give rise to suspicions and so Blake liked to plan his strategy well in advance and move carefully. This time, however, he had no choice if he was to get to the camp in time. For several minutes Blake sat still, outwardly calm, but inside a battle was raging. Someone had killed Coulter, and any false move on his part could direct attention to himself, something he had tried hard to avoid. On the other hand, killing Quock would seriously damage the effectiveness of the Viet Cong in this area. Was the chance of success and the potential gain high enough to outweigh the risk of suddenly breaking cover like this? Or should he pass up the chance, stay unobtrusive, and carry on with less pressured assignments?

Blake read the instructions, memorised them and then burnt them over the kitchen sink. He had to think quickly. He would need to hire a boat for this assignment and cross the Mekong delta. His English class was tomorrow night; he'd need to cancel it without raising the suspicions of whoever was taking a close interest in his affairs. He berated himself for having started the blasted lessons, picked up the telephone and rang the Embassy staff member hosting the lesson that week. Telling her he had to postpone the next class because of urgent Embassy business, he asked her to contact the others, give his apologies and say that he would see them in two weeks.

CHAPTER 13

Khien, dressed in pyjamas, opened the door, blinked and looked bleary-eyed at Blake. 'What time is it?'

Blake looked at his watch. 'Three minutes to midnight. Sorry to get you up so late,' he said.

'What is it? Something serious?' said Khien, frowning. 'Come in.'

Blake followed him into the living room where Khien turned on a small table lamp. He looked at Khien squarely and took a deep breath. He didn't want to involve Khien so closely in his affairs, but felt he no longer had a choice.

'I'll talk candidly. I'm under surveillance; I think somebody in the Embassy is on to me. I think I know who it is, but I can't say more. I've got an important job I need to do tomorrow. I'll be away all day.'

Khien stared at Blake. 'What else?' he asked.

'I think you should get Hoa and your family out of the way. They may come after me, but whatever the risks I've got to do this job.'

Khien rubbed his chin and walked briskly over to the window. He pulled the thick net curtain back and looked out at the street below.

'I've been wondering about getting the family away myself. It's getting worse and worse in town. You can't tell who's the VC and who isn't in Saigon these days. Only yesterday a Government office was bombed, twenty people dead,' he said.

'I think they should leave straight away.'

Khien took a long, sombre look at Blake.

'I agree. I'm not going to ask you what you're doing tomorrow, but there's no time to lose.'

'You said there's a place on Lang Doc island.'

'Yes, it's a villa owned by Ming's sister. I will tell Ming that she and the children must go there tomorrow.'

'And Hoa must leave with them as well,' said Blake.

'You know my daughter. She may be more of a problem. You know how defiant she can be, but I'll do what I can.'

'I will insist she leaves,' said Blake.

'But I am staying on, I have my accountancy business to attend to.'

'Don't put yourself at risk,' said Blake.

'I will do whatever is necessary,' said Khien.

* * *

When Khien arrived at Blake's flat Hoa and Blake were both in the living room. Hoa sat at her small table by the window turning her tarot cards over and over in her hands. Her face was down and her hair fell about her face.

'Hoa knows what she needs to do,' said Blake.

Khien paced up and down the room and jangled the coins in his pocket.

'There's a boat leaving for Lang Doc island, boarding tonight,' said Khien. 'Are you paying attention, Hoa?'

'I can hear you, father,' she said and gave her father a brief sideways glance.

'I want you to go on the boat. It's the school holiday, you have nothing to keep you here.'

'I have my husband.'

'I insist you go, Hoa,' said Blake as he continued gathering together what he needed for his jungle trip.

'All the family are going, including your cousin Lou. I have booked passage for us all,' said Khien. 'You need to get ready.'

'I will think about it, father,' she said and turned the cards over in her hands. Blake noticed her holding the *Hanged Man* card between her index finger and thumb. She looked at it intently, dropped it back into the pack and shuffled the pack again.

'You must come,' said Khien with frazzled intensity, his voice loud and forceful. His face turned red and he wiped his forehead with his handkerchief. He jangled the coins rapidly in his pocket; they clinked and rattled. 'You will need to pack and leave in one hour. Now I have other arrangements to make. I will be back for you soon and I expect you to be ready.'

Khien left, slamming the door behind him.

'You must go on the boat,' said Blake levelly. He stopped what he was doing for a moment, and looked at her.

'I don't want to go,' said Hoa. Her voice began to tremble. She laid several cards out on the table, face down in a diamond shape, and began turning each one over slowly, in sequence.

'It is not safe here. I order you to leave,' said Blake. He had never found it easy to persuade Hoa to do anything. His job was uppermost in his mind and he didn't want to waste energy and time with distractions. However, out of a sense of loyalty, obligation and just a smidgen of guilt, he persevered. 'Neither contact with your ancestors or your fortune-telling cards can help you now. Can't you see, they're all just projections of your own imagination? False prophets. Give up this mumbo-jumbo now and wake up and see the reality that's in front of you.'

Hoa gathered the cards together, held them in her hands and looked up at him defiantly.

'I will not. My husband cannot order me to do anything... my life is here.'

'It's the cards, isn't it?' said Blake. He felt himself brim with irritation and anger. 'You'd prefer to follow the predictions of the cards rather than the reasoning of your own family.'

As he held her gaze her expression of defiance slowly metamorphosed into one of consternation and fear.

'John, stop looking at me like that. You're so cold, so severe... you're scaring me.' Her voice began to crack. 'I knew you didn't love me when we married, but I hoped that in time... ' She stifled a sob. 'All these months we've been married I've tried, but failed. But now I know the truth, my dead ancestors have more heart than you.'

'Here,' said Blake. He walked straight across the room. 'Let me explain it to you in a language you'll understand... give me the bloody cards,' he said forcefully and wrenched them out of her hands. He picked out the *Death* card and slammed it down on the table in front of her. 'This is what you may bring upon yourself and us. Leave, Hoa, leave on the boat.'

'You are a cruel, callous man!' said Hoa and began to sob.

'See reason, Hoa, see reason. You are my wife. Listen to me, your husband, and keep yourself safe.'

'I can't leave... I won't leave,' she protested between sobs

Blake turned aside and continued assembling his backpack.

'You are a stubborn and headstrong girl,' he said, 'by staying here you're not helping, you're putting yourself in greater danger and hindering me…'

'Where are you going, John, what are you doing?'

'Your father and I are helping the South Vietnamese Army. You know that.'

Blake gathered his rations together and put them in a container. 'My assignment takes priority… I can't force you.' He placed his compass, torch and flares in the outer pocket of his backpack and zipped it up. 'But if you're stupid enough to stay, I don't want any whingeing, whining, complaining or any regrets.' Hoa sobbed profusely, her head in her hand. 'If you stay, I'll treat you like any other citizen caught up in this messy war… I won't be trying to rescue you or protect you, you'll be on your own.' He placed his camouflage clothing and war paint in the body of the rucksack and fastened it up. 'You must not get in the way.'

'I will not get in the way… but I will not leave!' said Hoa, almost hysterical.

He put his rifle in his rucksack, his handgun in his pocket and did a last check. Their eyes met and she looked at him distraught.

'I understand!' she screamed and in a fury of passion threw the tarot cards into the air, beside herself with emotion.

Blake was ready. He left by the front door. He didn't look back.

CHAPTER 14

London
October 1979

Cathy walked into the office and settled at her desk. Her eyes focused on a handwritten note from Blake clipped to a document. *As you know, I'm in Copenhagen this week. Here is my proposal. Please type it and send it to Mr Zachary. Blake.* She got on with it. She'd been typing for a couple of hours when Norman walked up. As he hovered over her desk she felt herself stiffen; there was a vague scent of aftershave. He peered at the papers on her desk and thumbed through them.

'So, this is Blake's proposal, is it?' he said.

'Yes, excuse me, I'm working with that,' said Cathy curtly. She pulled the pages closer.

'Well, it just so happens I've got my own proposal for you to type,' said Norman. With a flourish, he tossed a document attached with a bulldog clip into her in-tray. 'And once you've typed it I'd like you to send it to Dr Shaw, The Research Director.' There was a glint of smug satisfaction on his face. 'How soon can you do it?'

'I'll do it when I have time,' said Cathy.

'When will that be?' He studied her closely. She quickly glanced away.

'A couple of days, I expect,' said Cathy, looking at her typing.

'Perfect,' said Norman, 'I want it laid out in sections. The side headings are clearly marked, I'm sure you'll work it out. Thanks, Cathy, you're a star.'

He winked at her and meandered back to Blake's office, stopping to chat to Rose and Margot on the way and making them laugh.

Cathy scanned through the pages of Norman's proposal and then dropped them back into the in-tray. That can wait, she thought. Later that afternoon she took a short break at her desk with a cup of tea and a biscuit. She picked up Norman's paper: *Collaborative Proposal with Porton Down: The large-scale manufacturing of AJ gases.* She felt herself stiffen. Oh God, she mumbled under her breath. Even the title irked her. She thumbed idly through it. On first glance it was a mess, all jumbled up, with lots of crossings-out. Except for several sections that were neatly laid out and looked familiar. Cathy sat back in her chair frowning, trying to remember. Abruptly she got up and crossed the office to a cabinet labelled *Dormant*. She took out a file and went back to her desk. From the file she extricated a report, put it beside Norman's proposal and compared them. She looked up: several desks away Norman was locking his filing cabinet. She'd lost count of the number of times she'd seen him lock and unlock it. There were obviously things in there he didn't want others to see. He walked into Blake's office; he'd been using it all week. After some thought she got up and replaced the report in the *Dormant* cabinet, collected the proposal and walked to Blake's office. She took a deep breath, knocked on the door and went in. Norman was on the telephone. He waved her to a chair in front of the desk. She sat down and waited until he put down the phone.

'Yes, Cathy, what is it?'

'It's your proposal.'

'Oh, sorry, is it a bit too technical for you,' he said, 'that's the way of these things. You'll get used to them once you've seen a few more I expect. I'll help you sort it out.'

Cathy ignored his patronising tone.

'Actually, as it so happens, I've already seen that before. Part of it anyway.' She waved the proposal in front of him.

'What do you mean?' said Norman uneasily rubbing his neat short beard.

'I mean the data you've presented as preliminary findings in the introduction, and which you've also used in the results, and the Appendix, are identical to a report that Blake wrote about three months ago. All the data are the same, the tables and the graphs, except he was working with yeasts and yours is to do with bacteria.'

Norman fidgeted, running his fingers through his thick wavy hair.

'You're mistaken, Cathy,' he said.

'I'm not. I typed the report for him a few months ago and I've just checked it. They're the same.'

Cathy could feel her heart start to pound.

'Coincidence,' said Norman. His face had turned red and he twisted a pen between his fingers.

'No,' said Cathy firmly, 'every single data point is identical. That's more than coincidence. It's plagiarism, and it's dishonest.'

For a moment Cathy thought she had gone too far. But the thought of Norman, the odious Norman, stealing Blake's work was too much for her to take.

'Now see here,' Norman blustered. Beads of spittle flew out of his mouth and across the desk, just missing her. 'Your job is just to type what you're given. The content is none of your business. Now get out of here and type it up as it is if you know what's good for you.'

Still seething, Cathy stormed back to her desk and flung the proposal back into her in-tray, her hands shaking. She noticed Rose and Margot looking over at her, whispering to each other and sniggering. She finished Blake's proposal and sent it to Mr Zachary. With a groan, she took Norman's out of her in-tray and started typing it. There was a tight knot of frustration in her stomach. She managed to work out which bits went where and pulled it all together. Once she'd finished typing she read it through to the end and felt a wave of consternation. It was well-written and presented, comprehensive and compelling. Especially with Blake's data in it, giving it a real professional edge. It had a strong chance. No wonder Norman was so smug. Cathy gritted her teeth and sat back in her chair, deliberating.

'Deep in thought, Cathy?' said Ann as she walked past.

'Yes, I'm trying to work something out,' said Cathy.

What the hell, she thought. Taking a deep breath, she took a red pen out of her drawer and went through the document systematically crossing out all Blake's data to see what it looked like without his work in it. The document was now about two-thirds its original length and not nearly as impressive. Incensed, she removed the Treasury tag, separated all the pages and tore them into pieces one by one. Ann walked past again.

'Not happy with your typing?' she said.

'No, I've made a big mistake here.'

'Oh dear,' said Ann, and moved on.

Cathy retyped the document, leaving out all Blake's data and replacing those sections with blank paragraphs. Breathing deeply, she attached the compliment slip and wrote out the envelope for Dr Shaw. She hesitated as she stood over the tray for the internal post, momentarily uncertain, her heart pounding. Then she dropped it in. She walked out of the office feeling exhausted.

She finished off a whole bottle of wine by herself that evening and spent a sleepless night tossing and turning. She thought about handing in her resignation and starting a completely different career, but at what and as what? Times were hard and she needed the experience. Then she thought about Blake. She tried to be rational. What's in a smile, a look? What if I'm imagining everything? I'm just an employee and he's my boss. And he hasn't even asked me out. But her emotional voice was so loud it nearly deafened her. She felt instinctively that they'd bonded, that he had feelings for her. If he does, this is the weirdest courtship. What's holding him back, why wait? She grappled with her emotions for the next few days, feeling lonely and apprehensive. She knew what was coming, and this challenge wasn't going to involve Blake. Not directly.

On the morning of the 18th she skipped breakfast; she wasn't hungry. She went into the office, prepared to face the music come what may, and spent an unpleasant morning waiting for the showdown. She wasn't going to apologise, no, she'd stick up for herself, be resolute and strong. It was late morning when she saw Norman march in. His face was red and contorted with rage. She braced herself. He marched over to her desk, curtly summoned her into Blake's office, ordered her to sit down and closed the door. Cathy swallowed hard.

'I've just come from a meeting with the directors. What do you think you're doing leaving half my report out,' he said furiously, pacing up and down the office. 'Who the hell do you think you are to decide what goes into my reports and what doesn't? – a jumped-up little secretary like you. You've just ruined my chance of promotion.'

'I wasn't aware there was a vacancy,' said Cathy.

He glared at her. His face was like thunder and glistening with beads of sweat.

'You should have typed it exactly as I gave it to you. I'm your senior.'

'You knew I wasn't happy with it and I don't care who you are. I won't type what is wrong.'

'It's not for you to decide what's right and wrong. I tell you what to type and you type it.' He paced up and down, looking at her with disgust, contempt and hate. 'This is gross misconduct. I can't fire you without consulting Blake, although I know you've been trying to wrap him round your little finger. No doubt trying to improve your position here. We've all noticed.'

'Who, you and the girls? Have you nothing better to do?' said Cathy scathingly. 'All you do is gossip and scheme.'

'Be careful what you say.'

'No, I won't. I haven't finished yet,' said Cathy boldly, feeling her blood boil. 'I don't think Blake is likely to be influenced by anybody, and I resent your suggestions about my motives. We're not all out for the main chance like you. Blake and I are professionals, we respect each other as colleagues, as we should and you should.'

Norman leant over her menacingly. His lips were drawn back over gaping teeth. His nearness made her itch and a heat radiated from him. She pulled away and blinked. She could see the pools of spittle forming in the corners of his mouth. He almost spat in her ear.

'I've had enough of you and your cheek, young lady... As of now I'm suspending you. Get out of my sight!' he yelled. 'Collect your things and go.'

She left the office and walked briskly, although she was in no hurry and had nowhere to go but home. The last remnants of adrenalin coursed through her. She felt exhausted and battered. Lorries roared past her throwing dust up into her face. Tears sprang into her eyes, blinding her. Angrily she blinked them back. She wouldn't give way to self-pity. But her situation was grim. Despite her best efforts it had all gone wrong. Her first foray into the world of work was an unmitigated disaster. The office was seething with politics and unpleasantness, she'd fallen in love with her boss and been suspended, now most probably would be sacked. There was little chance of securing another job with that track record. Just a couple of days ago it seemed she was on the verge of having everything, the job and Blake. Now she had nothing. Only the dreadful realisation that not having Blake was so much more devastating than not having the job. She never meant it to be this way. She arrived home, changed into her long grey skirt and torn, baggy, green jumper. She sank into the sofa and wrapped herself in a blanket. She could hardly move. She was in a strange state of suspended animation, as if her life were on hold.

* * *

Several days passed. She got out of the bath and viewed herself in the mirror. She looked terrible. Her face was white and she had black bags under her dark eyes. Her hair looked wild and stood up in peaks; she ran her fingers through it. She poured some jasmine oil

144

into a burner and lit a tea light under it. After a few minutes the small living room was suffused with the smell; it was soothing and pleasant. She put on her *Easy Listening* LP. The smoochy *This Guy's in Love with You* by Herb Alpert was the first one to play. She indulged herself. It was the ultimate wish fulfilment record. As she listened her mood became more soporific at each complete circuit of the turntable. She moved the glass coffee table near to the G-plan sofa. The fabric had split and the yellow foam was bulging out, but it was still comfortable. She arranged a Thermos of tea, a glass, the bottle of vodka and coke and the packet of biscuits in a line and lay down. Everything was within easy reach. She watched the sunset, and through the window she could just see the grey roofs and chimneys of the houses opposite.

It was getting late when the doorbell went. Cathy didn't feel like moving. She dragged herself out of the sofa slowly like an exhausted swimmer dragging herself out of water, turned the music down low and went to open the door.

'Oh,' she said, aghast, and put her hand to her mouth; Blake stood there.

His tie was loose around his neck and his top shirt button unfastened as if he had got hot under the collar. Her heart began to throb.

'Any chance of that coffee?'

'Yes, come in. I'm sorry… I look terrible.'

'Not to me.'

He closed the door and followed her through to the kitchen. The simple activity of putting water into the kettle suddenly seemed impossibly difficult and she grabbed the teapot instead and started filling it.

'What am I doing, I'm stupid,' she said.

She shook her head and looked around for the kettle and filled it. He leant back against one of the kitchen units and watched her for a few moments. She could feel the intensity of his gaze.

'I need to say thanks for what you did with the research proposals.'

'Did it cause a lot of problems?' she said, trying to suppress the spasm in her voice.

'Only for Norman, who couldn't explain away the blanks in his proposal. I'm sorry, you were put in an impossible position. I found the draft he gave you; I know what he was trying to make you do.'

Cathy plugged in the kettle and flicked on the switch.

'How did you find it? He locks everything away in his filing cabinet every night and double checks it.'

'Simple, I picked the lock.'

'Well, won't he know?'

'No, I put everything back exactly as I found it. He won't even be suspicious.'

It took Cathy some time to take this in. She hadn't expected this from him. He was able to put it so simply, as if it were just part of going to work. Blake looked awkward suddenly.

'Morally reprehensible, I know, but it was the only way. I had my suspicions and needed to know why he'd suspended you. We argued. He wouldn't tell me himself but kept referring to your incompetence, which I knew wasn't the case,' said Blake.

'I'm sorry, sorry you argued… about me.'

'It was inevitable, anyway; it was a long time coming, simmering just below the surface.'

'You do look a bit… dishevelled.'

'Do I?'

'Your tie… is loose,' she said, pointing to it.

146

'Yes, well… Forget it, we didn't beat each other up.'

'And your SERC proposal? The IT and satellite communications?'

'Fully funded. Went through on the nod, if I want it,' said Blake.

'I'm relieved,' said Cathy.

'I only found out today about all this. He suspended you last Thursday was it, six days ago?' he asked softly.

'Yes.'

'How have you been?'

'Not bad, though it caused me some flak and stress. I've been drowning my sorrows on a cocktail of tea and vodka, the first things that came to hand. Oh, and coke.'

'You don't expect to have to deal with this when you come to work, do you?' he said. His voice was quiet and slow.

'It wasn't in the job description.'

The kettle hissed and steam escaped from the top. She put the coffee granules in the cup and poured on the hot water. As she poured the milk into the second cup she felt his hand touching her shoulder. She took a deep breath and put the milk carton on the work surface. He'd moved closer to her, his clothes touching hers. Her heart pounded. He was so near it almost took her breath away. She turned and looked at him and he held her gaze, his grey eyes welling with emotion.

'This wasn't in the job description either. Right now, the research is not what I really care about, Cathy. It's you, I care about you.'

Cathy fell into his arms and felt tears filling her eyes. At last. She felt the strength of him, the heat of his body, his breath on her face. He held her close. And her tears turned into a smile and then into laughter. They laughed together and looked into each other's eyes.

With his fingertips he tenderly brushed a teardrop away from her cheek. The music came to an end, the stylus on the turntable making a repetitive beep as it completed each circuit.

'You always knew how I felt as well?' she asked in a whisper.

'We've both known about this for a long time, haven't we?'

'Yes.'

'I love you,' he said, and gazed steadily at her, his grey eyes full of love.

'And I love you.'

'I've tried to stay professional with you, Cathy. I've failed.'

'You've made me wait so long. Why did you refuse my invitation for coffee?'

He didn't respond immediately. She snuggled into his shoulder and he gently ran his fingers through her hair.

'I was always sure about my feelings for you... But I'm not an easy man to know or be with,' he said at last.

'Surely that's up to me to decide, not you,' she said and looked up at him.

His expression was inscrutable. His mouth searched for hers. The kiss was warm and soft, just right. He pulled her close and they embraced for a long moment; he pressed her against him. She felt the hard bulge in his groin and the stirrings of her own passion. She looked into his eyes.

'Do you want to?' he asked.

'Make love?'

'Yes?... Is it too soon?'

'Yes, I want to,' she said softly.

He scooped her up into his arms and carried her through the flat until he found the bedroom, and placed her gently on the bed. He kissed the side of her neck, then below, then her ear lobe. She pulled at his tie, yanked it off and threw it across the room. They tugged and fumbled at each other's clothes. Then they kissed again and the clothes came off and they threw them anywhere. She was out of practice and sensed that he was the same. It was raw and spontaneous and urgent. His hands roaming her breasts, her belly, her legs, were more potently pleasurable than she could have imagined. She felt his warm, firm flesh under her hands. As he pushed his way inside her she gasped with the intensity of the physical experience and joyously accepted him, giving herself to him fully, trusting him, holding nothing back. Finished, they both gasped for breath. She could feel his throbbing heart slowly calm and they lay in silence. She moved her fingertips over the firm muscles of his shoulders, his biceps, his back, discovering him slowly with her senses, her mind. They kissed again, a long, slow, deep kiss. He turned on his side, resting on his forearm, his hand on his cheek, and looked down at her, his other hand caressing her.

'I hope you don't regret taking this job,' he said.

'No, of course not, but right from the start I thought I might like you too much to be my manager. I can tell you that now…'

'This isn't what I expected to happen, really. I've grown to love you over the months.'

'Why did you hire me?'

'Because of your qualifications and skills, of course,' he said. A smile formed on his face.

'The office is such a desolate, lonely place without you there, Blake. Besides, do I still have a job?'

'Of course. I'll have you reinstated.'

'But not yet; at the moment I still can't face it.'

'What would you like to do?'

'Just go away as far as possible.'

'I don't blame you.'

'With you.'

'How far away?'

'A long way?'

'What, on an aeroplane?'

'Yes, just like that.'

'Where would you like to go?'

'What, anywhere?' she laughed.

'Yes, anywhere.'

'There is somewhere I've always wanted to go.'

'Where's that?'

'Cairo, to see the pyramids.'

'Anywhere else?'

'To an exotic island – hot, with a beautiful beach.'

'You're serious about this?'

'Yes, of course.'

He looked towards the window for a few moments.

'Then let's do it… why not… We only live once after all. Let's see what I can arrange.'

'What!'

'Yes, we'll do that… Do you think you could put up with spending some time with me?'

'Of course… I've already put up with you for hours toiling away in the lab. And I nearly got killed. Dangerous places, labs. I managed that, didn't I? I'm stoic.'

'What you did was impressive, you were a heroine and saved the day… but I'm thinking of an adventure that's less risky. It's about time I spent some of this money I've been earning. Don't worry, you don't need any.'

He picked his shirt up off the floor, sat on the edge of the bed and put it on. Cathy looked lovingly at the toned muscles around his shoulders and back, although she noticed some scarring, especially round the back of his neck. She remembered her first impression of him as being rugged. As he stood up she flinched, shocked. There was a large and ugly disfigurement on the back of his left thigh, some sort of scar from a serious wound, which had healed badly.

'Are you wounded, Blake?' she asked.

'Oh, that. It was a long time ago. It's nothing,' he said dismissively, but there was a strange note in his voice. He pulled on his trousers. 'I've got to go to the office, I've left my passport there. Where's yours?'

'It's here.'

He turned and looked at her.

'Get a good night's sleep; you look as if you need it. I'll be back for you in the morning. Is that too soon for you?'

'No, I like spontaneity... I love it! Am I still suspended?'

'Until we get back, yes.'

'Good.'

He kissed her. She heard the front door close and her heart was full of unrestrained joy. All her suspicions were correct, her intuition hadn't let her down, all the waiting had been so hard but it had been worth it, just for this moment. She got up, walked into the living room, took the stylus off the turntable and went into the kitchen. The two coffees were on the work surface. She placed her fingers around the cups; they were cold. She tipped the liquid down the sink and poured herself a glass of vodka.

'Yes!' she said aloud, then raised her glass and downed the vodka in two gulps, drinking deep. The strong liquor burnt the back of her throat. She stopped suddenly. 'God, how things change!' she said.

CHAPTER 15

Cairo
October 1979

Blake pulled back the wooden shutters of their Edwardian hotel room; they creaked and banged into position and let the light in. Cathy gasped at the inspiring sight from the window. Before them lay an arcade of mosques and tall minarets pointing to the skies that projected from a spectrum of whitewashed, flat-roofed buildings. The sun was high, the air was hot, humid and tinged grey-pink from smog and dust. Below them cars honked and people shouted. The city was bustling with activity. There was a faint smell of spices.

'What a sight,' said Cathy, 'so exotic, so full of eastern promise.'

'I think we need some Turkish Delight to go with this,' said Blake and smiled mischievously.

Cathy turned round and looked into the room, which was now brightly lit. A crystal chandelier hung from the ceiling, an art deco lamp rested on a lace tablecloth on a corner table. Blake stretched and walked towards the bed; it creaked as he lay down on it. He relaxed with his hands behind his head and his legs crossed. She noticed him watching her as she unpacked, but she was more interested in his case on a side table than her own.

'Your case is very small. Do you mind if I ask what's in it?' she said.

'You can look if you like.'

'OK.'

She walked across the room, clicked the fastenings open and carefully sorted through the items, putting them back into position. There were the usual toiletries, one pair of trousers and three long-sleeved white shirts. She stopped and looked at him. He watched her, smiling.

'Do you have any shirts that aren't white?' she asked.

He hesitated, thought about it for a bit.

'No, I suppose I haven't.'

'Is this all you've got?' she asked.

'I travel light.'

'But look, you haven't got enough clothes. You need shorts and short-sleeved shirts and sandals.'

'That's more than I need.'

'*Oh reason not the need*, that's Shakespeare, isn't it?'

'King Lear, *Why need one*?' Blake quipped.

They grinned at each other and laughed.

'Look, you need clothes suitable for the weather or you'll boil.'

'I'll just cut the sleeves off,' he said.

'No, you won't.'

'Are you trying to organise me… I'm not used to being organised,' said Blake.

'Please, can we buy you some new clothes?'

'Alright, if you must. But not yet, I want to take you to the pyramids first. I'll go and order a taxi.'

He left the room and she hung her clothes in the cavernous mahogany wardrobe. It was heavy and ancient and looked as if it had been in position for as long as the great monument they had come to visit.

As their taxi wove its way through the chaos of the pedestrians and the other vehicles milling about in the crowded streets, Cathy sat close to Blake on the back seat, his hand firmly clasped in hers. She excitedly took in the unfamiliar sights and smells, turning this way and that to see all that she could. Rounding the last corner, suddenly she saw the Great Pyramid, directly in front of them. It was some way off but even so it was an imposing sight. She turned to Blake, her eyes shining. 'Wow,' she said, grinning at him. He smiled back.

'Impressed?' he asked.

'Very.'

Their taxi pulled up outside the Great Pyramid and they got out. Mohammed, their taxi driver, went to buy them tickets to get inside. Coachloads of tourists milled about adorned with sunhats and sunglasses, some had impressive-looking cameras swinging from their necks, but these tourists were angry. They heard vigorous but incoherent exchanges between some of the American tourists and their representative, who was dressed in yellow and held a yellow umbrella up high.

'Quiet, please,' she yelled above the general mayhem; this time her voice was clear and distinct.

Mohammed returned.

'I'm sorry, the pyramids are officially closed,' he said.

Blake studied Cathy. 'You're disappointed,' he said.

'I'm devastated,' Cathy said, her shoulders slumped. 'I was so looking forward to it.'

Blake dug inside his back pocket, produced a mass of bank notes, started counting them and looked at Mohammed. 'Do you know anyone who can help to get us inside? As a favour,' said Blake.

Mohammed raised his eyebrows, gave Blake a quick stare, said he'd see and walked away. The crowd was getting even more irate and were massing in a small, tight, menacing group around their representative. She used all her diplomatic skills to entice them back on the coach.

'I've come halfway round the world for this. Unhappy, you bet I am!' shouted a tall man with an enormous paunch.

'I'm sorry, there's nothing I can do,' said the representative.

A little grey-haired lady with a high-pitched shriek raised her voice. 'I've saved for years for this trip and I'm not going back without going inside the Great Pyramid.'

'Nor am I,' bellowed another female voice.

Mohammed returned.

'I have two friends who will help you,' he whispered, 'if the price is right.'

Cathy watched the crowd while the men negotiated. The yellow umbrella wafted precariously from side to side as if in some transient wind. Mohammed introduced them to a guide who led them up the steps in full view of the furious crowd below. The entrance lay about one-third of the way up on the side of the pyramid. As they approached the entrance, she was aware that several of the Americans had spied them.

'Look. They're going in,' a man shouted, raising his fist, his face contorted with rage.

Just as pandemonium and chaos was about to break out below, they entered the still silence of the Great Pyramid. A withered old cripple sat on a stone block in the shade inside the entrance. His face was dark and leathery, showing the creases of age and sun. A well-worn walking stick was propped up beside him. Blake passed him some cash. The man grinned, his open mouth was black and toothless. He put the cash into the pocket of his greasy ankle-length robe. The air was cool inside and it smelt of stone and subterranean space. Slowly Cathy's eyes adjusted to the darkness. She followed Blake along passages to a diagonal upward-sloping corridor and started the climb. Braided cord had been threaded through black metal hoops to make handrails. Bare bulbs strung on cable, which stretched into the distance, dimly lit the way. A Japanese couple passed them on the way down, looking bewildered and tense; the man's camera swung precariously from side to side as he negotiated the steep stairway. Nobody else could be seen or heard. The corridor levelled out but the ceiling suddenly dipped. It was too low for them to stand up so they stooped for the next few yards. The space opened up into a chamber, rectangular with dark granite walls and dimly lit with a single electric bulb on a stand set in one corner. It was hot, oppressive and airless, and bare apart from a grey sarcophagus. Cathy breathed deeply, taking it all in. She hugged herself, arms crossed in front of her, as she looked all around. An elderly Arab sat cross-legged on the floor against a wall moving his worry beads back and forth between his fingers.

'Where are we?' Cathy whispered.

Her voice had no echo; it just seemed to disappear, absorbed into the walls. Blake didn't reply. She watched him as he climbed into the sarcophagus, lay down flat and closed his eyes. The Arab didn't react. Cathy ran her hand along the side of the sarcophagus, feeling the roughness of the stone against her fingers. She reflected that it had lain here undisturbed for thousands of years, forgotten by the outside world. After an indeterminate amount of time that seemed like an age, Blake climbed out and took up the same posture as the Arab with his back against the wall and closed his eyes. Both men appeared completely relaxed, oblivious to the strangeness of their surroundings. Cathy stood

157

motionless, silent. The whole experience seemed surreal and oppressive. It was rock-climbing she liked, being out in the open, smelling the fresh mountain air. She began to feel faint and coughed. Blake opened his eyes; he was looking at her and seemed to say something but she didn't hear it. He stood up and came to her.

'Are you OK?'

'I'm hot, it's a bit claustrophobic.'

'Let's go. Do you want to do any more exploring inside?'

'No, it's enough. Thank you for bringing me here, but I'm ready to go now.'

He led her out, finding his way easily. The bright sun at the entrance was almost blinding. It took some time for her eyes to adjust. The Americans had gone and the Egyptians had set up a barrier, refusing anyone else entry.

* * *

Mohammed took them in his taxi to the souk in the old part of the city. As they stood at the entrance a labyrinth of pedestrian, narrow, cobble-stoned streets lay before them. It was heaving with stalls crammed with everything ranging from exotic to kitsch. Above them washing was suspended between tall buildings. They wandered along a street. Cathy lost count of the number of Great Pyramids and Sphinxes that were on display. Some were obviously made of cheap plastic, others were metal or wood. Some were studded with semi-precious stones. There was a delicious syrupy smell in the air; she followed the aroma. The stall had row upon row of sweets coloured pink, brown, green and yellow. As she stopped to look the stallholder proffered a sticky yellow ball for her to try.

'Eat, eat,' he said. 'You try, you like!'

He thrust it at her. She accepted it and took a bite out of it. She could taste the saffron, the cinnamon, then the honey, lots of honey, far too sweet and sickly. Cathy chewed and then swallowed with difficulty.

'Delicious,' she lied.

Before she could stop him, Blake had bought half a pound of the sickly sweets. At one stall, laden with shimmering fabrics of turquoise, azure, crimson and gold, Cathy admired a sheer silk scarf. Moments later Blake had bought it, without haggling, and draped it across her shoulders. Another time she made the mistake of admiring a delicate evening purse studded with tiny pearls and now it was nestling in one of the bags they were carrying.

'You mustn't keep buying all these things for me,' she said.

'Why not? I have the money and you like them, don't you?'

'Well, yes, but that's not the point,' she said feebly. 'It's just so extravagant.'

'I enjoy buying you things.'

'I know, it's very sweet of you, but you must stop doing it. Look, why don't you buy yourself something. You need more clothes, for instance.'

A corner of Blake's mouth contracted. He grinned.

'I'll do it for you, Cathy.'

Blake looked at clothes with indifference. She helped him choose two plain sky-blue shirts and a pair of shorts. When they were buying sandals for Blake she saw an exquisite pair that would have been ideal for her as evening wear. She was about to say how lovely they were but, looking up, she saw Blake pulling out his wallet and stayed silent.

'Blake, I could do with something to eat, we've had nothing since breakfast,' said Cathy.

'Let's follow the savoury smells,' said Blake.

They bought some strips of roast lamb stuffed into small crusty rolls with a spicy sauce and washed them down with chilled fruit juice. Up ahead, two burly Arabs carrying rifles stood either side of the alleyway. Set up high was a sign in several different languages. It was only when they were underneath that Cathy read in English: 'Gold and precious gem market'. A *Diner's Club* logo was hanging below it. Oh no, she thought. Once inside, the stalls positively sparkled in the afternoon sunshine. There were necklaces, brooches, bracelets and more rings than Cathy had ever seen. Here they were free of the crowds. There were just a few tourists standing quietly examining the items on display.

'Look,' gasped Cathy. 'It looks just like the treasure in Aladdin's cave.'

'Perhaps that's where they get their stock,' said Blake, smiling. 'Do you see anything you like?'

'I don't know,' she said, feeling overwhelmed. She wandered a bit. Her eye was drawn to a gold filigree necklace studded with closely spaced brilliant jewels inside a glass cabinet. She looked questioningly at the vendor, who nodded, beaming.

'Gold, with diamonds,' he said.

He unlocked the cabinet and placed the necklace into her hands. Cathy held it in the light and the gems sparkled brightly, almost blinding her.

'Do you think they're real diamonds?' she whispered to Blake.

'Look like it,' he said. 'Do you want it?'

Want it? thought Cathy. It's the most exquisite piece of jewellery I've ever seen, let alone touched. But if I say anything he'll buy it for me and that would be too much. Taking a deep breath, she handed the necklace back to the vendor.

'I don't think it is real. Although it is quite pretty,' she whispered to Blake.

Blake studied her for a long moment. 'Perhaps they aren't real,' he said eventually.

'Shall we go back to the hotel now?' said Cathy.

They turned around to leave. Two men wearing what looked like bulletproof vests were standing only two feet away and watched them as they left the alleyway.

* * *

The next day the taxi driver took them to some tombs on the outskirts of Cairo. The entrance was swarming with coachloads of Japanese and German tourists. They followed some Germans down a narrow staircase, single file only, into an underground tomb with brightly painted walls lit by small spotlights. It was noticeably cool compared with the heat outside despite the large numbers of people in the small space. They were trapped while the tour representative spoke, then hustled along through a narrow corridor into another tomb and up a single staircase into the open air. Blake held her hand through the tightly packed crowds and led them away from the group.

'I don't want you to feel claustrophobic,' he said.

As they stood in an open space between the tombs an Arab approached them. He was tall and dressed in a full-length white robe, his dark skin a stark contrast. He strode up and stood right in front of them, studying them with interest for some moments.

'Have you been here before?' he asked in clear English. His features were sculptured and his eyes were bright.

'No,' said Blake.

'Do you want to see some tombs the usual tourists don't see?' His expression was unreadable, as though there was nothing strange in the question.

Blake looked at her questioningly.

'What do you think?' he asked.

'Who are you?' enquired Cathy.

'I am a man of religion, a Sufi,' said the man and bowed. 'To fully appreciate the tombs you need to see them without crowds. I offer you this opportunity.'

'Well,' said Blake, 'are you up for it?'

Cathy shrugged. 'If you are.'

'Yes, we do,' said Blake.

They followed him away from the crowds past white limestone buildings and onto a concrete track between sand dunes which led out into the desert. The blazing sun on the sand radiated back at them. The journey continued and the track sloped downwards at a steep gradient. There was sand in every direction, only sand. It was softly undulating but seemingly petrified. There was not a breath of wind. She'd heard about the desert – the destination looks nearer than it is, but in this case they couldn't see it at all. She felt apprehensive, but didn't want to appear wimpish. For some reason she felt confident Blake knew what he was doing. After a further trek they reached a white brick building with a flat roof half buried in the sand. The sand had been removed from the entrance and was banked up on both sides.

'We have arrived,' the man said. They followed him inside down a steep stone stairway and out of the blazing heat of the sun. It was suddenly cooler. Cathy reached for her plastic bottle, gulped the water down and threw some over her face. Blake opened his bottle and offered to share it with the man, who refused, appearing completely unaffected by the heat. He led them from room to room, corridor to corridor through a complicated labyrinth of rooms that seemed endless. It was similar to the tomb they had just been in with the Germans but vaster. Little splinters of brilliant light broke through the ceiling in a number of different places so they were never in complete darkness. The walls reflected back the light with a strange luminosity. The half-light revealed the faded colours of Egyptian paintings on plasterwork. Empty tombs lay on either side at floor level. Cathy was aware of an eerie silence about the place. Only the sound of their footsteps, their breathing, pervaded it; the air was completely still. They stopped in one of the rooms, all three looking at each other, in silence. The man seemed fascinated with Blake and couldn't stop staring at him.

'Would you like to be left alone, to meditate?' the man asked.

Cathy glanced at Blake, waiting for his response.

'What do you think?' Blake asked and looked at her as if trying to read her expression.

'I think I've had enough, I'd rather get out. But you stay if you want,' she said.

'I will take you back to the entrance,' said the man.

'Is that OK?' asked Blake.

'Yes, of course.'

'You are sure about this?'

'Definitely,' she said confidently, 'but Blake, how will you find your way out?'

'I'll be alright,' he said.

She wasn't satisfied with his answer, but sensed that arguing with him would be futile. She followed the strange tall man through the labyrinth and back to the entrance. They stood in the shade and Cathy opened her water bottle once again.

'Your husband, he is a priest?' the man asked.

'Er... no,' said Cathy, taken by surprise. 'He's just ordinary.'

He looked at her searchingly. 'I don't think so... I have met men like him before, exceptional men.'

'Really there's nothing,' said Cathy, hardly knowing why she said it.

'Then you don't know your husband very well,' said the man.

He regarded her with a complicated mixture of curiosity and disdain. She noticed him looking down at her hand, searching for the wedding ring that wasn't there. There was an awkward silence between them. She splashed water on her face again, trying to relax and break the strained atmosphere as the enigmatic man studied her. She looked at her watch. Five, ten, fifteen minutes passed. She listened acutely for the sound of Blake's footsteps. When he emerged, the man's expression slowly metamorphosed into a smile and the two men shook hands warmly, as though they were old friends. Cathy watched them, intrigued. Blake offered him money, but he refused.

'That was an odd experience,' she said to Blake in the taxi.

'Was it OK for you? You seemed a bit anxious when I came out of the tomb.' He looked at her with concern.

'I'm fine… it was a bit hot and claustrophobic; as you know, I prefer wide open spaces. How was it for you?'

'Fascinating. He was right. It's much better exploring without crowds.'

'He was very interested in you, even though you hardly spoke to him.'

'Was he? He was interesting himself.'

'You're fearless, aren't you, Blake?' she said.

'No… what makes you think that?'

'Nothing fazes you.'

'Not true, fear is part of the human condition.'

'But you have less than most.'

'Less than some.' Blake was staring out of the window. 'Look, there are some wild camels over there in the distance.'

'We've got one more day in Cairo, haven't we?'

'Yes.'

'And then are we going home?'

'No. You wanted to visit an exotic island, didn't you?'

'Yes, I do. So…'

'When I was arranging this trip I did some research. I've booked for us to fly into Paris on Tuesday, take an overnight TWA plane to Miami, then a short flight to Abaco in the Bahamas and a boat to Little Goat Cay.'

'Little Goat Cay?

'Little Goat Cay, a small island; there's a new resort with huts over the water where you can take a ladder from the balcony straight into the ocean. I thought it looked interesting and it's the best I can do. The connections all work well. It's a long trip but…'

'I don't care how long it is. How wonderful, it sounds amazing. Being suspended is the best thing that's ever happened to me!'

She hugged him.

CHAPTER 16

Little Goat Cay

The sun was high in a clear blue sky as the boat approached the tiny Caribbean island of Little Goat Cay. There was a sign painted in bright colours *Welcome to Little Goat Cay* on the quay and an old man was waiting. A gangplank was shot out on to the jetty. The man reached down and lifted their cases, which were now full to bursting, off the boat. His hands were wrinkled and calloused.

'Mr Carter,' he said. His grin was engaging despite the row of broken teeth with metal fillings.

'I am Kenton, I will be looking after you. Come.'

He led them down a narrow path between tall, supple palm trees and simple wooden structures. The gravel crunched underfoot and a green lizard ran across the path. Cathy spotted several tiny yellow birds darting from tree to tree and chirping. It was humid and hotter than Cairo, but a gentle breeze made the temperature pleasant. They arrived at a beach with golden sand. Before them lay a single jetty pointing out to sea that branched into several smaller ones. Each separate jetty led to a platform on which sat a single beach hut on stilts set above shallow, still water.

'Most are empty,' he said. 'There are only two other tourists here, Americans, Alan and Joan. They have been looking forward to you coming. I have a hut for you at the end, but first I will show you where you eat and drink.'

They followed him to the end of the jetty. Several simple tables and chairs with colourful sun umbrellas were set out on a platform looking out to sea.

'That boat is mine,' he said and pointed downwards; the metal fillings in his teeth sparkled as he turned towards the sunlight.

They gazed over a railing. A small motorboat was tied up below. It looked like a converted fishing boat, too big and the wrong shape for a conventional motorboat and showing its age; the modern white plastic seating appeared incongruous. An old motor hung precariously from the back; the rotary blades lapped in the water.

'You can borrow it,' said Kenton.

'Well, hello,' said a man with an American drawl, his voice booming. They turned around. 'Good to see we're not alone at last. Alan and Joan from New York.' He grinned.

Both were corpulent. They wore his'n'hers designer sunglasses and his'n'hers flip-flops and his'n'hers brightly patterned shorts and top. Cathy shook his hand. It was enormous, hot, sweaty and firm.

'I'm Blake and this is Cathy.'

Cathy felt Joan's eyes scanning them with curiosity.

'Kenton has given you the hut with the best view over the ocean,' said Alan. He wiped his brow with a handkerchief.

'Well, I expect we'll see you around,' said Blake, 'once we've settled in.'

Alan laughed. 'You'll tell us when you've had enough of us I expect.'

'I'm sure there are nooks and crannies where we can hide away,' said Blake.

Kenton led them to their beach hut.

'They're bored,' said Cathy.

'Do you want company?'

'Only yours.'

'Come and join us,' said Alan.

Cathy and Blake drew up chairs at the table.

'Well, you've been here a couple of days now, what do you think?' asked Joan.

'What can I say, if this isn't paradise I don't know what is,' said Cathy.

'Ah, but you're young and you're together,' said Joan.

They heard the motor from Kenton's boat hiss and splutter and die again and again. Billowing smoke wafted upwards and was carried away on the breeze. A smell of petrol got down her nose and throat and made her cough.

'Kenton's got problems with the motor,' said Alan. 'Shame, we were hoping to take the boat out this afternoon.'

'I'm not getting on a dicky boat with you,' said Joan and frowned.

Kenton called. 'I have a trouble.'

They all got up and leant over the railing.

'I wasn't sure about that boat the first time I saw it,' said Joan, 'but Alan's decided he wants to go out on it. I wouldn't mind so much if it worked, but look at it. It looks as clapped out as its owner.'

Blake and Alan climbed down and the three men clustered around the boat.

'Well-meaning but not filling you with confidence,' said Cathy.

'Exactly. You know what men are. Alan always thinks he's more able to deal with mechanical things than he really is. He borrowed an enormous RV once, you call them camper vans, misjudged its size and drove it into a ditch. We both nearly came a cropper. Now he wants to take me out to sea in this. I'm not sure about it, not sure at all.' Her voice was tense with agitation.

They watched as Blake removed the nuts, bolts and parts from the motor and placed them in groups in the base of the boat.

'Look, Kenton and Alan haven't got a clue,' said Joan scathingly, 'it's your Blake who's doing it.'

'We'd hope Kenton knows something about his own motor,' said Cathy.

'But not as much as your Blake, who is tackling this, well… so systematically. I hope you don't think I'm intrusive,' she said, lowering her voice to a whisper, 'but are you on your honeymoon?'

'No… we're not.'

'Don't take this the wrong way, but at first I didn't think you went together.'

'Why is that?'

'I would have put him with a more glamorous woman.'

'That's just not who I am.'

'But I see I was wrong. You look very natural together, have you known him a long time?'

'I've known him for a number of months.'

'Is he an engineer? He seems to know what he's doing with that motor.'

'No, he's a scientist.'

'He must be one of those clever people who can turn their hand to anything.'

'Yes, I suppose so.'

'Where did you meet him?'

'He's my manager at work, but we've only just got together, this journey was a last-minute thing.'

'Alan was my manager at work and we've been together now for twenty years. I was in agonies trying to get him to notice me. I had to use all kind of ways and means to get him, you know, but us women, we do, don't we, when we really want a man.'

'I'm sure I would never want to manipulate him into caring for me.'

'My dear, I can see he's completely devoted to you. But what a man! Alan and I have been talking about it. He hasn't got Hollywood good looks exactly, but there's something about him. I'm no young woman, but when he speaks I could almost swoon. You're a very lucky girl.'

'Yes, he is an exceptional man,' said Cathy thoughtfully.

'Look, you're not unattractive yourself. You have a cute face and neat figure. Take my advice. If I were you, I would secure him as quickly as possible, before some other woman does.'

'I don't know what you mean by "secure him".'

'Make sure he makes a commitment to you, marries you! All this living together that goes on these days, it makes a woman very insecure. Men hate to commit.'

'I haven't even thought of that. I'm just enjoying being with him now. And I'm sure he would be ready to commit if he wanted to, he's that sort of man. I certainly wouldn't, and couldn't, trap him.'

'Then he's a lucky man,' said Joan, and gave Cathy a long, thoughtful look. 'I remember,' she said suddenly, 'there was something I wanted to ask you; what's that thing he does early in the morning 4.00 to 5.00 o'clock?'

'What thing?'

'Alan's a restless sleeper, you know... he wanders around in the night. Blake sits at the end of the jetty, completely still, cross-legged, just looking out to sea. He's there for quite a long time.'

'Are you sure he's looking out to sea?'

'Well, what else could he be doing?'

'I don't know.'

'You should ask him.'

The motor appeared to jump into life. Kenton gestured to them with thumbs up that there had been success.

'The boat's OK now,' called Alan to Joan. 'Blake has shown me how to fix it if it goes wrong again. Come along, let's go.'

'Over my dead body!' called Joan and stood rigid. 'I know you and your technical skills, we'll be lost out in the open ocean! If it was a hundred percent I might risk it... but doubtful... no, not on your life!'

Alan shrugged.

'I'd be confident with Blake, but not with Alan,' said Joan to Cathy.

'Would you like us to go with you?' asked Cathy.

'Would you?' asked Joan.

'Yes, I'm sure it's OK. I think Blake wants to go out on the boat anyway.' Cathy leaned over the railing and called to him. 'Blake, shall we go as well?'

'Yes, OK.'

'Where are we going?' asked Cathy.

'To that teensy little island on the horizon,' said Joan. 'Kenton says it's deserted, only insects and a few birds live there.'

The boat creaked and groaned as Joan and Alan climbed in; it seemed uncomfortably loaded and water splashed inside. They needed to find room for an enormous empty basket that Joan was carrying for 'souvenirs'.

'So, you'll go with Blake but not with me,' said Alan.

'That's right,' said Joan.

'She hasn't trusted me ever since I drove the RV into a ditch,' said Alan. He grimaced.

The boat chugged its way out into the open water and over to the island. They docked at the tiny jetty. Blake tied up the boat and Joan and Alan settled on the sand.

'Let's explore, shall we,' said Cathy. She took Blake's hand and led him into the island interior. Within a few minutes they'd reached the beach on the other side. Blake bent over, examining objects on the ground.

'What are you looking at?' she asked.

'Rock formations. See this one,' he pointed to it, 'basalt, from the Cambrian period I expect.'

'Fascinating,' said Cathy, 'but the beach is enticing me.'

Cathy ran to the shore and danced and sang with exuberance. She buried her toes in the sand and kicked it in the air. Finding a sheltered spot, she removed her bikini and squatted and urinated into the sand like an animal. Feeling totally uninhibited and carefree, she ran into the sea. The water was shallow and only reached her thighs. It was cool, clear and transparent. A small yellow and blue striped fish with an enormous tail like a fan darted around beneath her. She watched it until it swam out of view, walked further out to sea, then submerged herself. The warm water lapped against her and she felt sensuous.

'Blake... here... Blake!' she called and held her arms wide open and stood up.

He walked quickly across the sand towards her, waded into the water and lifted her up into his arms. She wrapped her arms and legs around him and held him tight.

'I want you,' she whispered in his ear.

'Good, that's both of us then,' he said and carried her towards the beach.

She could feel his heart racing and his breath against her cheek.

'I can tell,' she said.

He leant her up against a coconut tree and kissed her full on the mouth. His lips and tongue were soft, warm and demanding. He was drinking her in, pressing her against him. She could smell the subtle sweat of his body, feel the strength of him... she wanted him so much. As his hands supported her buttocks he plunged deep inside her and pumped. All inhibition gone, it was wild and reckless and thrilling. She trembled with the rush of passion, and from somewhere in her belly she noticed a sensation rising up to her throat and screamed out loud. She didn't know she'd made the sound until she'd heard it herself. It was spontaneous and completely unconscious. She heard him groan and pant. She giggled, and then they laughed together.

'This definitely has the edge over those rocks,' he said.

They were still laughing an hour later when they arrived back at the boat. Joan and Alan had had enough and were ready to return to the 'luxury' of Little Goat Cay. They climbed back into the boat and it creaked its way out into the open sea. Joan had discovered some interesting-looking shells, which she collected in her basket, and told them about a family of tiny bright red birds with white beaks she had watched dancing in the trees. She and Alan had also heard a strange noise.

'It sounded a bit like a monkey, but Kenton said there aren't any monkeys on the island,' said Joan.

'Can you describe it?' asked Blake.

'Like a loud mating call,' said Joan.

'Perhaps it was,' said Blake, with a hint of a smile.

'But how can it be if there aren't any monkeys here?' asked Joan.

'Maybe no indigenous ones,' said Blake.

'How would monkeys get here if they aren't native?' asked Joan, with a look of bafflement.

'By some artificial means,' said Blake.

Cathy giggled, covered her face with her hands and blushed. Alan laughed and winked saucily at her.

'It's not surprising there should be mating calls in a place like this,' said Alan, and all three roared with laughter.

'Now, I don't get this,' said Joan, crossly. 'I'm hot and I can't cope with all this jollity. Can you speed up the motor, Blake, I need a rest,' and she began to fan herself down with her hand.

Blake obliged, but the buoyant mood wouldn't be so easily extinguished. By the time they arrived back Joan had softened and was only a little disgruntled. Blake tied up the boat and Cathy waited for him on the jetty. Kenton came up and stood next to her. He flashed his dazzling smile.

'Did you enjoy your day on the island?' he asked.

'Yes, it was… exhilarating,' said Cathy.

'Nasty wound Mr Blake has,' he whispered. He slapped his left thigh and pointed in Blake's direction. 'Shark bite?'

'Er…yes, that's right,' said Cathy, at a loss what else to say. She was so used to seeing his disfigurement she hardly noticed it anymore. Kenton seemed satisfied with the answer and shook his head.

'Very bad,' he said.

Cathy wondered what had caused it. She decided to ask Blake, when the time was right.

* * *

'Well, this beats *Capascas* for freshness,' said Alan as he gorged himself on an enormous lobster that was spilling over both sides of the plate. Cathy felt the lobster's eyes were looking at her. Alan's face was red and shiny with sweat; he wiped his brow with his handkerchief.

'*Capascas*?' said Cathy.

'Yes, our local downtown restaurant, New York,' said Joan. 'I am feeling a bit homesick.'

Joan wriggled in her wicker chair, trying to get comfortable, and fanned herself down with her hand.

'She's missing the air conditioning,' said Alan as he crammed some more food into his mouth.

Cathy picked at her salad. Watching Alan was putting her off her food somehow. Blake and Joan had already finished. Blake sat back, relaxed in his chair, his hands behind his head.

'And the super-soft bed,' said Joan.

'There's nothing I miss, I think I could stay here forever,' said Cathy, 'and even live like those villagers. Not romantic or luxurious, I know. But uncomplicated, just working the land and being part of a community.'

'That would be hard physical graft,' said Blake. His expression was serious and thoughtful.

'It wouldn't do for me,' said Joan. 'This is nice for a short break, but I would miss the shops, restaurants, theatres and the services. Service is very quick and efficient in New York.'

'No, I could live without all that,' said Cathy.

'What, without the modern comforts that money can buy?'

'Yes, with a wage to cover just the necessities of life and a bit more.'

'My dear, you don't have to have glamour or look like a Broadway superstar, but you can never have too much money,' said Joan. She leaned towards Cathy and looked her straight in the eye.

'I don't agree,' replied Cathy, 'I think there's something obscene about excessive affluence… especially when half the world's starving.'

'We all have to look after ourselves, my dear, you can't worry about the rest of the world,' said Joan, frowning.

'I'm not worried about the rest of the world,' said Cathy, 'I just have humanitarian concerns. Surely consumption in the end just consumes itself. How much does one person need just to be happy?'

Alan burped and put his hand to his mouth. 'Sorry,' he said. They all looked at him for a moment.

'People are often misguided and think they can find happiness in material things alone,' said Blake.

'Well, I can see you'd both be very happy with very little,' said Alan, and he wiped his brow. 'My dear wife here has bled me dry my entire life, but New York is the place for us. You don't get very far in New York without money.'

'No, I daresay not,' said Cathy.

None of them had any inclination to continue with the conversation and it came to a natural but amicable close. Alan finished his lobster and wiped his mouth.

'I'm off to have a lie down,' said Alan, 'to let my dinner settle.'

Joan and Alan heaved themselves out of their chairs and ambled back to their beach hut.

Cathy relaxed back in her chair, relieved to be alone with Blake. The sun was setting; the sky was full of shades of luminous reds, pinks and yellows. They watched in silence as the sun dipped and the rich colours deepened, from pinks, to damask, to purple, in a slow rapture of nature. The breeze dropped. Cathy picked and chewed the odd grape from the bunch in a bamboo bowl on the table. She looked over at Blake and squeezed his hand.

'Do you know any other stories, apart from the one about the jade master? You said you might,' she asked.

'Probably... if I think hard enough... What sort of story?'

'A story about somewhere exotic, like this,' she said without thinking, and picked up a grape.

He tossed his head back and looked up at the sky for a few minutes, and then he sat forward.

'OK, this is a Zen story. A man was running in the savannah, being chased by a hungry lion. Suddenly he realised he had reached the cliff edge. He looked down and noticed a second hungry lion prowling around below. Then he noticed a branch jutting out of the cliff. Realising he was trapped, he jumped and grabbed hold of the branch, just before the lion that was chasing him reached the cliff edge. He noticed some grapes growing on a vine twisted around the branch. He reached for one of the grapes and put it in his mouth, tasting it. "Yum", he thought "it's delicious".'

Cathy grabbed another grape out of the bowl and stuffed it as quickly as possible into her mouth and chewed.

'Hmm, it's delicious,' she said exuberantly.

'Slow down,' said Blake. 'Feel it in your mouth, concentrate. What does it taste like? Sweet, sour or bitter? What is the texture like? Soft, stringy, chewy, hard? How much liquid is there in it? Feel it disintegrate. Feel it dissolve. Feel it on your teeth, your tongue, in the back of your throat. Experience every sensation as if eating the grape were the most important thing in your life!'

'Oh yes, it is!' she said, still chewing.

'You're rock-climbing. You've got to be perfectly aware of the present moment all the time, because your life depends on it, and then you feel really alive.'

She swallowed deep and gulped and looked at him and they both burst out laughing. She laughed so much that she nearly choked on the remnants of the grape and doubled over, tears flowed down her face.

'That's the most extraordinary taste sensation I've ever had,' she said. 'A grape will never taste the same again.'

After a long time the laughter eased. Cathy looked at him thoughtfully. 'You know, you're right about the rock-climbing. Every moment counts, every hand movement, every footfall. When I climb I am in the present; I am fully alive.' She regarded at him steadily for a few moments. 'You've got a lot of insight, Blake, about all sorts of things.' Her voice became quiet and trailed off.

They looked at each other lovingly. He put his hand in his pocket.

'My timing could be improved, I hope you won't find this excessive, but I've got something for you,' he said. He withdrew a small rectangular object wrapped in red tissue paper from his pocket and gave it to her.

She took the gift and unwrapped the paper. Inside was a delicate box covered in colourfully patterned silk, with gold catches. She unfastened them, opened the box and looked inside. The light from the setting sun caught it and the diamonds glistened, gold and brilliant white, blues and reds. She lifted out a filigree necklace. She recognised it from the Cairo gold market. She spread it out in her left hand and stared at it.

'Oh my God, are these real diamonds?'

'What do you think?' He waited patiently.

'You bought it at the gold market?'

'Yes, it's the one you liked, isn't it? I went back for it when you were sleeping.'

She touched it, almost disbelievingly.

'It was so expensive, you shouldn't have.' Her voice was quiet and thoughtful.

'Look, it's only money. I've got it at the moment, don't think about the cost,' he said.

She believed him. He really didn't care about money. He put it around her neck.

'It looks lovely on you, but with or without it, I love you just as you are.'

'Thank you,' she said.

She held his hand in silence. She felt loved, more loved than she had ever been.

* * *

'You know, Joan said when she first met us she would have put you with a more glamorous woman than me,' said Cathy.

'I'm not interested in glamour,' said Blake. 'I've got a real woman right here. I want a woman who will squat down and piss into the sand.'

'You saw that!' she said and put her hand to her mouth. He grinned.

'And a woman who will swim naked in the sea and make love in the open air. You are all I need,' he said.

She felt his breath on her cheek as he lay next to her on the bed. He undid the belt of her silk dressing gown and it fell loose away from her like water. He caressed her belly and her breasts and her legs. His touch was extremely light, and she felt all her nerves on end. She pulled him closer and kissed his cheek.

'You're the best lover I've ever had,' she said, 'although I haven't had many... really.' She looked at him anxiously.

'I believe you,' he said.

She remembered Peter, her shyness and his fumbling awkwardness. And Jack, who had roused her passions and left her feeling used and empty and cold.

'I don't need to hide or pretend with you. I can't, you'd know. I feel vulnerable, but I trust you completely,' she said.

'I love you,' he said.

'And I love you.'

It was a moment of sublime tenderness. He slowly explored her body, with his hands, his fingertips, his mouth, his tongue, sometimes touching her almost imperceptibly, sometimes more firmly. He wasn't following any set formula; she just sensed he was learning about her unique sexuality, aware of all her responses, totally present. She was being slowly filled with pleasure to saturation point as his hands, his mouth moved over her. She felt more acutely aware of her body than she ever had, almost as if the flow of blood was palpable and every cell in her body had been ignited. He was close but not close enough. Her passion peaked and she drew him inside her. As she melted into him, she felt their energy merge in a dynamic ecstatic union. For the first time her body exploded in timeless ecstasy, she heard herself gasp. She knew this was it; there was absolutely no doubt about it. It was a total mind-body experience involving all her senses in pleasure she hadn't dreamed possible. It was awesome and indescribable. She no longer knew who she was, only that he was with her and that the present moment and the sensation were real. Her body felt hot with energy of its own; she could almost feel it radiate out of her. She could hear the breath from her own long, deep exhalations and feel the rapid pounding of his heart. They lay there for some moments and quietened. She didn't want him to leave. She tried to hold on to him with her pelvic floor muscles but he slowly slipped out. As he held her in his arms, inexplicably her body quivered and jolted on the bed over and over again. It felt like warm, pleasant shock waves were pulsing through her. For the first time a warm afterglow saturated her. And it was better than being in uninhibited inebriation, and it was better than looking out at the rainbow colours of the sea at sunset, and it was better than her one misguided experience of taking cocaine. It was the best experience she'd ever had. After some time she looked into the infinite depths of his eyes. He held her gaze with consummate rapture.

'I didn't know making love could be this good,' she said.

'Neither did I.'

'Really!... You've blown me away,' she said, 'I've got no words.'

'You don't need to have words,' he said.

They didn't speak any more. She reproached herself for being so crass as to say anything at all, wrapped herself in his arms and dozed off to sleep, into a dreamy, heady heaven. When she woke the sun was setting but he wasn't there. She put on her dressing gown and went to look for him. She pushed back the fragile voile curtains and stepped onto the balcony. He was standing naked with his hands on the balustrade looking out to sea. For a long time she watched him in silence, appreciating his muscular figure, the curves of his body, the slight bronze of his skin. Her eyes were drawn to the deep scar on his left thigh. It didn't look ugly to her; she loved all of him, blemishes and all. She walked up to him and put her hand on his shoulder; he turned, looked into her eyes and smiled. She ran her hand down his back, over his buttocks and on to the deep scar. With a feather touch she ran her fingers over it, as if it were precious and fragile. He didn't flinch.

'Does this hurt?' she asked.

'I get the occasional twinge, that's all.'

'Does it slow you down?'

'Not much, the other muscles have compensated.'

'How did you get it?'

He was silent for a moment, regarding her reflectively. He turned and looked out to sea.

'I was shot,' he said at last.

She took in a deep breath. She felt uncertain, not ready for this answer.

'Where were you?' she whispered.

He was again silent for a while. Never before had she seen him so sombre or thoughtful.

'In the jungle, in Vietnam.'

He seemed locked in a deep space. She wanted to know more, but it felt like an intrusion. He looked out to sea, as if transfixed.

'How… why?' she asked, with measured sensitivity.

It seemed an age before he spoke again.

'I haven't told anybody before. It was a long time ago. Do you really want to know?'

'Yes.'

Another silence followed. He turned and looked into her eyes.

'Do you want to hear it as it really happened, the truth… you might find it hard to take?'

'I want to hear the truth. I love you, I can take it, whatever it is.'

Besides, she wasn't sure he would be able to tell it any other way.

And then Blake remembered. His story unfolded. And Cathy listened…

CHAPTER 17

Saigon, Vietnam
April 1968

As evening fell, Blake arrived at a quiet river on the Mekong delta; he saw an old man clearing out the fishing gear from a boat and approached him.

'I want to hire your boat,' Blake told him.

'What do you want it for?' The old man looked quizzically at Blake.

'Pleasure cruise,' said Blake, deadpan, and held out a bundle of bank notes.

The old man took the money.

'How long?' he asked.

'All night.'

'Not enough,' said the fisherman.

Blake handed him some more money.

'Alright,' said the man. 'But if you travel far you need more fuel.'

With a sigh Blake gave him some more bank notes and the man handed him a spare can of diesel and a toolbox. It was dark when Blake set off, travelling by the light of the moon.

As he pushed off, the boat sent ripples through the surface of the river and the reflection of the silver moon wobbled and danced. Up ahead the water was flat like a mirror, shimmering dim and surreal. The trees' silhouettes were jet black against the dark grey sky, stars appeared and flattened into blobs. The nocturnal jungle noises began erupting. After about two miles he cut the motor, pulled into a secluded recess along the riverbank, changed into his camouflage clothes and smeared brown and green war paint on his face. The water made sucking noises at the boat as he moved about. He swigged back some thick black coffee from his Thermos and pulled on the Evinrude motor; it jumped into life with a smell of diesel. He set off upriver. Just like the jungle, each twist and turn in the river looked the same as the last. Blake peered closely at his map by torchlight. Suddenly the boat was enveloped in mist; he cut the motor just in time to avoid crashing into the bank. Just as quickly the mist wafted upwards and he was able to see again by the light of the moon. He took the boat upriver for thirty-five miles and stopped at daybreak. The bank was thickly overgrown, hidden under bush ferns and yards of lianas. Blake scrambled off the boat and waded ashore. It was a bright, cool dawn; as the sun rose it reflected dazzling light off the flat river. He beached the boat and hid it in the undergrowth, leaving markers so that he could find it again. Checking his compass, he pushed off into the jungle towards the camp. Soon he was on high ground and the earth was relatively dry. The vegetation was less dense than in Borneo, but with the same heat, humidity and familiar sounds. This was primary jungle, with tall and strangely orderly trees. Each had found room to grow separately. The towering trees with tiny leaves rose to great heights like huge pillars, there were ferns and vines in between. Only the slightest patches of blue sky penetrated the curved roof and branches.

After three hours he approached a ridge and looking over the top he saw the camp laid out below. It was circular, with an outer rim of fortified bunkers. Blake could see only three positions set up for automatic weapons fire but guessed there would be several more. Further into the circle, there were more bunkers, interspersed with foxholes and sleeping platforms. At the centre were two wooden buildings. One was obviously the kitchen and Blake decided the other was probably living quarters. While he watched, the camp started to come to life. He crawled as silently as he could over the ridge and down towards the camp, making his way to a clump of bushes. Once there he lay completely still, waiting and watching for any signs that he had been spotted. After about ten minutes, satisfied he was undetected, he stealthily unpacked his rifle and binoculars and settled down to wait in the densest, shadiest part of the clump. Mosquitoes materialised seemingly from nowhere, whirring and whining around his head, and then sped off like aircraft in formation. As the heat of the day rose, his clothing became wet through with perspiration and began to cling to his skin.

After two hours had passed there was greater activity in the camp. He continually swept the area with his binoculars, trying to identify the officers. A further hour later a group of four men emerged from one of the larger bunkers and made their way to the living quarters. Even at this distance Blake could tell that two of the men were used to command. Unhurriedly he put down the binoculars and used the telescopic sight on his rifle to examine their faces. The first meant nothing to him, but when the second came into view there was no doubt that it was Lee Ho Quock. Blake's pulse quickened, then he felt the familiar mood of steely coldness. He waited, finger on the trigger as the first officer opened the door of the hut and motioned for Lee Ho Quock to precede him inside. As Lee Ho Quock approached the doorway Blake pulled the trigger, hitting the target. Sprayed by blood and brains, the remaining officer stood frozen in shock, then took an unsteady step backwards as the Colonel sank to the ground in front of him. Blake lowered his rifle, swiftly but calmly dismantled it, stowed it back in his rucksack and glanced back at the camp. Men were purposefully taking up defensive positions. They would know now there was a sniper covering the camp, but they would not know exactly where or how many enemy were present. At any moment soldiers might emerge from one of the tunnels that undoubtedly had exits far away from the camp. He had no choice. Blake broke cover and scrambled back over the ridge, gunfire stirring currents of air around him as he went. Adrenalin raced through his body. Soon he could hear the sounds of shouted orders as a group of men started to leave the camp. Blake half-slipped and half-fell down the ridge and made off into the jungle. He skittered away, snaked between the trees and disappeared into the forest, moving swiftly and quietly through the vegetation. He paused every now and then for breath and to listen for the sounds of pursuit. Far off in the distance he could hear the occasional shout as his pursuers searched for him. Eventually he got back to the boat's hiding place, noiselessly pulled it out and set it on the water. It was mid-afternoon and the sun was approaching the western horizon. He changed back into his shirt and trousers, threw the camouflage clothing into the river and washed off the war paint. He got in the boat and paddled for a mile or two, then started the engine and travelled downriver for a couple of hours.

As Blake slowly relaxed and exhaustion set in, his mood became speculative. By daylight the awesome tropical beauty of the river and thriving banks of vegetation were revealed in their full splendour. Here he felt it possible to disconnect from the devastating impact of the senseless war where man fought against man and life was cheap. No evidence of war here, here nature ruled, but respite was brief. The engine started to make spitting noises, a thin sliver of smoke rose and he could smell diesel. The boat began to vibrate; the engine gave a loud cough then was suddenly silent. Blake took the paddle, manoeuvred the boat into the lee of a small island and opened the metal toolbox. As the sun descended behind the horizon of the jungle giants, he set about trying to coax the engine back into life. Summoning up all his energy, he took the engine apart, examined it, cleaned and oiled it and then put it back together. His first couple of efforts failed then, in the gathering gloom, the engine spluttered back to life. After three more coughs it began to purr. Blake continued his journey downriver by moonlight, stopping every now and then and coaxing the engine along. About a half-mile short of the place where he'd hired the boat, Blake hoisted his rucksack on to his knee and opened it with one hand, keeping the other on the tiller, took out his wallet and Browning and put them in his pockets. He reached in to get his torch. At that moment the boat struck a half-submerged log and the shock of the collision tumbled the rucksack into the river, where it quickly sank out of sight. Blake cursed his luck but was thankful the boat had not capsized. By the time he returned the boat, dawn was breaking. After paying the irate fisherman extra as compensation for the delay, he set off for Saigon. Desperately hungry, he bought himself *pho* - a traditional Vietnamese breakfast from a street stall - stopped for a few minutes and ate it. His schedule was out. He'd hoped to be at his desk by early morning. Things hadn't gone according to plan.

A few streets away from his flat, Blake checked the designated lamp post as usual. Three pieces of red tape had been stuck to it – the emergency signal from Khien. Without breaking stride, he turned and crossed the road and made his way to the meeting-point, where Khien was waiting. Khien's face looked ashen and grave.

'I have been waiting up all night for you,' Khien said breathlessly.

'What's happened?'

'Somebody shot Hoa last night,' said Khien, and his eyes filled with tears.

'Shit!' exclaimed Blake. 'Where was she?'

'In your flat.'

'How is she?'

'She's alive, but injured... badly... she dragged herself into the street and somebody called for an ambulance.' His voice cracked, and his expression was full of anguish. 'They've taken her to Cho Ray Hospital.'

'I must go to her,' said Blake.

'No, no... I don't advise it, you must be a target yourself... you need to get away from here. They'll be watching for you. That's what I wanted to tell you,' said Khien urgently.

'It's vital I see her, I've got to know who shot her.'

'John, it's madness. You must get away.'

'No, I am going to her,' said Blake. 'You can stay out of it or come with me, just as you like. But I warn you, if you come it might be dangerous.'

'I'll come.' Khien said simply. 'Two of us together will stand more chance of success.'

They hired a rickshaw. Blake offered the driver ten times the normal fare if he could get them there swiftly. He had never travelled so fast in a rickshaw before, the man raced as though a horde of devils were pursuing them, tilting over dangerously at corners and barely slowing down at intersections. The hair-raising ride through town nearly had them killed. The town was in a state of chaos and commotion. Ambulances and police were swarming everywhere. They heard someone shouting about another car bomb explosion. They arrived within ten minutes and got out at Cho Ray Hospital; Khien had trouble walking on shaking legs.

CHAPTER 18

Crowds of people surrounded the entrance to the hospital, frantically jostling and shoving to get inside. Blake and Khien pushed their way through. At reception people shouted and wailed, desperate to talk to someone with information. Blake stopped a nurse in her tracks.

'We're looking for a young woman, Hoa Miller. She was shot and brought here in an ambulance. Do you know where she is?'

The nurse looked quizzically at Blake.

'Yes, I remember her... she's been admitted. Wing 4, on the first floor.'

Blake and Khien darted up the stairs. Following the signs, they quickly found Wing 4. Swarms of people moved in all directions and a small group elbowed for position at the nurses' station. Along the corridor a grim-faced orderly wheeled a trolley. On top was a long metal box, large enough to hold a body. Several people walked alongside with their hands on the box. A woman clung to it, wailing. Behind, a man supported another woman by the waist; he dragged her along while she beat her chest, her face contorted in despair.

Wards and single rooms led off the corridor. Blake and Khien dashed here and there searching for Hoa. The place was in such turmoil and panic that nobody seemed to notice them. Blake overheard two elderly men in the corridor talking about bombs and the injured. They found Hoa in a single room at the far end of the corridor; the room was dimly lit with translucent blinds across the window. A young nurse, checking the drip attached to Hoa's arm, looked anxiously at the two men as they burst in. They didn't bother to introduce themselves. Through the open window they could hear the noisy commotion outside.

'How bad is she?' said Blake.

'You are relatives?' she said.

'Yes,' said Khien.

Khien kissed his daughter tenderly on the brow, stroked a lock of hair away from her face, and stood back. He was trying hard to appear calm, but Blake could see the trial of agony he was in by the deep furrows on his face and his quivering lips.

'It is difficult to tell. She has some internal injuries and we will have to monitor her condition.'

The nurse continued to adjust the medical equipment next to Hoa's bed, absorbed in her task. Blake sat down on the chair beside the bed and bent over Hoa, who looked pale and still, so different from the strong and resilient woman he knew.

'Who were they?' he said quietly, his mouth close to her face. She slowly opened her eyes, struggled to focus, and managed a tentative smile. Her voice was so weak he hardly heard it.

'There were two or three... a man with red hair... man at the Embassy dinner, was there. It was very quick.'

'Anderson, was it Anderson?' asked Blake.

'Yes... it was him.' Hoa's eyes began to close.

'Rest now,' said Blake. He walked over to where Khien was standing by the window. Khien had pulled the blinds aside and was discreetly looking out.

'Anderson, I'll deal with him,' Blake whispered in Khien's ear.

'Later. Forget about Anderson,' said Khien. 'Look what's happening outside.' He pointed. 'The crowds have been pushed away. There are armed men, swarms of them; some have come inside, some are taking up position out here.'

'Who the hell are they?' said Blake.

'Looks like a hit squad,' said Khien, 'they're not in uniform.'

'Shit, shit,' said Blake under his breath, 'they're probably VC.'

Blake felt adrenalin course through his body. He made eye contact with Khien; there was an urgent, grim expression on the older man's face.

'They might be looking for you. We've got to get you out of here... But how?'

Blake looked out of the window again. He saw straight away there was no escape route that way.

'We'll have to smuggle you out,' Khien said decisively. He turned to the nurse; she had finished her work and looked panic-stricken. 'Those coffin-sized containers on trolleys, get me an empty one,' he ordered.

'No... please.' She started to sob, drew her hands to her face and backed up towards the door.

Khien pulled a handgun out of his pocket and pointed it at the nurse. She drew her breath in sharply and stood stock-still. She looked terrified.

'We'll get it together, I'll be behind you all the time. Just do as I say and I won't shoot,' said Khien. He grabbed the nurse's arm and marched her towards the door, gun in her back.

'Say whatever you need to get one,' he commanded.

They left the room, Khien closing the door firmly behind them. Blake sat next to Hoa, held her hand and half leant over her, his senses at fever pitch. He could tell that she was having trouble focusing; her eyes were glazing over. She used all her fading strength to squeeze his hand and whispered:

'John, is that you?'

'Yes.'

'I'm sorry... I'm a burden... You were right... I should have left. I was stubborn... selfish.'

'Save your strength. There's no need to talk.'

'I care about you, John, I don't know why, but I do.'

The door opened and the terrified nurse and Khien appeared with a container on a trolley. Khien closed the door.

'Where do they take the bodies?' said Khien.

'The mortuary in this hospital is full. There's a temporary mortuary elsewhere,' the nurse replied, her voice cracking.

'Where is the other mortuary?' asked Khien.

'In Pa Ghee village, north of the city.'

'How far is that?'

'About twelve miles,' said the nurse.

'How do the containers get there?' said Khien.

'On a truck from downstairs,' she replied.

'My friend here needs to get on that truck in this container,' said Khien.

'I will try,' the nurse said and broke into a sob.

Blake kissed Hoa gently on the forehead.

'I'm sorry... be strong... you can get through this,' he said.

'Save yourself, please go,' she whispered.

Blake squeezed her hand and looked at her one last time.

The container on the trolley was at a height of about three feet. Blake removed the lid and propped it up against the wall. He saw that the container was too small for him, but using a foothold on the bed he levered himself up to the right height and clambered inside. He noticed the sides of the upright metal panels were bloodstained. Dark hairs clung like glue to some unknown residue at the end on the horizontal base where he was about to place his head. It smelt strongly of disinfectant. This hiding place wasn't going to be pleasant. As he stretched himself out he realised he was right; it was too short and he needed to bend his legs to fit inside. His skin felt cold where the metal came in contact with his clothes. He shivered suddenly. Khien and the nurse got hold of the lid and levered it into position over the container, leaving Blake's face momentarily uncovered.

'Good luck, my dear friend, you are more than a friend, you are like a son to me, I will think of you, always.'

Khien's eyes watered; his voice was losing its clarity. He inhaled sharply and regained his composure.

'I'll be back when I can,' said Blake.

The next moment they slid the lid fully into position, its lip fitting snugly over the frame, and he was in darkness. He heard the door squeak open and felt the vibration and motion of being wheeled down a corridor, in a lift, along another corridor. He could hear frantic raised voices and the sound of heavy boots thudding along the linoleum floors, then a commanding male voice.

'Who has died? Let me see.'

'This one is not a pretty sight, she has bad injuries and her poor father here is very distressed. Please have some respect.'

Blake felt for the Browning in his pocket. There was a momentary silence.

'OK, go on.'

He was being wheeled further along a corridor, then abruptly came to a halt. Again he could hear voices, another male voice:

'We only have spaces for five. This one will have to wait.'

He recognised the nurse's voice:

'You would be advised to take this one. She is very badly mutilated and already smells unpleasant. A few more hours and the stench will be overwhelming.' There was a moment of silence.

'Alright, we'll take her.'

He could hear the clanging of metal on metal and the searing sound of metal sliding against a rough solid surface. Then he felt he was being lifted, turned left, right, diagonally, and finally horizontal again.

'This is very heavy for a girl,' he heard a man say.

'She was a big woman, very overweight,' the nurse replied.

There was an enormous bang, then silence. Nothing seemed to happen for hours. Blake gradually became aware of a putrid smell, which increased with the heat. He lifted the lid a fraction to create some airflow and stop himself from suffocating. Eventually he felt the vibration when the motor started up and was thrown from side to side as the truck bumped over uneven ground. Soon he felt sure they were making a steady speed on the open road. He was aware the container he was in was impacting against the one next to him and he could hear them grind together. He felt the metal vibrate at tremendous speed and it made his teeth chatter. He gritted them.

The truck slowly came to a halt and he could hear distant voices. He heard the sound of the lock on the back of the truck being undone and the doors being thrown open. The voices grew louder then faded away. Blake silently lifted the lid of the container and slid it away so he could peer out. It was dusk and the light was fading. In front he could see a large single-storey building that looked like a warehouse. He could hear the sounds of people weeping, mingling with the familiar drone of the jungle. He slid the lid off and climbed out. The jungle was only a few feet away. He jumped out of the truck and gulped the fresh air, ran into the dense undergrowth, bounded over the buttress root systems and dodged under the hanging vines. He moved as quickly as he could. They would realise what had happened soon. He needed to get as far away as possible.

'God, what a terrible experience,' said Cathy. She shuddered. As she looked at him her eyes were full of questions and mixed emotions. 'I couldn't have endured it.'

'I had to survive, I didn't have time to think.'

After a moment Cathy asked, 'What happened to Hoa?'

Blake sighed and looked into the distance for a moment. 'Do you want to hear more?'

'Yes, of course.'

CHAPTER 19

Blake walked fast and purposefully. He didn't know where he was going but he didn't look back. This was primary, not secondary jungle; he wouldn't need a machete here. Huge trees, spread metres apart, densely shaded the forest floor; he could easily walk between them. The ground was dry and clear, only one leaf thick, but the exertion in the heat made him pant. After ten minutes he stopped for breath and, with his hands on his knees, looked around. There were several layers of green jungle canopy far above him. At the lower levels abundant vine stems swept upwards, there were delicate tree ferns and bushes with spiky leaves several yards long. Dappled evening light filtered through the canopy on to the ground. As he walked on, deeper into the forest, the drone of the jungle got louder. There were animal tracks everywhere. He knelt down and examined them. He recognised the long, curvaceous impression of a snake's body, the swish of a lizard's tail, the prints of mice and a larger animal, perhaps a paca. With so much wildlife there were unlikely to be human hunters. This looked like virgin territory, which belonged to nature alone. Darkness was imminent. He would be safer off the jungle floor but had no time to prepare a shelter and there was nothing suitable to climb. He sat down on the bare earth with his back up against a tree and waited for darkness. He watched a solitary, enormous worker ant collect a leaf off the ground and carry it away. Further away there were several other ants at the same task. They all took their leaves in the same direction. Night invaded quickly and absolutely. It did not fall; it rose. It first cloaked the jungle floor, then the vines and ferns, and finally climbed the tree trunks to the canopy, far above.

It was so dark Blake couldn't see his hand in front of his face, only the small luminous specks on the jungle floor, maybe phosphorescent spores or nocturnal insects on the move. He hadn't slept for twenty-four hours. Sleep was essential, whatever the conditions. Without sleep he might hallucinate and, as he'd learnt in Borneo, in the jungle that could be fatal. He watched the specks, absorbed, until his eyes would stay open no longer. A shrill cry jolted him awake. He instinctively felt in his pocket for his Browning. He dozed for a while. A small creature ran across his legs, tickling him. He felt for his gun again. Now he was fully alert and tense, all his senses on edge. His mind raced. He felt strangely vulnerable. Here the night creatures had the advantage. In the darkness he could smell the jungle's strong earthy, pungent odour. His back and his buttocks ached from the journey in the metal box and he couldn't get comfortable. The night seemed endless. He longed for day.

The sun rose so quickly it woke Blake with a shock. The jungle suddenly burst with colour and energy. A great chorus of crickets, cicadas, exotic birds, tree frogs and monkeys welcomed the dawn exuberantly. Small creatures scuttled in the undergrowth. The sky lifted and the greyness revealed the full stature of the jungle giants. The sun tried to penetrate the canopy; shafts of bright light cut down to the jungle floor at an angle of about fifty degrees. Blake stood up and stretched his aching body. He was desperately thirsty and his mouth was dry. He licked his lips; they tasted salty from sweat. He looked around for old hollow bamboo stems. They were plentiful, and he broke them off at the base and poured the tepid rainwater down his throat. The priceless liquid was like nectar. He gulped down at least another ten shoots full until he was quenched. He knew he would not die of thirst.

Blake found a small patch of open ground in full sunlight. He broke off a straight stick about three feet long and stuck it upright in the ground. He put a stone at the tip of the shadow, waited fifteen minutes, then placed a second stone at the tip of the shadow. He knew that the line joining the two stones pointed east-west. He considered his options. All of them had their risks. He could make his way back to Saigon, but he would be a marked man and would probably be discovered and killed. Or he could lie low in the jungle, or make his way to another town. He estimated the trek through jungle to another town would take him weeks, but he couldn't survive for long without equipment. His stomach now ached with hunger. When he looked for it food wasn't difficult to find. He ate figs and olives and broke open coconuts and brazil nuts, using his gun as a hammer. He studied familiar and unfamiliar types of fruit, nut and vegetation; some he recognised as edible, others poisonous. As the long morning turned into a hot, humid afternoon, his clothes clung to him, saturated with perspiration, and his skin itched. The quick rainfall of the late afternoon cooled him down. He stopped at a wild olive tree and plucked the juiciest green fruits.

Visibility was about 20 yards but, peering through the vegetation, he noticed something unusual up ahead. He immediately crouched low and was completely still. Two large mounds of earth lay side by side, with rough-hewn crosses made of bamboo standing upright at one end of each mound. Dangling from each cross was a set of dog tags. They had been abandoned for a while, as vines had begun their relentless crawl to cloak and engulf them. He quickly scanned the area, went to the mounds and examined the dog tags. He read the names: *Gary H. Lovett* and *Wayne D. Franklyn.*

He looked around again. In a clearing to the left of the mounds was what looked like a crashed helicopter. Blake approached it cautiously. All his senses were alert to any slight difference in smell, sound or atmosphere. He hid behind a bamboo clump and peered through the first green wall of leaves and ferns to the next. He scanned for as small an abnormality as a single twig, or even a leaf, out of place. He listened for the least sound not made by nature, and was ready to identify the faintest whiff of, perhaps, cooking smells or deodorant, which could hang for hours in the lifeless air. He took the Browning from his pocket; his body and mind were focused, as sharp as a blade. After about ten minutes he noticed nothing wrong and stalked around the aircraft like an animal, hiding himself in the undergrowth. It had definitely been there for some time, a couple of months he guessed, judging by the vine growth. As his confidence increased, he walked up to it and touched it with his fingers. The metal felt cool, smooth and hard. He tugged at some vines covering it. They gave way easily, revealing the fuselage underneath. It was the wreck of a Bell UH-1 American helicopter, the workhorse aircraft of the US Forces. He rocked it, checking it for stability, found the pilot's door and wrenched it open. It was stiff and opened with a screech that set his teeth on edge, followed by a loud thud. The whole structure vibrated. He pulled the door back 180 degrees, rested it against the fuselage and clambered inside. It was dry; the rain had not penetrated here.

As his eyes adjusted to the light, he noticed the corner shadows were not black but were the darkest shade of green. Moss and unusual spindly vines were thriving inside, a machete lay in one corner. An unopened map still in its transparent plastic wrapper stuck out from under the pilot's seat. He picked it up, took it into the light of the doorway and opened it; it was in perfect condition. It showed the northern area around Saigon and the Mekong delta, detailing watercourses, tracks, primary and secondary jungle and areas under cultivation. It also showed the position of An Lac monastery. It lay to the north-east, near two villages. He studied the map meticulously, then carefully refolded it and put it back in its wrapper. He looked around again. Two rucksacks were hanging from ceiling hooks. He lifted them down onto the floor and into the light, loosened the cording of the first one and pulled out the contents. There was a strong smell of antiseptic. There was military clothing, medicines, fishing kit, firelighters, ponchos, a compass and, most importantly, a knife. Blake pulled it out of its sheath, laid the blade in his hand and gazed at with pleasure. As he tilted it, it caught the light and flashed. He ran his fingers lightly over it; it was smooth, hard and sharp. Blake rummaged again and laid everything out in front of him. 'Yes,' he said out loud. There was enough kit here to keep him going in the jungle for months. He reckoned the two mounds of earth he'd stumbled across must be the graves of US personnel who'd died in the crash, hence the kit he'd found. Whoever had dug the graves was long gone. He was a lucky man; so was Blake. The sun was going down. He went back out into the jungle, filled the water bottle he'd found with water from the bamboo stems and gathered together seeds, figs and coconuts. He changed out of his wet clothes and tossed them into the undergrowth and put on one of the sets of military clothing. He ate and drank then laid the poncho out flat inside the wreckage with a rucksack as a pillow. He considered a new possibility. If he could make it to An Lac he could ask for sanctuary from Ajahn Kai-Luat. If he could make it, and if Ajahn Kai-Luat would agree. If. It was risky, but then his options were limited. At least now he had another option. It had been a good day, better than he had expected. He relaxed and fell asleep quickly.

The dawn chorus woke Blake; he got up and stood in the doorway. He heard a yelp and saw a creature scuttle away down a hole. He ripped off the fuel pipe from the helicopter and cut it into several sections with the knife; he'd made a blowpipe. He put the knife back in its sheath and threaded the sheath onto his belt beside the Browning. According to SAS estimates he would be able to move 1000 yards an hour through bush that didn't need to be cut, and he hoped to be able to walk for six hours a day.

He walked at a steady pace in a north-easterly direction, looking at the compass at least once every five minutes. It wasn't possible to walk in a straight line; he always had to dodge round something and avoid tripping over roots. After a while he relaxed, satisfied that he was moving in the correct general direction. He stopped every now and then to check his compass. As he skirted around a tree to avoid a buttress root he felt a tug and was suddenly pulled backwards. He heard a rip and felt a sharp pain in his shoulder. He stopped and looked. A sagging vine had torn the back of his shirt. He put his fingers over the tear, brought them into view and smeared his own red blood between his fingers. He walked until he came across a slow stream, washed the blood off his hand and the clear water turned a subtle shade of pink. Blake watched as the pink became fainter and the water ran clear. His stomach rumbled and his feet ached. He sat down, removed his boots and socks and took out the fishing tackle from his rucksack. The ground where he was sitting was teeming with wildlife – insects, beetles and worms. He caught sight of a fat pink worm twisting and writhing in the red earth. He took it between his thumb and index finger and attached it to his hook. The hook met the water with a gentle plop. The first fish took the bait quickly, then another two in rapid succession. They had bulging eyes and long, streamlined, silver bodies. He laid them on the earth, where they writhed and flashed their tails. Their mouths pulsed open and shut until the life drained from them and they lay still. He couldn't identify them, but cleaned and gutted them anyway and wrapped them in large leaves. He used the flint and steel to light a fire over the primitive oven he'd made with stones and sticks and left the fish to cook. When they were soft he sprinkled salt on them. The yellow flesh was chewy and moist. They tasted peppery and tangy but not unpleasant and he felt replete. He put his socks and boots back on and trekked some more.

He walked for a couple of hours then set up shelter for the night. He constructed a pole bed high off the jungle floor with the poncho as a canopy, changed out of his wet clothes and hung them out to dry, then put on the other set of dry clothes. He placed his boots upside down on sticks to prevent insects from getting inside, then covered his face, neck and hands in insect repellent. Yet another day had been full of the practicalities of survival. As night fell he lay on his makeshift bed and reflected. He'd learnt in Borneo never to travel alone in the jungle. But here he was, totally alone. Nobody knew where he was and he couldn't signal for help. As he looked into the blackness he felt his muscles tense. He knew that fear was his worst enemy. He acknowledged his own fear and accepted it. It was close. Real.

The sun rose quickly and so did Blake, awakened by the dawn chorus. A large beetle was crawling up his arm underneath his sleeve. He rolled up his sleeve and flicked it off. His skin felt itchy and a rash began to form. He rubbed in some anti-histamine cream then removed his dry clothes and put them away, dressing himself in the damp ones. There was a slight mist in the air that made the jungle seem more claustrophobic than usual and bathed everything in a surreal white haze. He packed away his things and started to trek. There was a bitter stench in the air; he looked around for the durian tree and picked the big, spiky, ripened fruit. He ate wild bananas and olives as he went and collected young fruits of bamboo and jungle cabbage - he wasn't keen on this but there was plenty of it. By late morning the ground became waterlogged and water had collected in his boots. He took them off. Using the knife, he made a couple of holes above the sole, midway along the foot, to release the water. His progress was slow now as he squelched through the muddy terrain. There seemed to be more mud in his boots than water; he could feel the warm, putty-like substance between his toes. Thankfully he saw a way round the mud bath leading to higher ground and stopped at the nearest shallow pool. He removed his boots and socks and washed them out. His clothes were bathed in perspiration so he took them off. The cool air on his sticky skin was delectable. He rinsed them in the stream and washed himself with a minute amount of soap, just enough for hygiene but not enough to make him detectable to the VC, if there were any. He caught sight of the outline of a snake hanging in five bracelets from a low branch and watched it gather itself, slither along, drop into the water and swim away. He put his clothes back on wet and made his way over the bog for a couple of miles until he reached higher ground.

The rains came and had a refreshing effect on the whole jungle, dampening down the slightly putrid smell, which increased with the heat. He made a star fire and waited for it to die down until there were no flames, just embers. Using the cardboard backing from the map as a cooking pot he boiled the vegetables he'd gathered until they became pulp. He was aware a spider monkey had been watching; its face appeared and vanished from behind ferns and vines. Suddenly it felt confident enough to show itself. It leapt from high in the canopy to a lower bough, coiled its tail around a branch for support, stretched itself out and grabbed a small fruit ball from a nearby bush. It bounced straight back up, its tail swinging and clasping, chewed the outside of the ball, tore it open and sucked out the inside. Blake took note of the fruit ball it had been eating. He picked one, rubbed some on his skin and waited. There was no instant adverse reaction. He picked a few more and put them in his rucksack: he'd try them later.

With renewed energy he walked on and found a suitable space to camp for the night. He built himself a shelter and changed into his dry clothes. The whole process was much easier this time. He knew which size and length of bamboo to cut, how to make the best cording and knots. He collected two stones, about the size of his fist, sat on the platform with his legs dangling over the edge and rubbed the stones together. It was a slow, repetitive process, but he was not in a hurry. The emerging flat surface began to feel smooth under his fingers. He wet the stones, working the knife over them with a smooth action, sharpening the blade. It felt Neolithic, he felt Neolithic. His mind wandered. He remembered his conversations with Hoa when she refused to leave, his escape from the hospital and his journey incarcerated in the metal box. His mind replayed it over and over again like a tongue on an aching tooth. He resolved that it was futile to dwell on this; the past was gone. He had a more pressing assignment now: survival.

* * *

One, two, five, fifteen. He'd tried to keep track of the days, but somehow it didn't seem important anymore. What was important was that he'd adjusted to his jungle. He recognised the subtle variation in the differences in the temperature, smell, sounds and humidity at various times of the day. He learnt to use the blowpipe to kill small rodents and monkeys, shooting them with small pointed sticks he had hardened in the fire. He now knew how to gut, skin and smoke them. He understood his own needs, when to walk, when to rest, for how long. He recognised his own moods, how bright and alert he felt in the morning, how lazy and inert during mid-afternoon and the sudden rush of energy in the evening as he built his shelter. Before nightfall he sharpened his knife and cleaned his teeth using the fine fibres on the inside of tree bark. He used his knife to prise the ends off his nails. Every few days he washed out his day clothes and washed himself, but the soap was running out and the clothes were now torn and rotten. He needed to tighten his belt a few more notches. He was still sure he was in virgin forest, animal tracks were everywhere, but he couldn't afford to be complacent. He needed to remain alert, even though his senses experienced the same jungle, yard after yard, uniquely different but the same.

An odd-looking monkey followed him around for a few days, squawking at him but keeping safely out of sight. Blake was made aware of its presence by the sudden snapping of branches and rustling of leaves. He caught an odd glimpse of its shape flying through the trees. He squawked back, and they kept up an awkward kind of conversation. He became adept at squawking, and other inquisitive monkeys joined in. Some time ago he had mercilessly killed, skinned and eaten a monkey. These he made his friends. Maybe he'd just lost his appetite for monkey, or lost his appetite for killing. He felt more intimate with the teeming mass of creatures living and thriving in this vast, heaving, green, amorphous entity that was the jungle. It was no longer alien but breathing life, just like himself.

* * *

Blake felt he had been wandering in the jungle forever, but he knew it hadn't been more than a few weeks. He sat down on a rock and removed his boots and socks. He hadn't the energy to go on and his feet were raw and sore. He opened his backpack. The supply of salt was low. So were the medicinal potassium permanganate crystals he'd been using to treat the fungal infections in his feet. He took a frugal amount and rubbed it in. He had a dull, unrelenting pain in his back from the wound that hadn't healed properly. He removed his shirt. He'd had an uncomfortable prickly sensation on his chest for the last hour. A rash had appeared; he'd had a number of them over the last few weeks. And his neck itched. He applied the antihistamine and antiseptic. It didn't help. It rarely did. Stubble on his face and chin felt uncomfortable: he hadn't managed to have a close shave using his knife. He took the cut-off length of the root of the strangling fig plant that he'd collected earlier out of his backpack and set it alight. The strong, bitter taste made him cough, the smoke wafted around him and hung in the air. His eyes watered and stung. It helped with the pain, as he knew it would, but it made him feel vague and sleepy.

He trudged on and stopped at a pool to wash. He hesitated for a moment; as the surface of the water flattened like a mirror, he caught sight of his reflection. He held his breath in disbelief at the sight of his own image: his bitten, blemished, unshaven face framed by lumps of matted, greasy hair, wild, sunken eyes and gaunt cheeks, hollow like crevices, his torn, disintegrating clothes. He hardly recognised himself. He looked wild. He looked like a savage.

CHAPTER 20

Blake grabbed the gun and pointed it into the jungle. His eyes darted back and forth.

He shouted, 'Who's there? Show yourself!'

Waving the gun from side to side, he turned around 180 degrees and walked backwards. He jumped as he hit an obstacle; his heart raced and his body went rigid. Swinging round, he pointed his gun straight at the trunk of a jungle giant. A small creature ran in the undergrowth. Blake panted. Sweat dripped into his eyes. He wiped his brow and put his Browning back in his belt.

He walked on, noticing, suddenly and inexplicably as if for the first time, the colour green all around him. He stopped now and then and examined in minute detail leaves and stems. He analysed and compared the different hues of green in different-sized leaves; the different quality of the surfaces of green leaves, matt or shiny; whether droplets of water on leaves affected the quality of the green; and whether the green was different on leaves at different stages of maturity on the same plant. Wherever he went, 'green' was in front of him, at the side of him, behind him, demanding his attention. His heart thumped. His vindictive jailer was laughing at him. He tried to distract himself; he sang out loud, 'Hey Jo, where are you going with that gun in your hand, where are you gonna run to, I've gotta get out of here as fast as I can… in other words I've got to get out of here as fast as I can…de de de de de… de de de de… de de de de. Hey Jo, where you going with that gun in your hand…' He stopped abruptly. 'De de de de de, Hey Jo, you fucker,' he yelled.

Rebellious fury welled up inside him. He clenched his fists and held them in front of his face. His emaciated knuckles gleamed white and glistened through the skin. The sight sickened him. The sudden visual confirmation of his physical weakness acted like kindling. He may have noticed it before but right now it was intolerable. His whole body quivered in a livid rage. He reached a clearing in the forest, flung his rucksack to the ground, got out his knife and slashed indiscriminately at the vegetation around him.

'Fuck you jungle, fuck you, you endless bloody… fucking green… shit… shit… fucking green.'

He slashed and pulled at stems, leaves and vines and tossed them into a heap, which quickly grew in size. He laughed out loud and, with equally destructive relish, he grabbed the flint and steel, pulverised some dry tree bark and set the pile of vegetation alight. The fire whistled and sucked and flickered into life, the red flame danced, developing and consuming the debris, and a plume of smoke rose above it.

'You think you're king of the jungle, don't you… you green,' he shouted, his voice turning into an agonised shriek, 'well, I'll show you another colour that'll change your mind, then you won't be so bloody arrogant!'

He breathed deeply and, dripping with sweat, staggered from one side of the fire to another. As he watched the fire burn he smirked with satisfaction.

'See, I've got one over on you… you bastard!' he said. His voice seemed to echo in the clearing.

Panting with exhaustion, Blake collapsed to his knees. He looked vacantly at the ash and leaf litter scattered around him. Every muscle in his body ached. The sky darkened and he felt rain; lifting his head to the sky, he opened his mouth and felt the cool raindrops on his mouth and tongue. It cooled and soothed him. He watched as if in a trance as it put out the fire.

As his reason returned, his fragmented mind thought about control: being in control, being out of control. He remembered an old schoolmaster once saying to him, 'When sailing a boat you can control the sails, but you cannot control the direction of the wind'. He sat for some time watching the rain and the smouldering smoke of the fire. Water dripped off his forehead and into his eyes; his vision blurred.

'Idiot,' he shouted suddenly.

He remembered the poncho and quickly stretched it out to catch the pure, drinkable rainwater. He wondered about the fervour that had overwhelmed him, welling up from inside. He felt insecure: he hadn't known he was capable of it. He drank and ate, filled the water bottle, walked for a bit, then built a shelter for the night. He slept well and in the morning set out, making friends with the jungle again, the same jungle he had felt so angry about last night. He stopped to rest, to tend to the blisters and fungal infection on his feet. He was used to the permanent discomfort. An intermittent searing pain on his neck where he had been bitten was troubling him. He put his fingers on the wound and felt a vague sensation of something slippery, a jelly-like substance. He brought his fingers into view. They were covered with a bubbly white alien stuff. In horror, he realised something must have laid eggs in his neck. He stood stock still in his tracks and retched. Jones in Borneo had warned him about this kind of bug; it would need to be cut out by a medic. Blake's morale took an immediate nose dive; he sweated. Wounds festered quickly in the hot, humid atmosphere of the jungle. He sat down on the bare earth, drank and checked his compass. His backpack had been rubbing up against the wounds on his back, causing friction, pain and potential infection, and it felt heavy. He checked the contents. He removed the rotten, stinking clothes he was wearing, threw them away and put the dry clothes on, but they were never really dry anymore. He discarded his blowpipe; he no longer had the energy or inclination to catch rodents or monkeys. He needed to travel light. The backpack was easier to carry now and was no longer rubbing so hard on his wounds. He walked on. He took his Browning out of his belt and turned it over and over in his hands, full of indecision. His gun had become an integral part of himself; it was his friend, he would feel naked without it, naked and vulnerable. But now it had become an encumbrance; he didn't even want to use it for hunting. It was no good carrying stuff 'just in case'. Reluctantly and with regret he threw it into the undergrowth.

At the back of his consciousness was an ominous, sinking feeling. The dreadful realisation began to dawn upon him that he might not make it. He became aware of his own fear, fear that was raw and real, fear of sickness, weakness and his own death. The images of the Indonesians' corpses lying in the jungle of Borneo jumped into his awareness. He relived the moment suddenly and shivered. He expected those men would have had proper burials, but his death would be alone, no ceremony, no goodbyes, no mourners, no epitaph. Just death: he would die raw, like an animal, his corpse would rot, consumed by the jungle. A tight knot formed in the pit of his stomach, his heart thumped in his chest, he trembled and broke out in a cold sweat. He was terrified. No amount of jungle survival training had prepared him for this. No reasoning or analysis could help him to overcome it. He was face to face with the darkness of death. Who was he, who was it that was dying? He hardly recognised himself. A physicist, a spy, a translator, a husband; all that was meaningless now. He was a shadow of his former self, a sick, weak, almost broken man, just walking, walking. He was aware only of his senses and what he was sensing; only these had meaning. As he walked on, the fear slowly began to dissipate. He became alert, responsive, living in the present moment. He became aware of the jungle, abundant and alive. Strangely, he felt subtly possessed of a kind of transcendental serenity. And with it his consciousness expanded, time seemed to disappear and he became the vegetation and the jungle giants and the red earth and the rocks. And, although he was walking, he felt absolutely, completely still, yet more awake than he'd ever been. And he noticed that he was experiencing a kind of inner calm, an almost blissful state, not born of intellect or emotion but from somewhere else, something he couldn't describe in words but real nevertheless. Gradually the experience faded. He knew he had touched something timeless. But he couldn't dwell on it. His survival was paramount. He noticed slight changes in his environment: drier ground, and more sunlight penetrating through a less dense canopy.

In the night Blake woke with a start. He heard the loud crash of falling branches followed swiftly by a thud. He felt the ground vibrate and pain pulse through his body. He realised he'd landed on the jungle floor and his face was in leaf litter. Soaked through, he trembled in the pitch black, his hands instinctively protecting his head. High above him the branches creaked. Now and again bucketfuls of water fell after being dislodged. They bounced off the foliage on the way down and splashed onto him. Tentatively opening his eyes and lifting his head, he saw phosphorescent specks of light darting to and fro a few inches below his face. After a while he recognised them as tiny insects. He reached out to touch them and was startled as his hand plunged into the black pool of water they were swimming in. When he pulled his hand out some of the insects got trapped among the hairs on the back of his hand and lay there like tiny twinkling, stars. He watched them, mesmerised. A sudden crack, and more deadfall, jolted him from his trance-like state. He realised he'd been complacent, hadn't selected his shelter well. He felt shivery; he wasn't sure if he was feverish or just cold and a headache was developing.

At daybreak he started walking, and began muttering to himself about nothing in particular in a jumble of languages: English, French, Vietnamese, Thai, a thick stew of witch's soup like the strange mixture the army cadet troop once made. Each youth brought a can or packet of soup and they mixed them all together so a new breed of soup was born. So Blake brought forth a new language from his consciousness. And the ground beneath him seemed to slide and move as if in an earthquake. He stopped and pissed into the ground. A dark yellow dribble of urine with a sweetly pungent stench evacuated from his body and sprinkled on the earth. Blake looked at it and began to laugh. He heard his own laugh. It was hollow, brittle and hysterical. He studied his hands. They were drifting in and out of focus and looked as if they were under water. A bubble of reason descended from somewhere in his consciousness.

'Drink, you idiot, drink. De-hy-dra-tion... de-hy-dra-tion...' he repeated to himself in English, emphasising each syllable as if the word were too long and difficult to say all at once. He picked up the bottle and gulped water down to the last sip. He was in a frenzy. He tore at the bamboo stems and poured the water into his mouth, coughing and spluttering. Stretching out the poncho, he waited for the afternoon rains. When they came they fell like iron sticks out of a menacing dark sky, slicing, and pounding. A solid wall of rain thumped into the earth with such force it made mini craters and left flying branches and tattered leaves sprawling around chaotically. He collected water, drinking as much as he could. This time he selected the position for his shelter with great care. He looked upwards before spreading his poncho to make sure there was not going to be any deadfall from trees and downwards to make sure he was high enough away from any possible flash floods.

The next day he came across a fast-flowing river and identified it on the map as the river to the west of An Lac. Following the riverbank, it led all the way to Tan Ria village, near to the monastery. As he approached he could hear the sounds of the village. He hid in the undergrowth listening for the origin of the noise, keeping close to the riverbank, moving from one massive bamboo clump to the next: waiting, watching. He guessed he must be quite near the monastery now, maybe less than a mile away. His senses fully alert, he was seized with a vivid foreboding. He noticed a subtle change in the atmosphere; in the still air hung the slight trace of a scent that was not quite human nor jungle. Blake heard something moving through the undergrowth. It sounded like one of those monkeys whose company he had come to enjoy, but it hadn't taken to the trees as quickly as usual. Blake watched, crouched down beside a clump of bamboo, knife in hand. His heart thumped and the hairs on the back of his neck stood on end. Out of the corner of his eye he saw something moving, then there was a flash of sunlight off metal. Blake slowly turned his head. There was a VC standing a few feet away, just the other side of the bamboo. Blake couldn't tell if the man was alone. Retreat seemed the best option. He stealthily rose to his feet and, getting his balance, took one step back, stepping on a tree root, which snapped loudly under his weight. Instantly the VC spun round to face him. For a moment their eyes met. Blake saw the tell-tale narrowing of the VC's eyes, indicating he was ready to shoot. As the VC levelled his rifle, Blake threw his knife. It pierced the man's throat and blood gushed out, splattering the man's clothes and nearby bamboo and vines. The man seemed to hover in the air for a few seconds, his eyes fixed and glazed. As he fell to his knees the loud bang of a gunshot pierced the air. Blake felt a searing intense pain in his left thigh as the bullet tore through his flesh. The man slumped forwards and hit the ground with a thud. The stench of blood filled the air. The jungle went silent.

With trembling hands Blake tore the fabric of his trouser leg and examined his wound, blood welling through lacerated flesh. He took the surgical dressings from his rucksack, using the first to mop up the blood. With intense relief he realised that the bullet had missed his femoral artery. He applied another dressing in a tight knot and pressed firmly against the artery in his groin. He could feel the pulse throbbing against the edge of the wound; the bleeding stopped. He scrambled his way through the undergrowth over the dead man and removed the knife from his throat. There was a hiss as he yanked it out. Blake continued through the undergrowth, keeping to the riverbank. His leg throbbed; he could feel a rising nausea and his head swam. He kept going even though the effort needed was superhuman. He was nearly there; he saw An Lac coming into view. In a gesture which was completely uncharacteristic, he made the sign of the cross as his mother used to. He had no idea why; he hadn't done that since he was a small boy.

'So that's when you were shot... the wound in your left thigh?' asked Cathy.
'Yes, it was then,' replied Blake.

CHAPTER 21

June 1968

Blake heaved his aching body the last few yards up the hill, putting as little weight as possible on his ruined leg. The jungle finished suddenly and the clearing appeared; cultured grass lay like a soft carpet before him. The sun blazed out of an open blue sky on to the simple but substantial bamboo huts raised on low stilts. An Lac looked like an odd and unnatural oasis in the landscape and he was filled with a surge of joyous relief, which was so intense he almost wept. Blake sat down on a mound of earth, too exhausted to go on. He needed only a few small steps to make the transition from jungle to monastery, but at that moment the effort required was enormous and beyond him. The pounding in his heart echoed like a thud in his head.

His leg blazed with agony. Torn material from his trousers had become intertwined with tatters of bandage and blood was seeping through. His heart began to flutter, beating in a series of sharp, shallow fillips. He put his hands round his mouth and breathed deeply; moments later his heartbeat returned to a more familiar rhythm. As he gathered his energy, he noticed a small bald-headed figure dressed in saffron robes pass by one of the huts. He hardly had time to think, but stumbled out of the jungle and into the open. The brilliant sun hit him like a slap. He took a few steps then fell head first onto the grass as his wounded leg collapsed underneath him. The small figure rushed over and supported him as he struggled to sit upright. The monk was young, no more than a boy, and barely five foot tall, but well-built and muscular. He held Blake gently but firmly. As the boy loosened his grip Blake could no longer find the energy even to sit. He flopped backwards on to the grass.

'Stay here, I will get help,' said the boy in Vietnamese and ran off. Soon Blake heard voices above him.

'Yes, he is badly hurt.' The man's voice was vaguely familiar. 'Can you hear me?'

'Yes,' said Blake.

'Lie still.'

Blake was vaguely aware of someone pressing the pulse in his wrist, and hands on his chest, throat and neck.

'I am going to turn you over,' said the voice. He was so close that Blake could feel the man's breath on his cheek. Blake opened his eyes; the monk looked intently at him.

'I recognise you, brother. Are you Khien's son-in-law, John Miller?'

'I am, and you are Ajahn Kai-Luat.'

'Yes.' Ajahn Kai-Luat took a deep breath. He turned Blake over so that he lay prone.

'What happened to your leg?'

'I was shot.' Blake was aware of a pulling and prickling sensation as the bandage was removed from his leg. He could smell the stench of his own blood and wanted to retch. Another bandage was put in place. Ajahn Kai-Luat described to the boy everything he was doing. Blake only half-listened and only half-comprehended; this was medical language and his mind appeared to have momentarily ceased functioning, like his body. Ajahn Kai-Luat rolled him over.

'Lie here and rest,' he said.

Blake lay on the grass and allowed exhaustion to overcome him and all his muscles to go flaccid. His body felt heavy like a rock, sinking into the earth. He felt that he was at the end of his journey, and his need for rest was absolute. The sunlight burnt his raw, bruised face, but he had no energy to move his hands to shield his face from the sun. He was vaguely aware that the two monks had moved some yards away and were whispering together. He turned his head to get a better view. They were deep in conversation. The boy listened; nodding repeatedly, then ran off. Ajahn Kai-Luat knelt beside Blake, looking at him with compassion but also with a kind of troubled watchfulness and apprehension.

'Welcome, dear friend, to our humble monastery,' he said with a measured urgency. 'You have a nasty hole in your leg where the bullet came out. You have an infestation in your neck. You have a fever and your feet are covered in fungi and sores. But you cannot stay here. If you are seen here word may get out about you.'

'Where can I go?' said Blake. 'I can't travel far.'

'This young monk will take you to a shelter further up the hill. He is getting some provisions for you now. With your injuries the journey will take about one hour.' He hesitated. 'It will not be easy… but I think you can make it.'

'You are joking,' said Blake, incredulous. He took his weight through his forearm and propped himself up.

'You have to,' said Ajahn Kai-Luat, looking him straight in the eye. The message was clear: this or die.

'And my leg?' asked Blake.

'The boy will do what he can. He's very capable; as soon as he returns you must go. The other monks must not see you.' There was an authority in Ajahn Kai-Luat's voice that was final.

The boy raced towards them: his saffron robe flowed awkwardly behind him. Two large canvas brown bags were slung over his shoulder.

'Leave by the back way,' said Ajahn Kai-Luat. 'If you live, we will meet again.'

Ajahn Kai-Luat held the palms of his hands together in front of him and bowed to Blake, then left without further eye contact or looking back. The boy helped Blake to get up and pointed the way. When Blake put his weight on his injured leg it sent a rill of pain straight through him, making his teeth clench. For a second the pain was overpowering and threatened to take him away; the edges of his field of vision greyed. Then the darkness faded, he found his balance, he was on his feet.

As they went uphill from the monastery the jungle grew less dense, and dry underfoot. They followed an old overgrown footpath, which looked as if it had been abandoned months before. The boy took the lead, clearing undergrowth as he went. In parts it was a well-defined path, in others blocked by jungle vegetation. Each step he put weight on his wounded leg was physical anguish. It was throbbing slowly like a bass note from a string that never stops vibrating. The boy ripped off a thick, sturdy length of bamboo.

'Use this to help you walk,' he said and handed it to Blake.

Blake grasped the bamboo and heaved himself three more steps up the hill.

'How much longer?' he said.

'I need to see to your wound, we must keep moving.'

The boy put Blake's arm around his neck and supported him for the last hundred yards as his leg had gone rigid. They reached a clearing at the summit of the hill.

'We have arrived,' said the boy.

Blake looked round in consternation. The shack seemed dilapidated and at first glance not habitable. It was a few feet square and made from upright strips of bamboo lashed together with wooden corner posts, the doorway missing. Half of the pitched roof had caved in and one of the walls had partially collapsed. Bamboo and cording were scattered on the ground in a messy heap. Insects appeared seemingly from nowhere and began swarming around Blake's head. In his fragile state they seemed like dive-bombing fighter planes, appearing to cluster and veer away suddenly in formation. Then they buzzed around his injured leg, encircling it at speed. The boy waved a bag at them and they zipped away up into the canopy. The floor was thinly covered in leaves and undergrowth. As the boy cleared it away with his hands, tiny rodents scattered off into the undergrowth; underneath were slivers of decaying straw matting. Blake propped himself up against the nearest post. He felt sick and queasy; his head began to swim. He tried to jolt himself back into full consciousness, fighting to stay upright. Hanging from a nail on a wall and covered thinly with vegetation was a basic green army camp bed, canvas stretched over an alloy frame. The boy grabbed it and lifted it down. There was a shrill squeak as he pulled the supporting legs into position.

'I hoped it would be here,' he said, 'but I wasn't sure.'

He put it on the ground and checked the alloy frame structure and hinges, then he rubbed his stubby fingers back and forth against the green canvas, which was mottled brown with mould. Dust particles wafted in the air and tickled Blake's nose.

'It's a bit damp, but it will hold,' Blake thought he heard the boy say, but the voice was slow, laboured, indistinct. Then the voice repeated itself in Blake's head over and over again, like a stuck record, and burnt itself out.

Blake thought he saw the boy rummage in the bag, take out a large white cotton sheet and place it over the camp bed, but he wasn't sure, and he wasn't sure whether the side of the shack was moving or he was. He was experiencing a gentle to and fro motion of his body. His vision began to cloud over and the green mosaic of the leaves on the ground beneath him seemed momentarily to resemble the swirls on the green and red patterned carpet of his grandmother's living room in Aldershot. He thought he could hear his grandmother's voice and children laughing. He was just about to fall when he became aware of the boy's sturdy hands holding him by his upper arms. With his eyes half-open he could just make out the top of the boy's head which barely reached his own shoulders, but the boy stood stout and firm.

'Sit down on the bed... I will help you,' he heard the boy say, but the voice sounded faltering and distant.

The boy guided him over and assisted him onto the cot. It squeaked and groaned with the weight of Blake's body. Lying down was better; his mind cleared, he was almost alert.

'I am going to turn you onto your side,' the boy said and turned Blake. He heard the sound of the boy rummaging in his bag and then a sharp rip and felt him remove the dressing on his leg.

'Now you can rest,' the boy said.

Blake waited for the next thing to happen; he was aware that the boy had gone quiet. He thought maybe he had gone away until he heard the rustling of paper and plastic bags and then another sound, a tap, tap, tap as if the boy were flicking his finger. Momentary silence followed. Then he felt a pinprick, hardly discernible from the intense throbbing and almost unendurable pain in his leg. To his intense relief the pain faded. Blake began to doze and was only vaguely aware of the boy kneeling over him, doing something to his leg.

'Your leg is in a bit of a mess, I'm going to sew it up as best I can. It may hurt later.'

That was the last thing Blake heard as he passed out.

* * *

Blake drifted in and out of dreams and semi-consciousness. One moment his whole body was so hot he felt he was on fire and the next he felt so cold he shivered and shook. He was acutely aware of every sensation. His consciousness followed the path of a single droplet of water, which tickled his already super-sensitive skin receptors unbearably before it dripped onto the sheet underneath him. His body was shouting at him, and in his delirium he felt that tiny men with pickaxes were crawling over every inch of him, stabbing the sharp ends deep into his flesh. He felt as if his leg was being roasted and his neck held in a vice. Darkness and light came and went. Sometimes it was that same day, other times he thought two weeks had passed. He was vaguely aware that the boy was sometimes there and sometimes not there. Every now and then he was aware of being gently supported from behind to sit up and drink. In a more lucid moment he was able to open his eyes and half-focus on the boy.

'Ajahn Kai-Luat says you must take this,' the boy said. He placed a tablet in Blake's mouth and helped him to gulp it down with some water. Still supporting his head and neck, the boy said: 'Drink this. It is medicine.'

The boy poured into his mouth a sour-tasting thick, sticky, liquid with the consistency of cold custard, but which was also lumpy and stringy. It left an unpleasant residue in his mouth. Blake was uncertain how many times the boy had given him water, the tablets and the medicine. He knew that the boy changed his clothes and bedding and moved him into different positions on the camp bed. He was being moved carefully, as if he were a rare Ming vase. Sometimes he hallucinated that the boy was a nurse dressed in uniform or Hoa, and sometimes he thought it was his mother. Other times out of the corner of his eye he was aware that the boy was sitting and meditating, or walking rhythmically up and down the shack, and sometimes he could hear him chant. He hallucinated that he could see the boy levitate, suspended in mid-air with legs crossed, and his repetitive chanting had a soporific effect. Blake felt he was floating on gentle waves on a warm sea as the notes of the chant rose and fell.

Interwoven with these experiences was a Pandora's box with a cocktail of vivid, unpleasant dreams and random visions that had opened to haunt him. They would play themselves out like a film, in his mind. In his confused state Blake wasn't sure if they were authentic recollections or fevered dreams or hallucinations. He dreamt about mutilated bodies, the stench of death. He saw the bodies of the men he'd assassinated side by side, lined up against a wall. He was transported to the room where his mother was dying. He was twelve years old. His father's sister, Aunt Ruth, had dressed him in his best formal clothes before seeing his mother. The room was cast in half-light as most of the curtains were shut. Several older members of his mother's family were present, hovering in shadows, like death's sentinels. He felt terrified as he looked down at the bed at his mother's white face. As he clung on tight to her weak, outstretched hand his heart thumped furiously and there was a lump in his throat. She beckoned him to come nearer and whispered to him,

'You must find your own path in life now, your own truth.'

Aunt Ruth led him out of the room and into an annex nearby. He started to cry hysterically, almost gagging. His aunt's face was hard and unyielding; she shook him by the shoulders.

'Stop it! You are the eldest. You have a duty to be strong for your brothers.'

Blake choked back his tears, stifled his outward display of grief and became like a stone, emotionless, cold, feeling nothing but numbness inside. His aunt took his hand firmly and led him down a dark corridor. The door to another room was open. His father and his father's family were inside; it was a gloomy room with thick net curtains. They were sitting around in silence, their faces grim and gaunt, dressed in black.

Another time, another vision. It was later in the year after his mother had died. He had been summoned before Aunt Ruth and her friend Dora. Blake stood in front of them as they sat upright and tight in formal, high-backed armchairs. They were looking at him intently and telling him he had to do something; the words were indistinct, but he heard his own reply.

'Is this a command or a request?' he asked.

'A request I think, dear.'

'Why can't father talk to me himself?' said Blake.

'Your father's very busy,' said his aunt awkwardly.

'Father is always too busy for us,' said Blake.

'Don't be impertinent.'

'It's true, isn't it?' said Blake.

His aunt didn't reply, but Blake noticed her lip twitch.

'I want to be able to make up my own mind,' said Blake; his heart thumped in his chest.

'Your brothers have already agreed, you'll be showing them the way.'

'You told them, you didn't ask them, didn't give them a choice.'

His aunt shuffled in her seat. 'We'll talk about it again, dear, run along now and do your studies.'

Blake left the room and hid behind the door, listening to the conversation between the two women.

'He worries me that boy, so cold and distant. He won't let anyone near him. He feels he needs to take responsibility for his brothers,' said his aunt.

'And they idolise him, hanging on his every word,' said Dora.

'And he's becoming increasingly defiant.'

'His father needs to discipline him.'

'That's not easy, he's got his father's quick mind,' said his aunt.

'Too clever by half,' replied Dora.

Blake woke with a scream rising in his throat; he almost fell off the cot. As he moved, the alloy frame squealed for him, it made the noise he couldn't. He felt disorientated for a moment and wondered where he was. The dreams, the tortuous dreams. This purgatory was unendurable; he could bear it no longer. Sometimes he wished he were dead. He wished it would come soon. Sometimes he thought he was dead.

* * *

Blake raised his head, took his body weight through his forearm, heaved himself into a sitting position and eased his legs over the side of the cot. He puffed and panted with the exertion and his heart thumped. He smelt something in the air that meant rain. A few large droplets fell down from the canopy and splashed on the earth. He watched from his dry position as the solid wall of rain fell a few feet in front of him, bounced in tiny pools and trickled away in little gushing streams. As the rain eased he caught sight of a flash of bright saffron through the wall of green. The boy had an open umbrella in one hand and a large blue plastic bowl tucked under his arm. He ran, breathless, into the shack, shook out his umbrella, nodded, smiled, bowed and began the ritual Blake knew so well by now. Stooping, he removed a neatly folded small brown square of cloth from his bag, unfolded it and placed it, with patience and precision, on the ground then knelt on it. He chanted in Pali: '*Araham sammasambuddho bhagava, buddham bhagaavanyam abhivademi*', bowed and straightened up, his palms together as if in prayer. '*Svakkhoto bhagavata dhammo dhammam namassami*' he said and bowed, '*Supatipanno bhagavato savakasangho sangham namami*' and bowed again. Slowly and without hurry he turned and faced Blake.

'What was that chant?' asked Blake. This was the first fully formed sentence he had spoken to the boy. He heard his own voice: weak, small and frayed.

'I was taking refuge in the *Triple Gem*. Do you know what that is?'

'Yes, it's the *Buddha,* the *Dhamma,* the teachings expounded by him, and the *Sangha*, the monastic order.'

'That is quite right. Very good. I see you have sat up all by yourself,' said the boy eagerly. 'And you speak also,' he said and smiled.

'Now you've taken the bandages from my feet… I'm keen to walk… soon… very soon.'

'When you are strong enough. Here, I have brought you this bowl for urination.'

'A gift,' said Blake and smiled.

The boy smiled back.

'Some clean clothes, and here,' the boy removed a metal container from his shoulder bag. 'Today you have *banh trang* - rice paper wraps, and guavas sprinkled with salt.'

'A feast fit for a king,' said Blake.

'Here, let me open it for you.'

'No, I'll do it,' said Blake. He clenched his bony hand around the screw-top lid of the container and, using all his energy, unscrewed it. Hot steam and a starchy smell were released. He picked the fluffy, large, lukewarm grains of rice out of the wrap and placed a few of them in his mouth. Despite being hungry, he could only eat a morsel at a time. The boy filled Blake's cup from the large water butt he had put there a few days before. He sat down on his square of cloth and while Blake ate he meditated. Blake looked at him with appreciation and curiosity. He was a sort of Boy Friday, also surgeon and nurse and errand boy rolled into one. He had an intriguing, inscrutable, oriental serenity. The boy finished meditating, opened his eyes and bowed three times.

'Do you know what the date is?' said Blake.

'It is now July 7th.'

Blake knew he'd left Saigon on 25th April. So he'd been in the jungle for over two months. Two months that felt like two years.

'Thank you... for helping me,' said Blake. He'd been thinking about what to say to the boy and how to say it. He didn't want to say too much or too little. No words would ever be enough. If he had had any expectations the boy had exceeded them on every count. This diminutive, unassuming and steadfast boy had quite simply saved his life. And he had done it all unconditionally, with unwavering compassion. He'd been reliable, sensitive beyond his years, patient and tolerant beyond most people's capability. Blake felt strangely and uncomfortably unworthy of such attention. The stark contrast to the way he had so quickly and ruthlessly taken life irked him. He recognised how far he himself had moved away from the Christian simplicity of the 'sign of peace' and 'love thy neighbour as thyself' that his mother practised to becoming a player on the stage of death.

The boy looked him in the eye, with a smile on his lips, and nodded. 'You are most welcome,' he said.

They were silent for a few moments.

'You have looked after me well... like an expert,' Blake said.

'Ajahn Kai-Luat tells me.'

'How does he know?'

'Ajahn Kai-Luat knows many things. Before he became a monk he was a doctor of Western and, later, herbal medicine.'

'Was he now. And you're his apprentice?'

'Yes. I have helped him with surgical operations on other monks with minor injuries and also forest animals. I describe your ailment and he gives me your medicine.'

'What is in my medicine?'

'Antibiotics, pain-killers, fungicide, vitamins and minerals... other things as well. Sometimes he changes it. He tells me how to dress your wounds and how to look out for signs of your condition changing.'

'You learn well and you follow instructions well.'

'I have a good teacher.'

'How old are you?'

'I am nearly sixteen years old.'

'Only fifteen,' said Blake, startled.

'It is my birthday in ten days' time,' the boy said and smiled in delight.

'How long have you been an ordained monk?'

'Since I was twelve. Ajahn Kai-Luat took me in when I was eight. Some soldiers killed my parents and most of the people in my village. Then they burnt my village down. A monk found me wandering alone in the jungle.'

The boy looked away. For an instant Blake felt that he could detect in his expression something unbearable. He was tired and lay down. He didn't ask the boy any more questions.

* * *

Blake sat up and looked around, frustrated. He had time on his hands. Time that irked him. He knew every tree, every bush, every rock and stone, with an intimate familiarity. It was almost easier doing the jungle trek; then, he had had a mission to accomplish, he was going somewhere, he didn't have time to think, but now he was forced back into himself. He was no longer a nomad passing through a vast amorphous landscape, he was a convalescent fixed in a tiny space, which seemed to extend no farther than his eyes could see. There were creatures beyond his immediate field of vision he knew because he heard them; the edges of his auditory space were fuzzy, and visitors into it came and went, but he was stuck. More stuck than he had ever been in his life. There were only a few jungle giants up here. The sun was able to penetrate all around the shack onto open ground and fall in amoeba-like shapes between areas of vegetation. Blake watched the shapes move round with the sun. He knew exactly their form and position at each hour. A regular routine shaped his day: the boy's early morning visit, the boy's midday visit, his siesta, the late afternoon rains and the migration of the sun on the horizon. With stoic determination he took the weight through his legs and held on to a wooden post supporting the shack. The constant throbbing ache in his left leg had become a dull awareness, but when he flexed it the pain was intense. And he also knew the biting insects. Like little enemies invading his territory. The boy brought a robust-looking spade, dug a latrine some yards away from the shack and helped Blake hobble over and use it. Civilisation was dawning.

* * *

One morning the boy ran towards him frowning, his eyes fixed firmly on the ground. He promptly sat down in front of Blake and looked intently at him.

'What is it? Aren't you going to bow to the *Triple Gem*?' asked Blake.

'I need to speak with you.'

'Well?'

'Ajahn Kai-Luat says there are Viet Cong soldiers in the area. He says you must stay here. You must get strong.'

Blake had a sinking feeling; he hoped they weren't looking for him. He had been vaguely mulling his next move over in his mind and it wasn't this.

'I don't want to put you in danger. Leave me. I will survive alone,' said Blake.

'No, you are weak, like a skeleton. Soldiers are all around. Ajahn Kai-Luat says you must stay in this shelter if you are to live.'

Blake thought for a while. The boy was right. His arms and legs were wasted. He could see the outline of his bones and feel his ribs through the skin on his chest. Even hobbling over to the latrine was a monumental effort that sapped all his energy. Afterwards he lay down, exhausted. He couldn't go anywhere. Not yet.

'Only if there is no danger to yourself or the monastery,' said Blake.

The boy nodded and looked at him with relief.

'What was this place, this shelter?'

'Monks used this as a place for their solitary retreats.'

'Why did they stop using it?'

'Because of the biting insects.'

Blake laughed, a hollow, empty laugh.

'Yes, of course.'

They weren't there all the time: sometimes Blake would not see the insects for several days in a row. When they were there, the insects bit him relentlessly, particularly on his exposed face and hands. He heard their high-pitched buzz as they flew past his ear. He listened and watched with a kind of fascinated revulsion for hours at a time. He watched each one carefully, anticipated its landing and swatted it flat dead. At first it was a totally absorbing time-filler. The struts of bamboo were splattered with their remains, black with tinges of red. He felt a kind of sick satisfaction with each one he eliminated. An insect buzzed around his ear. He swatted it against a strut of bamboo and its carcass joined the others. One of its legs slipped gently down to the ground. The boy frowned, looked at him with compassion and went into deep meditation.

* * *

The insects. Their endless reinforcements wore him out. There seemed no end to the bloody things. And they bombarded him from too many directions. He imagined they were using tactics to try to demoralise him, and in a sick kind of way it reminded him of this crazy war. This crazy, mixed-up, chaotic jumble of a war, where there seemed to be no distinction between combatants and civilians and where appalling atrocities were commonplace. And for what? Did he know, and did it matter anymore? Blake had always been a bit of a perfectionist, liked to do his work well. His attitude towards his work at MI6 had been no different. Blake wanted to be proud of what he'd done. He'd had a clear assignment. He wanted to make a difference; they'd told him he would. By taking out the commanders he'd be breaking the back of the VC. He'd been resourceful, he'd been effective, he'd done his job well, but now he felt nothing but increasing regret. Why, he wasn't sure. He began slowly to hate himself; his self-hate gave him a griping sensation in his stomach. He wished he could change the past, but he couldn't. He couldn't reject it or

ignore it. He'd have to accept it somehow, but how?
He'd have to live with his own actions for the rest of his
life. The burden was awesome. He looked at it in the
cold light of day. He'd killed ordinary men like himself,
ruthlessly, without pity, leaving a trail of grief and loss
in his wake. These VC commanders at least knew who
their enemy was. They had a purpose, a mission, and it
was their country. It wasn't even his war. What was he,
some kind of killing machine on automatic pilot? Did he
feel invincible? Not anymore; he'd come close to death
himself. And he had experienced the bitter reality of
war. The reality was gruesome, gory, gut-wrenching,
dehumanising and horrific. Why had he been so ready to
accept the Vietnam assignment anyway? Perhaps it had
something to do with a fanciful notion: the mystique of
the solitary gunman, moving through a shadowy
landscape pouncing on his victim and then melting
away into the darkness. No, that wasn't him. Or did he
see himself as a hero, as his forebears were in the Boer
and the First World War? Doing his bit for Queen and
country? No, that didn't seem to work either. The
Americans were terrified of the spread of communism
and Britain needed to support them, all off the record.
Of course he'd had a choice; he'd agreed to it. He
wondered whether he'd become subtly institutionalised
perhaps, a cog in a dogmatic culture at MI6 where
awkward questions were avoided and orders followed.
The thought of not being self-determining appalled him.
The more he picked at it the hollower it became. There
didn't seem to be any heroism anywhere. And it was all
too late. He could no longer justify his actions on any
level, politically, ideologically, personally. It was all
trash… a sham… he was a sham.

'Sometimes you have to do the wrong thing for the right reasons' was one of the things he had learnt in MI6. In Blake's mind right and wrong had become shades of grey, drifting along a continuum like clouds drifting back and forth in gusts of wind. Blake examined his mission from every angle, every scenario. However hard he tried, he could no longer reassure himself of the legitimacy of his mission. If only he didn't have to think: it would be easier not to think. But here he was, stuck with his cogitation. Like a prisoner with a long-term sentence, Blake picked up the pen and paper he had asked the boy to bring and began to write down his thoughts and ideas as if for posterity, his embryonic ruminations about war and peace and freedom. Eventually he'd cogitated so much his ideas had all but extinguished themselves and there was nothing left to write. He was left with only a feeling. He was locked into a kind of self-imposed introspective misery, which made him feel inert and incapable. This was also a new feeling he didn't recognise and he didn't feel comfortable with it. Something was disturbing him. He was profoundly unhappy with himself, unhappy at the level of his bones. He couldn't budge this, couldn't ignore it. Like a deeply embedded thorn, which had been stuck for aeons, it was entrenched in his psyche. Yet somehow it was yielding, revealing itself. It needed to be drawn out, extinguished. It was quivering in him. Strong emotions tormented and overwhelmed him for days: loathing, anger and frustration came and went in varying intensities.

* * *

238

A biting insect landed on the sheet beside him. He watched it for a long time, absorbed in observing it. It was black and its body was streamlined like a rowing boat. It had a circular black head and six spindly legs. Like a helicopter it slowly lifted into the air, buzzed and zipped up into the canopy.

* * *

'How are you this morning?' said the boy as he walked into the shack, eyeing Blake curiously. 'You are not mindful?'

'I need to get away, from here, from this place.'

'There is nowhere to go.'

Blake clenched his fists, his voice at fever pitch, and breathed heavily.

'It's enough, tell Ajahn Kai-Luat, thank him. I can't do this anymore.'

With uncharacteristic impetuosity, as if he had suddenly lost his mind, he limped off into the jungle; he heard the boy shout after him.

'Come back, you won't get far.'

'I'm going,' Blake roared; he walked a few hundred yards with the boy close behind, then stumbled and fell over a buttress root, his weak leg collapsing underneath him. As Blake reeled with the pain and grabbed his thigh, the boy rushed over.

'Leave me!' shouted Blake.

He struck out at the boy, landing a blow on his chest. The boy looked startled, but Blake's blow had been weak and ineffective. Blake looked at his wasted arms and legs and his rage died. He lay for a moment in bitter and dismal resignation, then wordlessly let the boy lead him back to the shack and help him onto the cot. Blake slumped down, with the boy close by, watching. Vague ideas began to shape in his mind. His relationships had been a barren wasteland, and his indifference was so entrenched he didn't even know there was any other way of relating. He'd never really been happy, never at peace, never felt love, except, maybe, for his sickly mother. He had made her proud, she told him, but when he thought of her it was only of sadness and guilt that he couldn't have done more. Now his self-loathing was total. He was full of hopelessness, wretchedness and desolation. This bitter, empty life... Then there was the boy, loyal, consistent and supportive. Was he worth it? Was he worth saving? He looked at the boy with a kind of bewilderment. The boy sat in meditation, his eyes half open, his expression serene. Blake shifted on the cot; it squeaked and the boy looked up at him.

'Remind me,' he asked the boy. He was in a pit of despair. 'Why are you helping me?'

'Because you are my brother.'

The boy went back into meditation, serene and motionless in his lotus posture. The boy's tranquillity had a soporific effect on Blake. He dozed off to sleep.

* * *

Blake woke. The early morning air was still, the sky clear. For once there were no insects to torment him. He levered himself to his feet and tottered to the doorway. Holding on to the wooden post for support, he looked out. In the valley below there were patches of thin mist hanging in streamers. They looked ghostly in the dim light of the moon, now low down in the sky. Blake inhaled deeply, feeling the freshness of the cool air filling his lungs. He watched as the moon slowly moved even lower and the sky began to lighten. To the east there was a thin layer of cloud on the horizon. While he watched, it took on a rosy glow as the sun rose silently behind it. Soon the sun would be high in the sky, burning off the mist. Streaks of orange and pink suffused the bank of cloud, which now shone brightly. Blake stood upright, stretched in the warming rays of the sun and limped back to his cot. He sat down in the canvas dip, which had now become comfortable after hours of use.

The boy ran up the hill, bowed to the *Triple Gem* and looked at Blake intently, his expression inscrutable.

'What is it?' asked Blake.

'Ajahn Kai-Luat says that for us to continue to successfully hide you here you need... to become a monk.'

The boy looked at Blake and a smile began to play on his face. After a moment's delay, Blake burst out laughing, a genuine, full-blown belly laugh. He clutched his stomach and almost fell over as his body contorted; the laugh continued and tears trickled down his face. The boy's smile turned into hesitant giggles, then he too laughed fully and unselfconsciously and rocked back and forwards. They both laughed together, uncontrollably, and the laugh went on and on. Afterwards they looked warmly at each other; they had shared something basic to the human condition, which crossed all artificial boundaries. As their laughter slowly mellowed their mood became more thoughtful. Blake glanced down at the ground for a while, deep in thought, and then raised his eyes to look at the boy.

'What you're asking is impossible. I'm completely unworthy of wearing the robes,' he said, 'I'm not even fit to wash your feet.'

The boy looked at him fixedly. 'None of that matters now. You have to do this. Ajahn Kai-Luat says so, so please agree,' he said emphatically.

Blake was surprised at the passion and vehemence of the boy's response. They were silent for a few moments, locked in eye contact. With tremendous effort Blake heaved himself out of his negativity and within a few moments his mindset had flicked from self-deprecation to self-preservation.

'Tell me what's going on,' he said resignedly.

'Ajahn Kai-Luat has been told there are more and more Viet Cong soldiers wandering the forest. He is concerned about your safety.'

'Are they looking for me?' asked Blake.

'We don't know. They may find you anyway, by accident or not,' said the boy.

Blake frowned.

'Wouldn't it be suspicious for me to be a monk alone here, away from the monastery?'

'Many monks take an annual solitary retreat, and there are many places in the area where they hide away.'

'Do they leave monks alone?' asked Blake.

'Ajahn Kai-Luat says they will definitely kill you if you are not a monk. If you are a monk they may not bother with you.'

'Surely they would be suspicious of me, a Westerner?'

'No, they may not be. There are several Western monks here. Ajahn Kai-Luat has links with Ho Chi Min so the Viet Cong need to be careful. But to completely fool them Ajahn Kai-Luat says you have to be convincing as a monk. I will teach you,' said the boy, his voice quickening and becoming impassioned, 'he understands this may be difficult but he thinks it is the only way to save you. He urges you to agree to do this to save your life.'

Blake stood up slowly and laboriously. He held on to one of the wooden posts and looked out on to the horizon, sighing deeply. Never in his life before had his choices been so few or so challenging. He was a wanted man, he was still weak and he knew his chances of escape were slim. Blake thought for a moment.

'Well, in my condition, fighting or escape is out of the question, so it had better be camouflage,' he said despondently.

'This good decision,' the boy said and smiled.

Later that day the boy returned with a large meditation cushion, some chanting books and some books on the *Dhamma*, written in both Vietnamese and Pali. He fumbled in his bag, brought out a shining metal razor and placed a clean white towel around Blake's shoulders. He set to work and Blake felt the scrape of the razor from the back of his head up to his crown, his eyebrows, around his temples and his chin. The boy was experienced and it was all done quickly and efficiently. Blake was aware of his hair falling matted and filthy around him and passed his hand over his shaven head and face. It felt itchy but cool and he felt clean. It was good. The boy placed the clean saffron clothes on the bed and bowed respectfully. He showed Blake, with great care and attention to detail, how he wore his own robes. First the lower robe, *sabong,* with the simple cord tie around the waist, then the upper robe, *jiwon,* then finally the double-layered outer robe, *sanghati*, slung over the shoulder and twisted around the back to secure it in position. He explained that even getting dressed should be done mindfully, with full attention and precision. Blake removed his clothes and put on the robes according to the boy's instructions, followed by the second-hand sandals. After some time he was fully dressed as a monk. His next challenge was to behave like one.

'The boy sounds extraordinary, so young, so reliable, so mature. He saved your life,' mused Cathy.
'Him and Ajahn Kai-Luat, yes,' replied Blake.
'So… what happened next?'

CHAPTER 22

Blake again put his hand over his shaved head and looked down at himself, dressed in robes. He felt strange; never in his whole life could he have imagined himself so oddly attired.

'You look very much like a monk,' said the boy proudly.

'I don't feel much like one,' said Blake dismally. 'I've never done this before, tell me what I need to do to be convincing.'

The boy looked serious, deep in thought.

'There are two things you need to learn. One is the way we wear our robes and fold and unfold our meditation cloth. I will show you how, but if you don't do it precisely I'm sure nobody would notice except another monk,' he said.

'I'll be as precise as I can. Now, what's the second thing?'

'You need to learn how we do our spiritual practice: chanting and meditation. Mostly we do sitting meditation and walking meditation. This is where you need to look the most real.'

'You must teach me how to do it properly. No half-measures.'

'Yes, of course.'

'Where do I begin?'

'Shall we start with chanting?'

'I've heard you chant the *Triple Gem* so many times I think I know it already.'

'There are other chants at other times of the day, but the *Triple Gem* should be enough to start with. Let's try,' said the boy gently.

They bowed and chanted together, Blake mirroring the boy in gesture and chant almost exactly.

'This is very good,' said the boy, 'and now, the sitting meditation.'

The boy showed Blake how to sit on his meditation cushion, shifting his position when he became uncomfortable, which for Blake was frequent as his left thigh was painful.

'When we breathe, we pay attention to the slow inhalation and exhalation of breath.'

Blake closed his eyes and tried the breathing. 'This isn't working, my head is full of thoughts.'

'Of course: treat any thoughts like a fly in a bottle, to watch them come and watch them go, like a witness, but always bring your attention back to the breathing.' The boy studied him. 'You look doubtful.'

'I am.'

'This takes much practice. Start with only ten minutes then slowly increase the time. It will become easier then.'

After having sat and thought for ten minutes, Blake heard the boy chant a few words. He opened his eyes.

'How was it?'

'The fly is still trying to find its way out.'

The boy smiled. He stood up, walked a few yards and cleared undergrowth and stones from a strip of earth.

'What are you doing?' said Blake.

'We need somewhere for walking meditation.'

He marked each end with a large stone. It was about thirty feet long, just wide enough to walk along.

'This will do… are you ready?'

'Show me.'

Blake walked over to where the boy stood, at the first stone.

'This is how you do it,' said the boy, 'you walk between the stones; you start at one stone, walk slowly, paying full attention to each step, arrive at the second stone, turn around and walk back, over and over again. When you take each step don't think about the last step or the next step, you have to be focused on this step only.' The boy raised his foot in the air. 'You have to be aware of the sensation of your foot leaving the ground, moving through the air, how your weight is balanced and the sensation of your foot as it is placed back on the ground.' He put his foot slowly and carefully back on the ground. 'This concentration on the now is what we call mindfulness. But this mindfulness is not something we practise only during meditation, it is something we practise every waking moment.'

'That's a bit steep,' said Blake pensively, 'how long does it take to be adept at mindfulness?'

'It depends on the pupil. It can take many years.'

'That sounds challenging. I knew monks lived by strict rules but I imagined it was a fairly easy kind of life,' said Blake, frowning.

'Many people make this mistake; Ajahn Kai Luat says it is very hard.'

'Are there any techniques to help develop mindfulness?'

'To get you started I'll show you some techniques tomorrow.'

'OK, I'll try this walking meditation now.'

Blake felt cramp in his leg after standing still for so long. Getting from one stone to the other and back again exhausted him. He told the boy he had had enough for one day.

'All the practices are to help us develop full awareness in everything we do,' said the boy the next morning, 'getting dressed and undressed, standing up, sitting down, walking, eating, urinating, defecating. While we are defecating that should be the most important thing in our life. While we are eating that must be the most important thing in our life, while we are dressing, dressing should be the most important thing in our life. If while dressing we are thinking about sitting or eating, then we are incapable of living during that time we are dressing. We need to be mindful during every waking moment. Awareness is a life and death matter.'

Blake pondered for a moment that, ironically for him, it was.

'I will show you how to experience the taste of water,' said the boy. Blake raised one eyebrow, incredulous. The boy filled Blake's cup from the water butt and brought it over. 'Now you need to pay attention to the sensation of water in your mouth, and try to feel it as it leaves your mouth and travels in your body.'

Blake sipped the water, swirled it around in his mouth and swallowed it. He looked at the boy.

'Water is water,' said Blake, unimpressed.

'And now a mango. How does it feel, smell and taste? Try.'

Blake examined the mango with his hands. He felt the sensation of the smooth, rubbery, firm outer surface; he noted the mottled colours of red and orange and yellow and tinges of green. It was the size of his fist, with an elongated rounded shape; he lifted it to his nose and its smell was tropical and fragrant, with a hint of pine. Cutting it open with a knife, he examined the soft, firm flesh; it felt like putty when he pressed it with his finger. He cut away some peel and bit on the orange flesh. It tasted sweet and juicy and yielded easily when he bit on it. The texture was harder and stringier near the stone. He noticed the complexity of the mango; never before had a mango been so meaningful or relevant. He became aware of how many different sensations there were when he fully concentrated on the activity and slowed right down.

'I think I'm getting the hang of this,' said Blake.

The boy gave a slight smile. 'And now, outside,' said the boy.

The boy took his hand and led him at a snail's pace, blindfolded, into the jungle. Blake walked, aware of each bodily sensation, feeling the ground carefully before he set his foot down and put his weight on each leg.

'Let's stop here. Stand still and do nothing but listen,' said the boy.

Blake listened. He could identify many sounds: animals scampered, insects buzzed and hissed, birds sang far and near and leaves rustled.

'Now concentrate on only what you can smell,' said the boy after a few minutes.

Blake detected the smell of fresh jasmine, a faint waft of eucalyptus and the less pleasant, all- pervasive smell of rotting vegetation with which he was all too familiar. He could detect the freshness of rain on vegetation.

'When I take the blindfold off I want you to pretend you are an underground animal emerging from your hole for the first time,' said the boy.

The boy removed the blindfold and Blake stood with the sun behind him. It cast brilliant light onto the scene bursting with life in front of him. All at once he saw green vegetation of all varieties and hues, a mixture of trees, undergrowth and climbing plants all densely packed, wild and disorganised, a heap of living, thriving matter. The sun caught the occasional raindrop and made it shine like a sequin. The shadows of the trees behind him and his own elongated shadow in front of him striped the ground with grey. He had looked at nothing but jungle vegetation for months but, for whatever reason, in that moment, he saw everything with a kind of clarity and acute awareness uncluttered by his previous experience, raw, vibrant and alive. At the same instant he saw that everything was exactly in its right place. His mind didn't try to reorder it into something different, or label it into something meaningful. He accepted it for what it was, life in all its intensity. He became aware of the sun on his back warming his robes, and a small creature crawling up his leg; it tickled him, he brushed it off. They walked back in silence to the shack and meditated together. Then they did the ritual homage to the *Triple Gem*.

'You are a good pupil,' said the boy.

'I'm good at pretending, but I think I'm beginning to learn.'

'Yes, you are learning,' said the boy, and smiled confidently.

* * *

For the next few days Blake practised awareness of his senses. It made him feel alert and in touch with his surroundings and for the first time he experienced some quiet moments. But there was something else that kept troubling him.

Lust. It gripped him slowly but increasingly as the days passed. Normally he would be able to keep a lid on his urges; right now he felt his urges were bigger than him. This was new. His urges contained and sapped all his energy from anything else; he was in their vice. All his sensation was in his groin and all his attention submerged in lustful fantasies. First he thought of Hoa, then he imagined the many women of all shapes and sizes he'd had sex with. He longed to feel his hands on the soft curves and crevices of a woman's body, the smell and taste of her, and he longed for more and more... as his mind whipped him into a frenzy of erotic images, fuelling his distraction and his agony. He felt as desperate as a thirsty man in a desert, and nothing he did would satisfy. Any woman would do, however old or ugly he didn't care. This was lust at its most raw, at its instinctive level, as a force of nature. A Shakespeare sonnet that he had read at secondary school repeated itself in his agitated mind:

Th' expense of spirit in a waste of shame
Is lust in action; and, till action, lust
Is perjured, murd'rous, bloody, full of blame,
Savage, extreme, rude, cruel, not to trust;
Enjoyed no sooner than despised straight,
Past reason hunted, and no sooner had,
Past reason hated as a swallowed bait
On purpose laid, to make the taker mad;

Yes, he was going mad, absolutely mad. Still obsessed with his urges when the boy arrived, he hardly gave the boy time to go through his ritual.

'If I don't have a woman soon I shall go mad,' he blurted out. He stood up and paced around the shack. 'I am overwhelmed with lust. Night and day it obsesses me... I'm a slave to my body.'

As soon as he said it he was surprised he had, and to a boy of fifteen, what must he think? Usually so controlled, rational, logical, self-possessed, clear-headed and in command, he hardly recognised himself. He suddenly felt embarrassed and stupid. He stood still and took a deep breath.

'I've lost the plot, a moment of madness. I'm sorry, I should never have burdened you with this. Forget I said it.'

The boy's expression was inscrutable. He said nothing for a full two minutes, then raised his eyes to Blake and spoke quietly with a subtle, bashful smile on his face.

'Ajahn Kai-Luat says that when a prostitute comes to him she talks only of enlightenment, she says: "I hate my life, I only want enlightenment", but when a monk comes to him he speaks only about wanting sex.'

Blake broke into spontaneous, hilarious laughter. The incongruity of the situation grabbed him. All his consternation suddenly seemed irrelevant. The boy began to laugh and they laughed together unselfconsciously. Tears of hilarity streamed down their faces, the boy's infectious laughter fuelling his own.

'Ajahn Kai-Luat has a baffling worldly insight into our weaknesses. What else does Ajahn Kai-Luat say?' asked Blake.

'He says, the more you meditate and chant and practise mindfulness the more these urges will subside. He says one should contemplate the loathsomeness of the body. Examine the body as a corpse and imagine the process of decay or think of the parts of the body, the lungs, the intestines, fat, faeces, and so on. Think of these loathsome aspects of the body when lust arises.'

'I don't have a problem with that,' said Blake.

'There are also ways you can tap the sexual energy and take it to higher levels of consciousness,' the boy said, and demonstrated with his hand, moving it in the air from his groin area up to his head in a smooth, slow, delicate movement, 'but this takes much practise and discipline. Older monks know about this, and when I am older I will know about it too.'

'Is that so,' said Blake, unconvinced.

* * *

However, this was little reassurance or relief to Blake, who for several endlessly long days felt trapped in lust, which overwhelmed his mindfulness, his practices and his peace. He thought about the boy. He expected that he'd probably travelled less than a few miles from his birthplace during his entire life. But here he was with a kind of maturity that eclipsed that of many old people he'd met. Awareness was the key. *In the kingdom of the blind the one-eyed man is king.* Perhaps all men were blind, aware of only their own limited view of the world, and that being blind was a kind of complacent living death. Perhaps that was how he'd been most of his life. At times he felt sick inside himself, hated himself with a passion and thought of the relief of death. Being a monk was too challenging, being a spy and removing VC commanders anathema, and just staying alive in the body physically painful. Then after a while came the dawning realisation that he didn't have to become anything. This was the monk's way, just to be, no ego, no set identity, just mindful of the moment. And that the great contradiction was that just being was everything, when the conditioned was stripped away, the unconditioned was realised and this was the truth.

CHAPTER 23

Blake fixed his eyes on the path down the hill, his stomach rumbling with hunger. Every day the boy brought him his food at the same time, just before midday. Judging by the movement of the sun, Blake estimated the boy was two hours late. He had a nagging, uncomfortable feeling, and sensed things weren't right. Soon, he saw the boy's saffron robes amongst the green. As the boy walked up the hill his movements were laboured and his head hung low; he caught Blake's eye briefly then looked away. When the youngster paid homage to the *Triple Gem* his voice trembled and a tear trickled down his cheek. Blake waited.

'What's happened?'

The boy avoided Blake's gaze; his eyes were red and puffy.

'For goodness sake tell me!' said Blake.

As the boy turned to face him Blake could see his eyes full of pain; he felt a surge of compassion. The boy choked back some sobs and wiped away a tear.

'Something terrible has happened… It was last night, we had our all-night meditation, which we do each month when the moon is full.'

'Go on.'

'It starts about nine o'clock in the evening and continues until dawn. All the monks were in the hall and it was lit up by candlelight. If we had not been in meditation we could have all seen each other and we could have seen if monks came in or left the hall, but not much else.' His voice settled into a flat monotone as he tried to suppress his emotions. 'Well… it must have been about two o'clock in the morning; suddenly there was a big noise and many men… I don't know how many… rushed into the meditation hall with huge guns. They were all very loud, fierce and disrespectful. They took up positions along the walls, behind the lines of monks, who were all meditating. I was in the middle of the line of monks on the left so I could see them standing behind the monks in front of me… ', the boy tried to stifle a sob, 'but I could hear them behind me as well. Their leader came and stood at the front, near to Ajahn Kai-Luat. The man shouted in a loud voice that they knew that foreigners, enemies of Vietnam, were hidden in the monastery. He demanded that they should be brought to the temple and handed over to the Viet Cong.'

Blake's mouth tightened.

'They may have been looking for me,' he said quietly.

The boy shook his head.

'I don't know. The leader told his men to point their guns at the heads of some monks. I could see what was happening in front of me, five or six monks had guns pointed at their heads, but I don't know whether one was pointed at my head because they were behind me,' he said and suddenly gasped in anguish. 'After this there was silence in the hall as the monks continued their meditation. All the monks were completely still apart from a very young monk who began to cry. But I couldn't meditate, I just sat there with my eyes half open. I watched and waited; I was really terrified. "You will bring these enemies of Vietnam to me now," the leader shouted angrily, "or you will all die." Ajahn Kai-Luat stood up. "Your war lies outside the boundary of my monastery," he said; his voice was very calm and steady, "this is a place of peace. Look into your own heart. Leave your anger, hate and destruction behind, these only lead to suffering. Look around you. There are only Buddhist monks here, there are no enemies of Vietnam." The leader didn't seem to understand Ajahn Kai-Luat, he looked confused. "You are hiding foreigners here, enemies of Vietnam!" he repeated. He seemed agitated and didn't know what to do. He pointed his gun directly at Ajahn Kai-Luat. My heart was pounding in my chest; I was so scared. I thought he was going to kill Ajahn Kai-Luat!' The boy choked and tears welled up in his eyes. He paused briefly, pulled himself together and continued. 'The leader stood right in front of Ajahn Kai-Luat, still pointing the gun at him. They stared at each other for a very long time. Ajahn Kai-Luat was very brave. Everyone was silent. "Hand them over or I will kill you!" shouted the leader. "Even if you kill me that will not change the facts," said Ajahn Kai-Luat, he did not raise his voice but was very forceful with his words, "I told you, there are no enemies of Vietnam here."

There was another silence while they continued to stare at each other and then I was very, very surprised; the leader looked uncertain and lowered his gun. At last he looked away. "Very well," he said, "but if I find you have lied to me it will mean death for you all!" He told his men to put their guns down and then he went up to the nearest monk and kicked him in the shoulder. When the monk was on the ground he beat him with his gun on his chest and on his legs. The monk, I wasn't sure who it was at the time, I thought it might be Venerable Jayadhammo, a very pious monk, very quiet; he started to cry out in pain. It was really terrible to witness!' The boy's face screwed up in alarm. 'Ajahn Kai-Luat rushed over to help him and the leader spat on the fallen monk. Then he marched out of the hall with all his men behind him. Some of the other men beat more monks as they were leaving. Other monks were injured as well. It was so, so terrible,' the boy said, his eyes full of agony. 'Later I found out it was Venerable Thanissaro and I was pleased because he is a much stronger monk.' His voice trailed off and he sobbed quietly for a while.

Blake took a deep breath.

'I'm sorry, that was an ordeal for you,' he said. 'I need to leave.'

'No, we have a plan.'

'The best plan is that I leave,' said Blake decisively.

'No, please, this is Ajahn Kai-Luat's plan.'

Blake decided to listen, out of respect for Ajahn Kai-Luat and the boy.

'What's your plan?'

'You know this hut was used for retreats.'

'Yes.'

'In the usual tradition, the monk supplying food to the one on retreat leaves the food some yards away and the monk on retreat collects it. We do not see each other. From now on we must do this. I will only be able to visit once a day with your meal. If you need anything you can write me a message and leave it in your empty bowl. I can continue to leave you clean sheets. When it is safe I will come again.'

Blake sighed. He was still weak. The plan seemed plausible and he couldn't see that it would put the monastery in danger. He thought he'd be able to outwit the VC if it came to it.

'I owe my survival so far to you,' said Blake. 'I'll do it.'

The boy removed the food container from his shoulder bag and mindfully placed it on the ground.

'Today you have rice and vine leaves,' he said.

'Thank you.'

'I must go now. Ajahn Kai-Luat needs me to help with the injured monks.'

'Of course.'

'You are a very strong man,' said the boy.

'And you are a very good monk.'

* * *

Days later, one hot afternoon as Blake lay on his cot reading, something caught his attention. He put down the *Dhamma* book, lay still and listened. Then he realised: the crickets had suddenly fallen silent. Blake slowly sat upright, making as little noise as possible. He could not hear anyone approach but he knew someone was out there. Blake's heart raced. Minutes later the crickets started up again and Blake lay down. He practised one of the breathing exercises the boy had taught him.

A few hours later, the crickets were suddenly silent again. Blake bowed and paid homage to the *Triple Gem*. Finished, he mindfully folded his meditation cloth, placed it on the end of the cot, then went outside and practised the walking meditation. As he walked back and forth between the two stones he could see men in black clothes, moving slowly and crouching silently like wildcats in the undergrowth. They circled the shack, watching him. Blake's attention was razor sharp. All his instincts prepared him for battle, but in order to survive he had to be convincing as a monk; mindfulness and harmlessness had become his subtle weapons. He walked at a regular, unhurried pace, up and down, up and down. His leg ached, the pain increasing with each step; he ignored it. He felt as vulnerable as a sloth being stalked by a lion; no chance of escape here, the disguise had to hold. After what seemed like hours, the watchers slipped back into the jungle, as silently as they had come. Blake returned to the shack and lay down on the cot. He sensed this was not yet the end: he had managed to live another day at least.

Blake sat in meditation. He was still unable to sit properly cross-legged; he propped himself up, with his meditation cushion supporting his wounded leg. His eyes were half-open, his gaze unfocused. He suddenly became aware that there was a faint rustling sound outside. If he hadn't been so still he wouldn't have been able to hear it at all. The crickets chirped on. Whoever was outside had approached from the opposite direction to last time, four days ago. Suddenly two black-clad VC stepped boldly into the hut and stood in front of him; one of them aimed his rifle at Blake's head. Blake stifled his instinct to fight. He ignored them and continued to breathe steadily, maintaining the rhythm.

'He's a spy,' said the man pointing the rifle. Blake could hear the anger in his voice.

'No. He's another one of those monks on retreat. You can see his bones. He must have been starving himself,' said the second man more calmly.

'He's an impostor, a spy I tell you!' said the first man.

'No, he's a monk, you've been watching him, we all have,' the second man persisted. 'You've seen. He's a proper monk. Here from the monastery, on retreat.'

'Let's kill him anyway,' said the first venomously.

'No, we're not to kill Ajahn Kai-Luat's monks,' said the second.

'Are you lily-livered, scared of killing a monk? He's not a real monk anyway.'

'He is. Look. He's in deep meditation.'

'Meditation my arse,' snorted the first.

Without warning he swung round, unslung his rifle and thrust it towards Blake's head. Blake watched, detached, as the butt of the rifle came hurtling towards him and stopped a fraction of an inch in front of his nose. He kept on meditating, the rhythm unbroken, his gaze still unfocused.

'See,' said the second man. 'I told you; he's in deep meditation. He probably doesn't even know we're here. Come on, let's go.'

The second man walked a few paces outside the shack; the first man hovered over Blake, panting and snorting with anger. Blake thought he was about to die. He could feel the man's anger, it was like a force field, radiating outwards. It took all his will to sit quietly, to ignore the imminent danger, to overcome his instinct to lash out. The VC lowered his rifle, but instead of slinging its strap back over his shoulder he lunged, then jabbed the butt viciously into Blake's shoulder blade. The pain was excruciating. Blake fell over onto his side. The man kicked him, with full force, on his back and his legs. It took all Blake's strength not to shout out in pain. He felt the VC step over him and take a step to the doorway. He looked up and saw the malice on the man's face. The man turned and spat on Blake as he lay crumpled.

'Imposter,' he snarled contemptuously, turned and went out. 'Now he knows we're here,' he called out as he joined the other.

All was quiet once more. Blake dragged his battered body back onto the cot. He shuddered. The man had missed his wound. Only the lower part of that leg had been kicked. He felt dizzy and nauseous, but he had cheated death again, he could live another day. A headache developed, which turned into a migraine, and he vomited. The stench of his own vomit wafted and hovered in the air for hours. He couldn't move, his nerves were fragile. He thought he heard the men return, but it was only the thudding of heavy water on the roof of his shack. A violent thunderstorm cleared the air and the stench away. With trembling hands he scribbled a note for the boy for more painkillers and dragged himself down the hill. He spent a fretful night in agony; the pain seemed to be deep in his bones. The next day dark purple bruising appeared on his legs and shoulder and over the next few days turned black. He wondered when his ordeal would be over. He really had had enough.

* * *

Seven days later the boy ran up the hill, grinning. But when he saw Blake he frowned. He bowed, unfolded his sitting cloth and paid homage to the *Triple Gem*.

After the ritual he looked closely at Blake. 'You are bruised, have the Viet Cong been here?'

'You could say that… they beat me up over a week ago. Left me black and blue. That's why I needed the painkillers.'

'Do you need treatment?'

'It looks worse than it feels now. Don't bother with medicine, it's healing.'

'I'm sorry I couldn't be here for you.'

'And how are things in the monastery?'

'Better. I have some good news for you,' he said with lightly and his expression transformed into a smile.

'Ajahn Kai-Luat says you can come and join us at An Lac and recover there. It will be more comfortable.'

'This sounds good,' said Blake.

'The villagers have told him that the Viet Cong have gone. A French monk is similar to you in height and Ajahn Kai-Luat has sent him to a temple at Hue; he had wanted to go there for some time. So, for any outsider, there will be the same number of European monks.'

'So I'll take his place?'

'Not exactly. Ajahn Kai-Luat says you must arrive tomorrow morning. If the other monks talk to you, tell them you are in silence. For everybody's safety none of them must know the truth, so you must live amongst us like a monk.'

Blake sighed. 'I won't be convincing.'

'Watch how the other monks behave, and then you will learn and fit in quickly. Listen for the gong. The gong is sounded five times a day. When you hear the gong, leave what you are doing and follow the other monks. They will either be going to eat or meditate, to chant or to do work. Do not miss the daily meal in the main hall at noon as it is the last meal of the day.'

'I'm not used to living by rules.'

'Do you want to stay here?'

Blake had had enough of the hut. The boy was throwing him a lifeline to something new. It was the better option.

'No, I need a change.'

'Good. There are a few things you must do as a guest monk. In the queue to receive your midday meal you must stand after the ordained monks but before the novices, who are dressed in white. And you must sit at the back left-hand side of the hall for meditation, and be the last ordained monk to leave the hall. Oh, and you mustn't ask for anything, anything at all from anybody, apart from me, of course. You have to wait to be asked.'

'Tell Ajahn Kai-Luat I humbly accept his hospitality.'

The boy clapped his hands together with pleasure. He placed a clean, starched, saffron-coloured textile bag and a bowl and drinking cup on the ground. 'Here, now you have your own bowl and drinking cup,' he said, 'and you can keep them in this bag. I will come here for you at sunrise.'

'I will be ready,' Blake said.

'Oh, I nearly forgot, your name is to be Venerable Annando.'

'Thank you, and what is your name?'

'Venerable Sunnido.'

'It's nice to meet you, Venerable Sunnido,' said Blake and bowed.

The boy grinned.

* * *

In the morning Blake gathered his things together: the textile bag, sitting cloth, meditation cushion, toothbrush, toothpaste, the books, writing paper and biro, a towel, the bowl, drinking cup, and the ointment. These were now his entire worldly possessions. He placed them mindfully in the textile bag and soaked in the atmosphere of the dilapidated shack for the last time. He wasn't sure exactly how long it had been his shelter for, but he suspected it was nearly two months. He had changed. He realised that something had left him, like an old skin that a snake sheds.

Venerable Sunnido led Blake down the well-worn path and through a large wooden gateway. They passed huts and other larger buildings raised up off the ground on posts and went into a hall, then walked down a narrow corridor and into a small room. A monk with a crinkled face sat bent and stiff behind a desk. He stood up and bowed as they entered, holding onto the desk for support.

'This is Venerable Annando,' said the boy, 'Ajahn Kai-Luat has been expecting him, he has come to stay and he is in silence.'

'Welcome, my name is Venerable Seniya,' said the aged monk and smiled sublimely.

Blake smiled back and bowed.

The older monk put on his spectacles and turned over some papers.

'Yes, hut 45 has just been vacated. You are very welcome.'

Blake nodded and the men bowed and smiled again.

They reached the top of a small flight of steps and the boy gestured for Blake to enter the hut. Blake stepped out of his sandals, left them on the porch and went inside. He put his bag on the floor inside the entrance and stood for a moment in the doorway of the main room.

'How many people is this hut for?' he asked.

The boy smiled. 'One,' he said.

To Blake, used to being cramped in the shack, this seemed enormous. There was a mattress on a raised platform in one corner and a simple wooden table and chair in another. Several small straw mats were laid out on the floor like a mosaic, corner to corner. The walls were plain bamboo panels, lashed together. A large opening on one wall gave a view of tall green bushes beyond. The only other objects were a meditation cushion, a candle and an incense-holder on a small wooden stand.

'You like?' said the boy.

'Oh, I like very much,' said Blake.

'So, you were able to recuperate there for a while?' asked Cathy.

Blake smiled ambiguously, 'More than a while.'

'Go on...'

CHAPTER 24

An Lac Monastery
August 1968

Blake gasped as the cold water poured down over his head, running off his naked body onto the ground.

'More?' said Sunnido.

'No, that's enough,' said Blake. Sunnido lowered the bucket that he was holding above Blake's head and put it on the ground beside the rainwater butt. Sunnido passed him a primitive bar of coarse, grainy, jasmine-smelling soap. Blake rubbed it vigorously and covered himself with its thin froth. Fragments of dead skin and congealed blood sloughed off his body onto his hands. It seemed like an age before he felt clean; his body almost itched afterwards with the shock of it. Sunnido rinsed him off with another bucketful of cold water. Blake dried himself with a damp towel that hung on a nearby hook and dressed.

'Here, you can see you are a monk now,' said Sunnido and handed Blake a small shaving mirror.

Blake took a moment to absorb the image looking back at him. Pockmarked, gaunt face, no hair, no eyebrows, saffron robes. The last time he'd seen his reflection was in a pool of water in the jungle and then a savage had looked back at him. But now he looked like an emaciated monk. The transformation was astonishing even to him. He wandered back to settle into his hut, flopped onto his mattress and lay there relaxed and at peace.

It didn't take Blake long to realise that the huts surrounding hut 45 were occupied by more senior monks and that these huts were bigger than the others.

A French monk lived in the hut diagonally opposite from him. Blake noticed him grin at him whenever they passed each other on the path.

* * *

The gong sounded in the pitch black. Blake dressed by candlelight. Dawn was breaking as he walked towards the meditation hall with the other monks. He had seen the hall from a distance during his previous visits with Khien, but not gone in; at certain times of day it was out of bounds to all but monastics. In the half-darkness the mist gave the monastery grounds a surreal quality. As he approached, the hazy structure appeared as if out of a cloud looking like a large medieval barn. He climbed the few steps to the entrance. Huge rafters supported a bamboo roof, there were small windows and straw matting on the floor. Many large candles were dotted around, lighting the space. A statue of the Buddha stood on a plinth at the far end. Cushions were neatly piled up at the entrance of the hall. Each monk collected one as he came in and walked slowly and purposefully to a distinct place on the floor where they sat down. Blake picked up a cushion. Sunnido came up behind him and indicated for Blake to sit at a space at the back. The atmosphere inside was serene and peaceful. A woody aroma of incense wafted around. The monks slowly and silently filed in, taking up their positions in rows on the left- or right-hand side of the hall, facing each other. Four were definitely Westerners, towering over the Vietnamese. He watched the monks' composed, graceful movements, their gestures and their facial expressions. He studied how they mindfully unfolded their sitting cloths, how they moved as they sat down on the cushions, the way they bowed. There were four rows of monks, with ten or twelve to a row. Ajahn Kai-Luat entered, placed his own sitting cloth and cushion on the floor and sat down facing the Buddha statue in a prominent position at the head of the hall. In a ritual that seemed perfectly timed, and without being prompted, the monks took up a kneeling posture and bowed three times to the Buddha statue, taking refuge in the *Triple Gem*, and settled back into their sitting positions. Ajahn Kai-Luat turned on his cushion to face the monks; his sharp eyes scanned the hall. He nodded at Blake in such a subtle way it was almost imperceptible. Now Blake's next test was about to begin, from one covert role to another, he thought to himself.

* * *

'Ajahn Kai-Luat would like to meet with you. Follow me,' said Sunnido.

They walked through the monastery grounds to a quiet, secluded spot that had been cultivated like a garden. There was a large circular pond with a stone rim; carp glided through the water. Round the edge of the pond were clumps of water lilies, their wet green leaves shining in the sunshine. Colourful orchids grew on stems trailing from large earthenware pots. Ajahn Kai-Luat sat on a small bamboo bench. Blake approached and they greeted each other with a bow, Sunnido withdrew and Blake sat down.

'Words are not enough. I owe you my life, and will be forever in your debt.' said Blake.

Ajahn Kai-Luat smiled wryly at him.

'Ah words, words are never enough. It is in silence that we find the truth,' he said. After a pause he continued, 'Anyway, it is not me, it is the young monk, Sunnido, who saved you. I have to admit now; I didn't expect you to survive. His expert care probably prevented you from developing gangrene in your leg, which would probably have been fatal. He has shown dedication and courage.'

'He told me his parents were dead and his village had been burnt down.'

Ajahn Kai-Luat shook his head.

'We have had war in Vietnam for so many years. Firstly with the French, and now our country is being torn apart, North and South. When war is all around us it is even more important and even more difficult for us living in the community to remain rooted in stillness. For as long as there is war in men's hearts there will always be war in the world.'

'You have to start with yourself,' said Blake.

'Yes,' said Ajahn Kai-Luat, and regarded Blake with a gentle but piercing scrutiny.

'Tell me about Sunnido.'

'He was found wandering in the forest by one of our monks when he was eight years old. He had seen sights of destruction and mutilation unfit for one so young. I recognised his potential and have guided him myself for the last seven years. I chose him to be my medical assistant because he was keen and totally un-squeamish, young as he is,' he said with a chuckle.

'You were trained as a doctor, Sunnido told me.'

'Medical training is helpful in a remote place like this. We don't need to rely on outsiders.'

'I've come to the right place.'

'Yes. But you have helped Sunnido as well. His mindfulness and compassion have matured as a result of looking after you. I understand he has taught you to meditate. How do you find it?'

'It's not something I'd be inclined to do, but now I'm here in the monastery I am practising. If I'm to be convincing as a monk, needs must.'

'Try a different attitude. Allow yourself to experience meditation as the serene encounter with reality. It is a way of breaking through the illusion of the way things seem and realising that whatever arises passes away. Be as awake as a medieval knight walking weaponless in a forest of swords, or a mountain climber without a rope feeling for the next foothold. You need to be this alert to realise the awakening. The ultimate reality has neither gender, colour, culture or geography. In my humble opinion all the great religious traditions and scriptures help us towards the realisation of this same one universal truth. You don't need to become a Buddhist, you are not trying to become anything. In fact you must reject the concept of becoming a Buddhist. The rituals and practices we undertake are merely a vehicle to allow us to rise above who we think we are, to know what we are not. If you have any questions ask the more senior monks, they will help you. Ajahn Anaro, the French monk: he is a good person to ask and always willing to help,' said Ajahn Kai-Luat.

'Thank you,' said Blake.

Ajahn Kai-Luat nodded and closed his eyes and they sat in silence for a few moments.

'Do you have any news of Hoa?' asked Blake.

Ajahn Kai-Luat took a deep breath and sat forwards. He opened his eyes, looked into the pond and gently rolled his fingers over each other. When he looked Blake in the eye his expression was full of sorrow.

'I am sorry... she has died,' he said softly.

Blake had tried to put Hoa's fate out of his mind. Now he was unexpectedly full of emotion. Remorse, guilt and regret welled up in him. He hadn't known; he had wondered and hoped. For some unfathomable reason the grim reality hit him with the same acuteness as the shot in his thigh. Blake put his head in his hands.

'She started to recover, but there were complications.'

'How long ago?' asked Blake.

'She died over two months ago,' said Ajahn Kai-Luat.

'And you said nothing?'

'I felt it best to wait until you were stronger, until you were ready. And now is the time. Am I wrong?'

Blake sighed heavily. 'No.'

Ajahn Kai-Luat looked at Blake with a deeply penetrating gaze. He put his warm hand over Blake's and gently squeezed it.

'I can tell that you are full of pain,' said Ajahn Kai-Luat. They sat in silence for a moment.

'I'm not used to having strong feelings, but I have been experiencing all kind of emotions that I wasn't even aware I was capable of. It's almost better to feel nothing,' said Blake.

'To feel nothing is to be separated from the deep place of stillness inside you and to be separated from the world. As you become established in your meditation practice you will find the sense of separation lessens, you begin to realise that every other living creature and even inanimate objects are part of the same unconditioned permanent reality.'

Blake considered for a moment.

'I had some sense of that in the jungle,' he said.

'You are a different man from the man you were a few months ago. Your experience in the jungle has changed you.' Ajahn Kai-Luat spoke slowly and he closed his eyes, as if he was finding the words from somewhere deep inside himself. 'Then, you were ruthless and single-minded, driven only to achieve your goal; now you have a deeper knowledge of yourself and greater awareness. Lay people who come to the monastery often think the practices will make them invulnerable to pain. This is a mistake; as you develop you will feel more and with greater intensity, but the effect on your own life will be less; you will recover more quickly and become re-established in the deep place of stillness inside you.'

'Well, for whatever reason, I certainly feel different.'

'With awareness you will know what to do spontaneously: unselfish, good, honest and life-giving actions are done through awareness. See through yourself then you will be able to see through everyone else you meet. Then you will be able to love them,' said Ajahn Kai-Luat.

They sat in silence. Blake noticed a small exotic bird pecking at some seeds under a nearby bush. The vegetation rustled as the bird jumped about.

'You are still very tired and weak,' said Ajahn Kai-Luat. 'Please stay with us for a while in our monastery and regain your health. While you are here, try to build up your power of concentration, mindfulness and meditation to find an inner calmness and quiet your mind. Maybe you would like to do some translations for us, I understand you speak several languages.'

'Yes, I would like to do something for you and the community,' said Blake.

'You must not feel you have to repay any debt,' said Ajahn Kai-Luat.

'You are too generous,' Blake said, 'but I would like to help, just the same.'

'Discuss this with Venerable Vimalo in the library. He will know what we need to have translated and which texts will be suitable for a beginner,' said Ajahn Kai-Luat. 'Oh, and make sure you wear your robes correctly. You are observant and have copied Venerable Sunnido exactly, but he has made a slight mistake and you have copied it. I must remind him about it. I'm surprised the other monks haven't. See how the senior monks wear their robes.'

'Thank you, I will,' said Blake.

They stood up and bowed to each other. Blake went back to his hut and lay on the mattress. The news of Hoa's death affected him in a new way. He discovered he cared about her. Foolish, misguided Hoa. What was this feeling? Love perhaps? For the first time he loved her and she was dead. Had she expected something? Affection maybe? Had he even bothered to notice? Whatever her expectations, he had failed her. Their marriage had been a hollow, empty space. He'd used her for cover and sex. She was a convenience, nothing more than that. Suddenly having feelings for her now at this too-late stage was absurd and out of place. He wanted to remember her face; he could remember the fall of her hair, her figure, her defiant eyes, but her face seemed a smudge. He was supersensitive all of a sudden: grief, sorrow, compassion and affection came in waves. He let the emotions sit, didn't fight them, observed them and practised mindfulness. Eventually they passed.

* * *

'There is a lady who wishes to become your benefactor,' said Sunnido, grinning.

Blake felt like an imposter, that receiving this woman's generosity would be wrong, but he had no choice.

'Who is she?'

'Her name is Pham Thi Hong. She visits once a month from Hue. Her family are in the printing trade and wealthy. She's here and wants to meet you now.'

'Well, I suppose I'd better see her then.'

'You have to meet her in a public place: you are not allowed to be alone with a woman. Remember, do not ask for anything,' whispered Sunnido.

'I know.'

Mrs Hong wore an embroidered cream silk suit and bright red lipstick. Her smile was demure and her bow graceful. She looked Blake up and down, top to toe, without the least embarrassment. Blake knew what this relationship involved. He had watched with interest the strange one-sided conversations the other monks had with their benefactors. Blake bowed and she invited him to sit down next to her on a wooden bench near the hall. It was a thoroughfare, with monks and lay people going about their business.

'And now, would you like some new sandals?' she asked.

'If you like,' said Blake awkwardly.

'You have large feet,' she said, looking at them and frowning, 'I will get the largest I can find. I can see the

275

ones you are wearing are too small and almost worn out.'

'Thank you,' said Blake guardedly.

'Would you like some pencils and pens?'

'Yes,' said Blake and smiled. He really wanted these and had nearly run out. 'This would be very helpful.'

'And some paper?'

'Yes,' said Blake and nodded.

'And some toothpaste perhaps?'

'Yes, please.'

'And a new toothbrush?' she asked, smiling at him.

'If you like.'

'Some nail scissors?' she asked.

'Yes.' This would be a luxury.

'And a razor and shaving cream?'

Blake nodded. Mrs Hong giggled. Blake began to enjoy the experience in a perverse sort of way. They laughed together. She looked at him intently and frowned suddenly.

'You look very thin. Is there any special food you would like?'

'I have everything I need here,' said Blake.

'I think you need building up. I will see what I can get. I may be able to get some coconut candy. Would you like this?'

The thought of coconut candy suddenly sent his taste buds into overdrive. Strange because he was never that keen on sweets, but at that moment he craved it.

'You are very thoughtful,' said Blake.

'I will bring them on my next visit,' she said.

'Thank you,' said Blake.

They stood up and bowed to each other. The woman took a few steps backwards, then turned and joined a group of lay people. Never before had Blake had such a strange conversation. He was acutely aware of his role on the material level as the lowest of the low. Yes, he was truly in poverty, a beggar, and learning the ways of the monk.

Mrs Hong returned after a month with his 'essentials' and an unexpected bonus, deodorant. She had also thoughtfully included some coconut candy. He broke off a small piece and popped it into his mouth. It was deliciously sweet. He chewed it thoughtfully. If he wasn't careful this could become addictive. Blake visited the sink block to try out his new toothbrush and toothpaste. Never before in his life had these simple items taken on such significance.

The toothpaste tube was on the large size and boxed. He looked carefully at the packaging. Each of the four sides had different artwork on it. *Dr White's all-American toothpaste, made in Los Angeles,* he read. He rotated it to see the next panel, which had an enormous toothy grin with accompanying star and glitter logo. He turned the box another 90 degrees. *For that glamorous look,* he read. Blake began to chuckle. And then another 90 degrees; more text appeared: *You too can have that film star smile.* Blake started laughing, and the laugh went on and on, uncontrollably. Another monk noticed, and soon Blake found himself surrounded by a group of monks, who were so small in comparison to him he was looking over the tops of their heads and they seemed like children. They were all intrigued and wanted to join in the joke. Blake was laughing so much he couldn't speak. Ajahn Anaro, the French monk, appeared. Blake handed him the box and he did the translation. The monks laughed out loud. The box was passed from monk to monk and the infectious hilarity passed like a ripple in a pond to the surrounding group. Ajahn Kai-

Luat mentioned the incident with amusement in his discourse on attachment that evening.

* * *

For four mornings each week Blake worked on translations in the library. The humidity had made some of the books warp and mould grew on some of the more fragile specimens. The large hut, raised on stilts, had three desks and chairs and hundreds of scriptures from the world's religions stacked on shelves. Occasionally a copy of *The Washington Post* newspaper would be left behind by a visitor, but it was often three months out of date. Blake read it thoroughly. He took in the whole spectrum of international news, from the relatively trivial to the more directly relevant and consequential. From it, he learned that in November Richard Nixon had been elected President of the United States. And in December the Apollo 8 capsule with three men aboard orbited the moon: the first time any human had set eyes upon the far side. The newspaper was the only thing that kept him in touch with life outside. For now, he felt cocooned, remote from his familiar world, and no longer sure where he belonged, if anywhere.

Blake soon realised that this was a happy, but serious place. As the monks went about their business there were regular greetings, bowing and smiling. He began to recognise Ajahn Kai-Luat's changing moods and expressions. Sometimes he looked burdened with the problems and sufferings of the world, other times full of serenity and equanimity, and at other times would laugh uproariously at the smallest thing. Twice a month, on observance days of the new and full moon, the monks sat up meditating all night. Blake found himself entering

278

a dream state, almost fell over, then jolted himself back upright, at which point he tried to observe the process of falling asleep.

* * *

'Where did you meet Ajahn Kai-Luat? asked Blake.

'When we were both working at a hospital in India; he was a doctor and I was the chief pharmacist.'

'I see,' said Blake.

'I still practise. I have a supply of drugs here and dispense them as monks and villagers become ill,' said Ajahn Anaro.

They had stopped to rest and sat on the ground in a clearing while the other monks continued towards the village. Blake had walked with the others before but this was the first time he had broken silence.

'Where do you get the drugs from?'

'A lay person has been bringing us top-quality medicines from the USA. We are very fortunate,' said Anaro. 'Ajahn Kai-Luat is the spiritual director of several influential and wealthy people, we are not short of supplies. Some months ago I dispensed a very long course of antibiotics Ajahn Kai-Luat needed for somebody and a cocktail of complicated medicines. They must have been very ill. I never did find out who it was for,' he said, and shrugged his shoulders.

Blake said nothing.

'He often uses herbal medicine as well,' he continued, 'he makes some of these himself and has been training Sunnido in the identification of rare herbs. Do you know him, he's very young, sturdily built?'

'Yes, I know him,' said Blake.

'He's Ajahn Kai-Luat's medical apprentice. Very able and reliable.'

'Yes,' said Blake, 'it's almost like a small hospital. I'm surprised you're not swamped.'

'It's only the monks and local villagers we treat. We wouldn't have the resources to help more people than that.'

'Did Ajahn Kai-Luat teach you meditation?'

'Yes, in India. When I met him he was a wandering forest monk. Every morning he came with his alms bowl to the village I was staying in. I was travelling around Gujerat. I planned to go to Tamil Nadu but he was on his way to an ashram and I went with him. Later we both practised meditation with an Indian *Sanyassi* and a Benedictine monk. We are very cosmopolitan here at An Lac. I could have stayed in India but I wanted to be with Ajahn Kai-Luat. When he returned to Vietnam I accompanied him. I never expected to become a Buddhist monk, but over a decade later here I am.'

'I see,' said Blake.

'How did you become a Buddhist monk?'

Blake thought for a moment.

'Like you, I never expected to become a monk,' he said carefully. 'I haven't been practising very long. Maybe you could give me some advice about my meditation.'

'I am very pleased to,' said Anaro.

'Sometimes when I meditate I experience some unusual sensory distortions or hallucinations,' said Blake.

'This is very common. Try not to be distracted; relax and do not strain. If it happens when sitting try to take longer breaths, when walking increase the pace,' said Anaro.

'Thank you, I will try,' said Blake. 'Would you mind giving me other guidance if I need it?'

'Not at all, anything, any time,' he said and grinned enthusiastically.

'Thank you.'

They walked on and Anaro tried to engage Blake in more conversation. Blake said he wanted to be in silence. Anaro nodded; he didn't ask Blake any more questions. As they approached the village they heard children laughing and playing. They came to a set of simple thatched wooden huts arranged in a group around an open courtyard. Along two sides of the courtyard the other monks who had already arrived sat on wooden benches with their bowls in their laps. In the middle of the space two women were stirring a large pot with one handle either side, set over an open fire. Steam poured from the pot and there was a starchy smell of rice. An old man in a conical hat approached Blake and guided him to a vacant spot on one of the benches. He gestured for Blake to sit; Anaro squeezed in beside him. A few minutes later the two women each grabbed one handle of the pot and carried it over to the monks. As they stopped at each monk in turn a small child ladled rice into each bowl. Another child followed behind the first one and put some freshly cut pieces of Chinese broccoli, cucumber and bamboo shoots on top of the portion of rice. Another child handed out chopsticks. When all of the monks had been served, the most senior monk, Ajahn Nyananato, chanted a blessing. After the chant the senior monk began to eat and the others followed. Blake examined his food. The yellow rice was flavoured with some herbs he didn't recognise; there was a peppery smell. Blake gulped down the savoury-tasting rice. The chopsticks clinked and the children sat still, watching. When the monks had been served the villagers filled their own plates with the remaining food. All too soon Blake's bowl was completely empty. It was time to join the others on the walk back to the monastery.

Anaro's guidance seemed to work. Blake was no longer bothered by the strange experiences. Anaro taught him some other techniques. Some were to do with breathing, some with feeling the vibrations of the body and some with the body's energy centres. Blake was curious, sceptical but open-minded at the same time. This austere, disciplined life did seem to have some benefits, and Ajahn Kai-Luat was an inspiring teacher.

CHAPTER 25

Blake was sweeping the path. Nothing else. He wasn't daydreaming, dwelling on the past or planning the future. Just sweeping the path. He couldn't have told anyone how long he had been doing it for or how much there was left to do. He saw only his broom, the path in front of him and the dirt. Nothing else existed. When Blake saw feet appear in his field of view on the path in front of the broom he raised his eyes. Standing before him was a novice, dressed in white robes. Blake stopped sweeping. He looked into the novice's face.

'I am sorry to interrupt you, Venerable Annando. You have a visitor.'

'Is it Mrs Hong?' said Blake.

'No. It is a man and he has come a long way to see you, in private.'

Blake took a deep breath.

'Did he tell you his name?'

'No. He just said he's a friend.'

'Where is he?'

'He's by the carp pond.'

'Thank you. I will go to him.'

The novice bowed to Blake and walked away. Blake propped the broom against a post at the side of the path, ready for him to finish sweeping later. As he walked towards the pond he noticed his heart rate speeding up. He could just see the back of the man's head through the bushes. Blake instinctively reached for the non-existent Browning in his non-existent pocket. There could be only one genuine visitor; anybody else would surely be here simply to finish him off. A moment later a surge of relief overwhelmed him; he saw that it was Khien whose head was bent forward as he watched the fat carp swim lethargically round and round. Khien's face brightened when he saw Blake; he got up and embraced him. He had lost weight, his pot belly gone and his face was pale and drawn. His green shirt was tucked into his black trousers; both were dirty and smelt of stale sweat.

'I'm so pleased to see you, my son,' said Khien. 'About two months ago Ajahn Kai-Luat told me you were here. He said you had been shot and you were being cared for in a "place of safety". He told me to expect the worst. He didn't think you would survive.'

'Nor did I,' said Blake.

'Ajahn Kai-Luat has offered you his hospitality while you recover. And so,' he said proudly. Loosening the embrace, backing away a step and looking Blake up and down, 'now you live like a monk.'

'I do, a humbling and novel experience. I never in my wildest dreams imagined I would appear as I do or live like this,' said Blake with a chuckle.

They sat down on the bench.

'But... do not take offence, but you have lost your strength, you are thin and weak. It will take you months to recover, surely?' said Khien, his expression full of concern.

'Not that long, I'm sure. There's good food, I have rest and medicines on tap.'

'I don't think you could be in a better place.'

'But it's not an isolated paradise, of course. The conflict reaches us even here. Did you hear about the VC coming here?'

'Yes, I did,' Khien said and frowned. 'But I understand they haven't returned.'

'No, they haven't, the community carries on as normal,' said Blake.

'The Viet Cong are as numerous and elusive as mosquitoes. South Vietnam swarms with them,' said Khien with weary frustration.

'I know, I read it in *The Washington Post*.'

'It's good that you can get the newspaper, even if it's not very often.'

'It's always out of date, of course, but I'm thankful for it.'

'I have been thinking about your trek through the jungle. How could it have been? You made it here, but how?'

'The last part was very challenging, but as you see I have survived,' said Blake, suddenly feeling upbeat.

'It was meant to be, as Hoa would have said,' said Khien spontaneously. Suddenly tears began to well up in his eyes, as if he was surprised and upset at having mentioned her name. His bottom lip quivered and he began to sob.

'Khien, I'm sorry,' said Blake.

'But you, at least, have survived,' Khien said between sobs. 'I have had a wretched, wretched time.'

'I can see you have. You look thin yourself. Tell me what happened,' said Blake.

Khien regained his composure and shook his head.

'Well, all this happened immediately after you left the hospital, you understand. I saw the lorry disappear into the distance. I turned to the nurse and said, "If you speak of this to anybody it will be the worse for you." Her eyes were full of fear and she nodded, but said nothing. Then we both made our way back upstairs to Hoa's room. I bent over Hoa and the nurse checked the equipment again. I didn't realise that moments later she had left the room, and I never saw her again. I went to find another nurse, but the hospital was very poorly staffed and very busy and I found I was taking over the nursing role myself. Another nurse showed me how to check the equipment and gave me sheets to change the bed. They said they weren't able to give Hoa the medical attention she needed, so the more I could do for her myself, the better. A doctor visited twice a day on his rounds, but apart from that I hardly saw anybody. I lived at the hospital, hardly moving from Hoa's bedside for the next few days. She developed a fever and became delirious, and at different times called out for Ming, for you and for me. It was very, very distressing. I didn't know if she recognised me.' Khien paused for a moment and wiped his eyes. 'I bathed her with cool water to bring down her fever, gave her endless sips of water and changed her sweat-soaked bed linen. After two days of anxious waiting I noticed her fever had broken and she slept peacefully at last, and so did I. I thought the worst was over. Hoa was strong and making a good recovery, they told me. But her wound became infected.'

Khien stopped talking suddenly and sucked in his lips. His eyelids fluttered. 'They tried antibiotics, but they had little effect. Suddenly she developed septicaemia and died within a few hours.' Khien looked at Blake, deep pain in his eyes. 'I was desolate, weeping at her bedside. I hadn't left the hospital, hadn't even told Ming. The doctors sedated me and I fell asleep. Hours later I awoke and found myself in an unfamiliar bed in the hospital. For a moment I thought I had had a nightmare in which Hoa had died. And then I remembered.' Khien wept quietly for a while and then composed himself again. 'The next day I went to my office. Post was piled up behind the doorway, I could hardly open the door. The place looked like a mortuary to me, the shutters closed and papers and files stacked up on desks. I had never felt less like work than I did at that moment. I wandered upstairs to your flat, unlocked the door, although strangely, the key didn't turn easily in the lock. I pushed the door open and was faced with a scene of devastation. Chairs were upturned; tables smashed, every cupboard and drawer was open and the contents spewed over the floor like litter. The bedroom was the same. Some of Hoa's dresses had been torn and were in tatters. This really upset me, the breath caught in my throat, I couldn't stay. I turned and dashed down the stairs, I could hardly see where I was going, my eyes were blinded by tears. Once outside, I stood for a few moments, leant against a wall and took in great gulps of air.

After a while I became calmer and decided to go for a walk to clear my head. I didn't know where, just away from there. As I walked past *Les Croissants* I suddenly stopped dead. There, sitting at a roadside table, sipping coffee and watching your flat, was a man with distinctive red hair. My heart nearly skipped a beat. It was Anderson! I walked on and ducked into a nearby alley beside the café where there were only boarded-up, abandoned buildings. I stood, in a complete quandary wondering what to do then settled down to wait. As I waited my mood settled and I became calmer. I watched dispassionately as the passers-by came into view, crossed the entrance to the alley and then went on their way. Nobody came into the alley itself, it had nothing to offer. I hid in the shadows. After three or four hours, I don't know how long, I had lost track of time, an obvious foreigner appeared with that distinctive red hair. With a speed and strength I didn't know I had, I grabbed him from behind and dragged him into the alley, my hand over his mouth. I swung him round and his head struck the brick wall. Anderson sank to his knees with a low groan, dazed. Blood trickled from a cut on his temple. All the time I had been waiting I had been calm and still, like a cat waiting to spring on a mouse. Now my rage and anger welled up inside me. I was in a frenzy. I picked up a heavy stone from the ground and before Anderson had recovered his senses I brought it down with both hands and began beating him on his head and neck and shoulders. He slumped forwards and slid to the ground. I knelt down and smashed the stone again and again and again. That's for Hoa! That's for John! That's for me! I felt nausea rising in my throat, I dropped the stone and staggered to my feet. I had no idea whether Anderson was dead or alive and at that moment I didn't care. I just knew I'd put him out of action. I went to the other end of the alley and forced my way through a wooden fence enclosing an abandoned shop. The whole of my body was shaking. I hardly know how I made my way home... afterwards I felt that justice had been done... you see I am a very poor Buddhist.' Khien's voice trailed off. As if in physical pain, his brows contracted, his lips compressed and his eyes were feverish. Then he burst into tears again and sobbed uncontrollably for a few minutes.

'I am very, very sorry,' said Blake, feeling intense pity for Khien.

'I thought you would be pleased I have put Anderson out of action,' said Khien.

Blake wasn't. For some reason he found himself recoiling from the brutality of it. He was silent, deep in thought. After a while he turned and caught Khien's eye.

'Son, you are looking at me in the same way Ajahn Kai-Luat does, full of pity and compassion. What are you thinking?' asked Khien.

'I am very, very sorry,' repeated Blake. 'There is no victory, only suffering.'

Khien looked at Blake with a strange and sudden interest and studied him closely.

'My son, your face looks different. No, not the fact that you have no hair, your expression... you've changed, you're more... how can I say... receptive, more aware. You have been here only a few months living in community with Ajahn Kai-Luat and you have already changed,' said Khien.

'Maybe I have changed, just a bit... but it was the trek through the jungle that changed me, my own insights, not Ajahn Kai-Luat,' said Blake.

There was a moment's pause.

'Is it possible to live with Ajahn Kai-Luat and not be affected?' Khien asked rhetorically, and studied Blake curiously. Blake was silent. 'What are your plans now?'

'To stay here for a while. I'm making myself useful doing some translations for the monastery. There's a lot to do. I'll wait until I'm stronger, then I'll see. I've no immediate plans to move on.'

'The operation you were involved in has been shut down.'

'Has it? Do you know why?'

'They questioned me as to your whereabouts, but all I could tell them was that I last saw you escaping on the back of a lorry and I had heard nothing since. Apparently they decided you were probably dead, as you didn't return. It was becoming too risky, you and Coulter both killed, so they wound the whole thing up.

Do you want me to let them know that you're still alive?'

Blake took a deep breath and thought for a moment.

'No, let John Miller rest in peace.'

Khien sighed. 'Maybe that is wise.'

'And yourself?' asked Blake.

'We're still recovering,' said Khien with resignation and pain. 'Ming and the children returned about a month ago. She was devastated. The worse thing for her was that I hadn't told her. She can't forgive me for that. I am trying very hard to be the best husband I can for her; hopefully in time... And I'm concentrating on the business, keeping myself busy. We are thinking of moving to Lang Doc island. It's quieter and more peaceful there, for now at least, and the memories are too painful at the moment for Ming. We'll see... '

They stood up and spontaneously embraced.

'I am pleased to see you and sorry about your ordeal,' said Blake. 'I wish you and your family the very best.'

'Thank you, my son, and the same to you.'

'When will you come here again?'

'Maybe three months' time or so, I need to spend as much time as possible with Ming.'

'Of course,' said Blake. 'When are you leaving?'

'Later today. I want to see Ajahn Kai-Luat first.'

'Have a safe journey,' said Blake.

Blake returned to his hut and lay down on the bed. He felt completely drained. He hardly moved for the rest of the day.

* * *

290

Blake continued with his translations. It was not uncommon for visitors to stay for a few days, often on retreat. Inevitably they were a source of rumours and gossip. For reliable reports about the wider world, international events, Blake relied on what he read in *The Washington Post*. In one edition he saw that a rumour he had heard some weeks earlier was confirmed: in October 1968 US President Nixon had stopped all bombing and shelling of North Vietnam, and peace talks to end the war were taking place in Paris. Blake also read of the death of former President Eisenhower, in March of 1969.

On clear nights Blake often used the sight of the moon as a focus for his meditation. One September he learnt that the rumour had been true: man had stepped foot on another celestial body. While he had been gazing at the moon in July 1969, Armstrong and Aldrin had been bravely exploring a new world.

Reading in December 1969 about the My Lai massacre from 1968 he found dispiriting. He noticed that in April 1970 Captain Medina was charged with war crimes committed at that time. Blake was disappointed but not surprised that Medina was acquitted. However, Lt William Calley was convicted of murder and given a life sentence in March 1971. He was the only person to be convicted for the crimes committed at My Lai.

As the months slowly passed, mainly uneventfully, he began to teach himself Pali and Sanskrit and translated in these languages as well. He gave *Dharma* discourses in the evening to the *Sangha* and lay people; he pored diligently over the texts, trying to convey the meaning of the scriptures as succinctly as possible. The audience liked them. As time went by he no longer needed to study or use a script. Like the other more senior monks, he was able to give discourses spontaneously from his own experiences and realisations.

Despite the routines of the monastery, it wasn't possible for anyone to forget they were living in a country at war. There were frequent reminders. A monk wandering in the jungle didn't return; monks were sent out to scour the area for him. They found him and carried him home. His leg had been caught in a Viet Cong booby-trap; it took months before he was able to walk again. Every couple of months a VIP with military escort came for spiritual direction from Ajahn Kai-Luat. The community seemed tense during these visits. Two American GIs made weekend visits; one spoke good Vietnamese. More and more American items began appearing. Lay people brought in top-quality American steel for repairing the kitchen roof. Blake suspected it was meant for the American military warehouses of South Vietnam but had somehow found its way on to the local black market.

After three years of living in the monastery, Blake found his position of seniority had increased. As new monks joined, his position in the meditation hall changed and he sat nearer to Ajahn Kai-Luat. Some of the young monks were deferential towards him. Blake had settled comfortably in hut 45 and the routine was familiar. Apart from the usual small conflicts, which arise as an inevitable part of community living, he felt at home. After months of personal search and deliberation he'd made a decision. He was brimming with confidence and optimism and it was in this upbeat mood that he decided to make his wishes known to Ajahn Kai-Luat.

CHAPTER 26

June 1971

'You have made good progress. Your translations have been well received,' said Ajahn Kai-Luat. 'I encourage all monks to study texts from the different religious traditions. When guided to read the scriptures in the proper historical context and in an open, receptive way they will be able to discern the same mystery, the same unconditioned permanent reality, Tao, Brahman, Godhead, Yahweh, God by many names, described within the scriptures. But to do this takes a special kind of approach.'

'You need to read the scriptures as metaphor,' said Blake.

'Exactly,' said Ajahn Kai-Luat, and gave Blake a searching look. 'You have a finely-tuned understanding, as I always thought you would. I recognised early on your potential to achieve high states of awareness although you didn't know it yourself then.'

'You did?' said Blake, surprised.

Ajahn Kai-Luat smiled wryly at him. 'And our many conversations over the years have confirmed this. It takes some of my monks several years to reach the understanding and realisations you already have. The young monks have also enjoyed your evening discourses on impermanence, mindfulness and the four noble truths, which resonate with wisdom,' said Ajahn Kai-Luat.

'I'm pleased to hear it,' said Blake.

Blake was used to meeting Ajahn Kai-Luat at the carp pond. The colourful orchids were mature and abundant. The carp in the pond seemed lazier than usual, dozing under the water lilies. Blake gazed idly at them. Ajahn Kai-Luat was silent for a while with a thoughtful and serious expression.

'Judging by your bearing and countenance, some of the monks think you have achieved profound states of equanimity. You spend much of your time in silence,' said Ajahn Kai-Luat.

'There have been moments when I have experienced a kind of stillness and peace beyond anything I understand,' said Blake.

'You have practised well,' said Ajahn Kai-Luat, 'but you know stillness and peace, as you describe them, are not definitive indicators of our progress.'

'How do you judge progress, if there is such a thing?'

'It is difficult to know if we are making progress or not,' said Ajahn Kai-Luat, and was silent for a few moments. 'It is often when we return to the secular life, even if just for a few days, that we realise that experiences, like stillness and peace were temporary, arising because of an environment conducive to these, such as here, in the monastery. It is only when we are established in our practice that we are able to return quickly to that place of equanimity, whatever our situation.'

'I realise that the way I lived my life before was as a shadow, I was only half-alive, blinkered to the reality around me by my own fixed concepts, my own sense of self-importance.'

'Ah yes,' said Ajahn Kai-Luat.

'Now I feel more alert and awake than I ever have,' said Blake.

'The experience of *Nirvana*, as the Hindu scriptures would describe it, will come slowly and steadily,' said

Ajahn Kai-Luat. 'Spiritual progress can be measured by what we have lost, noticing what is not there anymore. The truth is inside you. In order to find it you have to put away your books and plunge into your own depths; ultimately you have to give up all doctrine. It is when we have lost the sense of control of our individuality that we discover its greatest dimensions,' he said, and raised his arms in the air. 'I am whole when I am completely demolished,' he exclaimed exuberantly. 'So while our intelligence considers options, our being is immersed in choice-less awareness and we respond out of total oneness with reality. Wherever we are, we are always at home. Our progress is subtle and noticeable in our thoughts, speech, and serenity arising from the greatest depths. The unconditioned permanent reality is pure consciousness; it is completely beyond the mind and intellect... but we can experience it.' Ajahn Kai-Luat spoke passionately. 'I know you understand this.'

'Yes, I do,' said Blake.

'Wisdom arises from awareness and mindfulness of the present moment. This is why mindfulness is so important. You can only find *Nirvana* right now. Not in reminiscing about the past or in fantasising about the future. This is the great paradox. The change comes slowly, but it can only be experienced right now. Only this moment is real. You can spend a lifetime exploring this.'

They sat in silence for a moment. Ajahn Kai-Luat looked at Blake.

'You have a question for me, brother?' he asked.

'Yes. I have lived here in the monastery for three years now, and I have come to ask to stay here, to take on the precepts and become a fully-ordained monk. As far as the *Sangha* knows I am already an ordained

295

monk, so I would ask you to do this privately for me. I know there was always the expectation that my stay would only be short-term, but this is what I want to do.'

Ajahn Kai-Luat rocked back in his chair and laughed heartily. Just as quickly, his expression became solemn and he was silent for a moment.

'You didn't arrive at the monastery through the traditional route. It was by necessity, not choice, that you came here. Is this what you truly want? I am not doubting your spiritual intention or your progress, but has living in the monastery become too comfortable? We must always guard against complacency,' said Ajahn Kai-Luat.

'I have no wish for a secular life,' said Blake.

'If you were to return to your Western lifestyle the stillness and peace you have experienced here might drop away. In the secular world, where your senses are tempted by all kinds of attractions, status and material wealth, the equanimity you have found here may seem but a distant memory. You may begin to question whether you really want the monastic life at all. The spiritual journey is almost never straightforward.'

'I don't think that would be the case,' Blake answered confidently. 'In fact, you have said yourself, "a bird freed from its cage does not return for the remnants at the bottom of the cage". When we have the freedom of knowing our life is a spiritual journey we won't return to what gave us pleasure when we were living in a cage.'

Ajahn Kai-Luat chuckled. 'You have a sharp insight, and have made your point, but... my dear, dear brother, I hear what you are saying and I feel it in my heart. In my humble opinion it would be best for you to resume your life in the West for a while, then you would be sure. And if you return, you will know what it is that you no longer need or desire.'

'I do not need to test this, I already know it,' said Blake decisively.

'Not until you try, then you will know for sure,' said Ajahn Kai-Luat with equal conviction.

'So just as I decide to stay I need to leave?'

'As I said, the spiritual path is almost never straightforward. Think about this. It's your decision, but I believe this would be for the best. And if you leave do this soon, before you become too comfortable with stillness and peace.' Ajahn Kai-Luat regarded Blake attentively. 'You look disappointed, my brother,' he said.

'This isn't what I was expecting,' said Blake, feeling disconcerted, all his plans undone.

'Contemplate what I have said and we will meet again.'

Blake took a deep breath, and sat back on the bench. 'I will give it some thought,' he said.

Blake bowed to Ajahn Kai-Luat. He wandered back to his comfortable, familiar hut and meditated for a while. Then he contemplated life back in the West and all the complexity. He was a different man, he'd changed, he didn't recognise his old self and he didn't feel ready to resume a secular life. But he realised that he had become comfortable. The disciplines of the monastery had lost their vitality as spiritual practices. They had become comfortable, comfortable like a familiar chair, safe and certain and reliable. He took a few days in slow preparation. It was common for monks to robe and disrobe and none of them seemed surprised that he was to leave. Ajahn Kai-Luat often suggested that his monks leave, some to resume their lives as lay people, some to other monasteries and some to wander in the forest from village to village, to survive only with their robes, bowls and water bottles. The guidance he gave to each monk was individual. The monk in charge of the laypersons' retreat centre looked hard to find clothes big enough to fit Blake. The best fit were a pair of faded and tattered stone-coloured trousers and a white shirt. The trousers reached just below his knees and the shirt could only be done up with one button, the sleeves reaching midway between his elbow and wrist. The monk apologised profusely that these garments were all he could offer. With no large mirrors, Blake couldn't imagine what he looked like. A novice monk handed Blake a small amount of money. He accepted a lift with some visitors who were returning to Nha Trang and on the day of his departure Sunnido walked with him to the car.

'I will miss your companionship,' said Sunnido, his eyes welling with tears. They hugged each other warmly.

'Thank you for all you have done for me,' said Blake, and for a moment he felt the sorrow of parting, but he was ready for Saigon and whatever else lay ahead.

CHAPTER 27

Blake sat back. He sank into the soft but unbearably hot leather upholstery of the car. The leather hissed under his weight as the seat was compressed. He could feel the heat radiating like hot cinders through the back of his clothes. Within a short time they were saturated, wet through with sweat, and stuck to the seat. He shifted his position; it didn't help. As he bent forward his clothes sucked away from the leather, and when he sat back, they stuck again. He was seated in the back, next to one of the visitors, a short, squat woman with bad breath. Her name was Ly; the driver was her brother Dhan. His wife Kim occupied the front passenger seat. All three were excited. As soon as the car set off they talked about what they had experienced during their three-day stay at the monastery. It didn't take Blake long to realise just how important the silence and contemplative nature of monastic life was to him. Ly tried to draw him into the animated discussions she was having with her brother and sister-in-law, asking him about the customs and practices that she had seen for the first time. Blake did his best to discourage this by replying in monosyllables. They were obviously fascinated by Blake's presence, and only the almost inviolable Oriental politeness kept them from pestering him with questions about how and why he was leaving to return to a secular life.

After several hours they stopped at a small village and bought some *bahn mi*, pork sandwiches with pickled vegetables, at a roadside shack. His companions insisted on paying for all the food, and as he had very little money he accepted. Blake noticed that while they were eating they couldn't jabber as much, allowing him some respite from the constant chatter. Gradually some of the peace and stillness he was so used to, began to return. Having fed well, when they set off again the atmosphere in the car was more subdued, much to Blake's relief. Ly went to sleep and after a while began to snore loudly. Her head lolled towards him, tilted upwards and came to rest on his shoulder. With her mouth open her bad breath was literally in his face, loathsome and repulsive. He tried hard to be mindful.

They arrived at Nha Trang village and Blake clambered out. He could breathe fresh air at last. Thanking them for the lift, he told them politely how much he had enjoyed their company and the journey. He went to the ticket office and purchased a ticket for the bus journey to Saigon including overnight stay in a hostel at Bao Loc. The official explained that the journey would be very slow; the roads were in poor condition and it was too dangerous to travel at night with Viet Cong everywhere. The first part of the journey was three hours, tomorrow another four. He boarded the bus along with a frail, elderly woman with a stick, wearing a shapeless black dress. Her grey hair was gathered into a small tight bun. There was also a mother with her son. The elderly woman seemed oblivious to his odd appearance, but the mother looked him up and down inquisitively. Her son was about eight years old; he kept turning around to look at Blake, who was in the seat directly behind.

'What happened to your hair?' the small boy asked.

'I'm very sorry,' said the mother to Blake. To her son she said, 'You mustn't ask such questions. It's very impolite.'

'I don't mind,' said Blake. 'I've been a monk at An Lac for the past three years and we all have shaved heads.'

'Where are your robes?'

'I'm not a monk anymore.'

'Why not?'

'That's difficult to explain.'

'I am so very sorry,' said the mother, 'sometimes he has no manners at all.'

'I don't mind,' said Blake.

'No, he must learn to respect his elders, and especially monks.'

Blake had nothing more to say. He stared out of the window as the bus lurched along the road, grinding its way towards Bao Loc. The driver switched on the radio and out blared the latest, at least Blake assumed they were the latest, Western pop songs. The noise was unpleasantly loud and scratchy with a rapid and regular booming bass beat. Within a few minutes the old lady got up and gingerly made her way towards the front of the bus, clinging on to the back of the seats to keep her balance. Once at the front she spoke to the driver. As she made her way back she muttered under her breath and frowned.

'What did he say?' asked the young mother as the old woman struggled back to her seat.

'He says it's his bus, he's in charge and he'll play music if he wants to.'

'How rude,' said the mother.

'He has the manners of a pig and smells worse than one too,' said the old woman, angrily.

'Did he say anything else?'

'He said he'll turn it down a bit.'

The music was turned down a smidgen, but when they arrived at the next bus stop he turned it up again. A mother with three young children and many other people, some with chickens in cages and goats, crowded into the bus. Unpleasant smells wafted around in the airless, humid atmosphere. Another twenty minutes of jarring noise ensued, pop music overlaid with chicken squawks. The road was rough and they were shoved from side to side as the bus lurched over débris and in and out of potholes. The old lady clung on to the rail in front with both hands, struggling to stay upright. Thankfully the people with the farmyard animals alighted at the next stop, but this didn't help with the grating pop music, which was wearisome and unremitting. The three children were over-excited and began to fret and cry. The old lady made the hazardous journey to the front of the bus for a second time. As she walked back to her seat she looked pale and anguished.

'What did he say?' asked the mother.

'That I should mind my own business and if I didn't like the music I could get off the bus. *Troi oi,*' she said and turned to Blake. 'What do you think?'

'I think it's an appalling racket,' said Blake.

In reality Blake was gritting his teeth and he was suffering. His finely-tuned senses were alert to every vibration, sight, smell and sound. The experience of being on the bus was abrasive, coarse and jarring. His nerves were completely frayed. No chance for contemplation here; this was sensory overload and discord. Thoughts or scraps of thoughts passed through his mind, vague ideas without order or connection. They followed each other in a chaotic way and raced round and round like a tornado. He tried to be as mindful and accepting as possible but was failing miserably. He

302

longed for hut 45; he tried to bring to mind the gentle sounds of the chanting, the running water in the stream, the cries of the wild birds and the sounds of nature that had been the only music he had heard for so long. It didn't work, however, and Blake felt his equanimity and inner peace draining away like sand through his fingers. He wasn't sure how much more he could stand when, suddenly, shortly before dusk, thankfully, the bus pulled in for the night stop. The passengers got off and went into the hostel.

The next morning the bus was quiet for the first fifteen minutes, then the driver turned on the radio. Pop music blared out loudly as before. Blake was dismayed and surprised; this wasn't what he was expecting. Five minutes later one of the front wheels of the bus fell into a pot-hole. They all lurched to one side and at the same time the radio sizzled and the music gave way to random crackles and static. Blake smiled silently to himself. The wire he had loosened on the radio last night had come away at last. The driver emitted a snort of annoyance, gave the radio a couple of heavy thumps, muttered some obscenities under his breath and turned it off in disgust. The two women looked around at each other in pleasure and the old woman caught Blake's eye.

'It's broken!' she exclaimed exuberantly, and grinned.

Blake gave her a subtle wink. She looked at him in astonishment and laughed. They spent the rest of the journey in comparative peace and quiet.

At last they reached the outskirts of Saigon. The noise and bustle of this vibrant Oriental city had been part of its original attraction for Blake. Now it was anathema to him. He longed for the peace and tranquillity of the monastery. Instead there was cacophonous noise everywhere: people shouting in an incoherent medley of voices, the noise of the traffic, the squawks of the wildfowl in the markets, pop music blaring from loudspeakers in the bars and clubs. He looked round. Not much had changed in the last three years. Blake felt his nerves jangling, all vestiges of calm having vanished. Stillness and peace were mere phantoms of the past.

CHAPTER 28

Saigon
June 1971

Blake went straight to Khien's house and then his office. Both were deserted and locked up. Khien had said that he was thinking of moving to Lan Doc Island, at least for a while. It looked like a permanent move. Blake sensed he looked a sight because on the street people were staring at him. He had little of the travelling money left. Without any form of identification he couldn't get money from the bank. Besides, no doubt his account had been made dormant after all this time. Blake decided that John Miller would have to return from the dead at the British Embassy.

When he arrived he was passed from one bewildered and disbelieving official to another and eventually one official told him to wait, the Ambassador would see him in due course. After two hours he was led upstairs to that same intimate Ambassador's office he recognised from over three years ago. Blake walked in and shut the door. It closed with a sharp click. A ceiling electric fan whirred and buzzed far above but produced only slight respite from the overbearing heat and humidity. The youngish, well-dressed and groomed Ambassador didn't look up as Blake entered but continued scrutinising the paperwork on his desk. An oriental wooden carved cabinet stood in a corner. The portrait of the Queen he recognised from three years ago, which used to grace the reception area, gazed down on him from behind the Ambassador's desk. And there was something new. Blake noticed with surprise that on the wall, in a frame, was an MBE, obviously belonging to the self-important man behind the desk. Only someone imbued with more pride than taste would display his awards so blatantly, thought Blake. Despite all efforts to look debonair, the Ambassador's face was red and he was sweating, clearly suffering from the heat. He looked a curious sight. Blake quickly decided that his own goals were most likely to be achieved by adopting a mildly deferential approach.

'Look, I'm a very busy man. I haven't got time to waste. Now what do you want…,' he said in a cut-glass English accent. He raised his eyes and looked at Blake. 'Good God!' he said, after a moment's deliberation, and rocked back in his chair. 'You look like a vagrant!'

His voice was so forceful that the small Union Jack held in a marble ornament on the desk swayed as if in a wind. The Ambassador remained speechless for another full minute while he looked Blake up and down, examining him unceremoniously and minutely. He was wide-eyed and his mouth gaped open. Blake felt like a quirky modern art exhibit that had clearly failed the test and was not to the gentleman's taste.

'Look,' the Ambassador said, composing himself, 'you say your name is John Miller.'

'Yes, sir, it is,' said Blake.

'Nobody here remembers you, although one person remembers hearing of you. We've had a complete change of staff. Nobody wants to stay in Saigon more than a year, you understand. I've been here six months and I've already had enough.'

'Yes, I can understand that.'

'I've had to have a clerk go through the archive's personnel files even to find you. According to these records your last day of work here was 24th April 1968, more than three years ago. The day after your

Vietnamese wife was shot in mysterious circumstances. Efforts were made to find you, but they were all in vain. Am I right so far?'

'Yes, sir, but I had no idea efforts were made to find me.'

The Ambassador studied him quizzically. There was a shrill squeak as his chair swivelled round. He picked up some paperwork and scanned it briefly.

'You worked here as a translator. You speak three languages very well and two others well. You used to hold language lessons here,' said the Ambassador. 'The officials only let you in because you are obviously European. How do I know you are who you say you are?' he said sternly, his brows knitted.

'Would you like me to demonstrate my languages, sir?' asked Blake.

The Ambassador scrutinised him.

'No, that won't be necessary,' he said, 'you've already spoken in perfect French and Vietnamese to my officers downstairs, and obviously now English.'

He looked at Blake and his eyes narrowed. Blake sensed the Ambassador still wasn't convinced that he was John Miller.

'You'll find my fingerprints match the ones on the file.'

'Very well, we'll get them checked.' He rang a bell. There was a knock on the door.

'Enter,' commanded the Ambassador. An official came in. 'Walter, would you check this gentleman's fingerprints against the ones on the file for John Miller?'

'Certainly. Now, sir?'

'Yes, now.'

Walter opened a drawer and removed a black inkpad. Blake rocked his index finger from left to right on the pad and pressed his inked finger on a piece of paper. Walter scrutinised the paper and compared the print with the one from the file.

'Yes, he's definitely John Miller, sir.'

'Thank you, Walter. I'll let you know if there's anything else.'

'Very good, sir.'

Walter left and closed the door behind him. Blake stood in front of the desk. The Ambassador looked at his papers again, then up at Blake.

'On 25th April 1970, exactly two years after you disappeared, you were officially recorded as "missing presumed dead",' he looked at Blake with piercing scrutiny.

'As you can see, I am no ghost,' said Blake calmly.

The Ambassador studied Blake again. He removed a carefully folded white handkerchief from the breast pocket of his jacket and wiped his brow. He refolded it and placed it back in the pocket, ensuring a corner of it was visible.

'Apart from your bizarre appearance, you look fit and well.'

'Yes, I am, sir.'

The Ambassador turned over the last page in the file and read it. He looked up sharply at Blake.

'It says here that you were seconded from a Government Department in London.'

'Yes, Department 25.'

The Ambassador's look was long and thoughtful now.

'Well, in that case I think we may be able to help you after all,' he said. 'Although you don't look much like

the people we normally get from that Department...'
The Ambassador closed the file in front of him and
rocked back in his chair. 'Why aren't you wearing
clothes that fit you?' he asked bluntly.

'These were given to me, I don't have any others.'

'Don't have any others?' the Ambassador repeated in
disbelief.

'No, sir.'

'And why is it necessary for you to shave your head
and eyebrows? It looks most peculiar.'

'With respect, sir, my appearance is of no
consequence to you,' said Blake, remaining calm and
composed.

'Then what do you want from me?' the Ambassador
asked irritably.

'I need papers, sir.'

'Papers?'

'Yes, ID.'

'No papers, no ID? Where are your papers?'

'Lost, sir.'

'Lost!'

The Ambassador looked at him incredulously. 'How
much money do you have?' he asked.

Blake felt in his pockets, pulled out a few coins and
counted them.

'Three dollars, sir.'

'Three dollars! Is that all?'

'Yes, I have a bank account but I have no ID. So I
can't access it,' said Blake. 'All I have are the clothes I
stand up in and three dollars.'

'All you have are the clothes you stand up in and
three dollars,' the Ambassador repeated in
astonishment. 'This is the most irregular... the most

extraordinary thing I've ever heard! Where are you staying?'

'Nowhere, sir.'

'Nowhere! Where have you come from?'

'I arrived today from the Central Highlands.'

'The Central Highlands?' the Ambassador repeated, now more thoughtfully.

'Yes, sir.'

'Good God!' he said under his breath, perplexed and completely at a loss. 'How have you been living?'

'Undercover, sir,' said Blake, quietly.

'And why have you hidden yourself all these years? Not told anyone you're still alive?'

'I'm sorry, sir, but I'm not at liberty to divulge that. I know it's awkward for you, but I can only report to the Department.'

'Yes, damned awkward.'

The Ambassador gave Blake a long, hard stare. He walked over to the cabinet, opened it and poured himself a whisky from a crystal decanter. He swished the whisky around in the glass for a while, looking at it, gulped it down in one and placed the glass back on the cabinet.

'Well,' he said at last. He put his hand in his pocket and pulled out some twenty-dollar notes. He counted five. 'Here, take this,' he said, 'and buy yourself some clothes.'

'Thank you, sir, but I would prefer to use my own money once I have access to my bank account.'

'Yes, yes. But that may take a while,' the Ambassador said impatiently.

'I will take the money only on loan,' said Blake.

'Just as you like,' said the Ambassador and handed Blake the notes. 'There's a very good tailor I can recommend on the Tu Do Street called Pierre Beaucamp. The shop name is easy to find. He can knock up a suit for you in no time. I recommend the Thai silk... very good quality.'

The Ambassador rang the bell and Walter came in.

'Book Mr Miller into the Hotel Continental for tonight and, well, until I instruct otherwise,' he said, 'expenses on account.'

'Yes, sir,' said Walter, looking surprised. He left and closed the door behind him.

'Well, as you're officially dead, until we get this sorted you'd better charge what you need to expenses. Make sure you get receipts for everything and pass them on to Mr Yeo, the Treasurer's administrator.'

'Yes, sir, you've been very helpful.'

'Well, I'm going to have to contact London, let them know you've turned up. Glad you're alive, but all this is a bally nuisance.'

'Thank you, sir,' said Blake. 'And I would appreciate your discretion in this matter.'

'Very well,' said the Ambassador, his mood now more relaxed. 'I will be in touch when I have made the necessary contacts.'

It was a humiliating experience but he had achieved his objective. As Blake turned to leave he noticed the Ambassador at the cabinet, pouring himself another drink. Blake walked into a nearby men's clothes shop and bought himself some casual clothes off the peg.

'Go on, tell me the rest,' urged Cathy.

CHAPTER 29

Little Goat Cay
November 1979

'Coming back from the dead in Saigon caused quite a stir,' said Blake.

'I bet.'

'The Ambassador sent a communication to London and they sent two men over who interrogated me for three days. I felt as if I was on trial, I was flitting between being in an agitated state and a supersensitive, perceptive one, and sometimes experiencing both at the same time. It was gruelling and exhausting. One of the men told me he thought my disguising myself as a Buddhist monk was a shrewd way of avoiding detection,' mused Blake.

'And you still meditate now?' asked Cathy.

'Yes, it's something I never stopped doing,' said Blake.

'Carry on,' said Cathy. She was listening intently to every word and at that moment repressing the fact that in the past he had been a ruthless, cold and calculating assassin. She saw only her courageous, capable, decisive, single-minded, generous and sensitive lover. She curled her arms around him and laid her cheek on the dark hairs of his chest. The seawater lapped around the speedboat and rocked it slowly and lightly from side to side as it drifted on soft currents. The sun was dipping in the sky. They could just see Little Goat Cay on the horizon.

'They told me they wanted to redeploy me in Burma. There was some rogue dignitary on their target list, but I protested that I'd been living as a monk in a Buddhist monastery for the last three years and couldn't kill anymore. Then they tried to give me a job as an agent with no assassination agenda. They told me I was a valuable Government asset and wanted me to contribute to the war effort; there was still work to do in Vietnam. But I had seen how the Americans and the South Vietnamese operated: I wanted no part of that whole mess. In fact I didn't want to do any work for them anywhere. Not anymore, I insisted on resigning. They put up a fight and reminded me of my contract of employment; I held my ground. It took weeks before they realised I was a lost cause. I spent two months at a cheap hotel while the wheels of bureaucracy turned then finally got access to my bank account. If someone dies in service their estate gets a substantial lump sum. My brothers had got their hands on mine, but luckily they gave me the money when I resurfaced. I thought that MI6 might try to claw it back since I was alive after all, but they decided to let sleeping dogs lie. They even agreed to pay my airfare back to England. I rented a room with my brother George and did nothing for a while, then got a job as a van driver. I wasn't up to doing anything much.'

'How long did you do nothing for?' said Cathy.

Blake thought for a while.

'About a month, I think.'

'How long were you a van driver for?'

'About three months.'

'What then?'

'Well, I got bored with the driving and decided to do something useful with my life. So I got a job at the Institute of Developing Technologies.'

'Is that the same as the Centre for Alternative Technology?'

313

'No – no connection with them at all. Anyway, the Institute had a number of projects on the go. One was making solar ovens out of aluminium foil for the third world. It was quite interesting. Good work in theory. So I did field trips to Ethiopia and Somalia and Uttar Pradesh in India. For a while it went well, then after about six months the money suddenly dried up and we were recalled to Wales to do more fundraising. I knew something suspicious was going on because I'd seen the accounts only a month before in Wales and there was plenty of money, so I decided to find out. When I got back to the office I spent three months collecting evidence on the staff and discovered that 60% of the charity donations went into the pockets of the directors and only 40% where it was needed.'

'Disgraceful.'

'I was just about to confront the Managing Director when I discovered that he was embezzling money as well. It was fraud. They had some trusts and off-shore accounts, unknown to the Inland Revenue and were filtering money into their own accounts. Anyway, I did confront him, we had an argument and I resigned in disgust.

'Did you inform the Inland Revenue about the fraud?'

'I informed the authorities: I don't know if they investigated, no-one ever called me for interview. I sometimes gave money to selected charities until I discovered how corrupt a lot of the people in them are. One of them was the Leptis Trust. You may remember, back in 1975 I think it was, that the Treasurer was given a prison sentence for embezzling two to three million from their bank account.'

'Yes, I remember that. Go on.'

'I was disillusioned; I decided to go back into research. I went to Cambridge and became a Research Assistant. I had a chance to do a PhD in theoretical physics but got offered this job with BCS through the University so I took it. And what do I find, just more profiteering: the research efforts are geared towards making money for the company and lining the pockets of the directors rather than advancing the state of human knowledge. It seemed a good decision at the time. You know the rest.' Blake paused for a moment and looked pensively up at the sky. 'It's ironic, it seems even at BCS I can't shake off my role as a spy... you know, picking the lock in Norman's filing cabinet... I don't want to keep doing undercover investigation, I just can't avoid it; it seems my lot to remain a spy even when I'm not on the payroll.' Blake chuckled weakly.

'Did you ever see Khien again?'

'Yes, he comes to London every now and then and we have dinner together. You'd like him.'

'He has a tendency towards violence, doesn't he?' said Cathy uneasily.

'Well, you've heard my history and you like me, don't you?' said Blake mischievously.

Cathy sat up, straddled her legs over his hips and looked down at him.

'Oh God, you always have this way of turning my ideas around and making me question everything. Like I don't know anything for sure anymore.'

'That's the best way to be, not to know anything, to unlearn anything certain you've ever been taught about the way things are, to be open to whatever comes, to live in the moment like the wise Chinaman.'

'Chinaman? Another story?' asked Cathy.

'Do you want to hear it?' asked Blake.

'Well, why not, you're the best teller of naff stories I know,' said Cathy, laughing. 'Yes, I'm all ears.'

'About 200 BC in China an old farmer lived in a small village. He was a simple man of few words, but he had his horse and his son and both were important to him; they helped him with his farm. One day his horse ran away. The elders of the village came to him and commiserated with him: "We are so sorry for you, what bad luck." The man of few words replied, "Is that so." Then some days later the horse returned with six other wild horses. The elders of the village came to him and told him how fortunate they thought he was as he now had seven horses. The farmer looked inquisitively at them and replied, "Is that so." A few days later his son decided to ride one of these wild horses bareback. The horse threw the boy off and he broke his leg in three places. The elders of the village came to him to show their pity. "You are so unlucky. How will your son help you with the farm when he can only walk on crutches? We are so sorry for you, your only son." The farmer replied impassively, "Is that so." A year later soldiers from the High Commission came and rounded up all the men of the village between the ages of 15 and 55 to help build the Great Wall of China. All the women were left alone and all the men were dragged away in chains. All, that is, except the farmer's son, who was not fit to work on the wall. The elders of the village gathered together and decided that the farmer of few words really was a very wise man. They came to him and offered him the chance of being Mayor of the village. The farmer listened carefully to them with a totally composed expression and answered in an almost inaudible whisper, "Is that so."''

Cathy jumped up and stood in the middle of the boat. She moved her weight from one leg to the other, making the boat wobble. She flung her arms in the air with exuberance and shouted:

'I love you, Blake, I love your stories, I love you, I love you!' She threw herself on him and hugged him. He wound his arms around her.

'And I love you,' he whispered tenderly.

They laughed, and were still in high spirits when the boat docked. Joan and Alan were on the pier.

'You've been very scarce the last few days,' said Joan. 'We've missed you; what have you been doing?'

'We've been talking,' said Cathy.

'Talking!' repeated Alan and burst out laughing. 'Ha! Ha! Ha! Now why would you two want to bother to spend time talking in a place like this?'

'Stop your teasing banter, Alan. I'm very pleased to see them both, and if you two wouldn't mind joining us for dinner I'd like your company,' said Joan, 'he's been driving me mad.'

* * *

In the heat of the afternoon Blake dozed next to her on the bed, his breathing deep and slow. Inexplicably, rather than feeling peace and joy at his closeness, love and intimacy, for some reason Cathy suddenly found his presence unbearable. Abruptly she sat up in bed.

'You're too close to me, too overwhelming,' she gasped, trying to suppress the spasm in her voice. 'I can't cope with this.'

Her heart pounded slowly and heavily and her head began to swim. She half expected him to say something to her but he didn't. He got up, got dressed in his T-shirt

317

and shorts and, without looking at her, quietly left the hut, closing the door softly behind him. As soon as he left she flopped back down and breathed deeply. Oh God, I'm not handling this, she thought, a woman isn't supposed to have this kind of relationship with a man, it's suffocating and claustrophobic, not because he's possessive but because it's too close, too deep, too honest!

She heard the roar of the speedboat as it sped away from the jetty. It was only yesterday that he'd finished telling her about his experiences in Vietnam. She'd not spoken to him about it since. She'd listened to him openly and uncritically, as a child listens to a story told by a loving relative. When he'd told her the stories from the Far East he'd told them expressively, enlivening them with the tone and volume of his voice, facial expression, body language, gestures. And he was always light-hearted. Over the days he'd told this completely differently. He expressed it thoughtfully and carefully, taking his time. When he'd touched on painful memories she knew it. It was all too evident in his gestures, his tone of voice, the look in his eyes. Yet he still remained composed, as if there were a comfortable space between his past and his present, as if he'd worked through everything, come to terms with it all. It had been lying dormant in her mind, but suddenly it was almost too powerful to touch. The revelation remained as a contradiction, the vile mixed in with the profound. She found the two irreconcilable. The rational, logical part of her rejected him; he had been, after all, by his own admission, a ruthless assassin, and his use of prostitutes disgusted and sickened her. She visualised it in her imagination and it was too, too horrible. She'd wanted the truth and she'd got it. He'd asked her repeatedly if she wanted him to stop. No, she wanted it as it was. It didn't seem shocking at the time, somehow disconnected from the man she knew and loved. But it felt shocking now. She felt completely out of her depth. She briefly imagined life with a simple, predictable man she could feel cosy and safe with. But no, she'd fallen for this complicated, unpredictable man who would never be satisfied with the superficial. But she wouldn't change him for anybody else. She knew that, not for anything. Never. And nobody else would ever come near. She knew that too. As she lay on the bed she mulled over her thoughts and feelings. She tried to deal with the numerous conflicting emotions welling up from her depths, caught within a turmoil of uncertainty and doubt. She found it difficult to move; her body felt tight and uncomfortable. She lay there on the bed for an indeterminate amount of time: hours and hours. The golden parallelogram the sunlight made on the wooden floor as it came through the patio doors shifted from one side of the room to the other and dulled in intensity as the daylight faded. Gradually the tightness left her and she began to feel unbelievably lonely.

As the sun began to dip in the sky she looked for him on the jetty and in the bar. Now she missed him. Joan and Alan were at a table having supper and the motorboat was gone. There was a strong smell of grilled fish. An enormous, half-eaten barracuda steak covered Alan's plate.

'He went out on the boat hours ago. Run off and left you then, has he?' said Alan. He had a napkin tucked in the collar of his T-shirt. He took another bite of fish off the end of his fork, chewed and licked his lips. 'Had a tiff?'

Cathy saw Joan kick him under the table.

'No, nothing like that,' said Cathy, although she knew it was meant as a joke. 'Blake likes to be on his own for a while now and then.'

'I know how he feels,' said Alan.

Joan glared at him.

'He doesn't need much sleep, does he? Up all night sitting at the end of the jetty,' said Alan.

'No, not much,' said Cathy, distracted; she looked out to sea.

'Sit down and have some food, dear,' said Joan in a motherly tone.

'I'm not hungry.'

'A glass of wine then?' said Joan.

'OK,' said Cathy, and sat. Alan poured her a glass of wine and she sipped it.

'How much longer will he be?' said Alan.

'Not much longer,' said Cathy, scanning the horizon.

'Unless he's stopped off at a bar on one of those other islands and is having a few drinks.'

'Do be serious, Alan' snapped Joan, glaring at him again.

Cathy idly twisted the stem of the glass in her fingers and watched the liquid swirl back and forth. 'Such a lovely view.' She looked out to sea where the sun was rapidly setting and had painted the sky with bright reds and oranges.

'Once you've seen one sunset you've seen them all, I'd say,' said Alan.

Cathy gave him a withering look. She watched the slow, dynamic sunset. Behind her was the sound of someone running. She turned. Kenton came towards her, panting.

'Mr Blake,' said Kenton anxiously. 'He is out on the boat and it is nearly dark. I worry for him!' He stretched

320

his arms out in front of him as if looking for divine guidance.

'I don't know why but I just know he's OK,' said Cathy quietly.

'So do I,' said Joan. 'I have complete confidence in him.'

Cathy heard the boat before she saw it; the reassuring distant rumble of the motor. It was almost dark.

'You see, here he is,' said Joan. 'Come on Alan let's go for a walk.' She grabbed Alan by the arm and pulled him along the jetty towards the shore.

As the boat drew up the water wobbled and splashed against the jetty. Blake moored it and came and stood beside her.

'Mr Blake, you are back!' said Kenton.

'Yes, no problem,' said Blake.

'I worry about you.'

'No need.'

'You are hungry?'

'No, I've got my own food right here. Go home, you're off duty,' said Blake.

'Oh, Mr Blake, many thanks,' said Kenton and scuttled off down the jetty.

'I missed you, I missed you almost as soon as you'd left,' said Cathy.

He looked at her with affection and let out a muted laugh.

'Your basket's nice, where did you get it?' she asked.

'I made it.'

'Made it!'

'Yes, from tree bark and twine. You can learn to be creative in all kinds of ways in the jungle.'

'It looks really professional, good enough to sell in the market.'

'It's not bad.'

'What's in it?'

'Papaya, kiwi fruit, coconut... Brazil nuts... here, I'll cut up some papaya for you, you like this, don't you.'

They sat side by side cross-legged on the jetty. He cut a papaya into strips with his penknife and passed her a piece. The juice dripped onto her legs and the wooden platform.

'Look, Blake,' she said, her voice faltering, 'I'd just like you to know that I've been thinking. Just like my past isn't important, your past isn't either because I love the man you are now, I didn't know that man who worked for MI6. I don't recognise him, he's not you.'

Blake was silent. He stared at his penknife and the papaya.

'Thank you. I'm sorry if I've been overbearing.'

She detected a hint of vulnerability in his voice.

'No, you've just been natural, yourself, it's me, I'm all uptight,' she said suddenly, not knowing why. They sat in silence and continued sharing the over-ripe papaya.

'Look, I'm all covered in fruit juice,' she said, and climbed down the ladder into the sea.

She waded into the sea and splashed water on her legs. He followed her; the sea was warm and he embraced her in the dark.

CHAPTER 30

London
November 1979

Oh no, thought Cathy. She took a deep breath; Rose and Margot strode up and stood each side of her desk. Rose studied her with an intensity that made her prickle.

'So, Norman's just told us. Blake has reinstated you. We thought you were going to be sacked.'

'Sorry to disappoint you if that's what you were hoping,' said Cathy with a chuckle, trying to make light of it, 'it was all a misunderstanding.'

'We're pleased to see you, aren't we, Margot?' said Rose.

'Of course,' said Margot. 'So... what have you been doing while you've been "on suspension?"'

'That's my own business. Look, I'm flattered that you take such an interest in me, but I can't imagine why,' said Cathy, bristling.

'Because Blake has been away at exactly the same time... Funny that,' said Rose.

Cathy felt her cheeks burn.

'Well, what's he like then, Cathy?' Margot said, and a malevolent smile began to creep over her powdered face. 'Norman says he saw you both standing really close in the lab after the fire thing happened, just before he suspended you.'

Cathy gave Margot an annoyed look. 'You have got active imaginations... maybe you've been watching too much *Dallas*. And look, although you obviously haven't, I've got work to do.'

'Cor... that's a very nice necklace you're wearing,' said Rose. Her eyes widened and she leaned over, peering at the string of glittering jewels around Cathy's neck. 'Is it gold? And look... they're not diamonds, are they? Look how they sparkle.'

Cathy twisted the necklace between her fingers. 'Oh no, it's just a bit of junk jewellery I bought from Selfridges. A good imitation, isn't it?'

'I suppose so. Was it expensive?' asked Margot.

'Yes... for junk jewellery,' said Cathy.

'How much?'

'Oh, I can't remember. A few quid.'

'Which department?'

'The jewellery department on the ground floor, but it was some time ago,' lied Cathy.

'I really like that. I'm going to see if I can get one,' said Margot.

There was some noise in the background and Mr Zachary appeared with two strangers.

'Come on Margot, let's get back to work,' said Rose.

They went back to their desks and Cathy breathed a sigh of relief.

* * *

'The office is such a cold, desolate, place, and the girls are so obnoxious... and intrusive.' Cathy sighed and dropped back into her G-plan sofa.

'So they're giving you a hard time,' said Blake. He sat relaxed on the chair opposite, his sockless feet on the footstool.

'It's not easy. I'd really like to tell them what I think of them,' said Cathy.

'You could.'

'No, not yet. Maybe when the time is right.'

324

'Try not to let them bother you.' He looked at her sympathetically. 'But, while we're on the subject, I've been trying to find you some more things to do in the laboratory, then you can spend less time in the office, maybe some work with Roger on the new SERC project... satellite technology.'

'Roger?'

'He's been seconded from engineering. A nice chap.'

'That small, thin guy with dark hair who wears the green tweed jacket?'

'Yes, I'll discuss it with him.'

'I can handle them in the office, Blake, really. They just got me on a bad day. The SERC work with Roger sounds interesting anyway. But if I'm doing that, who will type out all your reports?'

'I'll ask Ann, or else second the work to the typing pool.'

'OK, sounds good.' She took a sip of her tea. 'What work is Norman doing at the moment?'

'Some project work for Dr Shaw on navigation equipment, but he's not handling it very well. Dr Shaw asked me to look at it; it seems fairly straightforward. It's odd... sometimes Norman finds grasping an idea or concept difficult. I didn't hire him myself, but he got a first from Bristol and more than one academic award, or so he keeps telling us. He should have been able to. Sometimes I do wonder.'

'No, he didn't get a first from Bristol, he got a third from Salford,' said Cathy.

Blake looked momentarily stunned and stared at her. He burst out laughing and rocked back in his chair.

'Anyway, I couldn't care less what qualifications he has if he can do the job. It's his scheming dishonesty I can't stand. Why, you're better qualified than him!' said

Blake and laughed uproariously again. 'How do you know?'

'I've seen his Personnel records,' Cathy said awkwardly.

'Have you now... How?'

'I had to go up to Personnel and fill in all these forms when I started. Well, Barbara gave me the forms but told me she had to rush off to the GP, so she asked me to lock all the filing cabinets. So, scandalous though it was, I had a peep.'

'In his Personnel file?'

'Yes,' said Cathy sheepishly.

Blake laughed again.

'I don't know what's more surprising, your audacity or Norman's deceit. Well, I always did have my doubts about him... But that's a good one, well done, MI6 would be proud of you.'

'I've heard Mr Shaw is quite astute, surely Norman won't be able to fool him for that much longer.'

'Dennis Shaw only focuses on results. The balance sheet is all he sees.' Blake was grinning and studying her. 'What is it, you have an odd, evasive expression,' he said.

'I've got another admission to make.' Cathy felt like coming clean at last. She looked sideways at him and bit her lip. 'I looked at yours as well,' she said, 'your reference said your work was "ground-breaking," and "outstanding".'

Blake laughed out loud again. 'I doubt it's that.'

'I think that's a pretty accurate description of your performance in bed.'

They laughed.

'It takes two to tango,' he said and looked at her tenderly.

'I know.' She looked away coyly and took a deep breath. They were silent for a moment while they both sipped their teas. 'You're not very interested in your career at BCS, are you? Loads of potential and not much motivation, that's the sum of it, isn't it?'

He shrugged. 'Something like that, I suppose.'

'Norman's the opposite, loads of motivation and not much potential.'

'Norman's got some good qualities and skills.'

'What do you want to do, Blake?'

Blake took a long, slow swig of his tea.

'Be here now,' he said; his expression was enigmatic.

'I suppose I should know better than to ask you such a stupid question.' She bit her lip, took a deep breath and asked the question that had been brewing for a while. 'I'd like to see your flat in Brandon Wood sometime. You've never invited me. I love you coming here and I don't have to travel to Brandon Wood, but I'd like to see it.'

Blake looked down at the floor for a few moments, avoiding her gaze. 'It's not comfortable,' he said, 'I don't think you'd want to.'

'If it's part of you, of course I'd want to. Surely you don't need to hide things from me?'

Blake looked at her seriously and she immediately knew she'd said the wrong thing.

'Really, it's not comfortable... not like this.' Blake sat forwards in his chair and gulped down the rest of his tea. 'Well, I'd better get on my way. I've got things to do.' He got to his feet, hugged and kissed her and picked up his coat. She followed him to the door. 'I'm going to Frankfurt tomorrow for a couple of days.'

'Will I see you at the weekend?'

'Yes, I'll be back by then.' He smiled, but she sensed there was something ambivalent in his expression. He closed the front door behind him.

* * *

'Sorry to bother you. Could you tell me when you're expecting Blake back in the office? I've got some things I need to discuss with him.'

Cathy was standing at Ann's desk. Ann had her head buried in paperwork and was sifting through it.

'Blake. Oh yes, he phoned in a day or so ago. He's taken some more annual leave.' She looked up. 'Hasn't he told you?'

'No.'

Ann buried her face in her work again.

'He sometimes takes leave on a whim. He doesn't give us any notice, but then we're used to him, you see. He's got some family or friends in the Far East. I expect he's gone there.'

Cathy felt a sharp pain in her chest. Ann was talking to her as if she, Ann, knew him better than Cathy did. Ann was able to roll back the years; she understood his quirky behaviour, his unpredictable but familiar routines.

'How long has he gone for?' she managed to ask, and stifled the crack in her voice.

'Another two weeks, I think.' Ann looked up at her and frowned. 'Are you alright, you suddenly look very pale, are you ill?'

'No, I'm fine.'

'Something urgent, was it? Maybe you can talk to Norman about it.'

'Yes, I will. Thanks.'

She walked back to her desk and sat down. She felt sick in the pit of her stomach. Why, why hadn't he told her? Had she pushed him too far, wanted too much too soon? She was full of doubt and searing pain. A welter of possibilities and scenarios sped through her mind; none relieved her feeling of utter dejection. She went home early, said she was unwell. She poured herself a vodka and put lemonade in it, then made a cup of tea and put both drinks on her bedside table, along with the Cheddar biscuits, still in the packet. She put on her long grey skirt and torn, baggy, green jumper and snuggled down into her bed with the phone nearby; she waited every moment for his call that didn't come. And from deep, deep in her bed she counted the moments to eternity. A desperate emptiness pervaded her. She had never felt so wretched, desolate, lonely, or so abandoned.

CHAPTER 31

Cathy looked up at the block of flats with the name *Conway Place* through the sheet of November rain and her heart pounded. Normally she would not have noticed this solid-looking, two-storey building, but for her, at that moment, it meant everything. A seam in her umbrella had split; a stream of cold droplets slipped down the nape of her neck and made her shiver. Blake had said only a few words on the telephone, said he would explain everything. She crossed the quiet road, arrived at the porch of the building and shook out her umbrella before entering. The foyer was warm and spacious, the décor welcoming. She took a deep breath and climbed the stairs to the first floor, found Flat 6, and rang the bell. He opened the door.

'Cathy, come in,' he said and took her umbrella and coat. An unzipped suitcase was propped up against a wall, the Heathrow sticker still attached.

'When did you get back... and from where?' she asked.

'A few hours ago... from Vietnam,' he said awkwardly.

'Oh.'

'How are you?'

'Pleased to be here with you,' she said.

'And, er... how has it been for you, in the office, since I've been away?'

'OK. Roger and I have been installing some new equipment for developing the satellite prototype.'

'Good... I've been thinking about you, wondering how it was going,' he said quietly. 'I'll show you the flat.'

She looked around. 'Is it 1920s? It seems large and solidly built.'

'1930s. It was built by *Regents and Son*, premier builders of their time. There's no problem with soundproofing or insulation.'

He led her down a high-ceilinged long corridor, which had several doors leading off it, and into the kitchen, which smelt of fresh laundry. A clothes horse was tucked into one corner; she recognised his white shirts drying on hangers. There were clean, minimalist cupboards and empty work surfaces, only a kettle hinted that the kitchen was in use.

'Do you ever cook in here?' she asked.

'I don't eat in the evening when I'm at home; I cook lunch sometimes at the weekends.'

'Never eat in the evening?'

'Not at home. When I'm away and there's an evening meal laid on at a conference, then I do.'

'But we did eat out together, in the evening, when we were away.'

'I was keeping you company, otherwise I wouldn't have.'

'You never said.' She looked at him curiously. 'You don't get hungry?'

'No, I'm used to it,' he said awkwardly.

'How odd. How long have you done this for?'

'A few years now.'

A pair of canvas chairs was tucked underneath a round table; two more were folded up against a wall. A transistor radio was plugged in at the wall, switched off. A window was slightly ajar.

'I rattle around in the flat a bit. There's more space than I need. I bought the flat thinking my brother George was going to be living here with me. I use one of the rooms as an office; here, let me show you.' He led her into the next room.

The desk was smaller than his one at work but the surface was arranged identically, with papers and books laid out in neat piles. Floor to ceiling shelves filled with books covered the length of one wall.

'What work are you doing here?'

'Translations.'

'Oh, yes, of course.'

'Here, come with me,' he said.

He took her hand in his and led her into the next room. The room was large but there was almost nothing in it except a camp bed folded up in one corner with blankets and sheets in a pile nearby.

'When George comes to stay, which isn't often, he uses this room,' he said, 'but apart from that I almost never go in here.' He led her into the next room. 'This is where I sleep.'

Like the other rooms, the walls were bare. A white blind, half-pulled, lay against the window and a duvet was spread on a single mattress on the carpet. Also on the carpet, nearby, was an alarm clock along with a pile of books, newspapers and a desk lamp.

'So this is a three-bedroomed flat?'

'Yes.'

'It looks sparse. You haven't got much furniture.'

'No, I suppose not... I'll show you the main room.'

He led her into a large rectangular room with several tall windows. Four mature, healthy-looking plants in ceramic pots were placed up against the walls on the beige-coloured carpet. A green cushion lay near the doorway; its bright colour stood out against the blank walls. A large candle on a plinth was in the centre of the room. She looked around for some moments in silence, taking it in. The room had a peaceful, quiet and serene atmosphere.

'This is where I meditate,' he said.

She didn't look at him; she looked at the space. They were both silent, standing, for several moments.

'You're right...' she said, after a while, '... it's not comfortable here. The atmosphere is nice but there's nowhere to sit.'

'Come into the kitchen, Cathy,' he said, 'I've got chairs in there... I'll make you a drink, what do you want?'

'Tea will do.'

'I've got no vodka to put in it.'

'Just tea will be fine.'

He pulled out the table and indicated for her to sit on one of the canvas chairs; he filled the kettle and stood with his back to the sink, looking at her.

'You didn't tell me you were going away. Why not? I felt rejected... and desolate. I thought we were going to spend the weekend together.'

Blake took a deep breath.

'I didn't deliberately not tell you. I just couldn't get through on the phone. I flew in from Frankfurt, arrived at Heathrow, tried to phone you several times, but you didn't answer. Then I phoned Ann and told her I was taking another ten day's annual leave... last year's in fact. Three hours later I was on the plane to Vietnam.'

'So you never left the airport?'

'No, my feet hardly touched the ground. I tried to phone you from Ho Chi Min City, but I couldn't make the connection. It's difficult making international calls from there.'

'You could have tried harder,' she said.

Blake made the teas, put the plain white mugs on the table and sat down opposite her. He sighed.

'Yes, you're right. I could have tried harder. I'm sorry, I never meant to hurt you,' he said, 'I'm not used to being accountable to anybody. It doesn't excuse my behaviour... but yes, I should have been more thoughtful.'

'When did you decide to go to Vietnam?'

'When I was in Frankfurt.'

'Why?'

'I needed to take some space... to do some thinking,' he said.

'I see... What did you do in Vietnam?'

'I went to An Lac.'

'What, the same monastery you spent three years in?'

'Yes.'

'Oh,' she said.

They were silent. She took a sip of tea.

'So, it seems to me, looking around, that you've never really stopped living like a monk then...' she mused thoughtfully.

'I have kept up a lot of the practices from An Lac... yes.'

'You certainly never seemed to fit in at BCS, even though Mr Zachary has tried to make you one of them; but you'll never be one of them, will you?'

Blake twisted his mug in his fingers.

'No. Not at BCS. My commitment could never be to status or power or money alone.'

'In fact you have a kind of contempt for wretched money, don't you?'

'Not as a means of exchange, but for the excessive and meaningless pursuit of it and for the gods of consumerism, yes. You know what I mean.'

'Yes, I do… but with me you're extravagant.'

'That's a spontaneous expression of my love for you,' he said, and looked at her affectionately.

She smiled at him.

'Apart from the people bit, you do your job well.'

He sighed and shuffled in his chair.

'I enjoy the conferences but I'm not doing what they want me to do. I even tried to say the right things to the right people in the past, but I don't like being hypocritical. It's a hollow, empty façade.'

'I can't imagine you ever being sycophantic to anybody.'

'That's not what it was; I was just trying to play the game I suppose. That was when I believed in what I was doing. I had an idealistic view that my research would make a difference. BCS does collaborate with other research bodies and universities, but, in reality, only to improve its image.'

'But maybe you could make them see things differently, go for ethical production, change the company from inside, so to speak? Become a director, which Mr Zachary talked about, then you'd have influence.'

'I have encouraged them to fund research into various products with a principled bias over the years. It's an enormous company… and I'd have to toe the line first.'

'You're so capable, Blake, you could do whatever you want. Look what you've achieved through sheer grit, determination and courage. This doesn't sound like you. You sound almost… defeatist.'

'No... it's just realism.'

'I believe that if there was a cause you were passionate about you would do whatever you needed to in order to achieve it.'

'Yes, I would... but not in this context. I'm not saying that things can't change, just that I'm not the right person to do it'.

'You could, but you don't want to.'

'That's right.'

'I didn't know you felt so strongly about it, Blake, so... so... what are you saying then?'

Blake got up from his seat.

'It's getting a bit cold in here, isn't it? It's been unusually warm for November but you notice it getting cool in the evening.' He walked to the other side of the kitchen and closed the window with a thud.

'Blake, tell me!'

Blake swung round.

'That's one of the things I've been thinking about. I wanted to tell you first... I've decided to resign.'

'To resign!' She sat for a few moments immobile in her chair.

He stood with his back against the sink, facing her, his expression intense.

'What else, Blake, there's something else, isn't there, what is it?'

'I'm sorry... there's no easy way of saying this... I'm going to go back and live in Vietnam.'

'Going back to live in Vietnam... why would you want to do that? You nearly died in Vietnam... there's no research in Vietnam!'

He said nothing for a few moments, just looked at her. She couldn't read his expression.

'I'm not going back to Vietnam to do research,' he said quietly.

'What are you going back to Vietnam for then?' Her voice was hoarse.

He took a deep breath.

'I'm going to go and live in An Lac,' he said.

She gasped.

'OK... How long are you going back for?

After a few moments he said, 'Indefinitely.'

'Indefinitely!' she echoed with incredulity, 'you are joking, aren't you?' She studied him. His look was earnest, serious and unwavering. 'Oh God... you're not!' Her heart pounded. 'Surely this is too drastic a step, isn't it?' she said in disbelief. 'Join a university, become an academic, then you can do whatever research you want...'

Blake paced about the kitchen.

'No. This isn't a bolt reaction. I'm not getting away from something I dislike. This is a positive decision. I've got unfinished business in An Lac.'

'Unfinished business... ?' she said, mystified.

'Don't think I haven't thought about you... about us... I have... a lot. This is hard for me... so hard.' His eyes were anguished and his voice trailed off as if talking were painful. 'I love you, Cathy,' he said in a whisper and with deep sincerity, 'you're the only woman I've ever loved. I wasn't capable of love until... until recently. But if I didn't do this now I'd do it later and that wouldn't be fair on you.'

Cathy stood up.

'So where does this leave me then?' she said, 'So... so you come into my life, make me fall wildly in love with you, fuck me, buy me diamonds and then piss off back to your monastery, yet you say you love me! It's like that, is it! You don't make sense, Blake!'

She rushed out of the kitchen, not conscious of where she was going, and ended up in the room with the candle and the houseplants.

He followed her.

'No. It wasn't like that. That was never my intention. I didn't plan it that way. You know that.'

She tried to steady herself, to prop herself up against a wall, but her energy failed her. She slowly dropped to the floor and curled herself up with her arms over her knees.

'Go on then. Tell me. What's your unfinished business?' She looked up at him.

He paced about the room, and looked out of the window. He sighed and stood motionless for a few minutes then paced about again.

'Those last three days in the jungle before I reached the monastery were the turning point for me. I was certain I was going to die and my whole consciousness began to unravel. It's almost impossible to describe... You know when you're a child and you see a tree and the tree is just a tree, and then a teacher comes along and gives it a name... a label. You don't see the tree in the same way again, you see the tree with the name, the label. Well, when my consciousness began to unravel the labels fell away, and there was clarity, a transcendent moment when I knew what was and what wasn't. There weren't any labels anymore, there was only completion, and I wasn't separate anymore. It was me and I was it, and it was perfect. It was a subtle experience of joy, peace, serenity and love, but these were only feelings... The experience itself was beyond feelings, beyond intellect... totally beyond...

indescribable. And then the pain and ravages of my body overwhelmed me again. So when the boy finally found me I was receptive and ripe for contemplation, although I didn't know it at first.'

'How do you know you weren't just going out of your mind?'

'I know, I just know. That was only the beginning. I spent the next three years learning and trying to perfect the practices of mindfulness and contemplation, except that I was always a fraud... I was sent away last time... It wasn't my choice to leave. I need to know if it's the right place for me. I can only find out by going back... going back authentically, taking the precepts and living by them... being a fully ordained monk... this is what I need to do.'

She stared at him for a long time, trying hard to fathom him, but felt only the pain of rejection.

'So you're going to contemplate your navel in the jungle with a whole load of other celibate men, are you?' She almost spat the words out as if they disgusted her. 'It beggars belief! In fact I can't even believe we're having this conversation!' They stared at each other for a few moments, his expression one of profound pain and suffering. 'I'm sorry, I should never have said that... I'm just a selfish, vacant, shallow girl with no appreciation of anything beyond the mundane... I'm ashamed of myself.'

'Rubbish... you're none of these things.'

'Maybe I'm not spiritual enough for you. Maybe I should take up meditation or Buddhism or something.'

'No, I'm not expecting you to adapt or change to suit me. I love you just as you are. It's me...'

'Oh, you really are too good to be true, aren't you, Blake!' she said suddenly. She got up; her eyes welled up with tears. 'You may have cheated death in the jungle, lived as a monk and had spiritual realisations, but your passions are just as intense and raw as mine. Celibate... It's denial and repression you'll be practising!' She heard her voice crack with emotion.

She walked straight up to him, tugged at his trouser belt and tried to yank it off. She fumbled helplessly with the fastening, pulling and tugging with all her might, but it wouldn't yield. He remained immobile, rooted to the spot. Frustrated, she backed slowly away from him, panting and exhausted. She felt a mixture of defiance, anger and anguish. She noticed he was breathing heavily and looking at her with an intense passion, devouring her with his eyes.

'You're just an ordinary man, Blake... just an ordinary man!'

'Cathy,' he said, in a tone that was so sensual and mellow and full of desire that she almost swooned. With a kind of raw determination he walked towards her and grabbed her up in his arms.

'No!' She pushed him away but he found her mouth and kissed her. She pushed and shoved and kicked him but he held her fast. With no fight left passion overwhelmed her; she yielded and melted into him. He lifted and carried her through to his bedroom and they sank onto his mattress on the floor.

The afterglow came on her slowly, by degrees, and rather than diminishing it changed in quality and essence. The sensation of pleasure became warm and comfortable and ethereal, then light and peaceful until she experienced a deep peace unlike anything she recognised. It permeated her whole body and seemed to go on and on. She fell asleep.

When she woke, she went to find him. He was sitting in his meditation posture in the main room. He looked up as she stood in the doorway then came and stood before her. He said nothing, but in his eyes was both searing pain and intense love, together with something indefinable that was unfathomably deep. The veil lifted. She suddenly saw, with devastating clarity, that the man standing in front of her was a mystic. This was what was enigmatic about him. It was what the Sufi at the tomb in Egypt had seen instantly, but what she'd missed until now. Although why she saw it now, and not until now, she didn't know. And she understood everything.

CHAPTER 32

An Lac Monastery, Vietnam
February 1980

Why am I doing this? Cathy asked herself as she alighted from the rickety bus with the horde of other people from Ho Chi Min City. The sun splintered through the green canopy of rattan trees far above. Silent black insects hovered and danced in the humid air and there was a scent of eucalyptus. She waved the hem of her loose linen dress; the air circulated between it and her skin and briefly cooled her down. She covered her shoulders with a white scarf and tied it in the front, aware of the need for modesty. The other people were also dressed discreetly, some colourfully, some in white. As she followed the group of exhausted travellers along a gravel path up the hill the stones crunched under her cork sandals. A monkey squealed in the distance.

They reached an imposing arched wooden gateway. A carving of the Buddha sat at its pinnacle. Everyone poured through. A small monk dressed in saffron robes stood at the entrance; he nodded and smiled sublimely at each person. Inside, hordes of people milled around a large courtyard, some talking in small groups. There was an atmosphere of celebration; the monastery was decorated in paper flags. Exotically painted lanterns hung in neat rows on strings, like Christmas decorations, between buildings. Tiny bells were ringing in the distance and a smell of incense hung in the still air.

Blake had wanted her to come and she'd agreed, although it felt like he was marrying someone else and had invited her to the wedding. She was reluctant, but as

342

the days passed she had felt compelled to come. Maybe it was sheer curiosity or her need for closure. She wanted to accept what he was doing. But the journey had been an ordeal. Somehow she'd found her way through this foreign country and strange culture to his remote monastery without speaking a word of the Vietnamese language. He'd told her she could do it and she had. Knowing a bit of French had helped.

They were escorted into a large hall, which looked a bit like a medieval barn on stilts. Like everyone else, she removed her sandals and put them at the side of a large pile of footwear. Inside it was bright and light, with numerous unglazed openings in the walls where the light flooded in. At the other end several dozen monks, kneeling, their backs to the walls, were lined up in neat rows facing each other. The spectators were ushered in and sat, packed tightly, on the wooden floor near the entrance. She jostled for a space to sit down and squeezed into a tiny gap; someone was so close his knee pressed into her leg.

'*Français ou Anglais?*' said the Oriental man crouched beside her, who stared at her with kindly curiosity.

'*Anglais*,' said Cathy.

The man stood up and swapped places with the Oriental woman sitting on his other side. The woman shifted slowly and gracefully as if she was well practised at moving in such a small space. As she sat down her chiffon scarf brushed Cathy's arm.

'Do you understand the ceremony?' she said. Her voice was very soft. The woman's features were fine and her expression serene. Several delicate bangles around her wrists jingled softly.

'No I don't,' said Cathy.

'Is this your first time here?'

'Yes.'

'I thought so. Would you like me to explain?'

'Yes, that would be helpful.' Chanting began and the audience fell silent. An elderly frail monk knelt, facing everyone, in prime position at the head of the hall.

'That is Ajahn Kai-Luat, the most senior monk, the Abbot,' the woman whispered.

The ceremony began, all in incomprehensible Vietnamese, and then there was a chant.

'This is the introductory chant asking for blessings,' said the woman. 'Soon the novice monks will enter, dressed in white. Six novices are being ordained today.'

'I know one of them,' said Cathy.

'Is that why you're here?'

'Yes.'

The woman nodded.

Six monks entered, dressed in white robes. There were three white men, who looked tall and ungainly in comparison to the Oriental novices. At first she didn't recognise Blake in his white robes and with his head shaved. The change in his appearance shocked her.

'Which one do you know?' whispered the woman.

'The tallest one.'

'The tallest one. That is Venerable Annando, who was here a few years ago. He has returned; this is very good.'

'Really.'

'Venerable Annando was highly regarded. He gave very good discourses.'

'Did he?'

Cathy visualised him teaching. He looked so different from the charismatic Research Manager behind a desk. The six men bowed and took their places in a row in front of Ajahn Kai-Luat while the chanting continued. Each of the novices chanted individually and was given neatly folded saffron robes.

'The novice monks are taking the precepts,' said the woman.

'The precepts?' said Cathy.

'Yes, the rules by which they must live from now on.'

'How many precepts are there?'

'For an ordained monk there are 227.'

'That's a lot.'

'It is a very disciplined life. Discipline leads to freedom,' said the woman.

The novice monks stood up and left the hall. The interval was filled with chants and bell ringing. They returned dressed in the saffron robes and sat next to the other monks.

'The monks have now made their commitment and are full members of the community, the *Sangha*. They have now withdrawn from the outside world,' said the woman.

Cathy looked at Blake, feeling a mixture of awe and love. Although they were in the same room, the gulf between them seemed impenetrably vast. She had the aching realisation that she had lost him forever. Yet the atmosphere in the hall was peaceful and the woman's presence serene. She felt the hardness of bitter resignation soften to a wistful acceptance of the inevitable. He was, after all, doing what he needed and wanted. He had chosen this austere life.

'It is a very beautiful ceremony, isn't it?' said the woman.

'Yes, it is,' said Cathy.

Ajahn Kai-Luat withdrew a brush from a bowl of water and flicked it several times. The droplets of water sparkled as they flew through the air and landed on the monks.

'Now we will all meditate,' said the woman, 'do you know how?'

'No.'

'Close your eyes and concentrate on your breathing. This is the simplest thing to do.'

A gong sounded and the whole hall fell silent. After a few minutes a fly knocked against a wall and began to buzz. It settled and there was silence again. An atmosphere of peace and stillness permeated the hall and Cathy felt herself relax. She had a fleeting experience of a deeper peace; she'd experienced something like it once before. The gong sounded, quietly. Cathy looked around; the woman next to her had opened her eyes and smiled at her benignly.

'So that's the end of the meditation?' said Cathy.

'Yes. That was a beautiful group meditation. This is a very special place,' she said. The gong sounded twice again and people began to stir. 'Now Ajahn Kai-Luat will give a speech.'

He did, and it was long and incomprehensible. The floor was hard and uncomfortable and her back ached. Without warning it all seemed to finish; the monks bowed and filed out followed by the spectators. She collected her sandals.

'Thank you for your explanation, it was helpful,' said Cathy.

'You are very welcome,' said the woman and smiled graciously. 'There is food and drink now in the *sala*, will you join us?'

'Maybe later,' said Cathy.

Unexpectedly, tears welled up in Cathy's eyes and she tried to blink them back. She pushed her way through the crowd and aimlessly followed a trail into a lush, green, tropical garden. Above, woody climbing plants meshed the whole canopy together, trailing from one tree to another. The ground had been cleared at the lower levels; there were a few shrubs and bushes with large flat leaves. She followed the sound of a bubbling stream, which took her along a path to a small clearing. She sat down on a bench, pleased to be alone. A rake was propped up neatly against a tree trunk. A thorny bush nearby had branches covered in resin and threw out a delicate perfume. The atmosphere was meditative and she gazed vacantly at the clear water as it trickled over yellow stones; some were covered in a carpet of bright green moss. For some unfathomable reason she didn't want him to see her. She was full of volatile emotions and it was all too much. She decided to slip away from the monastery unnoticed and returned to the main courtyard. The number of people had thinned out and some headed towards the entrance. A small group of Western monks were talking in French, smiling and laughing. As soon as she recognised Blake her heart pounded. How do you address a monk? She watched him from a distance. He looked completely at ease within the group; she had never seen him look so relaxed with other people before. He was 'home'. She procrastinated for a while, not sure what to do, then turned away, feeling like an impostor.

'Cathy.' She heard her lover's voice from behind her. A monk was calling her. She felt weak at the knees at the sound of his voice; she turned round.

'I've been looking for you.' He walked up to her.

'It's crowded here.'

'I'm pleased you came, you attended the ceremony?'

'Yes, I did.'

He looked at her steadily. 'Are you OK?' He adjusted the saffron robe over his shoulder.

She coughed, clearing her throat.

'I'm OK. You look just right as a monk,' she said suddenly.

'Thank you,' he said. They gazed at each other. The other monks fell silent. They were watching, but discreetly, as if respecting whatever was taking place. But there was no chance for intimacy here.

'I need to catch my bus,' she said. Her voice almost cracked.

She noticed him swallow hard.

'Why don't you stay the night in the women's guest centre, I'm sure they'll find space for you, you must be really tired.' He took a pace towards her. His saffron robes wafted around him.

Him a monk and her a guest, it wasn't something she could even get her head around. The leap was too enormous.

'No, I've got a hotel reservation.'

'The *Hotel Continental*?'

'Yes.'

'I remember it,' he said and smiled.

'Well, then,' she said. She felt her face redden and looked away.

'OK, Cathy.'

He walked up as if to embrace her, then stopped suddenly as if realising his mistake: monks don't touch women.

'I love you,' he whispered.

'And I love you. Always will.' She forced back tears.

As she backed away the group of monks all watched her, their faces radiating serenity and compassion. Blake's radiated love.

Tears gushed into her eyes and her vision blurred. She rushed towards the entrance, desperate to get away. Following the crowd down the hill, she joined a group of people chatting and laughing at the bus stop. She felt completely alone, not lonely, but just like an alien in a strange land. When the rickety bus arrived and the doors opened the people pushed and shoved, jostling for position. Cathy pushed her way into a window seat, but realised she had chosen to sit on the wrong side of the bus. The sun had been beating down on the plastic coating on the seat; the heat was almost unbearable where it came in contact with her linen dress and made her skin burn. The bus was filling up: it was too late to move now. The vibration of the motor went searing through her body, the abrasive noise pounded her ears. It was airless and difficult to breathe. She opened the tiny window at the top and a breeze wafted in, cooling her down slightly. An Oriental man came and sat beside her.

'Excuse the intrusion,' he said in English. The Oriental intonation was strong. 'Your name is Cathy, isn't it?'

Cathy looked at the stranger.

'May I introduce myself?' He smiled warmly at her, 'Khien is my name.'

He held out his hand. After some hesitation Cathy shook the firm, warm hand. She recognised his name and came out in a cold sweat.

'It was easy to pick you out from the crowd; Blake has told me so much about you. I'm sure he was pleased that you came today... you look surprised.'

349

Cathy breathed deeply, clutching the bar in front of her.

'I am… I never thought I'd meet you,' she said after a few moments. 'He's told me a lot about you too.'

'I saw Blake when he was here a few months ago. I knew something was on his mind. He spent so many days in silence.'

'Days in silence?' said Cathy.

'Yes.'

'Why?'

'He had to make a decision. I was always sure he would return to An Lac sometime. He's found it very hard settling in the West. But he'd met you. What was he to do?'

Cathy's heart began to pound. 'A decision?'

'Yes.'

She stared into the distance.

'Something is on your mind?' asked Khien.

'No,' she said and composed herself. 'Well, yes, there is,' she said after a few moments. 'Do many monks leave?'

'Yes, many.'

'And do they sometimes come back?'

'Yes, you can leave and return several times.'

'How many times?'

'Seven times.'

'Seven.'

'Ah, you are thinking about Blake,' he said. 'Only time can tell. He is a deeply spiritual man,' he said thoughtfully and looked into space. 'He wasn't always, but he is now.'

'I know,' said Cathy.

Khien studied her carefully.

'Then you also know he would not have left you for anything else.'

'Yes, I do,' said Cathy. 'Nothing else would have been important enough.'

'But he would not have told you how much pain this caused him.'

Cathy stifled a sob and tears welled up. Khien put his arm around her, withdrew a clean handkerchief from his pocket and gave it to her. She took it and wiped her eyes.

'Thank you.'

'Be certain,' he said. 'Whether he leaves or not he will always love you. His love is drawn from deep inside himself, from the source, as Ajahn Kai-Luat would say.' His face was full of compassion. He put his hand over hers and held it firmly. 'I love him... and now I love you too,' he said with delight and laughed heartily. He took her hand to his lips and kissed it. 'Now you look shocked. It's this English reserve I've been hearing about.' He laughed again. He handed her a business card. 'If you are ever in Vietnam again visit me. I will welcome you as I would my own daughter.'

Cathy took the card. *Khien, Accountant.* The card was small but the writing bold.

'I will bother you no longer. It was a pleasure meeting you.'

He got up and moved to another seat. Cathy breathed deeply. The unexpected meeting was disconcerting, but she'd found Khien genuine and warm and in a strange way felt soothed and reassured. She put her scarf over her head and closed her eyes, not sure she could cope with another conversation.

After half an hour they reached the main road. The ride was smooth and fast. She dozed. It was dark when they arrived at Ho Chi Min City. She was starving hungry and bought some rice noodles from a street vendor and ate them then and there. She made her way to her hotel and headed straight to the bar decorated with black and white tiles. Soothing piano music played in the background and there was a smell of cigarette smoke; as she breathed in she could taste it. A few scantily clad women sat at the bar, a few men loitered. She ordered a long, cold lager.

The barman looked awkwardly at her. 'I think Madam would be more comfortable in the hotel's other bar.'

'No, I want to be here,' said Cathy.

'I think you are making a mistake, Madam,' he said and shook his head.

'It's fine. I only want a drink,' said Cathy, feeling impatient now. 'I'll be sitting over there,' and she pointed to a quiet dark corner, went over and settled herself into it.

An Oriental man sitting on a barstool followed her with his eyes. Moments later he pulled up a chair and sat down opposite her. He smelt of a mixture of eau-de-cologne and whisky; his greased hair was plastered against his scalp. Cathy recoiled. He said something. She shook her head. He spoke again.

'*Je ne comprends pas*,' she said.

He looked her up and down.

'English, you're accent is English' he said, smiling at her, 'and you are, and charming. I have not seen you before.' He plunged his hand deep into his pocket, pulled out some bank notes and waved them in front of her. 'I have a room upstairs.'

Cathy felt every muscle in her body go rigid; she realised her naivety and glared at him. The man's smile metamorphosed into one of agitation. He squirmed in his seat and stood up.

'Go away, little man, I'm not for sale.'

'Well, you're in the wrong bar then.' She could feel the man's hostility radiate like electricity.

He hastily made his way back to the bar. Her lager arrived.

'Thank you for your advice,' she said to the barman.

'You're welcome,' he said without looking at her.

She noticed the man making conversation with a scantily clad Vietnamese girl. Moments later they left the bar together. She felt as if she were in a time warp. She took the lager up to her room, and snuggled down in bed. Vietnam, goddamn country. It was an exotic land full of extremes. This was her direct experience. It had been one of the most challenging days of her life. She had surprised herself. She was more capable and resilient than she had realised. Norman and Mr Zachary, they'd be putty in her fingers. She could handle anything now.

CHAPTER 33

London
March 1980

'Cathy... Cathy,' echoed in her head. She came to with a jolt. Roger was standing at the other side of her desk. 'Are you alright?'

'Yes of course, sorry, I must have been daydreaming.'

It wasn't the first time Roger had caught her staring out of the window. She'd done a lot of it over the last three weeks although he'd tried to engage her in the work. He had been patient. Sometimes she needed an almost superhuman effort just to open the post; when she tried reading the contents there was only a blur.

'I would like you to check something out for me.'

'Yes, what is it?'

'There's a laboratory that's become vacant in the annex. I think it's the one where we used to keep the lasers, but as you know they've moved to laboratory eleven. Will you go and have a look? Find out what's in it, if anything, and how many power sockets there are. We need more space for testing the prototype satellites.'

'OK.' She stood up from behind her desk.

'Here's the key.' He handed it to her. It was heavy and felt cold and smooth. 'If you have any problems finding it ask the caretaker.'

Cathy looked at the key and a cold shiver went through her; it was labelled 12. This was the key to the lab where she had worked with Blake. She put it in her pocket. It rattled against the key chain as she walked along. The tinkling echoed in the corridors of the annex. As she approached door 12 she swallowed hard, remembering when they had stood there together. She put the key in the lock, opened the door and closed it behind her. The room was just as she remembered, except it was now hollow, an empty chasm. All evidence of Blake and their work together was gone. She stood in the space for a long time, looking, taking in the atmosphere. She remembered the special hours they'd spent together, their teamwork, their discoveries, not just about the lasers but about each other. Now the room was empty and sad, a memorial to the past, full of only memories.

Scraps of thoughts and emotions came to her in a random order. She heard a door bang further down the corridor; she heard the echo of distant voices and the sound of people walking away. She stood silently, in the space. She felt the acute emptiness of the absence of him, but she didn't feel rejected or abandoned or used. No, there was something else. She felt empowered. His love had made her strong. It was the job, the place, which was wrong. She left the room, closed the door and locked it behind her.

She returned to her desk. Norman and the girls joked and giggled on the other side of the office. Roger was talking to Mr Zachary. As Norman walked over to her desk she glanced up. He had a twinkle in his eye.

'You've been very quiet the last few weeks since Blake left. Missing him, are you?' Cathy looked at him, but said nothing. 'I think I know how to put a smile back on your face. It just so happens I've got tickets for the Jimmy Tarbuck show for tomorrow night in Piccadilly. How about it, Cathy?'

He winked.

'You're married, aren't you?'

'She's away. A few days with the girls. Come on, Cathy. You know you've always wanted to – you and me.'

Cathy flinched. Something inside her snapped. She stood up.

'You're staggering. Your arrogance is breathtaking. I know more than I wish to about you. Even the sight of you makes me nauseous. You think you can smarm your way around anybody, but you're deluded, you're just a nuisance and a prat. You are the most egocentric, charmless, small-minded, bombastic, sycophantic, deceitful creep that I've ever had the misfortune to come across. And as for your empty-headed, vain and pitiful friends over there who only have time for trivia and gossip, well, you deserve each other.' Cathy's voice gained in strength and volume. Everyone stared at her open-mouthed. 'And you, Mr Zachary, you can stuff your bloody job as well. I'm fed up working in a place where bluffing and sucking up get results and nothing has any real value.'

Cathy grabbed her handbag and her coat. She felt stronger and more purposeful than she ever had.

'Enjoy the theatre, that's all you understand around here anyway, isn't it, things that aren't real.'

Cathy strode out of the office with her head in the air. She felt her heart thump. She'd surprised herself; she'd done something brave and bold and it felt good. There was a skip in her step and lightness in her heart. She'd thrown off the chains of the past and made a gesture to embrace the future, something better, something new. She turned left and took the familiar route towards the river. The air was cool and the sky blue with streaks of white cloud. Everything looked the same. The shops, the bus stop, the trees, the road, the cars, the bland, expressionless faces of the passers-by as they went about their business. But she felt different. Her speech had acted as a kind of cathartic sloughing off of the old, like a snake disposing of an old skin; she had quite literally thrown away her job and her livelihood.

Her route took her along the south bank of the Thames. She slowed her pace. A passenger boat passed by; sunlight flashed off her polished brightwork. A small boy waved enthusiastically at her from the rear and she waved back. She was aware that she was acutely in the present moment; she wasn't reminiscing or daydreaming but watching and listening, alert to all around her. She saw the old tramp in his familiar place. Blake's tramp, as she thought of him. She stopped suddenly, as if caught unawares. He seemed to recognise her.

'G'day, miss, 'aven't seen your friend 'ere of late, 'e alright, is 'e?' He looked at her benignly.

'He's gone away.'

''E's dead then, or in prison.'

'No.'

'If 'e's not dead or in prison 'e'll be comin' back then.'

'I doubt it, not where he's gone,' she said, 'he's a beggar like you now.'

The old man looked at her perplexed.

His filthy and battered old cap lay upside down beside him. A few coins had been thrown inside. I need to give him some money, she thought. She opened her handbag, fumbled for her purse and looked inside. Nothing. No coins, no cash. She felt a surge of guilt; she couldn't give 'nothing'. For a moment she stood in indecision. Then she felt for the necklace, hidden underneath her high-necked shirt. No longer reassuring, it suddenly felt unbearably heavy and cumbersome. A reminder of love lost. She opened the clasp, took it off and held it in her hand for a moment. She admired its exquisite filigree design, the glittering diamonds. But it too belonged to the past.

'Here, I haven't any money, but please, take this.' She knelt down and put the necklace in his open hand.

'I can't take this, miss, you need this,' he said, and looked at her doubtfully.

'No, this is more than I need,' she said, and cupped his fingers around it. 'I travel light.'

The tramp opened his fingers and looked at it, frowning.

'Make sure you get a good price for it. They're real gems,' she said.

He slowly slipped it into the dark, cavernous pocket of his grimy greatcoat.

'You a mighty kind lady, miss, thanks. I wish you a 'appy day.'

Cathy smiled with satisfaction. She walked on. She was alert to the present moment, caught between the past and the future. She had always hoped that she'd settle down with a decent, reliable man with good prospects who would provide her with a reasonable standard of living. All this now seemed too limited, too restrictive, and it wasn't enough, it was just a dream. She no longer had any clear expectations. Blake had taken her to a new dimension of experience, in her thoughts, her emotions, physically, in her being. She felt as if her whole life she had been like an egg encased in a neat, safe shell and he'd taken a hammer and smashed the shell into a thousand pieces and scattered them over an unfathomably wide area. She'd been liberated from her narrow view of herself, liberated from her fearfulness, her fixed view of the world. She would never cling to fixed hopes or ideals ever again, but embrace life just as it unfolded. As these thoughts raced through her mind she started to skip, run, she felt happy, carefree. She grinned, stretched her arms upwards towards the sky, and waved her handbag around in the air, oblivious to the stares of passers-by. She felt her joy rising.

'I'm free', she shouted, 'I'm free!'

Author's Note

The Asymmetric Man is chronologically the first part of the Blake Carter trilogy. The other two parts are already published and continue the story.

They are:

The Girl at Conway Place
ISBN 978-0950059136

Followed by:

Sunrise at An Lac
ISBN 978-0956249470

Both are available from Amazon.